STRANGER
IN THE
LAKE

KIMBERLY BELLE

PARK
ROW
BOOKS

PARK
ROW
BOOKS™

Recycling programs
for this product may
not exist in your area.

ISBN-13: 978-0-7783-1113-3

Stranger in the Lake

First published in 2020. This edition published in 2021.

Copyright © 2020 by Kimberle S. Belle Books, LLC

This edition published by arrangement with Harlequin Books S.A.

Park Row Books
22 Adelaide St. West, 40th Floor
Toronto, Ontario M5H 4E3, Canada
ParkRowBooks.com
BookClubbish.com

Printed in Lithuania

MIX
Paper from
responsible sources
FSC® C021394

For Ewoud, *voor altijd.*

STRANGER
IN THE
LAKE

1

I untie the dock cleats and shove the boat into water as gray as the sky. Sometime in the past few hours, gunmetal clouds have rolled over the mountaintops, shooting down icy gusts that froth the surface of Lake Crosby into a million white peaks. My stomach churns, and not from the water's chop.

Maybe morning sickness, maybe nerves at the words I need to say to my new husband out loud.

Surprise! I'm pregnant.

I sink onto the helm seat and shove my hands into the pockets of my new down jacket. A gift from Paul, who has impeccable taste—the kind that comes from good breeding and a big bank account. We've only ever spoken about children in the vaguest of terms. Things like "this room would make a good nursery" or "we would make pretty babies," the "one day" silent but implied. He and his first wife never tried for a baby before she died, a little over four years ago. I haven't known him a year. This wasn't exactly the plan.

But neither was falling for a man eleven years older than me, a man who always claimed he'd never marry again. The thirty-seven-year-old wealthy widower falls for a gas station clerk from the muddy side of the mountain, both of us touched by tragedy. A combination that everybody from our town said would never work.

"I don't give a damn what people think," Paul is constantly telling me. "I love you and you love me, and that's all that matters."

But now… My hand feels under the jacket to my still-flat stomach. What will he think about this little surprise blooming inside my belly? I have no idea.

His mother, the people in town, friends who've known him all his life. I know exactly what they'll say.

They'll say that this baby was no accident. That the littlest Keller will cement my place at the family dinner table in a way the three carats on my ring finger can't. That marriages are temporary, but children are until the end of time. That now he's *really* trapped.

Sugar daddy, sugar baby, baby daddy.

By now the wind has pushed me away from the dock, and I start the engine and swing the boat around. Paul and I live on a cove, but the currents here are swift, the water dangerously deep. The hill his house is perched on doesn't stop at the shoreline, but plunges to depths of up to three hundred feet. There's a whole town buried down there, tucked in the hills of what was once a thriving valley. Homes, roads, farms, schools. Graveyards. Whenever anything manages to wriggle loose—a battered shingle, an algae-covered shoe, a slimy dog collar—it ends up here, in Skeleton Cove.

Halfway to the town's center, I ease up on the throttle going around the point to Buck Knob Cove and look westward, over the water and mountains and endless smoky skies. I've never lived anywhere else but Lake Crosby, North Carolina—have never even considered it—and still the raw beauty of this place can take my breath away. These mountains are as much a part of me as my own skin and bones, the connection as real as the cells multiplying in my belly. If I close my eyes, I can feel the plates shifting under my feet. I am the mountains and the mountains are me. I couldn't live anyplace else if I tried.

It's the one thing I can't resent my mother for, I suppose, choosing this place to have a family—not that she was much of a parent. I mostly raised myself, and then I raised my brother, Chet, which is how I know love can only go so far. Love doesn't put food on the table. Love doesn't pay the rent or the creditors who come banging at the door. A baby needs so much more than love.

People say I married Paul for the money, but that's just not true. I married him because I love him, and I love him for all the things he provides. A mortgage-free roof over my head and a belly stuffed with nutritious, organic food. Health insurance and car insurance and cell phone and internet. The freedom of never having to choose between going cold or going hungry again. A life that is safe and stable and secure.

And really, when you think about it, isn't *security* just another word for *love*?

2

The town of Lake Crosby isn't much, just three square blocks and some change, but it's the only town in the southern Appalachians perched at the edge of the water, which makes it a popular tourist spot. Paul's office is at the far end of the first block, tucked between a fudge shop and Stuart's Craft Cocktails, which, as far as I can tell, is just another way to say "pretentious bar." Most of the businesses here are pretentious, farm-to-table restaurants and specialty boutiques selling all things overpriced and unnecessary.

For people like Paul, town is a place to socialize and make money—in his case, by selling custom house designs for the million-dollar lots that sit high on the hills or line the lakeshores. My old friends serve his drinks and wait his tables—but only the lucky ones. There are ten times more locals than there are jobs.

The covered terrace for the cocktail lounge is quiet, a

result of the off-season and the incoming weather, the sign on the door still flipped to Closed. I'm passing the empty hostess stand when I notice movement at the very back, a tattered shadow peeling away from the wall. Jax—the town loon, the crazy old man who lives in the woods. Most people turn away from him, either out of pity or fear, but not me. For some reason I can't put into words, I've never been afraid to look him straight on.

He takes a couple of halting steps, like he doesn't want to be seen—and he probably doesn't. Jax is like a deer you come up on in a meadow, one blink and he's gone. But this time he doesn't run.

His gaze flicks around, searching the street behind me. "Where's Paul." A statement, not a question.

Slowly, so not to spook him, I point to the sleek double doors on the next building, golden light spilling out the windows of Keller Architecture. "Did you check inside?"

Jax shakes his head. "I need to talk to him. It's important."

Like every time he emerges from out of the woods, curiosity bubbles in my chest. Once upon a time, Jax had everything going for him. High school prom king and star quarterback, the golden boy with a golden future, and one of Paul's two best friends. Their picture still sits atop his desk in the study, Paul and Jax and Micah, all tanned chests and straightened smiles, three teenage boys with the world at their feet.

Now he's Batty Jax, the raggedy, bearded boogeyman parents use as a warning. Do your homework, stay out of trouble, and don't end up like Jax.

He clings to the murky back of the terrace, sticking to the shaded spots where it's too dark for me to make out much more than a halo of matted hair, the jutting edges of an oversized jacket, long, lean thighs. His face is dark, too, the combination of a life outdoors and dirt.

"Do you want me to give Paul a message? Or if you stay right there, I can send him out. I know he'll want to see you."

Actually, I don't know; I only assume. Jax is the source of a slew of rumors and petty gossip, but for Paul, he's a painful subject, one he doesn't like to talk about. As far as I know, the two haven't spoken since high school graduation—not an easy thing to do in a town where everybody knows everybody.

Jax glances up the street, in the direction of far-off voices floating on the icy wind. I don't follow his gaze, but I can tell from the way his body turns skittish that someone is coming this way, moving closer.

"Do you need anything? Some money, maybe?"

Good thing those people aren't within earshot, because they would laugh at the absurdity of the trailer-park girl turned married-up wifey offering the son of an insurance tycoon some cash. Not that Jax's father didn't disown him ages ago or that I have more than a couple of bucks in my pocket, but still.

Jax shakes his head again. "Tell Paul I need to talk to him. Tell him to hurry."

Before I can ask what for, he's off, planting a palm on the railing and springing over in one easy leap, his body light as a pole vaulter. He hits the cement and takes off up the alley. I dash forward until I'm flush with the railing, peering down the long passage between Paul's building and the cocktail lounge, but it's empty. Jax is already gone.

I push through the doors of Keller Architecture, an open space with cleared desks and darkened computer screens. The whiteboard on the back wall has already been wiped clean, too, one of the many tasks Paul requires his staff to do daily. It's nearing five, and other than his lead designer, Gwen, hunched over a drawing at her drafting table, the office is empty.

She nods at my desk. "Perfect timing. I just finished the Curtis Cottage drawings."

Calling a seven-thousand-square-foot house a "cottage" is ridiculous, as are whatever reasons Tom Curtis and his wife, a couple well into their seventies, gave Paul for wanting six bedrooms and two kitchens in what is essentially a weekend home. But the Curtises are typical Keller Architecture clients—privileged, demanding and more than a little entitled. They like Paul because he's one of them. Having a desk is probably ridiculous, too, since I only work twenty hours a week, and for most of them I'm anywhere but here. My role is client relations, which consists mainly of hauling my ass to wherever the clients are so I can put out fires and talk them off the latest ledge. The job and the desk are one of the many perks of being married to a Keller.

"Thanks." I tuck the Curtis designs under an arm and move toward the hallway to my left, a sleek tunnel of wood and steel that ends in Paul's glass-walled office. "I'm here to pick up Paul. There's something wrong with his car."

When he called earlier to tell me his car was dead in the lot, I thought he was joking. Engine trouble is what happens to my ancient Civic, not Paul's fancy Range Rover, a brand-new supercharged machine with a dashboard that belongs in a cockpit. *More money than sense*, my mother would say about Paul if she were here, and now, I guess, about me.

Gwen leans back in her chair, wagging a mechanical pencil between two slim fingers. "Yeah, the dealer is sending a tow truck and a replacement car, but they just called to say they're delayed. He said he had a couple of errands to run."

I frown. "Who, the tow truck driver?"

"No, Paul." She swivels in her chair, reaching across the desk behind her for a straightedge. "He should be back any sec."

I thank her and head for the door.

On the sidewalk, I fire off a quick text to Paul. I'm here, where are you?

I wait for a reply that doesn't come. The screen goes dark, then black. I slip the phone into my jacket pocket and start walking.

In a town like Lake Crosby, there are only so many places Paul could be. The market, the pharmacy, the shop where he buys his ties and socks. I pop into all of them, but no one's seen him since this morning. Back on the sidewalk, I pull out my phone and give him a call. It rings once, then shoots me to voice mail. I hit End and look up and down the mostly deserted street.

"Hey, Charlie," somebody calls from across the road, two single lanes separated by a parking strip, and I whirl around, spotting Wade's familiar face over the cars and SUVs. One of my brother's former classmates, a known troublemaker who dropped out sophomore year because he was too busy cooking meth and raising hell. He leans against the ivory siding of the bed-and-breakfast, holding what I sincerely hope is a hand-rolled cigarette.

"It's Charlotte," I say, but I don't know why I bother.

On my sixteenth birthday, I plunked down more than a hundred hard-earned dollars at the courthouse to change my name. But no matter how many times I correct the people who knew me back when—people who populate the trailer parks and shacks along the mountain range, people like Wade and me—no matter how many times I tell them I'm not that person anymore, to them I'll always be Charlie.

He flicks the cigarette butt into the gutter and tilts his head up the street. "I just saw your old man coming out of the coffee shop." Emphasis on the *old man*. "If you hurry, you can probably catch him."

I mumble a thanks, then head in that direction.

Just past the market, I spot Paul at the far end of a side street, a paper cup clutched in his hand. He's wearing the clothes I watched him pull on this morning—a North Face fleece, a navy cashmere sweater, dark jeans, leather lace-up boots, but no coat. No hat or scarf or gloves. Paul always dresses like this, without a second thought as to the elements. That fleece might be fine for the quick jogs from the house to his car to the office door, but with the wind skimming up the lake, he must be freezing.

The woman he's talking to is more properly dressed. Boots and a black wool coat, the big buttons fastened all the way to a neck cloaked in a double-wrapped scarf. A knitted hat is pulled low over her ears and hair, leaving only a slice of her face—from this angle, her profile—exposed.

"There you are," I say, and they both turn.

A short but awkward silence. If I didn't know better, I'd think he looks surprised to see me.

"Charlotte, hi. I was just…" He glances at the woman, then back to me. "What are you doing here?"

"You asked me to pick you up. Didn't you get my text?"

With his free hand, he wriggles his cell from his pocket and checks the screen. "Oh. Sorry, I must have had it on Silent. I was on my way back to the office, but then I got to talking and…well, you know how that goes." He gives me a sheepish smile. It's a known fact that Paul is a talker, and like in most small towns, there's always someone to talk to.

But I don't know this woman.

I take in her milky skin and sky blue eyes, the light smattering of freckles across her nose and high cheekbones, and I'm positive I've never seen her before. She's the kind of pretty a person would remember, almost beautiful even, though she's nothing like his type. Paul likes his women curvy and exotic, with dark hair and ambiguous coloring. This woman is bony, her skin so pale it's almost translucent.

I step closer, holding up my hand in a wave. "Hi, I'm Charlotte Keller. Paul's wife."

The woman gives me a polite smile, but her gaze flits to Paul. She murmurs something, and I'm pretty sure it's "Keller."

The hairs soldier on the back of my neck, even though I've never been the jealous type. It's always seemed like such a waste of energy to me, being possessive and suspicious of a man who claims to love you. Either you believe him or you don't—or so I've always thought. Paul tells me he loves me all the time, and I believe him.

But this woman wouldn't be the first around these parts to try to snag herself a Keller.

"Are you ready?" I say, looking at Paul. "Because I came in the boat, and we need to get home before this weather blows in."

The talk of rain does the trick, and Paul snaps out of whatever I walked into here. He gives me that smile he saves only for me, and a rush of something warm hits me hard, right behind the knees.

People who say Paul and I are wrong together don't get that we've been waiting for each other all our lives. His first wife's death, my convict father and meth-head mother, they broke us for a reason, so all these years later our jagged edges would fit together perfectly, like two pieces of the same fractured puzzle. The first time Paul took my hand, the world just…started making sense.

And now there's a baby, a perfect little piece of Paul and me, an accidental miracle that somehow busted through the birth control. Maybe it's not a fluke but a sign, the universe's way of telling me something good is coming. A new life. A new chance to get things right.

All of a sudden and out of nowhere I feel it, this burning in my chest, an overwhelming, desperate fire for this baby that's taken root in my belly. I want it to grow and kick and thrive. I want it with everything inside me.

"Let's go home." Without so much as a backward glance at the woman, Paul takes my hand and leads me to the boat.

We're smack in the middle of Lake Crosby when it starts to snow, lazy fat flakes dancing down from a canopy of white. Flurries, but there's more coming. Those are snow clouds spilling over the mountaintops.

Paul has the bow pointed to home and the throttle buried, and I don't blame him. His fleece was bad enough in town, where there were warm shops to duck in and brick buildings to huddle behind. Out here on the open water the wind is fierce, and he might as well be shirtless.

He's hunched low behind the windshield, steering the boat with his knees, his hands shoved deep in his pits for warmth. I take in his blue lips, his chattering teeth, and wince. I should have brought his coat.

Tell him. Just open your mouth and say I'm pregnant. *Do it now.*

"Hey, Paul?" The words get lost in the roar of the engine, but there's no stopping now. Not when I've finally summoned my courage. I tap him on the shoulder and try again. *"Paul."*

He pulls back on the throttle, slowing the boat to a crawl. "What's wrong? Did you forget something?"

I shake my head. An hour ago, I left the house with exactly two items, the boat keys and my cell phone, both of which are here with me now. The keys dangle from the ignition, and I tucked my cell in the cubby by my seat, along with the Curtis Cottage drawings.

"You know how I've been feeling kinda out of sorts?" I don't have to tick off my symptoms—the bouts of nausea, the bone-tiredness I can't seem to shake. Paul brought me chicken soup from the market in town, covered me with blankets whenever I'd nap on the couch.

"You had the flu."

"That's what I thought, too. But who has the flu for three whole weeks?"

I stare at him hard, waiting for the realization to hit, but Paul's face is a complete blank. I can't tell if it's because he doesn't understand where I'm going with this, or if he's trying to contain his panic—or worse, suspicion. Will he accuse me of flicking my pills into the toilet, of forgetting to take them on purpose? His mother certainly will.

I look away. "Anyway, it wasn't the flu."

He reaches up and kills the engine. All around us, the air goes quiet the way it can only here, in the middle of a lake cradled between mountains and trees. A strange kind of muffled silence punctuated by the far-off cry of a hawk.

Paul swivels on his seat to face me, his voice laced with worry. "What is it? Are you sick?"

"No." My answer is swift, and I make sure to look him in the eyes. Paul's already lost one wife. Of course his mind would go there. I probably should have led with my good health. "No, I'm fine. Better than fine. Healthy as can be."

My heart is pounding now, but that's to be expected. I

think of the matching pink lines on the sticks, wrapped in toilet paper and buried at the bottom of the wastebasket. The instructions said one line may come out lighter than the other, but any hint of a second line meant I was pregnant. All three times I pulled a new one from the wrapper and peed on it just in case the ones before it were defective, the lines were so pink they were almost purple.

I see the second the quarter drops. Paul huffs out a breath, and the twin lines between his eyebrows smooth out. "Are you saying what I think you're saying?" He sounds stunned, not angry. In fact, he kind of sounds the opposite, happy and hopeful—but maybe that's just me.

Still. I bite down on a smile. "That depends. What do you think I'm saying?"

"Charlotte McCreedy Keller, don't play games with me. My brittle old heart can't take it." He stands, reaching for me with icy hands, pulling me out of my chair. "Are you going to make me the happiest man on the planet? Are you going to make me a father?" He wraps his hands around my biceps and gives them a little jiggle. His eyes are gleaming, his smile stretched clear to his sideburns. "Are you?"

After a second or two, I nod.

Paul whoops, and a flock of swallows bursts from a bush on the shore, birds and batting wings swirling in the air. Suddenly I'm in the air, too, my legs wrapped around Paul's waist, his hands firm on my backside. He twirls me around in the tiny space between the seats, and I laugh, from relief and at Paul's reaction—a stunned but unapologetic joy.

"You're pretty strong for an old man."

"I'm not an old man. I am *the* man. My swimmers are bad*ass*. They are *fierce*." I laugh, and he puts me down. "How do you feel? Any other symptoms?"

"A little tired still, and kinda pukey in the mornings. Once I eat something, I'm usually fine."

"This is…this is amazing. I can't wait to tell everybody. Let's go home and make some calls."

"Paul, can we just… I don't know…keep this quiet for a little while longer? At least until I see the doctor and she gives us the green light. I want to know everything's okay before we go telling the whole world."

Worry flits across his brow. "What, you think this baby might not stick?"

"No, but it's still so early. I want to see this baby with my own two eyes and be sure. Let's just wait until after the first ultrasound, okay?"

"Okay, but so you know, I have a good feeling about this little guy. He's going to be fine."

I lift a brow. "Little *guy*?"

"Well, yeah. An adorable baby Keller to carry on the name." He presses a hand over my lower stomach and smiles. "Paul Junior."

Now, *that* his mother would approve of, a carbon copy of her precious son. I think back to Diana's reaction when we told her we were getting married, the fake smile that tried to crack open her cheeks when Chet walked me down the aisle. I am not what she pictured for Paul—I'm too young, too unpolished, too poor and crass. She thinks that sometime very soon, her son will snap to his senses.

But a baby… A baby changes everything.

"What if it's a Paulette?"

Paul makes a face. "*God*, no. I can't saddle my daughter with a name like Paulette. She'll grow up and go on *Dr. Phil*, talking about how we ruined her life. She'll never speak to us again."

Neglect, alcoholism, a felon father and a mother who had

no business ever pushing out kids—now, those are some things to bellyache about on national television. This baby will have everything Chet and I didn't: a real house with real walls to keep out of the cold, a fridge filled with food, clothes that don't come from a church basement bin. Two parents who stick around, who don't disappear for days at a time or get carted off to jail.

And, as corny as it sounds, love.

I smile over our hands at my husband. "I do have one more request."

"For the love of my life? The mother of my child?" He lifts my hand to his lips, presses a frosty kiss to my knuckle. "Absolutely anything."

"When it's time, you get to tell your mother."

3

When I wake up the next morning, I'm alone.

I stare at the black sky pouring through the bedroom window and listen for the sounds of Paul, pulling on clothes in the closet or banging around in the kitchen downstairs. There's nothing but silence. An empty house, holding its breath.

Already left for his daily morning run, a six-mile trek around the hills to the west of our house, which means there must not be much snow on the ground. When we went to bed last night, it was really coming down, but the ground was probably too warm still for it to stick.

The clock on the nightstand reads 6:04, earlier than usual for Paul, but not unheard of, though I wouldn't have expected it today. Not after the glass of red he downed with dinner, followed by a gold-labeled bottle he pulled from the wine fridge, champagne that costs as much as a month's worth of groceries.

Paul's not normally much of a drinker, but yesterday's news sent him sailing far past his tipping point. I picture him huffing up Suicide Hill, cursing himself for that last glass, and maybe the one before. Poor guy must really be hurting.

My untouched flute stands full on the nightstand—"for toasting," Paul said as he poured, "not drinking." The last of the carbonation clings in tiny bubbles to the glass, next to Paul's empty one. I eye the liquid in the bottle, only a few inches or so. Paul is the only person I know who recuperates from a hangover with an early-morning run. One good hill, and his metabolism will have burned through the alcohol like propane, which, now that I think about it, is probably why he looks so good.

But all last night, he googled and drank, googled and drank.

"It says here there's only one percent chance of getting pregnant on the pill," he'd said, looking up from his laptop.

We were in bed, our backs propped up by pillows and the headboard, our bare feet tangled on top of the comforter.

He grinned, his eyes shining with pride and champagne. "One point three, to be exact. That's some pretty shitty odds, but I really cracked that nut, didn't I? I really got in there."

I laughed. "You really did."

He reached for the bottle and topped off his glass—his third by my count—then plunked it back to the nightstand. "Apparently, you calculate the due date by the first day of your last period. When was that?"

I shrugged, not considering my calendar but whether or not I should suggest going easy on the booze. My father used to drink like that, in greedy pulls that turned his words mushy around the edges and sent Chet and me skittering for the opposite end of the trailer. He was a mean drunk, but a lazy one, too. The trick was to stay out of range.

Paul frowned. "You don't know, or you don't remember?"

"My periods have always been wonky. But I can figure out when it was supposed to be if I count the pills left in the pack."

He read aloud a long, boring article about folic acid, and how I should be taking it to prevent birth defects. He searched out every local ob-gyn and settled on one in nearby Highlands with a degree from Johns Hopkins and a five-star rating on healthgrades.com. He declared ginger tea the best remedy for morning sickness and that it's important to hydrate, even though one of the symptoms of early pregnancy is more trips than usual to the bathroom. He claimed sex was allowed and so was cheese, as long as it's pasteurized, but no more sushi for me.

By eleven, he'd passed out, smiling.

I push back the comforter and step out of bed, padding naked across the plush carpet. Paul designed every room in this house to showcase natural light and killer views, which means one entire wall of our bedroom is shiny black glass—the glossy blackness another sign we didn't get much snow. A solid coating on the ground would lighten things up to a foggy gray, even though the sun won't rise for another half hour.

I press my face to the glass, gazing out on woods that are still dark and raw. A ghostly steam hangs over the water like smoke, creepy and picture-perfect.

But I was right about the snow; we only got a light dusting.

I grab my robe from a hook in the closet, wrap it around me and head downstairs.

Another sign Paul drank too much—the normally pristine kitchen is a disaster. Dirty dishes, crumpled napkins, food wrappers and a forgotten carton of milk on the counter. I pour it down the drain and straighten the mess while I wait for the espresso machine to warm up. It's Paul's prize possession, a complicated Italian gadget that cost more than a normal person pays for their whole kitchen. But I've got to give it to him—the coffee is divine.

While the machine spits out a foamy dark stream, I lean a hip against the counter and think through my day. Paul should be back soon, and then he'll need a ride to town to pick up the replacement car, which should be waiting in the office lot. On the way back, I can drop off the drawings for the Curtis Cottage at the client's current home.

And that's when it occurs to me. The drawings are still in the boat. Right where I chucked them, along with my cell phone, in the cubby under my seat. In our hurry to get up the hill and into the house so we could start the celebrating in earnest, I left them there.

I look out the window. The sky is brighter now, daylight lighting up tree branches sifted with snow, even though it's dry for now. But if some of that snow made its way onto those drawings, Gwen is going to have a fit.

I set my coffee cup on the counter and rush to the mudroom—a space I never knew existed before I started dating Paul. And honestly, what's the point? A whole room specifically for muddy shoes and jackets—is that really necessary? Ours is a rectangular space with a slate floor, a wall of custom cabinets and cubbies, and exactly zero mud. No Keller Architecture house comes without one.

I shove my feet into a pair of snow boots, faux fur–lined and with a steady, deep tread, and pluck my coat from the hook.

Outside on the upper deck, the wind hits me, and I duck

my head and hurry down the stairs to the lower level. Icy currents billow my robe around my legs, skating up my bare skin and prickling in my nose with the scent of moss and pine.

I think of Paul, conquering the hills on the other side of our house, and shiver. A hundred bucks says he didn't think to take his gloves.

I'm careful navigating the hill's steep steps, pressed gravel held together with reclaimed railroad ties. The treads are uneven, and the snow has coated the ties in slick patches, making the descent slow going.

Above my head, a hawk calls out, and I look up to see him tracing lazy figure eights just above the tree line. There must be something dead nearby, because an animal with any sort of sense would be hunkered down somewhere warm.

The dock is a skating rink, and it doesn't help my balance any that it's floating, the waters here too deep to drive in stakes. I grip the posts and move across it with cautious, steady steps. There's good fishing under this dock, but things that fall in here don't always come back up, not until much later. It's called Skeleton Cove for a reason.

My teeth are chattering and my fingers numb by the time I lower myself onto the boat. Paul left the keys dangling in the ignition, and I jiggle them loose and drop them into my pocket. The drawings are right where I left them, a little damp but not soggy, thank God.

I feel around the bottom of the cubby until my fingers connect with a smooth, icy object. My cell phone. I pull it out and poke at the screen, but nothing happens. The battery is dead, probably frozen to death. I slip it in my pocket with the keys, grab the drawings and step to the bow.

I'm hoisting myself onto the dock when I see it. Something long and white in the water below me, drifting like seaweed on the surface.

I lower one foot back onto the leather seat, then the other. Bend down and look again.

I shriek and scramble backward.

Not seaweed. Hair. *Human* hair. It fans out from the back of a blond head, twisting and swirling in the water like smoke.

I take another step backward, putting some space between me and the corpse, but there's nothing behind me but air. My body pitches off the seat and onto the carpet of the bow's cockpit, my back slamming into the opposite seat. I land on my right hip with a thud. Automatically, my hand goes to my belly.

Don't you come unstuck, little guy. Don't you dare.

I pause, waiting for what comes next. A dull cramping, a searing pain. I wait, not moving for the span of five full breaths, but there's nothing but a throbbing in my upper back where I hit the hard edge of the seat.

Carefully, I push to my feet. I step to the starboard side and lean my entire upper body over the side of the boat.

It's a woman, floating facedown in the water. I can tell from her hair, her slim shoulders and slight build, the designer jeans and thin black sweater. Her arms and legs are spread wide like motionless spider legs, her hands and feet disappearing into the murky water. It's a stance that's instantly familiar.

Dead man's float.

The urge to vomit comes on hard and fast, and sweat breaks out on my skin, even though I'm still freezing. I swallow the sick down and tell myself this is not the first time I've seen a dead body. When I was twelve, my grandma dropped dead right next to me, right in the middle of ordering from the Home Shopping Channel. She was a bit of a hoarder, her trailer crammed full with crap she didn't need and probably couldn't afford, but the point is, I didn't panic. I pried the phone out of her hand and called 9-1-1 without producing a tear, even though afterward I cried for days.

But this is different. This time it feels like watching a horror movie, like seeing something forbidden and monstrous. Another faceless, lifeless woman bobbing in the reeds under our dock, only this time… Is it an accident? Or something worse? I watch her hair swirl in a gust of water and it's like staring into the sun—painful but impossible to look away.

Not here, under Paul's dock. Not again.

My blood runs hot and I glance up the hill, the world shifting back into focus. Should I flip her over? Drag her into the boat and perform CPR?

Then again, I'm probably not strong enough to lift her out, and it's too deep under the dock to wade in, not to mention too late. I'm no expert, but it looks like she's been there a while. The skin that I can see—the tops of her ears, a sliver at the back of her neck—is waxy and luridly white, gleaming like it's coated in frost.

I decide to leave her be. I can't help her, and as far as the lake is concerned, this is the end of the line. The currents that live in these waters, powerful undertows and swift updrafts that swirl up muck from the depths, burp everything up here, in the reeds under our dock. Whoever this woman is, she's not going anywhere.

I reach for my phone, only to remember that it's dead. My gaze tracks up the hill, searching for a light in a window, maybe, or the ones that flank the back door. But our house is dark, and so is Micah's farther up the cove. Nothing but a big black blotch behind the trees.

With one last look at the dead woman, I climb out of the boat and shuffle carefully across the dock, then take off running up the hill.

There are seventy-six steps from the dock to the house, a steep hike of almost fifty vertical yards—half a football field. Paul chose the highest hill on purpose, and I'll admit, the views are spectacular. Lake and forest and mountains rolling into a smoky blue sky that goes on forever.

The climb from the dock, on the other hand, is a real buzzkill. Seventy-six slogging steps of muscle-burning, lung-wheezing hell. By the time I make it to the back door, I can barely breathe.

It doesn't help that the clouds are spitting snow again, or the whole time I was clambering up the slippery staircase, I was hollering for our neighbor Micah when I saw that the light above his back deck had popped on. I pictured him sipping a cup of coffee on the back deck, but then just as suddenly, the light faded and I realized it was a motion sensor. A bird, maybe, or an opossum scrounging for food set it off. I ducked my head and kept climbing.

I bust through the door and race into Paul's study, the closest room with a landline.

I fall into the chair at his desk, a giant slab of walnut and brushed steel, with nothing on it but a lamp and a phone. Its surface is spotless, a gleaming example of Paul's clean-desk policy that applies both at work and at home.

I pick up the receiver and dial with freezing, fumbling fingers. Micah's cell rings four eternal times, then flips me to voice mail. At the end of the beep, I start talking.

"Micah, it's Charlotte. I was just down at the dock, and

there's a body under it. A real body, a woman. I don't know who she is or how she got there, but she's clearly dead, so I didn't dare touch her." Saying the words out loud makes my stomach go eely with morning sickness, with shock. "Anyway, get over here as soon as you hear this, will you? I'm hanging up and calling 9-1-1 now. Bye."

Micah is our neighbor and friend, but also son of the police chief and badass diver specializing in underwater investigations and evidence recovery. Whoever I talk to at emergency services will be calling him next anyway. I hang up and dial 9-1-1.

Though… I suppose it's not technically an emergency—not anymore since she's obviously dead. But the sooner the police know, the better chances are they can retrieve whatever evidence she might still be carrying. Micah told me once that the lake's currents work like a washing machine, agitating everything in it. If there's evidence on her body and the fabric of her clothes—skin under her fingernails, a hair that's not from her head stuck in her sweater—it's probably already been knocked loose.

The line connects, and I give the operator my name and address, describe the scene down at the dock. I sound remarkably calm, if not a little out of breath still. He tells me the police are on the way and asks me to stay on the line, but I tell him I have to go. Paul will be home from his run soon, and he'll need my support. I think of him out there, jogging around the hills in blissful ignorance, and I hang up the phone.

There's nothing I can do now but wait.

4

Jax Edwards tromped through the woods behind his house, his rifle slung carelessly over a shoulder. Thanks to a week of nonstop rain, the air was so thick it had a weight to it, solid and sticky in his lungs. The damp brought out the bugs and turned the path into a tangled mass of branches and undergrowth, new shoots slapping at the bare skin of his legs with clammy fronds.

He probably should have changed into jeans. Better shoes, too, instead of these ancient sneakers, a holdout from his high school track days. He kept stepping out of them, kept having to double back to rescue one from where it got suction-cupped to a muddy spot in the path. Like most things these days, it really pissed him off.

The backs of his thighs burned, but it was a good kind of pain. The kind that came after hours of trekking through the forest, scaling trees and clambering up mountainsides. In his seventeen years, he'd explored every inch of these woods, looked behind every log and under every rock. He'd watched beavers chew bushes down to tiny nubs for their dam and almost stepped on two copperheads mating. Yesterday a deer let him come so close he could see the veins in its ears. Funny, when he first started coming out here, he thought it was because he wanted to be alone, but somehow, being out here with all these animals, with the wilderness…well, he never minded the company.

The dense path gave way, opening up to a patch of velvet grass an army of gardeners mowed and raked and fertilized into perfection every Tuesday afternoon, blinding green against the glittering lake. The house in the middle was a faded gray shingle, big and square with shiny black shutters on the windows. It sat on the water, so close you could drive the boat right into the attached garage, a yawning hole carved into an extension of the house that stuck out over the lake like a long finger. When they were younger, his mom had installed a slide to the deck up top, and all summer long you could hear squeals and splashes as he and his sister, Pamela, took turns skidding down. Jax had never lived anywhere else.

Now home was the last place on earth he wanted to be.

He banged through the back door into the kitchen, where Pamela was preparing dinner. "Where have you been? Dad's home, and he's been calling all over for you."

Jax could hear him on the other end of the house, yelling at some poor sucker through the phone, ruining his Saturday afternoon. That call had nothing to do with Jax. It was a business call, and an angry one at that. It was the one thing he and his father had in common, this constant, all-consuming rage.

Jax leaned his rifle against the wall. "Hasn't anybody ever told you? Lyin's a sin, Pammy."

"I'm not lying. And what are you doing out there in the woods all day, anyway?"

A year ago he would have brushed her off with *Why do you care? You're not my mother*, but even Jax wasn't that much of an asshole. Their mother was a sensitive subject these days. "You wouldn't understand."

He pushed past her for the stairs, and she skittered after him. "'The Lord is close to the brokenhearted and saves those who are crushed in spirit.' Pastor Williams says if we keep that verse in mind, we won't feel so alone."

She was always doing that, flinging Bible verses at anybody who was close enough, waving them around like some magic potion for whatever ailed you. It was maddening, especially since up until a few years ago they'd been twice-a-year churchgoers at best—sunrise service on Easter morning and candlelight worship on Christmas Eve. Mom never hung crosses on the walls, never taught them to pray before meals or bedtimes. He'd lost count of how many times he'd heard his dad say *goddamn*.

And then the diagnosis came—ALS, the quick kind—and his sister discovered the Lord. She let some pastor dunk her in a muddy cove of Lake Crosby, and then she wanted everybody else to do the same. To be "saved." Mom humored her, even though she was in a wheelchair by then and probably could have drowned. He and his father watched from the shoreline, both of them stewing in a combination of frustration and hope even though every doctor, every specialist and quack they'd talked to told them his mom couldn't be saved.

At night, Pamela would huddle by their mother's bedside for hours at a time, eyes screwed shut, lips moving in silent prayer like a chant. Mom might have had ALS but Pamela was diseased, consumed with what she swore was the healing power of prayer. For a while there, Jax had believed his sister's nonsense in that way that if you wish for something hard enough, you become convinced it should happen. A miracle. It happened all the time in the Bible, right? That's what Pamela promised, but his mom only got weaker.

Jax tried not to roll his eyes. "Prayers only work if you believe, which I don't."

Pamela blanched. "I pray for your soul, Jax Edwards. I really do."

"That makes one of us."

"I miss her, too, you know." Her words stabbed Jax in the heart, and he felt that heaviness in his gut like a tapeworm, eating away at him from the inside out. He almost turned around, almost laid his soul bare until, as usual, his sister ruined the moment. "If you knew what was good for you, you'd drop to your knees and beg for forgiveness right this second. Don't you want eternal life? Don't you want to see Mom again?"

"I don't have time for this."

"It's called faith. You should try it sometime."

Her words made him want to punch the wall, because he *had* tried, damn it. He'd prayed to his sister's Lord for faith—how messed up was that? Every night before he fell asleep and a million times during the day, he'd beg for even a smidge of belief in this higher power his sister was always yammering on about, if for no other reason than the promise of some of Pamela's peace. What a relief it must be to know that all this was just temporary, to think that life on earth was only an annoying stepping-stone to something better, a place where no one dies and no one has to miss anyone.

But Jax didn't believe in Pamela's Lord, just like he didn't believe in bigfoot or aliens or the tooth fairy. His mom was buried under a pile of dirt and rock at Whiteside Cemetery, not sitting like a guardian angel on his shoulder. How do you make yourself believe in something when you don't? How do you convince yourself of things you can't see? Jax had no freaking clue.

He wanted his family back, damn it. Not just his mother but the way things used to be, when the house was filled with laughter and music and the smell of freshly baked cookies. He wanted the sister who didn't preach at him all the time, and the dad who looked up from his computer for more than five seconds, a dad who bothered to be a father. He knew they were suffering, but damn it, so was he, and they were too self-absorbed to notice. He wanted to live in this big house full of people and not feel so alone.

Oh, and while he was at it, Jax might as well admit that he'd really like to cry. A good son would have shed some tears for his dead mother, wouldn't he? He would have stood at her graveside and felt something other than stone-cold fury.

But so far, not one measly fucking tear.

5

Sam Kincaid is the first officer to arrive and the last person I want to see. I spot his familiar face through the front window, his eyes steady on the driveway as he zigzags his way down the snarled strip of concrete, and a flash of heat lingers on my skin like sunburn.

He scrapes to a halt at the flat stretch of driveway, and I open the door, stepping out into the cold. I've changed into jeans and my warmest sweater, but I left my shoes upstairs. The wind has picked up since I raced up the hill, dipping the temperature into what must be single digits, carrying with it a heavy whiff of snow. Already my feet are like ice, the tips of my toes tingling with frostbite.

Sam unfolds himself from the car, all long limbs and the surly expression I've gotten used to seeing take over his face whenever his gaze lands on mine. His siren is off, but the lights swirl with urgency, painting the house and the hill in blood red and bruise blue.

"Charlie," he says, greeting me with a formal nod.

Like everybody else I grew up with, Sam knows that calling me Charlie is the best way to piss me off. I bite down on my lips and hold my tongue. If Sam's looking to get a rise out of me, then I refuse to give it to him.

"It had to be you, huh?" I say, folding my arms across my chest. "Of all the people Chief Hunt could have sent over, I guess he couldn't find anybody else?"

Sam slams the door with his hip, tugging a wool cap from his pocket against the cold. The Kincaid men are all bald as eagles, and whatever hair Sam has left he keeps shaved close to his head. This way, he once told me, he won't have to know when it happens to him.

"Come on. You're kidding me, right?" Sam says in his solid, mountain man accent, the kind that says he hasn't ventured far outside these hills. "Another body washed up under the Keller dock. You better believe I volunteered."

I clamp down on my poker face because the words sting. A year ago I would have called him on it. I would have punched him on the shoulder and told him to stop being such an ass. I sift through all the things I could say instead—that this is different and he knows it, that the first woman was an accident, a crazy, tragic fluke that despite Sam's best efforts he couldn't prove was a crime—but we've had this conversation before. Sam is a cop, which means he needs someone to vilify, to lock in a cell so Lake Crosby can feel safe again. He needs someone to play the part of the monster.

And he thinks that someone is Paul.

He steps away from his car, his big boots thumping on the drive. "You didn't touch her, did you?"

"Come on, Sam. You know I didn't."

"I don't know that. I used to think I knew you, but then…"

"But then what?" I know what, but I want to hear him say it. I want him to look me in the eye and say those ugly words again. I've had five months to prepare for this. This time I'm ready.

He holds my gaze for a second or two, then shakes his head and looks away.

In a flash, an image of Sam leaning an elbow on my counter at the gas station, back when we were best friends. Of him chugging cup after cup of stale coffee, using it to wash down enough powdered doughnuts to win a county fair contest. Of me teasing him about his hollow leg as I rang him up, wondering with the other customers where he put it all. He joked that he burned off the calories chasing bad guys.

And just like that, I feel it, that pang of missing him. Despite all the ugly words he said. Despite all the tears I cried. I still miss the guy, damn it. I do.

I shut the door in his face.

Ten minutes later, the hill is swarming with cops. They march up and down the back steps with their bags and equipment, dumping everything onto the ground and stringing yellow tape around the edges of the water. They clomp up the dock and hang their upper bodies over the edge, shaking their heads and exchanging grim looks. They tip their faces up the hill to mine, watching from the living room window, and their expressions look much like Sam's.

I step back from the glass, a giant solid plate overlooking the lake and trees that stretch up into smoky blue mountains. Like most people from the muddy side of the mountain, those cops down there resent my newfound life. They think I've abandoned my friends and my family and my morals for the comforts of a fancy house up on a hill.

Even worse, they make all kinds of assumptions about how I got here—by singling out a rich, older man and stalking him like prey, by offering up my body to a person I'm only pretending to love, by swiping aside every last lick of good sense to lay my head down next to a man everybody says got away with murder. Doesn't matter that nobody could ever prove he had anything to do with Katherine's death, or that he didn't love her. As far as Sam and those cops are concerned, my sins are unforgivable.

There's a rap at the mudroom door, a creak as Micah pushes it open a crack. "Hey, Charlotte."

"In the kitchen." I beat him there, pulling a cup from the cabinet and settling it under the spout, pressing the button without asking. When it comes to coffee, Micah's answer is always yes.

Micah is a big bear of a guy who looks more like an overgrown computer nerd than a master diver. Tortoise-shell glasses, a swoop of muddy brown hair, a nose that on anyone else would be too large but that somehow works on him. Like Paul, he was born in high cotton, with looks and charm and money from a long line of tobacco farmers on his mother's side. But he's the only one of Paul's friends who's never—not ever, not even once—made me feel like Paul's slumming by choosing me, which in my book means he can do no wrong.

"Sorry it took me so long. I was halfway to Sylva when you called." Micah lumbers across the kitchen, taking in my hair thrown back in a messy ponytail, my makeup-free face and rumpled clothes. "Damn, girl, you look like hell."

The comment is typical Micah, and I make a sound in the back of my throat—part laugh, part relief. He wraps me in one of his hugs, and tears prick at my eyes—and not because of the pregnancy hormones. He's warm and he smells nice, and I'm just so damn glad he's here.

He cranes his head back to look at me. "How you holding up?"

I shake my head, pressing my face into his chest. "Paul's on a run."

By now Micah knows me well enough to hear all the words I'm not saying. That my husband's not here at the worst possible time, that he doesn't know what happened because he never takes his dang phone, that I could use a little emotional support. He holds me for longer than he has to, waiting for me to be the one to untangle us.

When I do, he digs out his phone, pulling up the number for his father on his screen. "Hey, you think you could get some of your guys to sweep the roads around Nantahala Peak for Paul? He's gonna need some advance warning before coming home to a crime scene."

I smile a silent thank-you. Micah's father is police chief—the only cop in the station from this side of the hill. Both men know that a house full of cops would trigger old trauma in Paul.

Micah's conversation with his father turns testy, a regular occurrence whenever those two talk. Never mind that Micah is the best underwater criminal investigator in hundreds of miles, he'll never be good enough for Chief Hunt, who, from the sounds of things, would rather wait for a team of divers he's called in from Asheville to move the body. Micah turns up the heat, arguing he's already here, standing by in his wet suit, and I flash a grin at his little white lie. Another reason why I like Micah Hunt; his daddy issues are even worse than mine.

He hangs up, tossing his phone onto the counter. "You know, I'm really starting to wonder if he's been paying any attention at all. He just told me to send him my qualifications."

I laugh, because Chief Hunt only need consult a newspaper. Weighted-down bodies, weapons flung from a bridge, some rusty hunk of metal that solves a forty-year-old crime. If it's down there, Micah has dredged it up and held it up for some camera. He's semifamous, and not just in these hills. Last year, *USA TODAY* ran a front-page feature on Lake Hunters for their Life section.

I hand him his coffee, and he sinks with it onto a counter stool. "So, you want to fill me in on what happened?"

"Okay. Well, when I got up this morning, I realized I left a couple of things down in the boat, so—"

"What time was that?"

Behind me on the kitchen charger, my cell phone springs to life, buzzing with a string of incoming texts. I ignore it, and so does Micah.

"What time was what, when I got up?"

"No. When you went down to get whatever it was you left in the boat."

"Oh. Sometime just after six thirty, I think. The sky was still dark, but it was beginning to lighten up at the bottom. I yelled for you on the way up the hill, but I'm pretty sure you were already gone."

He sips his coffee and nods, both as confirmation and as a sign for me to continue.

"Anyway, I didn't see her until I was climbing out of the boat. She was facedown under the dock, and like I told the operator, she looked like she's been there a while. I didn't touch her."

My cell phone starts up again, the ringtone for my brother, and Micah tips his head in its direction. "You need to get that?"

I shake my head. "It's just Chet."

Micah knows Chet, too, and he can probably guess what he's calling to say. A long-winded account of some self-inflicted disaster, a desperate plea for a loan—and he always calls it a loan even though everybody on the planet knows he'll never pay me back. Like everyone else in this mountain town, Chet thinks I've hit the jackpot.

I step around the counter to my phone, tap the screen to Ignore and flip the side button to Silent. Two seconds later, it lights up again.

I let it clatter back onto the charger just in time for Micah's next question. "Were y'all home last night?"

"Yes. We got home around five, I think. Maybe a little later. We came by boat, and before you ask, she wasn't there when we docked. Paul was driving, and he would have seen."

I think back to how carefully he slid the boat up to the dock, how he leaned over the edge to tie the ropes and hoist me out, and I'm sure of my answer. I didn't notice anything in the water, but Paul would have. He pays attention to everything.

"Okay, so how about once you were inside? Did either of you hear anything out of the ordinary on the lake? Voices. Splashing, maybe, or the hum of a boat engine?"

"It was cold, and there aren't that many boats still out on the water, so I definitely would have noticed the sound of an engine." I pause, trying to remember. "I don't think so. Did you?"

The question is a valid one. Micah's house is at the top of
the cove, and though it's tucked behind some trees and sits
back farther from the waterline, the back deck offers an un-
interrupted view down the length of the lake. If anybody'd
been out there on the water, or even smack in front of our
dock, he would have seen and heard it, too.

"No. Didn't see anything, either. No boat lights, or the
flickering of a flashlight."

Again, I shake my head. "But we went upstairs earlier
than usual. I don't know what time, exactly. It was dark, I
remember that much."

Dark falls early behind the pines, but still. Thanks to our
champagne celebration, we went to bed soon after supper.

Micah is gearing up for his next question when the front
door opens and in runs Paul, covered in sweat and mud.
He sees me and skids to a stop, leaving orange and brown
smears on the hardwoods. The mud is caked down his entire
right side, from his hair all the way down to his shoes like
he slid feetfirst down a clay slide, and there's a cut above
his right eye, smack in the middle of a nasty purple lump.

"What happened to you? Are you okay?"

"Are you?" He takes me in with wide, bulging eyes. "I
saw the cars outside and I thought..." A tremor makes its
way up his spine, and he slumps against a table, leaning on
it with a filthy palm. *"Jesus."*

Paul's reaction might seem extreme, if he hadn't been
here before, returning from a run to find a horde of cops
fishing a body out of the water. Only the last time it happened, it was summer and the body belonged to his wife.
She drowned during an early-morning swim.

"Are you okay?" I say, moving closer. "That cut looks—"

The words dissolve into a squeal when he snatches me to
him, jerking me against his body, hard with cold and fear.

"You could have warned me, asshole," he says to Micah over my head. "Those cars out there about gave me a heart attack."

I press my palm to Paul's chest, where his heart thumps hard against the skin. His remark may have carried a hint of jest, but his tone didn't. It came out sharp and angry, but Micah doesn't take the bait. That's another great thing about Micah Hunt; he never takes the bait—except maybe with his father.

His voice is calm and matter-of-fact. "I had my father send someone out looking for you, but I'm guessing by your reaction they didn't have much luck. Take your phone with you next time like a normal person, so people can reach you in case of an emergency."

Paul's eyes narrow on the last word. He releases me, sending me a look heavy with meaning.

"I'm fine. Everything's fine." I smile to let him know I understand he's not just asking about me. He's asking about the baby, too. I push up on my toes, leaning in for a better look at the cut, dirty and oozing fresh blood down his brow. "Honey, this looks bad. It's deep, and it needs to be cleaned."

"It's nothing. It barely hurts." He dabs a sleeve to his brow, winces when it comes away red.

Micah steps closer, squinting at Paul's forehead. "Charlotte's right. That looks like it could use some iodine and a stitch or two. What happened?"

"The trails were icy, and I slid straight down Fontana Ridge. Looks worse than it is. Somebody want to tell me what the hell is going on?" Paul says, losing patience. "What's the big emergency?"

"Charlotte found a body under your dock."

It's not how I would have delivered the news, so abrupt

and matter-of-fact. Paul should be sitting down first. He should get a warning that what's coming is bad, that it will reopen old and aching wounds. As Paul's best friend, Micah should know this.

Paul doesn't blink. He looks at me, then back to Micah. "Who?"

It's the question all of Micah's earlier ones were leading up to, the one he didn't get to ask before Paul busted through the door. Who is the stranger in the lake?

"I don't know," I say, my gaze bouncing between the two men. "When I found her, she was facedown. All I could see was her back and hair. It's long and blond."

Which could describe half the women in this town. Fewer when you add in the dead woman's build—thin, petite—but still. I can think of a dozen possible names, right off the top of my head, and that's not even taking into account all the tourists who come through this place. It's no longer high season, the summer and fall months so busy you can't get a table at the restaurants in town, but the winter is still bustling. Floridians, mostly, traveling north in search of some snow. That woman down there could be anyone.

"Could it have been an accident?" I say, my mind scrambling for an explanation. "I mean, it's too cold for her to have been swimming, but maybe she was boating and fell over the side. Maybe she just… I don't know…hit her head or something and drowned."

Micah's eyes fix on mine, and they almost seem to glow. They probe into mine like searchlights, slamming me with the message he doesn't say aloud.

Not an accident.

She didn't drown.

And that's when I feel it. The bottom opens up, the earth drops out from under me. I think about who could have put her there and why, and my skin tingles with dread. Something very bad has happened, right outside our door.

Again.

I look at Paul, and he feels it, too. "Show me."

6

Paul and I march down the back steps in silence, our coats pulled tight against a mean kind of cold, one that doesn't typically happen until months from now, with gusting winds and temperatures stuck in the teens. The kind of cold that chafes the skin and burns the inside of the nose.

Above our heads, a thick layer of overstuffed clouds spits an occasional spell of swirling snow, dousing the mountain's browns and greens and golds. My gaze tracks to the lake, churning silver peaks on water that's a gloomy, bottomless black. I think of the poor woman under the dock and shiver.

He pulls me to a stop on the last step. "Are you okay with this?" He tips his head to the lake, white clouds whirling from his lips. "With seeing her again, I mean. I can clear things with Sam if you don't think you can handle it. You don't have to be here."

The truth is, I'm not looking forward to seeing her again. It was bad enough the first time, and the closer we get to the dock, the more the presence of her lodges underneath my ribs, gnawing at me from the inside. Honestly, I'm barely holding my shit together.

But I also know I need to be here, holding Paul's hand when they pull that poor woman out of the water. Lake Crosby delivered another woman to Paul's dock, to his *door*, and I can already hear the whispers worming their way through the hills. I already know what people will say.

"I'm more worried about you," I say. "This can't be easy."

His hand shakes in mine, and I'm pretty sure it's not from the cold. Paul needs me here, standing next to him when they pull her out, if for nothing else than a reminder I'm still safe and here.

He swings an arm around my shoulders and pulls me into his warmth, planting a kiss in my hair. "Don't tell Micah, but I'm kinda freaked out. I just hope it's a stranger, and not—" He hears himself and winces. "Oh, God, that sounded awful. I just meant..."

"I know what you meant. I hope it, too."

The wind lifts a curl from his forehead, the end matted with blood and sweat, and I get a clear and close-up view of the cut on his brow. He tried to clean himself up with some water and soap in the bathroom upstairs, but he didn't do a very good job. His efforts only smeared the blood and dirt around, shoved the gunk deep into an even deeper gash.

"As soon as we're done here, I'm taking you to urgent care. Even with stitches, you're going to have a nasty scar."

My words disappear into sirens wailing in the distance. More cops on the way, and it's a good thing, because the ones here have their hands full. Sometime in the past few minutes, a crime scene tech has arrived, stepping over the yellow tape strung around a U-shaped chunk of yard. Another is crouched low to the ground just outside it, reattaching the tape to branches or weighting it down with rocks, fastening it around wooden stakes he hammers into the frozen ground. They might as well be wrapping the dock in flashing neon lights.

Crime scene. Do not cross. Death happened here.

A chill runs down my spine, and my gaze scans the yard, the shoreline. I feel the cops watching us, feel their disapproving sneers and silent judgment, even though every time I stare back, they turn the other way. I feel their eyes everywhere.

Or maybe it's just Sam, his face pressed to a camera he fetched from Lord knows where, clicking away. He aims the lens at the wooden planks, the rocky path leading down to the water, the boat and the lake and the shoreline littered with rocks and tangled tree roots. At Paul and me, huddled close enough to share body heat.

"Where is she?" Paul asks, his gaze locked on the slice of lake between the boat and the dock. Micah stands in the very middle, talking to someone on his cell. There's nothing surrounding him but water.

"You can't see her from this angle. Not with the boat where it is and her so well under the dock. If I hadn't happened to look down when I'd been climbing out, I wouldn't have seen her, either."

Sam straightens, looking up the hill to where I'm standing, just outside the crime scene tape. "Hey, Charlie, what shoes were you wearing this morning when you came down here?"

I point to my snow boots, wag one around above the dirt. "These."

He moves closer, stepping carefully over a couple of markers placed in the soil. "Let me see the sole."

I hold on to Paul's shoulder for balance and show Sam the bottom. There's a piece of gravel lodged in one of the thick treads, but otherwise they look fresh out of the box.

He nods. "Looks like the one I spotted. Ground's probably too cold for it to be recent, but we'll take a casting just in case."

I shove my hands deep inside my pockets and frown. "What, do you think she marched into the lake from our backyard or something?"

The sirens are louder now, echoing across the water, the cars coming around the bend on the opposite side of the lake. Five, six minutes, tops.

"Just covering all the bases," Sam says, but his look tells me the real answer. He's not looking for the woman's prints. He's looking for the prints of whoever put her in the lake, and in a yard Paul and I have walked through a thousand times. Sam's gaze dips to Paul's running shoes, but he doesn't ask to see the tread.

"Give it up, Sam. Paul was with me."

"Are you saying you know time of death?"

"I'm saying whenever it was, Paul had nothing to do with it."

Paul threads a hand through my arm, gives an insistent tug. "Charlotte, let it go," he mumbles, even though I can't. How can he stand being accused of something so vile, something he had no part in? How can he let Sam barge into his house, onto his *property*, and treat him like a criminal?

Micah hollers across the dock. "Hey, Sam, can I get you up here with that camera?"

With one last look in my direction, Sam turns for the dock, jogging up the wooden planks and handing Micah the camera. He loops the strap around his neck, moves to the edge and lowers himself to his hands and knees, leaning his entire upper body over the water.

"Five foot five, maybe six, in the neighborhood of a hundred and twenty-five pounds. Light blond hair, looks natural. No roots. She's wearing jeans and a sweater but no coat."

He's right, I realize, something I didn't pick up on in the shock of spotting her. She wasn't wearing a coat when she slid into the lake. Even if she'd fallen in from a boat or another dock, she would have needed some protection from the cold. What happened to her coat?

Micah lies on his belly and snaps away, scooting up and down the dock for different angles.

"No scrapes or cuts that I can tell," he says when he's done, handing the camera back. "What I can see of her looks intact. Skin has a grayish cast, but that could just be from the water temperature. We won't know for sure until we haul her out."

"What does that mean?" When Paul doesn't answer, I glance over. "Does he think maybe she *did* drown?"

"Maybe," he says, but he doesn't sound at all convinced. I pull one hand from my pocket, slide it around his freezing one and hold on tight.

Micah pushes to a stand, and he and Sam stand there for a minute, discussing the best way to proceed. Micah wants her out of the water, like *yesterday*, but I don't see how. There are all sorts of obstacles in the way—the boat, the dock posts and floats, a patch of alligator weed Paul thought he got rid of last summer, spiky fingers reaching up from the water. There's no direct way to get her on land without going around one of them. Micah eyes the distance to shore, a good twenty feet, debating the flattest, most gradual spot.

Finally, they come up with a plan.

Paul is to let the boat drift far enough away from the dock to not disturb her, then start the motor and steer over to Micah's dock. Once the boat is gone, Micah will lower himself into the water, swim her as gently as possible to shore and slide her onto an awaiting tarp.

"That lake must be, what—fifty degrees?" I raised a wild-haired brother known up and down these hills for his talent for making dumbass decisions, but not even Chet would dip a toe in the lake this morning. Not in this weather, and not on purpose.

Micah shrugs. "More like forty, probably. And that's what the wet suit and towels are for, so I can dry off as soon as I get out."

"That's crazy. You're crazy. Even in a wet suit you're going to freeze to death. You're literally going to get hypothermia and die." I look to Paul for support, but he lifts a shoulder. "Excellent. So you're *both* completely out of your minds, and now we're gonna have two dead bodies instead of one."

"I'll be fine," Micah says.

Paul backs him up on it. "Seriously, Charlotte. He'll be fine. In and out before you know it."

I shake my head, roll my eyes. "What is it with you Southern men? Y'all aren't made of rubber, you know. You don't have nine lives."

Something catches Micah's attention at the top of the hill, and I turn to spot two more uniformed officers, new recruits the chief poached last month from the county sheriff's office, hustling around the side of the house. They're young, no older than me, which means they're probably straight out of police academy. I wonder how many crime scenes they've worked. How many dead people they've seen. They're about to get on-the-fly, on-the-job training.

Sam pulls a radio from a clip on his belt and calls up to them, rattling off a list of supplies they are to bring down from the cars.

He slides the radio back onto his belt. "Charlie, if you don't mind, the towels?"

"I'll get them," Paul offers. "I need to grab the boat keys anyway." He turns for the house, kicking into an easy jog up the stairs.

"There has to be a better way," I say to Micah.

Micah shoots me a sideways look. "If you think of one, I'm all ears." He sighs, and his voice softens. "Look, Char, I appreciate your concern, but somebody out there is wondering where this woman is and why she hasn't called home to check in. My goal is to get her back to them as quickly and honorably as possible, while also preserving whatever evidence she's still carrying. Even if that means I have to freeze my balls off to do it."

He's right, of course. If that were Chet or Paul under that dock, I'd want someone to cradle his head and swim him to shore, too. And I'd want him to do it now.

"You're a good man, Micah Hunt. Crazy, but good." I step back and let him get to work.

7

The recruits make it down the hill first, arms heavy with equipment and supplies.

Chief Hunt is here, too, an older, paunchier, grumpier version of Micah pacing the shoreline, barking out orders at anybody who comes within hollering distance. The chief's temper is well-known in these parts, a micromanaging control freak who terrorizes his staff with shouted commands and icy stares and doors slammed hard enough to fall off their hinges.

I'm sitting on a backyard step, watching the activity farther down the hill, when Paul sinks down next to me. A thick stack of towels is pressed to his chest. "Oh, good, you brought the big ones."

The ones we use on the boat or take to the beach, the ones I can wind three full times around my torso. They're like blankets, big enough for Micah's bulk, and plenty warm, too.

Paul studies my face. The wind whips the bare branches on the trees above his head, making an awful clacking sound, like a wind chime made of bones. His gaze dips to my stomach, toasty under the goose down. "You okay? I'm worried about you."

"Because of Sam?"

Paul tilts his head, solemn. "This isn't your fight. It's mine. You shouldn't let him get to you."

"I married you, which means it is my fight, and Sam's always been a sore loser. He needs to let this grudge go, especially when he's standing in your backyard."

Paul reaches for my hand, warms it in both of his. "It's yours, too, you know. The yard. The house. My heart. All of me belongs to you."

I melt, despite the icy air. Paul is so good at this part, at spoken sentiments and physical touch, at outward displays of affection. Kisses when he comes through the door, hand squeezes across the car console. Whispered I-love-yous in the dark. An aftereffect of losing Katherine so suddenly, he told me once. He's learned the hard way not to waste any time.

But after growing up in a household where people were either screaming, throwing things or passed out cold, Paul's brand of affection is something I'm still getting used to. Whenever we fight, which isn't all that often, it always feels like the end. Every time he leaves, a not-so-tiny part of me holds my breath until he comes back. As easy as it was to fall in love with Paul, I'm still getting the hang of how to be a married couple.

"Hey, *Paul*," Micah hollers up the hill. He shifts from foot to foot on the middle of the dock, tipping his head to the boat in an obvious *let's go*. He's already in his wet suit, his clothes and jacket in a heap on the dock, the golden necklace I watched him tuck carefully into a pocket. Paul has one just like it under all those layers, and so does Jax— Oh, crap, *Jax*.

"Paul, I forgot to tell you. I—"

"Can it wait?" Paul drops the towels onto my lap and stands, wriggling the boat keys from his pocket, casting an impatient glance down the hill.

"Of course. Go."

"I'll be back as soon as I can." He leans in for a lightning kiss, then takes off for the dock.

I clutch the towels to my chest, stuffing my hands into the folds, searching for a warm spot. The snow has started up again, tiny white flakes that swirl in the wind like confetti. Not the kind that sticks or does much damage, just a visible and annoying reminder of the cold.

Micah waits for Paul at the mouth of the ramp, and together they walk up to the boat. I can't hear them from here, but I see the focused tilt of Paul's head, his solemn nods, and I know he's listening hard. Instructions, I'm guessing.

Paul takes his seat at the helm, and Micah unties the ropes. He gives the vessel a gentle shove, and the currents catch the draft, the wind and the water carrying the boat away from the dock. Once Paul's made enough distance, he leans over the side, craning his neck for a better look. He catches sight of her, and his entire body stiffens.

Aw, hell.

I should have insisted on going on that boat with him. I should have known the dead woman would be a trigger. There's something distinctly different about being told there's a body and seeing it for yourself, feeling the horror—especially for Paul. He tries very hard not to talk about

Katherine with me, but there's no way this isn't digging up old wounds, pulling at painful threads. As awful as this is on me, for him this has to be a million times worse.

Micah gives the signal, and Paul starts the engine, swings the boat around, inches forward on the throttle and motors away, careful not to leave a wake.

Micah's descent down the ladder is just as quick. Quiet, too, all but the sucking in of a hard breath before his head disappears below the dock.

I shiver and inch closer, stepping right up to the lake's edge, doing the math. Fifteen seconds to swim under the dock to her, another fifteen to drag her out, maybe more. Behind me, the techs are antsy, too. They shift their boots in the dirt at the top of the tarp, their arms loose by their sides. The body bag is spread across the ground behind them. I stare at the empty water and hold my breath, the glare of snow and daylight rippling across the lake's surface making my eyes burn. What's taking him so long?

Micah's head reappears from under the dock, his hair slicked back, his face fish-belly white. So is the hand he's got hooked around the dead girl, who he carefully wrests from under the dock. He hasn't flipped her over yet. She floats facedown beside him in steady dips and bobs, white hair skimming the water.

Thanks to the cold and the dead weight, it takes him way too long to drag her to shore. He frog-kicks and drags his free arm through the water, his breath wet and sharp with effort, but he's still a good thirty feet from shore.

Hurry up hurry up hurry up.

The waiting tightens the back of my throat.

"Get back," Chief Hunt snaps, and I look down to see one of my boots has landed inside the tape. "I don't need you contaminating the crime scene."

I move a few steps back up the hill.

Paul jogs up, panting lightly from his sprint back from Micah's dock, right as Micah makes land. He plants his feet on the lake's slippery bottom and shifts her so she's in front of him, steering her carefully to shore. The techs run down the hill, wading a good couple of feet into the water.

"Grab her under the arms," Micah says, his voice tight, his teeth chattering loud enough to be heard clear across the lake.

"Gently," Chief Hunt yells. "Be careful with her, for crap's sake."

Between the four of them, they guide her up and out of the water, sliding her carefully onto the tarp. She settles at an awkward angle, hair hanging on either side of her face like a slick white curtain, smothering all but a sliver of porcelain jaw.

Micah hugs his sopping arms around his belly and leans over the body, careful not to drip on her. "I can't tell if this rigor is from mortis or the temperature, but the ME will know. Skin's intact, as far as I can see. Clothes and shoes look expensive." He's so cold his body is practically vibrating.

I rush down the hill, shaking out the towels on the way.

Sam stops me at the edge of the tarp with a hand in the air. "Stay back," he says, but he passes the towels to Micah.

He wraps one around his shoulders, but tosses the others on the ground. He turns to the two techs. "Okay, let's get her into the bag. Sam and I lift her up, and y'all slide the bag underneath. You two—" he points a finger at the recruits, flinging them with icy water "—hold the bottom edge of the tarp so whatever's on her doesn't wash back into the lake. Everybody clear on what they'll be doing?"

Head nods all around. Everybody moves into position. Chief Hunt moves to where he can get a better look.

"One…" Micah wedges an arm under her hips. "…two… three."

What happens next is a blur of hurried movements and moving limbs, of male grunts and shouted orders. From their voices, I get that it's not her weight but her rigidity that's making the task difficult, and they handle her like a piece of their grandma's best crystal. They lift her body in the air like it weighs nothing, cradling her to their chests and shuffling until she's hovering over the body bag. I try to get a peek at her face, but they're clustered all around her, a wall of shoulders and backs, and I'm standing at the wrong end. All I see are the bottom half of her pants and her shoes. Micah was right; they do look expensive.

Brown suede ankle boots with a thick stacked heel, not too high, fastened with a dark leather strap at the top. Like nothing in my closet, or anything I'd ever buy for myself—too prim, far too impractical on these muddy hills. City shoes.

Something slips across my mind, something important, but I'm too much in shock to catch it.

"Gentle now," Micah says.

They lower her into the awaiting body bag, tucking her hands and feet inside. I take in their words with a silent sigh of relief. They don't know her. A stranger from out of town.

I toss a relieved look to Paul, but he doesn't look up. He's standing at the top edge of the tarp, staring down at the woman nestled in shiny black plastic. His face is as white as the terry cloth slung over Micah's shoulders, and I wonder whose face Paul is seeing—this woman's, or Katherine's?

"Oh, baby." I shove past the other officers, moving up and around to the other side of the tarp. "Oh, Paul."

"I'm fine," he mumbles, his face a death mask. He takes a step backward, his sneakers slipping on a patch of rock and dirt. "I'm fine."

He's not fine. This is Paul from last March, when he took to bed claiming to be under the weather, when I brought him hot tea and chicken soup that he left untouched on the nightstand, on a day I later found out was Katherine's birthday. This is him pretending to be asleep so I wouldn't worry, even though under the covers his entire body was trembling. Most days, it's just me and Paul in our relationship, but for a few days a year, on her birthday or their anniversary or the anniversary of her death, there's a third. The beautiful, funny, sexy, smart, perfect ghost of Katherine.

"What's wrong?" At first I think Sam's question is directed at me, until I see the way he's watching Paul. I can see Sam thinking, processing Paul's distress, landing on the most obvious reason. "Mr. Keller, do you know this woman? Do you know her name?"

Paul swallows, and then he shakes his head. "No. I just thought…"

"You thought what?"

A gust of sudden wind blows up the hill, whipping Paul's hair. He looks at me, and his cheeks, already pink from the cold, turn even pinker. We don't talk about Katherine; that is the unspoken agreement between us, and now here she is, standing between us like a live grenade.

"You thought what?" Sam says again.

I take a step to my left, blocking Paul's view of the body. "Shut up, Sam. If you'd stop to think for one freaking second, you'd know what he thought. Just let it go, will you…"

The words die in my throat, because it's then I happen to look down. To get my first good look at the face half-hidden beneath plastic and a weedy fall of wet hair. Milky skin with a smattering of freckles across her nose. Pale lips parted on a silent gasp. Sunken, clouded eyes open in a lifeless stare with pupils the color of a late-summer sky.

It's the woman from yesterday, the one I found Paul talking to in town. The one who was trying to get her hooks in my Keller.

"Get to town," Chief Hunt is saying to Sam. "Find out her name, where she was from, anything you can about who she was and what she was doing here, including where she was staying. Start with the hotels, and if they don't know her, work your way through the rental agencies. Or on second thought, start there, at the agencies. If she came here looking for a quiet getaway, she'll be in one of the cabins."

Start with the hotels. The thought slices through my mind, but I somehow force myself not to say it out loud. Whatever that woman came to Lake Crosby looking for, it wasn't quiet. I think of the way she looked at me yesterday, her strange reaction when I introduced myself as a Keller. A flash of surprise, and her gaze went immediately to Paul. "Keller," she'd murmured, and something about the way she looked at him put me on edge. She knew the name, knew its significance in this town. I'm certain of it.

I whirl around, and Paul is staring at me silently, urgently, from a few feet away. I meet his gaze, and everything goes still. My entire body changes in that moment of understanding. At his message, sharp and sparkling.

Stop talking.

"Call me as soon as you've got an address," Chief Hunt is saying, "but do *not* go inside. Until we know otherwise, we'll be treating her last known location as a potential crime scene. Now scoot. Micah, I'll be waiting for your paperwork." He turns and lumbers back up the hill.

Maybe I misunderstood. Maybe Paul is just embarrassed

at his reaction, at this sudden swell of post-traumatic stress he tries so hard to stuff down. Maybe I'm reading more into this.

No. No, that's not right. Paul looked her straight in the eye, and he *talked* to her. Even if she only asked him for directions or a restaurant recommendation, he would remember. Her face is too pretty not to be noticed, and Paul notices *everything*.

So why did he just lie?

By now Micah is dressed. He clomps down the ramp in his boots, pointing to the techs. "Seal the bag and take her up to Harris Regional. I'll call the medical examiner, let her know you're on the way. Don't forget the tarp. She's gonna want that, too."

The creak of the body bag's zipper is like a knife, cutting through the cold and crawling all over my skin. The tech pulls it snug, then slips a plastic tag through the pull and draws it tight, essentially padlocking the bag until the next person to touch her clips the tag. Chain of custody, Sam told me it's called, during one of our gas station talks.

"You okay?" Micah's lips are blue, but his eyes are bright with excitement. He's itching to strap on an oxygen tank, sink to the bottom of the lake and dredge up whatever the woman dropped. He probably doesn't even notice the cold.

Paul nods. His expression is parked in Neutral. His face is completely closed off, like those metal shutters people roll down the windows of their summer cabins, familiar but guarded. He glances up the hill at the house. "I'm gonna grab a shower."

Micah shifts his gaze to mine. "You don't have to stay down here, either. I'll call up if I run into any snags. Just keep your cell close. The cops'll need an official statement at some point, so don't go anywhere without telling them, got it?"

I nod. Paul grabs my hand and tugs me toward the stairs, but I tug back.

Micah may be back in his clothes, but his hair is still sopping, the ends clumped and turning white with ice. I reach out and squeeze his arm. "I'll bring down some coffee and whatever else I can scrounge up, okay? I'll also make sure the basement door is open, in case y'all need a bathroom or you want to warm up in the shower."

Micah gives me a smile, purple lips against bright white skin. "Thanks, Char. You're the best."

Paul looks relieved when I turn for the house, and he leads me up the hill at a pace that sends my heart hurtling. Thanks to his daily trots up and down these hills, this climb is just a quick jaunt for him, barely any effort at all. I've already run up these steps once today, and it wiped me out.

"Babe, babe," I say, pulling on his arm. We're four steps in and I'm already panting. "Slow down. I can't—"

"Hey, Charlie," Sam says, not a question.

Paul and I pause, sharing a fleeting look that dumps me back into my body. I feel Sam's gaze on me like an army of ants, biting and stinging my skin. He's coming up the hill behind us, a duffel slung over his shoulder.

"I need an answer from you, too. Do you have an ID on the body?"

Paul squeezes my hand so tight it's almost painful, and if I had any doubts as to what's going on here, I don't anymore. This is where things could get sticky.

Because I don't have to think too hard about what would happen if I were to blurt out the truth. If I were to tell Sam that, no, I don't *know* her, but we did have a fleeting encounter. That I only noticed her because she was talking to

Paul, who was not too traumatized from his memories of Katherine like I first thought, but aware enough to look a cop in the eyes and lie.

Sam would pounce on my confession, on the way it would implicate Paul. *If nothing else, I've got him for lying to a police officer during an investigation. He won't walk away from this one, not this time. Not again. I told Charlie, and she went and married him anyway.* I feel Sam's eyes on mine now, conjuring up all the rumors that could come from this very moment. All the stories taking shape in his head, taking on a life of their own.

And Paul.

Paul might say he understands, he might tell me we are fine, but would we be? Would he love me just the same? Lie or implicate your new husband and there goes the marriage, the money, the stability. And really, what's one tiny, silly, inconsequential lie compared to everything Paul has given me? It's not a difficult decision.

Especially since I *don't* know her; I don't have anything to add other than that she was in town yesterday afternoon. Something that whoever else ran into her will surely tell Sam, as soon as he makes it to town. Self-preservation, I've only been doing it my whole life. The lie comes with surprising ease.

"Sorry. I've never seen her before, either."

8

June 12, 1999
5:53 p.m.

For those first few months after his mother's funeral, it hurt to see Mrs. Keller again. She was constantly dropping by the house or calling him up to check in, and every time, her voice would hit him like a surprise punch to the underbelly, that moment before you could tighten up your muscles to absorb some of the blow. If he were a funny guy, he'd say it hurt like a mother.

Jax had known Mrs. K all his life, but now he couldn't talk to her without remembering those days when his mom was withering away and his heart wouldn't stop pounding. When Mrs. K was a constant presence in their house, taking charge in that way of hers, doing the laundry and making sure the house was clean and everybody got where they needed to be. She was the one who set up the food deliveries, bossing the other moms around and working the sign-up sheet like a four-star general. Jax's mother wasted away in her wheelchair while their refrigerator busted at the seams. Talk about some sick irony.

She was there at the funeral, too, hugging him so hard with those skinny arms of hers that he felt like his bones might pop, then hounding him constantly in the dark days afterward. *We're all hurting. Please don't suffer in silence. Talk to me, sweetheart. I'm here for you, always.* He loved Mrs. K, but she was the kind of mother you didn't want as your own, needy and demanding and completely relentless. When he'd pulled back, when he'd stopped taking her calls and made himself scarce whenever she dropped by, she marched up the stairs and barged into his room.

"Jax Edwards, where the hell have you been?"

He shot upright on his bed, grateful he wasn't naked or—Jesus, what if he'd been jerking off? It was bad enough that a pair of his underwear was stuck to her left heel. He tried to ignore it, but he couldn't keep his eyes off the damn thing.

"Here. Around." He shrugged his shoulders up to his ears. "I don't know."

"You don't know."

He shook his head.

Mrs. K sighed, a heavy, put-out sound, and moved closer, dragging the underwear for a few steps before she kicked it aside. "Your mother warned me this would happen. She asked me to look after you—did you know that?"

Nobody had ever told him as much, but Jax wasn't surprised. Why else would Mrs. K be coming over here all the time? Certainly not because he was such great company. Hell, the only person besides Mrs. K who wanted to spend time with him was Paul.

She sank onto the edge of his bed, draping a hand over his knee. "She was so worried about you, sweetheart. About you doing exactly this. She always said you were the more sensitive child."

The pity on her face brought tears to his eyes, but he blinked them away. He wasn't about to cry now. No way. Not happening. Not with Mrs. K looking at him like that, like he might break apart or something.

"Uh, what am I doing?"

"Sitting up here all alone, punishing yourself for something that isn't your fault. Pulling away from the people who love you most, pushing us away. Your family and Paul and me. We love you and we know you're hurting, and we want to be there for you. Please let us be there for you."

Jax couldn't talk. His lungs were filled with concrete, his tongue weighted down with rocks. He wanted to tell her about all those times in the woods when he stared at his rifle and wondered if what Pammy believed was true—that there was a better life after this one, that his mom was living it up on some fluffy cloud up in the sky. He wondered what it felt like when your heart stopped beating and your lungs stopped pulling air, when all those horrible, awful thoughts going through your head just…stopped. He wondered if death hurt or if it was a relief.

"I adore you, Jax, and not because Paul does or because your sweet mother told me to. I've loved you since that first day at kindergarten, when you walked up to Paul and asked if he wanted to be friends. There's sweetness at the core of you, and that's how I know how much you're hurting. Because you're a good man who loves with all his heart and soul."

Well, hell. What was he supposed to say to that? Nice words and all, but coming from the wrong mother, they didn't stick. He didn't feel sweet at his core. He felt mean and ugly and wrong.

"You will survive this, I promise." Mrs. K leaned forward, grabbed his face in both hands. "I will see to it. Whatever you need, wherever you end up, I'll always be here for you, sweetheart. Always."

Ever since, he'd been making more of an effort to show up, mostly so she wouldn't ever barge into his room again. Once a week he dragged his ass out of the woods, scrubbed off the dirt and grime, and came here, to Paul's. He said all the right words. He made sure to smile at least once. And judging by Mrs. K's reaction, it seemed to be working.

She spotted him coming up her back deck, calling to him through the open double doors. "Jax Edwards, you hurry up and get your behind in here. How are you, sweetheart? Come here and give me a hug."

Mrs. K was a hugger, one of those people who liked physical contact. She was always patting his shoulder and squeezing his hand. Never creepy or inappropriate, just… nice. He'd learned a long time ago it was easier to just stand there and take it. She smelled like flowers and honey.

"Hi, Mrs. K. Thanks for the key chain."

She was generous, too, always giving him things—Tshirts from places she visited, souvenirs and little keepsakes, anything to let him know she was thinking of him. Mostly little trinkets like this silver ring with the Town of Lake Crosby seal, but she had great taste, and occasionally she'd splurge on something nice, like the gold necklace she gave him for graduation. Her gifts often came in threes, for him and Paul and Micah.

"You're so welcome, sugar. I figured you could use one for your dorm room this fall. How's your summer going? Did you find a job yet?"

Jax shook his head. "Still looking."

He wasn't looking. The last summer before college, and the only thing he could get even remotely excited about was getting the hell out of this place. Sixty-six days until freshman orientation at Duke University, two hundred and eighty-eight miles of space between there and here. Jax couldn't wait.

"I'm sure you'll find something soon," she said, leading him into the kitchen. "How's your father?"

"He's fine." It was what everybody wanted to hear when they asked that question, but not Mrs. K. She stopped walking to give him a look, and he amended, "He's a robot. My sister's a Jesus freak. And they think I'm the one having difficulty adjusting."

Her expression softened. "Everybody grieves in their own way, sugar. There's no right or wrong to it, just… different. I realize it's difficult, but try to remember that they're hurting, too." She reached out, patted his arm. "I'll talk to your father and see if I can't get him to be a little more supportive."

The idea of Mrs. K dressing down his father made Jax laugh out loud, even though he was torn between amusement and hope she could actually do something to fix it.

He pointed to the music thumping on the ceiling. "Is that Paul?"

She rolled her eyes. "Yes, it's Paul. Tell him to turn it down, will you? Oh, and here." She grabbed three Cokes from the fridge, shoved the icy cans at his chest along with a bag of chips from the pantry. "Take these up with you."

"Who's the third one for?"

"Micah." She sighed. "Do me a favor and try not to kill him."

9

We're all the way to the top of the yard before Paul pulls me to a stop. "It's not what you think."

I laugh—both at the way the climb has me huffing like I've just run a marathon, and at the absurdity of his statement. "Paul, even *I* don't know what I'm thinking. Like, zero clue. I just watched you lie to a police officer for reasons I can't figure out, and then you made it pretty obvious you wanted me to do the same."

"I didn't lie. Not technically. I said I don't know her, and I *don't*." He shakes his head, corrects himself. "Didn't. I don't know her name or where she's from. I don't know anything about her, other than that she stopped me yesterday to ask where I got my coffee."

"Well, *I* lied. I said I'd never seen her before."

He winces. "You said that, didn't you?"

"Yes, I did. And I'd really like it if you told me why."

Paul gazes down the hill to where Micah is huddled with the others at the edge of the crime scene. He stands a good head above the rest, his wet hair gleaming in the light. The cops around him stand rapt, nodding at whatever Micah's saying. The hometown hero.

"I panicked, okay? When they flipped her over and I saw her face, I panicked. Because you know exactly what would have happened if I'd told them the truth. You know what everyone down there would have thought."

I *do* know, because I thought the same thing myself: that's two dead bodies under the same dock. Four years apart, but still. Surely, *surely*, that must be a horrible co-incidence.

"Just so we're clear, I'm not mad about the lie per se. When you grow up like Chet and I did, stretching the truth is pretty much the same thing as surviving."

Yes, sir, our mama will be home later tonight. No, sir, we don't live here alone. We're children.

But this wasn't my lie; it was Paul's.

If only it had been anyone other than Sam who was doing the asking. Anybody else, and maybe I would have come clean. I could have reminded Paul of their fleeting encounter and everyone would have brushed it off as a blunder.

But it wasn't anyone else; it was Sam. Sam with his pursed lips and squinty eyes. With his silent judgment and retracted friendship. A year ago, he was capping off his workday with a glass of iced tea on my front step, and now suddenly I'm Mrs. Keller.

I reach out, touch Paul's sleeve. "Paul, who was that woman? What did she say to you yesterday?"

He sighs, a rush of breath I can feel on my forehead. "Can we finish this upstairs? I really could use a shower."

He really could. The cut on his forehead needs a good,

deep scrubbing before it scabs over, and I can't tell if the mud from his slide down Fontana Ridge is dried or just frozen. He smells like cold and earth and sweat.

I point him to the outdoor staircase that leads to the mud-room—the route we usually take to the house. "I'll meet you up there. I need to open the downstairs first."

Paul heads for the stairs, and I step around the outdoor furniture and tap in the code on the pad next to the base-ment door, a feature I've never once used until now. This door is one we usually unlock from inside, sliding the glass panels back into deep pockets that disappear into the walls and turn the indoors into outside. This entire level is made for summertime entertaining—a kitchen and fully stocked bar, a TV screen as big as the wall, his-and-hers powder rooms and a walk-in shower big enough for twenty people. In a stroke of genius, Paul painted the ceilings on the over-hang a metallic bronze, so when the sun hits the lake just right, it bathes everything in an orange glow.

The lock releases with a metallic thunk, and I step inside and slide the door closed behind me. The air is warmer than outside, but just barely. I flip on the lights and crank the thermostat to toasty. In the bathrooms, I restock the toilet paper and lay out fresh towels for Micah and whoever else needs them, then haul my ass up some more stairs.

I toss my coat on the bed and step to the bathroom, where Paul is coming out of what must have been a two-second shower. Fresh rivulets of water drip down his skin, naked except for a waterproof runner's watch and a twin to the golden necklace Micah unlooped from his neck and tucked in a pocket. A rectangular pendant engraved with the town's coordinates hanging from a gold ball chain, a graduation gift from Paul's mother so they could always find their way home.

My gaze dips to the fresh bruise on Paul's hip, a dark smudge of red and purple surrounding a melon-sized lump and curling down onto his thigh. I pull a towel off the bar and hand it to him. "That must have been some tumble. I guess Noland Ridge is pretty treacherous this time of year."

He swipes the towel over his back, scrubs it over his hair. "It wasn't so much a tumble as a skid straight down. And it was Fontana, not Noland." He wraps the towel around his waist, his fingers freezing on the terry cloth. "But I said that already. That was a test."

I grin. Both ridges are nearby, and both can be dicey, but Paul would never confuse the two, not unless he was lying about how he got hurt. Of course it was a test—one I'm happy to say he passed.

I rummage through a drawer and pull out some supplies, cotton swabs and antiseptic and a tube of liquid bandage, lining everything up on the vanity. I point him to the padded seat by the mirror. "Now sit down and start talking."

He shifts on his feet, glancing at his watch. "Can I get dressed first?"

"Not until I clean that thing on your forehead." I drape a hand over his damp shoulder and press down, and he drops to the seat. I hook a finger under his chin and tilt his face toward mine.

His eyes drift closed. "Well, I was headed back to the office to meet you when she stopped me. She saw my coffee cup and she wanted to know if it was any good. She said she hadn't scoped out the shops in town yet and was dying for a decent cappuccino."

I reach for the bottle of antiseptic, making a humming sound for him to continue.

"I remember thinking I hadn't seen her in the restaurants or on the streets. Not that I notice every tourist, but you saw her. She's pretty—*was* pretty."

I douse the cut with liquid, and he hisses at the sting. "Sorry." Not sorry. Not jealous, but not sorry, either. "Keep going."

Paul winces as I dab a cotton swab around the wound. "Anyway, I told her to skip the coffee shop for the counter at the back of the organic market, that their beans are way better. She thanked me, and that's when you walked up. She stopped talking."

"No, Paul. That's when *you* stopped talking. *She* perked up when I introduced myself, remember? It was like a light bulb went off in her head when I said the name Keller. I think she recognized it or something."

His eyes open. "Maybe she was house hunting. Even if she didn't come here looking for me specifically, my name's on at least a dozen lot signs. Maybe she didn't make the connection until you said the name."

It wouldn't be the first time Paul was approached by a stranger in town, someone who saw his homes in *Dwell* or *Architectural Digest* or on Houzz and wanted to meet the wizard behind the curtain. In the architecture world, Paul is kind of a rock star. People drive hundreds of miles just to beg him to design their dream house.

I pinch the skin around the cut and seal the wound with liquid bandage, then toss the tube on the counter. "Even more reason to just admit you ran into her randomly on the street. What if they find your name in her search history? What if she, I don't know, has pictures of some of your houses on her phone? At least then you won't look like you've got something to hide."

"Is that what you think, that I'm hiding something? Because I told you everything. There's nothing else going on here."

The hurt in his voice straightens my spine. "That's not what I said at all. I know you're not the reason that woman ended up in the lake. You have an alibi, remember? We were together all night."

Paul leans into the mirror to inspect his forehead. "This looks great, babe. Thanks." He squeezes my arm and brushes by, dropping his towel over the bar on his way out of the room.

I watch his naked form disappear into the closet, my chest going hot with exasperation, with aggravation. Paul is a great communicator when he wants to be, but other times—like now—he plies me with only the basics. *My first wife died unexpectedly. My dad left when I was ten. My mother can be a little controlling. Jax was once a friend.* Flat, nonspecific answers that tell me nothing but the facts.

I hustle after Paul into the closet. "What happens if somebody saw us talking? What if nosy old Wanda Whitaker was looking out her upstairs window and spotted the three of us standing in the alley? Sam's already halfway to town. He'll be questioning everybody."

Paul steps into a pair of navy boxer shorts, digs around in a drawer for a long-sleeved shirt. "Mrs. Whitaker is in Ohio, visiting her daughter. She's not back until after Thanksgiving."

"Somebody else, then."

"Who? It was freezing yesterday. Nobody was out." Paul pulls the shirt over his head and reaches for a pair of pants. "Let's just give it a day or two. See if anybody comes forward."

I fold my arms across my chest, leaning a hip against the wall. "By then it'll only be worse. Why can't we just tell the truth? It'll look better coming now, and from us rather than somebody else."

"If I thought it would help the investigation in any way, I would call Sam right this second, but I just…" His shoulders slump, a sock dangling from each hand. "I can't, Char. I can't go through that again. The suspicion. The rumors. I just can't."

His pained expression, the way his voice goes raw and real… My heart cracks wide open, and I stop pushing.

He thanks me with a thin smile, then opens a door at the far end of the closet, pulls out a backpack and leans it up against the wall. It's the big one he uses for multiday hiking trips, the one he once lugged two thousand miles up the Appalachian Trail. He yanks open some drawers and shoves in clothes much like the ones he's wearing—waterproof pants, a thermal shirt and socks, hats and gloves and fleece neck warmers. He stuffs his feet into his brand-new leather clodhoppers, leaving them untied. The laces slither like bright red snakes across the hardwood floor.

A dull pounding starts up behind my eyes. "Paul, why does it look like you're going camping?"

"I realize the timing's not ideal. That I'm leaving you to deal with all this." He swipes a hand in the general direction of the lake. "But I'll only be gone a day, maybe two. Three at the most." He closes the backpack with one smooth tug on the string, picks it up and slings it over a shoulder.

"Paul." I pause, trying to pull my shit together. Failing. I press two fingers to my temples. "You have got to be kidding me. You're *leaving*? Where are you going?"

"Walk with me, will you?" Paul brushes past me, moving in long strides through the bedroom and into the hall, so fast I have to jog to keep up. "With the storm blowing in, they're going to have to push Pause on the investigation anyway. I probably won't miss much. I'll be back before they even notice I'm gone."

Like hell. I rush down the stairs, picturing Paul in that hammock of his, a thin sheet of nylon wrapped around a Paul-sized chunk of ice. "Micah will notice, and you're going to freeze to death out there. And how are you going to get anywhere? You don't have a car, remember?"

I don't offer up my old Honda, both because I don't want him to go, and even if I did, he'd never get it out of the driveway. There are police cars parked every which way out there, ten tons of metal blocking the garage door. There's no way he'd ever sneak past.

By the time I make it to the kitchen, Paul is already in the pantry, snatching items off the shelves and dropping them into his backpack in no apparent order. Granola, energy bars, some soups, an industrial-sized bag of beef jerky. Hiking food, enough to last him for days. This is a man who loads the dishwasher with mechanical precision, who after I put away the groceries rearranges the pantry so all labels are facing out. He doesn't throw anything in anywhere willy-nilly.

A jackhammer starts up in my chest, rushing blood to my head so fast it makes me dizzy. "You know how this looks, right? What am I supposed to say? How do I explain you taking off as soon as a dead woman washes up?"

"I know how it looks, which is why I'm asking you— no, *begging* you—to just sit tight and not say anything. If Micah asks, which he will, make something up. Tell him I'm on a work trip or something."

I trail Paul back into the kitchen, watching him rummage through a cabinet by the sink, pulling out a reusable bottle and clipping it to a hook on the backpack. "At least tell me where you're going. What's so urgent you have to leave right now?"

Now, finally, Paul stops moving. He reaches for my hands, holding them firmly in both of his. "Do you trust me, Charlotte?"

I don't have to think about it, not even for a second. I nod.

"I'm going to find Jax." I open my mouth to tell him Jax was looking for him, but Paul stops me. "When I get back, you and I are going to sit down, and I am going to tell you everything. I promise. But right now I really don't have time." He releases me, hefting the backpack onto his shoulders. "There's money in the safe. The code's 3-0-3-1-9. If you forget, I wrote it on the inside flap of the Le Corbusier book."

I flinch, and automatically, my hand goes to his ring on my finger. I feel the weight of it, the significance. The day Paul slid it over my knuckle was the day I swore to never give anyone, least of all Paul, reason to think I only want him for his wealth. Yes, I like living in a pretty house. No, I never have to choose between going cold or going hungry again. But there are enough people in this town who think I traded my morals for money, and it would kill me if Paul were one of them.

"Paul, I don't want your money."

He stops, turns back. "That's not what I— Come on, Charlotte. You know that's not what I meant. What's mine is yours is ours. You work just as hard as I do for that money. It's there for *both* of us, just in case."

I ignore the first part, even though I don't know. Not really. It's true I work hard, but we both know I wouldn't have a job if not for Paul. I am a guest here, living off the back of my all-too-generous husband.

But a more pressing point is, what would Paul do if I held out my hand right now? Would he smile and slap some bills in my palm? Would it make me a different person in his eyes? Paul once told me he admired me for the way I worked two jobs at sixteen, paying the bills for Chet and me, pulling us both up by the bootstraps. He said he loved how my penniless past shaped me into a person he wished he could be.

But like I explained to him then, I wouldn't wish my past on anyone. You have to come from nothing to be like me. You have to suffer. And one thing I know about my husband is that he's never suffered, not that way. He has no idea what it's like to eat nothing but ramen noodles for thirteen days in a row, or to have your electricity cut off in the dead of winter. He's never felt that kind of worry. Privilege will do that to a person, make you blind to the struggles of those who exist outside your bubble.

"In case of what?"

"Emergency. Disaster." He lifts his hands in the air, lets them fall to his sides with a slap. Money is his love language, and he can't see a single thing wrong with him offering it to me now in place of himself. "I don't know. The point is, it's there for whatever you need while I'm gone."

"What I need is for you to stay here, with me."

"I wish I could do that." He looks sincere enough, but I don't believe him. There's too much here I don't understand, too much he's not telling me. He might not say all of what he's thinking, but he's not supposed to lie.

He presses both hands to my face, his palms cupping my cheeks. "Promise me you'll sit tight until I get back. Promise me you won't tell anyone where I'm going."

"Not even your mother?"

"*Especially* not her. Promise me."

I shake my head, not because I don't want to make that promise, but because I've already seen the gleam in his eyes, the determined set of his chin, and I know I can't stop him. It's the same expression he wears on a build site, where he can look at a pile of bricks and already see the finished walls. For Paul, there is an answer to every problem, a neat and logical path to every solution. In his head, at least, he's halfway around the lake already.

But I can't make myself say the words. I can't make that promise.

"What about Friday?" I say instead.

"What happens Friday?"

"The appointment with the doctor. The ultrasound."

Paul grimaces. "I will do my best, my very, very best, to be back." He pauses, glancing over his shoulder at the door. "But I can't make any promises."

"Then neither can I."

Paul threads a hand around my neck and pulls me in for a kiss, then drops to his knees and presses his lips to my stomach. I stand there like a statue, the room spinning like the world has shifted on its axis and I don't know how to stop it.

"I love you." He pushes himself to his feet. "I'll be home before you know it. Take care of yourself and our baby."

"I love you, too," I whisper, but he's already gone—off like a rabbit released from a trap.

I watch him through the front window, backpack bobbing as he kicks into an easy jog up the drive, and think of my mother. Shoving Chet in my arms and leaving us in a trailer with nothing but crumbs. Ordering me to stop fussing, that she'd be right back. The way my lungs locked up when I looked through the window to see her dropping into some stranger's car.

Now I sink onto a stool and look around Paul's big, fancy house—a place with everything I thought I ever wanted, only now it feels empty and cold. It doesn't take me long to realize why.

In the thirteen months I've lived here, I've never slept in this big house alone.

Paul and I were on our fourth date, halfway up the trail to High Falls, when he told me about Katherine.

"We met in college, at one of those dives that serves hot wings and PBR in pitchers. She was on a date with some other guy, but I didn't care. He went to the bathroom, and I slid into his seat. Later she told me they were just friends, but it was obvious they were close. I assumed they were together." He grinned over his shoulder. "I'm persistent, but then again, you already know that."

I smiled, thinking back to the first day he walked into the gas station, how he made me ring him up three times— for gas, then for gum, then for a $100 prepay card I knew he'd never use because clearly he was the type of guy who could afford a monthly plan. *I promise not to buy one of those*, he'd said, pointing to a giant jar of pickled eggs I had to fish out with a ladle, *but only if you tell me your name*. He was persistent, all right, and already I was smitten. Our fourth date, and I would have followed him anywhere.

"We were married eleven years, all of them happy. Until one day, a Thursday, Katherine went for a swim. Her daily morning ritual, like me and my runs. She went out the back door, me out the front. Do you know her last words to me? 'The raccoon pooped on the back deck again.' I wish I could say it was something more poignant, but we talked about raccoon shit. If nothing else, I've learned never to leave someone without a proper goodbye."

He didn't look back this time, but I could hear the emotion in his words, the way pain had turned his voice vulnerable. Every other sound faded away—the water pounding the rocks below, my lungs sucking air, the blood thudding in my ears. It was just me and Paul on that hill, and his love for her was flaying my heart.

"I loved her for every day of our time together. I would have loved her the rest of our lives. That's why all the talk afterward was so infuriating, so unbelievably appalling. Those people don't know me at all. They didn't see how I suffered."

"God, Paul. I'm so sorry."

He stopped in the middle of path then, turning back. "No, *I'm* sorry for burdening you with all this. But I know I'm the elephant in every room in this town. I know how people talk, and I wanted you to hear it from me, not them. Even though, obviously, it's still a painful subject."

Obviously. And he'd waited until he was here, leading me up a hiking trail, rather than face-to-face across a dinner table. A group of rowdy hikers came bounding down the trail, and Paul slapped on a smile for them, for me. By the time they disappeared into the woods, the moment had passed.

We started back up the hill, and that was when I knew.

The thing I wanted more than anything, the *only* thing, was for Paul to love me like he had once loved Katherine.

10

A half-dozen trips up and down the hill later and I am officially done. Spaghetti legs, freezer-burn lungs, skin tingling like I've been slapped all over. I can't keep up with the thirst of Micah and the others, at last count seven hungry bodies who've sucked down the coffee faster than I can make it, along with five packs of cookies and two banana breads I dug out of the freezer, defrosted and slathered in cream cheese.

By now the body is long gone, laid out on some cold metal slab at Harris Regional, being poked and prodded by the medical examiner. The cops have made a mess of the back hill, a crisscross of muddy tracks and footprints fanning out from a blue party tent they erected over a flat spot at the bottom. They've dragged over a teak table and some chairs, arranged them around a firepit they coaxed into a roaring bonfire. It sends up smoke signals people can see for miles. *Dead woman found here. Rubberneckers welcome.*

The mess inside is not much better, wrappers and crumbs and coffee grounds scattered like dirt across the marble of the kitchen island. I swipe the trash into the can and the grounds into the sink along with my breakfast, a bowl of oatmeal now congealed into a gooey chunk. I shove it down the disposal, and the way it clings to my spoon sends a wave of nausea rolling through. Eat or puke, I can't decide. So far this pregnancy hasn't been much fun.

Especially since there's no one here for me to share it with. I think of Paul, of his trek to find Jax, and the tears rise unexpectedly, hot and sudden. Paul has told me almost nothing about his former best friend, why the summer after their senior year Jax went off the deep end, walked away from his family and friends, and disappeared into the woods.

Paul's silence makes it all too easy to believe the rumors. That Jax cheated Paul out of money or popularity, or he slept with one of Paul's girlfriends. That there was a fight that got out of control, a fit of jealousy, a push too hard. That Jax hit his head, knocked something loose. That the devil made him do it. Lake Crosby gossip and speculation because the people who know—Paul and Micah and Jax—aren't talking.

I hate that Paul left me here to deal with Micah and Sam, with work and clients, with his mother, who has surely spotted the smoke signals by now. I hate that in a few hours, the sun is going to sink behind the trees and everybody will pack up and leave. The windows will go black with night, and I'll be in this big house all alone.

The front door swings open, and I jump. "Hey, Charlie, what's with all the cop cars?"

My brother, Chet, the only soul on the planet still allowed to call me Charlie. My cell has been lighting up with his messages all morning, and the truth is I've been expecting him. My brother is a needy guy, and he doesn't take well to anybody ignoring him, least of all me.

I swipe my eyes with my sleeves, clear the tears from my throat. "In the kitchen."

There's the thump of him kicking the heavy door with a boot, the thuds of his soles echoing in the high atrium of the house as he heads straight for the back window. He presses his face to the glass, looking down the hill to where Micah and the others are trampling what's left of the summer grass. "What's going on? Did somebody get arrested or something?"

"No. Somebody died."

His head whips around, his eyes bulging. "No shit. Like *died*, died?"

I nod, flipping on the water and rinsing out my bowl. "She washed up sometime last night."

He glances back out the window, down the hill to the dock. "Popular spot."

I don't want to feel that little niggle of doubt, but it nudges me between the ribs anyway. One body under the dock is a tragedy. Two is a pattern. I tell myself that it is a coincidence, that Paul had nothing to do with either. He was in bed with me all last night, and he loved Katherine. Her death was an accident, one he mourns to this day.

And yet I still hear all Sam's awful, horrible arguments, the words he said the night before I walked down the aisle to marry Paul. That former competitive swimmers don't just sink to the bottom of the lake. That drowning is the hardest murder to prove. That one of the reasons Paul is so loaded is because he inherited all her wealth. I don't know how much, but it's got to be millions. Her family had even more money than Paul's, and she got it all when they passed.

"Chet, stop. This is serious. They think she was murdered."

"Seriously? Why? Who was she?"

"I don't know. A tourist, I guess."

He whistles between his teeth. "Talk about a crappy vacation."

I smile despite myself, a particular talent of Chet's. The other is the way his eyes, big and green and framed with a thick fringe of lashes, really open up his face, make it seem like he's paying attention even when he's not, which is pretty much the only reason he made it through school. His teachers liked him enough to let him squeak by with a C minus.

He steps away from the window, clomping in his boots across the rug and into the kitchen. He doesn't bother to ask, just moves around the island and flips the switch on the coffee machine. Chet knows his way around Paul's kitchen, and the two share a taste for strong espresso, which is about the only thing they have in common.

I sink onto a stool at the counter, taking in his grungy jeans and the ring of scruff around his mouth and along his chin. His hair is even shaggier, long and slicked back off his face, curling up where it hits the collar of his coat. I know we live in the Appalachians, but still. He's taking the mountain man look a little too far.

"What's up with the hair? Are you interviewing for Hells Angels or something?"

He rears back, frowning down his nose at me. "What's wrong with my hair? You never complained about it before."

No need to define what he means by *before*. Before Paul,

when my boyfriends looked just like Chet, all denim and leather and hair one week away from shaggy. Sometime in the past year, Paul's style, short and well clipped, has grown on me.

"Besides, you're one to talk. You don't look so great, either."

Chet doesn't have to tell me. I saw myself in the hallway mirror earlier, the unwashed hair I worked into a messy braid down one shoulder, the clothes that look dug from the bottom of the laundry basket, my face pale and shiny with sweat. I know I look like hell. I feel like it, too.

"Yeah, well, *you* walk up on a dead body in your backyard and let's see how you look afterward. She was under the dock, Chet, just…bobbing there. She looked like a mannequin or something. Her skin was practically see-through. And then they flipped her over and I saw her face." I shudder, a chill hijacking my spine at the memory of her one-eyed stare into the sky, at the shock of Paul's words: *No, I don't know her.* "I'm pretty sure my heart stopped."

Chet frowns. "What, had you seen her around or something?"

I shake my head. "I just meant it freaked me out, is all."

That's the thing about lies, that they demand commitment. Once you spout one off, you have to stick to your story, to think before blurting the next words. Even at home, and even with Chet. *Especially* with him. He's the last person in Lake Crosby capable of keeping a secret.

He brushes it off with a shrug. "Understandable, I guess. Remember all those nightmares I had after Uncle Jerry's funeral? The way they just laid him out on that refrigerated table, his eyes all sunken in and stuck together with glue. I don't care what anybody says—he didn't look asleep. Creeped me way the hell out, too."

"Exactly." I steer us to a safer subject. "So what's the big emergency?"

"Who says there's an emergency? Can't a guy drop by to see his favorite sister?" Chet steps to the fridge, sticks his whole head inside. "Hey, you got any of that pumpkin spice creamer? That stuff was the shit."

"I'm your only sister, and it's gone." I don't mention that Paul dumped it after he spotted it at the very back of the fridge, half-hidden behind a tub of Greek yogurt and some organic orange juice. As long as I've known him, Paul's position has been, if it doesn't come from a farm or the organic market, it has no business going in the body.

"Palm oil, cane sugar, artificial flavoring," Paul said, squinting at the back label, "but you know what this stuff doesn't have? Milk." He twisted open the top, turned it upside down in the drain. "Imagine that, a coffee creamer without so much as a drop of dairy. You're going to grow a third ear if you keep drinking this crap."

The carton went in the recycling bin and Paul on a mission, rummaging through the kitchen for more Piggly Wiggly contraband. He found all the good stuff—the cheese in a can, the toaster pastries, the fruit rollups and snack cakes.

"Not the Moon Pies," I said, laughing even though I was serious. When you grow up like Chet and I did, you don't waste food, and you *definitely* don't throw any away. I came up behind him as he rummaged through the pantry, distracting him with a kiss between his shoulder blades. "Just as long as you don't find the SpaghettiOs I'm making for dinner."

He turned in my arms, and the side of his mouth quirked up. "You're joking, right?"

"Yes, Paul. I'm joking." I tried to give him a serious look, but I couldn't hold back my giggle. "We're having Spam."

The memory gives me a pang, both sweet and sour at the same time. I calculate how long he's been gone, picture the map of Lake Crosby in my mind. Twenty-six miles of shoreline—the equivalent of a marathon if you go all the way around, which Paul won't, and he can't be moving that fast, not after a run and with that backpack strapped to his shoulders. Still, even with tired legs, he can cover a lot of ground in three days.

But my brother's right. That pumpkin stuff was the shit.

"Please don't tell me Annalee threw you out again."

It's a logical assumption, because ever since Chet moved into her house, a tiny ranch on the outskirts of town, the two of them have spent half their time breaking up and the other half getting back together—most often loudly and in public. Annalee loves drama, and she loves when others share in hers. He makes a face and I know that I'm right.

"Oh my God, y'all are the most wishy-washy couple I've ever met. At what point do you just throw in the towel and take the loss?"

He scratches his head. "Have you two been talking on the phone or something? Because now you're sounding just like her."

I inhale long and slow, blow it out even slower. I love my brother, honestly I do, but sometimes I wonder if I'm going to be the only one. Oh, women like him well enough, but then the initial glow fades and shines a spotlight on all his faults. He's messy. Immature. Aimless and possibly very lazy. But he loves with his whole, enthusiastic heart, which is both his best and his worst quality. He's constantly getting it smashed to pieces.

I soften my tone. "Want to tell me what happened?"

He grabs the cups from under the dispenser, slides one across the island to me and leans on the counter with both elbows. "Okay, so you know how I thought Ted was looking to expand, buy up that other shop in Cashiers and let me run it?"

"Yeah." Ted is his boss, the ancient mechanic who owns Lake Crosby Automotive.

"Well, he wasn't looking to *buy*, but to sell. Some chain out of Asheville swooped in and bought up a whole bunch of shops, including his. They sent everybody home but the master mechanics."

"So go back to school, get a certificate." Up to now, Chet's training has consisted mostly of YouTube videos and trial and error on my old clunker, which he's managed to keep running for fourteen years and over two hundred thousand miles. That's got to count for something. "And you know more obscure car facts than anyone I've ever met. You're like the car version of the Rain Man. You can always learn."

He gives me a look over his coffee cup. "Nobody's ever accused me of being smart except you, which is how I know you're full of it. And even if I was smart enough, what am I gonna do in the meantime? I can't pay my share of the rent until I get another job, and even then, it'll take a couple of weeks before the pay kicks in."

"So she just kicked you out? Not cool."

At the same time, the realization he's got nowhere to stay wilts that hard knot between my shoulder blades. This house is too big, too made of glass to sleep in alone—especially with a murderer on the loose. With Chet here, maybe I won't look out the darkened windows and feel eyes, watching my every move. Maybe I'll actually sleep.

"It wasn't just the job. It's also..." He winces and shifts from foot to foot, boots scraping against wood. "Okay, so Annalee's been dying to go to Disney for, like, ever. It's her dream vacation, to drive down to Florida and spend a week visiting all the parks. Every Sunday night, she'd make us empty our wallets into the cookie jar. She said after a while, we'd have enough. She even made a little sign she taped onto it, with drawings and everything. She called it Mickey Money."

"Cute."

"But I've been asking around, and do you know what that place costs? Not just the tickets for the parks, but the hotel and the gas and these special passes so you don't have to stand around in line, and apparently everybody walks around with these giant turkey legs that cost ten bucks a pop." He shakes his head. "How am I supposed to pay for all that?"

For people like Chet, living month to month, vacations are not a luxury but a liability. What if his roof springs a leak or he needs a new refrigerator? Any money left over at the end of the month should go into an emergency fund, and Chet's question was rhetorical. He can't pay for a Disney vacation. He shouldn't.

Chet sighs. "And then the rent came due and I couldn't make my share, and there was that cookie jar full of cash, just sitting there on the counter…" His words dissolve into a shrug.

"Chet. You didn't."

"What? Half of it was mine anyway, and I was going to put her half back as soon as I found another job. I'm gonna pay her back. I just need for her to give me a minute."

This is the part where I'm supposed to reach for my wallet, to offer up some cash he'll never spend a second thinking about repaying. Chet pauses, waiting. I press my lips together and say nothing.

He sighs. "Honestly, Char, in this weird-ass way, it feels

like maybe the universe is giving me a sign. I mean, that mechanic thing felt like something I just fell into, you know? I'm decent at it, but it's not what I love to do. Maybe it's time for me to branch out. To find my passion."

A mechanic, a concrete pourer, a leaf blower, a valet, a window washer. Chet changes jobs like other people change out their toothbrushes. I try to be supportive, but he's running out of new professions to try.

"What's your passion?" I say, my voice dubious. Sometimes I wonder how we're related. All I've ever wanted out of life is stability, but Chet seems to thrive on upheaval.

His gaze roams the kitchen, landing on the cup of coffee in his hands. "Okay, but you gotta promise not to laugh."

"I promise."

"I'm serious, Charlie. Not so much as a snicker."

"I promise, Chet. Now tell me."

"Fine. Okay." A pause, his gaze wandering away from mine, then sticking. "I think I want to be a chef."

At the thought of food, my mouth waters, and a stab of hunger slices through the acid churning in my empty stomach. I think of last night's dinner, shrimp stir-fry I was too excited to eat much of, and the oatmeal I just stuffed down the drain. I need food, and fast, and Chet's taste buds are like mine. He likes things deep-fried and smothered in cheese.

"What? Why are you looking at me like that? I like to cook."

"I know you do." I smile across the kitchen at my baby brother. "You can start by making me an omelet."

11

I tear into the eggs like I haven't eaten in days, gobbling half of them down before Chet has cracked his own into a bowl. The omelet is delicious, light and fluffy and perfectly salted, without even the tiniest touch of browning. And just like I knew it would be, it's heavy on the cheese.

"You know, this chef thing isn't such a bad idea," I say, working off another bite with the side of my fork. Hot goo gushes out of the center, an avalanche of cheese and tomato and translucent onion. "Where'd you learn to cook like this?"

Chet shrugs. "TV. YouTube. It's not that hard."

The toaster pops, shooting up two slices of bread, and he cuts them into perfect triangles while rattling off his repertoire. Eggs and hash browns wrapped in bacon, anything that can be fried in a pan or grilled, fat cheese dogs smothered in chili. Behind him, onions sizzle in the pan.

I am digging out some organic jam from the top refrigerator shelf when the mudroom door opens, and Micah's voice calls out, "Hey, Charlotte."

"In the kitchen."

A few seconds later he appears in the doorway in his socks, a thermos dangling from a finger. "Why does it smell so good in here? Hey, Chet. How's it hanging?"

Chet eyes him from across the island. "Sheriff."

Micah gives him a good-natured smile. "Better not let Chief Hunt hear you say that. He likes being the only sheriff in town. And you know neither of us are sheriffs, right? I'm not even officially a cop."

Chet knows all this, of course, but he also knows that Micah's father is scary as hell, and that at the first sign of trouble, he and his deputies will roll through the trailer parks on the other side of the mountain and whoop their sirens at anybody who happens to be sitting outside. He knows they'll search the trunk of an old hooptie but let a BMW fly by without so much as a warning. He's grown up fearing men like Chief Hunt with their guns and billy clubs and handcuffs chinking from their uniform belts. Micah may not be a cop, but he's still connected to law enforcement, and not only because he's the police chief's son. He worked in search and rescue for years until founding his underwater criminal investigations training and consulting company, Lake Hunters.

Chet turns back to the stove with a shrug. "If you say so."

Micah lets it go, lifting the thermos into the air. "Can I bother you for a refill?"

"Of course." I motion him over, abandoning the rest of my breakfast. "You look like you've warmed up some."

He's no longer corpse-white but pink from the chill, his lips no longer a vibrating blue. If he was smart, he used one of the towels I laid out downstairs to soak up some of the lake water.

"The coffee helped some. Thanks." He hands me the thermos and I settle it in the sink, rinsing it out along with the dripper cone. "Sam just called with a lead on the woman. She was staying at one of the B and Bs in town."

"Oh. That's good news, right?"

"Mostly, it is. It's good news that they know her name and where she's from, which means they can contact her next of kin. But word's gonna get out soon, if it hasn't already. Sam's trying to get out in front of it. It's better for everybody if her family doesn't hear about it from the news."

He'll have to hurry. It doesn't take much to ignite talk in this town, and a tourist found floating in the lake will be a fast flame. As soon as the cops show up at that B and B, as soon as they start slinging around the crime tape and interviewing witnesses, conjecture will spread through these hills like a late-summer forest fire. I give it until the end of the day before people start showing up here.

I look up, and Micah is watching me. "'No comment.' Dad asked me to impress upon you that those are the only two words he would like to hear coming out of your mouth—except he didn't say it that nice and he didn't ask. He wants you to say it to friends, to family, to whoever comes knocking on your door wanting to know what you saw down there at the lake. If somebody won't take no for an answer, maybe don't send them to Dad. Send them to Sam instead. Let him deal with them."

I nod, settling the dripper on the thermos rim. "Sounds easy enough."

"Don't be so sure. Reporters are a persistent bunch, and they will go to all kinds of crazy lengths to make you think they're not one. They'll pretend to be a friend or a prospective client. They'll ambush you in parking lots and at the grocery store. They will follow you around town like your shadow if they think they're gonna get the first word out of you. Dad says his team is going to be strategic in which details of this investigation they release to the public, and he doesn't want things getting out there he's not ready to talk about, okay?"

"Okay, okay, I get it. 'No comment' to anyone and everyone."

He nods, satisfied. "Where's Paul?"

"He had a work thing. He left about an hour ago." I reach for the electric grinder, pry open the plastic top. I can't quite make myself look Micah in the eye.

"How?"

I frown, my fingers freezing on the cord. "How what?"

"How did he get to his work thing?" Micah clarifies. "I thought his car was in the shop."

Shit. It's a point Paul and I didn't think through, how we'd explain his transportation. I can't say he went bobbing up the driveway with a thirty-pound backpack on his shoulders. Micah knows Paul too well, and he'll know if there's something I'm not telling him.

Out on that hill, Paul and I made a decision, a silent pact. Our lie tipped over that first domino, setting off an avalanche that now there's no stopping. The only way forward is to spout off another one, cloak it in an occasional truth to serve as a decoy, pile on the details to build a believable story. My pulse flickers under my skin, turning it hot and sticky—or maybe that's the heat of Micah's stare.

I clear my throat. "He didn't say. I just assumed somebody was picking him up. There's a replacement car waiting for him at the office."

I busy myself with the coffee while Chet finishes up

his omelet, sliding it onto a plate he carries in a wide arc around Micah, now tapping away at his cell phone screen. He presses the phone to his ear and I know who he's calling. I also know there's no way in hell Paul is going to pick up. Not after he made me swear not to tell Micah where he was going. Better to ignore the call and make up some excuse when he gets back.

Micah hangs up without leaving a voice mail, and I feel him in the room, taking up space, sucking up all the air. This is a man who knows how to dig up the truth, and from dangerous and watery depths. If he thought I was keeping something from him, he would poke poke poke at me until he cracked me like one of Chet's eggs. That's why he's so good at finding things people want to stay hidden, he's relentless, and why I clamp down on my expression.

Micah slips the phone back into his pocket. "When you see Paul, tell him to give me a call, will you? I need to talk to him about something. It's pretty urgent."

I smile. "Sure thing."

He fetches his boots from the mudroom, puts them on by the back door. "I'll check in before heading home tonight, see how y'all are doing."

"Sounds good," I say, even though it doesn't sound good at all. I don't want Micah swinging by, not without Paul here as a buffer. Every second I spend alone with that man is another chance for me to lie or worse—to talk myself into a corner. A flash of anger blooms in my chest at Paul for leaving me here, for trekking off into the woods for who knows where or how long. When he gets home, I'm going to kill him.

"Hey, Charlotte?"

I look to where Micah is standing, one foot in the mudroom.

"Keep the doors locked and the alarm on at all times, okay? And maybe have Chet check the windows. Until we figure out who put that woman in the lake and why, nobody's safe."

Nobody's safe.

The words punch a panic button in my chest. Even with a backyard full of cops, even with big, badass Micah in the house next door, the murderer could show up here. My breath comes in a shallow spurt, hollowing out the room and my lungs and my stomach. But somehow I manage a nod.

As soon as Micah leaves, Chet turns to me. "Wanna tell me what that was all about?"

"What was what all about?"

He reaches across the counter for the pot of jam. "Don't you play coy with me, Charlie Delilah McCreedy. Where is Paul, really? And why did you just lie to the sheriff about it?"

I don't correct Chet or ask what gave me away. It could be any one of a number of things—my shaky hands, my twitchy gaze, the unambiguous pauses while I thought through my string of lies. Chet knows all of my tells.

I pour the beans in the grinder and flip it on with a thumb. "No comment."

12

June 12, 1999
7:07 p.m.

Jax didn't want to be here. While Paul and Micah talked nonsense, sports and parties, and debated which was the superior food group, pizza or hamburgers, Jax leaned back on the lounger and stared out the window at the tops of the trees, wishing he was anywhere but here, at Paul's house. The top of Leafy Knoll, maybe, or crawling through the caves on the western end of the lake. Paul was cool, but Mrs. K was right about there being something going on between Jax and Micah. For the past hour, Micah had worked Jax's every last nerve.

He bragged about girls, the ones he'd slept with and the ones he planned to, and how the ones at Clemson, where Micah was starting as a freshman this coming fall, were supposed to be hot and rich and easy. He ticked off his accomplishments like they were nothing, the cliffs he'd climbed and the pounds he'd bench-pressed, boasting and blowing steam until Jax couldn't take another second.

"I have a question," Jax said, interrupting an endless soliloquy about the size of his trust fund. Micah stopped flipping through the CDs on the far shelf and swung his gaze around. "Have you always been this obnoxious, or am I just now picking up on it?"

Paul snorted, but Micah didn't crack a smile. He just stared at Jax in that way of his, his face a concrete slab. "Better than being a buzzkill."

That familiar angry fire, Jax's old friend, flicked to life in his chest. "What's that supposed to mean?"

"It means the whole time we've been up here, all you've done is stare out the window. You haven't cracked a smile. You haven't said more than three words. It's pretty obvious you don't want to be here, so do us all a favor, will you, and go home." Micah turned back to the CDs.

"Fuck you."

Micah whirled around. "What did you just say?"

This time, Jax said it louder, exaggerating the words. "I said fuck. You. Fuck you."

"Stop it, both of you." Paul, playing the peacemaker as usual. He leaned forward in his favorite chair, a leather-lined acrylic bubble that hung from a giant hook in the ceiling, big enough for two people. It was modern and ridiculously cool, just like Paul. "Nobody's going home, so, Jax, chill. Micah, put on a new CD."

Micah managed one last glare in Jax's direction before selecting one from the pile. "Please tell me you don't really listen to this shit. Where's the Zeppelin? The Skynyrd and

Steve Miller? This is some girlie-ass music you got here, dude. Who the hell is Coldplay?"

Predictable. Ever since Jax's mother died, this had been Paul's strategy whenever the two argued, to distract and provide cover by drawing Micah's fire. Paul knew Micah would rag on Paul's music, because he *always* ragged on Paul's music. And Micah fell for it every time. He was blind to the way Paul was always ten steps ahead of the trends. His music, his clothes and hair, even his bedroom, sleek and shiny and the opposite of the overstuffed house downstairs. Whatever Paul surrounded himself with was what everybody wanted years from now.

"They're already huge in the UK." Paul grinned, sounding not the least bit offended. "A major German label just signed them. Put it on and you'll see."

Micah chucked the CD back onto the shelf. "Who cares about the UK? We live in America, remember?"

"Led Zeppelin is British."

Micah frowned. "No, they're not."

"They are. Look it up."

"Whatever." Micah flopped onto Paul's bed, swinging his dirty shoes up onto the white duvet, leaving twin streaks across the bottom. "This is boring. I'm bored."

Only boring people get bored. Jax's mother's words whispered through his mind with a painful pang. If she were here, she'd be bothered by Micah, too. He was eighteen, six months older and the son of the man everybody said was buying his way to the top of the town's police force. Mom wouldn't like the way Micah thought it gave him permission to do whatever he wanted, either.

"What do you want to do?" Paul said, rocking the swing with a toe. "You want to go somewhere?"

"This is Lake Crosby," Jax reminded them. "There's nothing *to* do."

Micah reached behind him for a pillow, threw it at Jax's head. "It's Saturday night, dumbass. There's bound to be some people out. Let's go to town, see what everybody's up to."

"Micah's right. I think I'm just going to go home." Jax made like he was leaving, sitting up on the lounger, looking around for his keys, even though home was the very last place he wanted to be. The thought of going back there, of another minute in that house, made his chest hot all over again. Everybody here knew it was an empty threat.

Paul unfolded himself from the chair, stilling it with a hand. "Don't go home, Jax. Come with us."

"Come with you where?"

"To town. Out."

"The only people in town this time of year are the tourists."

"Even better." Micah sat up on the bed, plunking his feet onto the floor. "Let's see if we can find a bachelorette party. Those girls are always up for a good time."

Jax rolled his eyes. "Those girls are also ten years older."

"So?"

"So you're being ridiculous."

"And you're being a buzzkill. Again."

"Would both of you just stop?" Paul said, stepping directly between them. "We've been friends for too long for this kind of hostility. Where's this coming from?"

Jax glared at his friends, and he didn't know, either, though full disclosure, it wasn't all that sudden and lately Jax harbored a hostility for everything and everyone. The three of them had been friends for ages, and for most of that time, he actually liked hanging out with Micah. Micah was fun and funny and a little crazy but in a good way, the kind of guy who was always the life of the party.

But lately, Jax had started noticing a streak that shot through the core of Micah, like the coal that used to snake through the Appalachians before they tore it all out. The way he was always hanging upside down from bridges or rappelling down waterfalls, how he always had to be the loudest person in the room. It was like Micah always had something to prove, and the older they got, the more Jax thought it was stupid.

Paul held out a hand, his body poised to haul Jax off the lounger. "Come on, man. It'll be like old times."

Old times as in: before your mom died, before you became such an angry troll. If Micah had said it, Jax would have punched him in the face, but not Paul. For some reason Jax didn't fully understand, he never got angry at Paul.

"And if we can't find a party, we'll just make our own." Micah grinned and spread his arms wide. "We'll *be* the motherfucking party."

Jax sighed, slapping his hand in Paul's. "Fine, but I'm driving."

13

The rest of the afternoon flies by in a blur.

I make gallons of tea and coffee that, in a surprise move, Chet offers to cart down to the water. After the first trip I figure out why—so he can eavesdrop on the cops, trading hot drinks and homemade snacks for snippets of information he carries back up the hill to share with me.

Chet tells me that the Asheville divers arrived with cold-water gear and are taking turns scouring the lake bottom around the dock for evidence, but the waters are deep, the lake so dark they can't see beyond their own flashlight beams. So far they've found nothing but a shoe and some old junk, and the chunk of hill cordoned off with crime tape and a neat grid of stakes and string hasn't yielded any clues, either. If she came through our backyard, she didn't drop any evidence.

When I'm not playing hostess or getting updates from

Chet, I stand at the window and watch. Two men stand guard by the shoreline, gripping coiled leashes that snake into the murky water. Currents under the dock are a living, breathing thing. The ropes are there in case they get swept away, a tether that will guide them to shore.

But none of the men Chet overheard are holding out much hope of finding anything useful. Fifteen hundred acres of water in Lake Crosby, with craggy depths of up to three hundred feet. No wonder Micah wanted to get her out so quickly, and to preserve whatever evidence washed off onto the tarp. If something drifted off that woman into the water, it could be anywhere, and it won't be sitting still. Needle, meet haystack.

Thanks to the cloud cover swirling with coming snow, darkness comes earlier than normal, at well before five. The pines and Fraser firs are quick to filter the light with their dense needles, and shadows clot under the trees. They creep ever closer to the house, the branches above leaning in to shut out the sky. This place is built for looking out, no curtains or blinds to block its showstopper views, but when the lights come on and the windows turn black with night, I always wonder who's looking in.

Micah pops to the surface, then another diver. They move onto shore, shaking their heads and peeling off their wet suits, drying off with towels someone fetched from upstairs. The cops gather up their trash and toss dirt on the fire. They're packing up for the day and, by the looks of things, leaving empty-handed.

Chet bangs through the back door moments later, his cheeks chapped from the wind. "All that for a big, fat nothing. Can you believe it? Wait'll I tell the guys down at the bar."

"Micah told us not to talk to anyone, remember? If anybody asks, we're supposed to say 'no comment.'"

"No. He told you to say 'no comment.'" Chet peels off his coat, drops it on a hook and jimmies off one boot, then the next, letting them fall to the floor with a thud.

"Chet, you know as well as I do he meant you, too. You can't go around talking about this all over town, not until we get the okay. You know how Chief Hunt is. If you mess up this case for him, he's going to toss your ass in jail without a second thought."

A flash of something crosses his face, fear mixed with resignation. "Oh, come on. It's not like I can say anything that people don't already know by now. By now there's not a soul in town who doesn't know about the dead tourist, or that Micah's been searching for evidence all day."

My phone beeps with a text from Micah. Done for the day. What do you want me to do with the towels?

My thumbs fly across the keyboard. Just leave them by the back door, I'll take care of it. Go home. Get warm. All good up here.

I walk to the window and press my face to the glass, cupping my hands to see everyone's gone, nothing but dark massing shapes of the trees and mountains against a slightly luminous sky. Paul is out there somewhere, in woods that come alive at night. Fox and coyotes and bats, tiny rodents that scurry between his legs as he crashes through. Night animals and people like Jax, who don't mind the darkness.

Speaking of Jax, where is he? Has Paul found him yet? And how does he know where to look? Jax roams the hills during the day and sleeps in caves or rotted-out logs. He doesn't exactly have an address.

The lake is a sea of swirling black, swollen and churning from a rainy fall. Even from here, even in the coming darkness, I can see the muddy streaks.

"I wonder why they didn't shut down the dam."

Lake Crosby isn't a natural lake but a reservoir, its waters boxed in on the southern end by a dam that controls both water levels and underwater currents. The engineers are like gods, holding back the currents or letting them rip, manipulating everything with a flip of a switch. Their gate releases are a major happening in these parts, announced well in advance to give the falls watchers and adventure sporters time to plan. But the hike to the top of High Falls Trail is steep and overcrowded, a long line of suicidal crazies carting kayaks they use to shoot down the five-plus miles of class-four rapids. Once you've seen one thunderous tsunami barrel over a cliff, you've seen them all.

"The dam *is* shut down," Chet says, flopping down on one of the matching white couches, plucking off his socks. If he could get away with going through life barefoot, Chet would throw away all his shoes. "There's not been a release since July. The lake's just choppy from all the rain."

"So now what?"

Chet shrugs. "I heard one of the cops say it was time to call in the big guns."

"Meaning?"

He shrugs again. "I was hoping you could tell me."

I don't know, either. The state police? The FBI? Earlier this year, when a couple of recreational divers swam up on a rusted-out Camaro containing a skeleton on the other end of the lake, Chief Hunt's team got sidelined by state investigators. But that was because the divers called the media before alerting the cops, and some reporter had already connected the body to a decades-old missing persons case. Who are the big guns for a murder case?

I haven't thought of that skeleton in months, even though for three weeks this past spring, it was all anybody could talk about. We're a town that's used to things living and dying underneath us, but the idea of a human trapped under our waters, a person rotting away in a car we didn't know was there…well, it freaked us way the hell out.

I stare out the window into the fading light, watching shadows dance on the surface of the lake. That's three back-to-back bodies the water has sent up from the darkness, three mysteries since I've lived near Lake Crosby's shores. Decades apart, but still.

If I were a superstitious person, I'd call it an omen.

I don't know what time it is when I come downstairs, only that it's good and dark, the hills and the lake a smudge of blackness on the other side of the glass. Light from the kitchen shines on the back deck boards sparkling with frost, and I think of Paul, freezing in his hammock.

The dishwasher is already going, water humming through the pipes along with the shower under my feet— Chet in the guest bathroom downstairs. I'm cleaning up the last of the dinner mess, wiping down countertops and scrubbing cooked-on grease from the stove, when I feel it—a body stepping onto the back deck. A distinct but subtle vibration on the floorboards under my feet, there and gone in an instant.

I whirl toward the window, thinking about who it could be. Not Paul, who's not been gone a day. Micah, maybe, swinging by for the promised check-in. Definitely not one of the cops; they left ages ago, and even if one of them came back, he'd ring the doorbell like a proper visitor.

More vibrations, more movement. My gaze tracks to the far end of the glass, bumping up against a wall between me and the stairs. Another ten steps at least. I wait, the footsteps sparking shivers of alarm up my spine.

I'm patting the counter behind me for my phone when it happens. A passing figure at the far corner of the window, a person stepping into view on the deck. A slip of mud-spattered pants, the cuff of a filthy sleeve, and then: Jax. Dirty, shaggy, bedraggled, batty Jax, lit up by the porch light. I feel a stab of relief, and then...fear.

Not fear for my safety, but for Paul's. That something's happened to him.

"Is Paul okay?" I say, shouting so he can hear me through the glass. "Did you see him?"

Jax frowns, the skin of his forehead crinkling up like ancient leather. The past twenty years have not been kind, the wind and sun and living outside. He looks old—ten years older than Paul at least.

I stare at him through the thin pane of glass, taking in every detail. His blond beard threaded with pine needles and leaves but otherwise surprisingly clean, the way his big shoulders seem sharp under his Georgia Tech sweatshirt, the hiking boots that look just like the ones Paul claimed to have thrown away. A hand-me-down scarf, creamy fringed wool and too dainty for his big frame, is wrapped around his neck. He watches me with eyes that are a pretty, bright blue. Is this the face of a killer?

A memory hovers just out of reach, somewhere beyond my fingertips.

He leans into the glass, cupping a hand to his ear. I point to the mudroom, a silent signal to meet me there, then beat him to the door. I was wrong before, when I said he reeked. He smells like earth and pine.

"Is Paul okay?"

"There's a cut on his face." Jax waves a finger above

his eye, on the same spot where Paul has a lump. "I didn't put it there."

"I know you didn't. He fell down Fontana Ridge."

"Oh. That's good, then."

I pause, confused. It's good that Paul fell and hit his head? Or Jax saw Paul but they didn't talk?

Jax holds up two fingers. "That's twice now."

"Two cuts?"

"No." He gestures behind him, to the black smear glittering in the darkness. "Two women in the lake. First Katherine, then Sienna."

I pull in a sharp breath, and my heart bounces against my ribs. Jax knows the woman's name. I want to ask how he knows—did he *talk* to her?—but I'm more traumatized by his message. This horrible, awful thing he's implying.

"Paul didn't hurt those women, Jax. He loved Katherine, and he was with me all last night. He couldn't have hurt either one. He *wouldn't*."

Jax doesn't look convinced. "But Micah…" He frowns.

"Micah what?"

Jax looks to his left, to Micah's porch lights flickering through the trees, and I wonder if he came from there, if he maybe banged on Micah's door first. But then Jax turns back, and his expression sends an uneasy feeling climbing up my spine. He looks jittery again, and I don't know what's changed. I don't understand any of this.

"Jax. What about Micah?"

But Jax has never been one for conversation, and I can tell I've already lost him. He takes a step backward, then another, moving in the direction he came. "I wasn't here. You never saw me." He turns in long strides for the stairs.

I step onto the deck, the boards icy under my bare feet. "Jax, wait."

He's all the way to the corner when he stops. He slaps a palm to the siding, but his body leans for the stairs. It's like he's literally holding himself back. Slowly, reluctantly, he looks over his shoulder.

"Do you need anything? Food, maybe, or a coat? Some warm socks?"

His beard tugs in a way that makes me wonder if he's smiling, and I think for a second or two that he might turn back. And then what? Do I invite him in? Raid Paul's closet while I make Chet whip him up dinner?

And then Jax makes the decision for me. He ducks his head and takes off, disappearing in one long stride around the corner. I'm turning for the door when his voice floats up from the stairs.

"Watch your back."

14

Jax follows me around the rest of the night. Not literally, of course, but every time the house goes quiet I feel him there, whispering in my ear. Chet settles in, taking over the entire downstairs. He blares ESPN while I putter around the house, replaying every word of the conversation over and over in my head.

That's twice now.

I wasn't here.

You never saw me.

I gather the laundry from the hamper in the closet and carry it downstairs to the laundry room.

Watch your back, he said, one humdinger of a closer. Was it a threat? A warning? His conversation skills could use some help, but Jax certainly knows how to end with a bang.

I'm coming down the hallway when the door in front

of me pops open. I shriek and lunge backward into the wall, clutching the laundry to my chest like a shield. Paul's mother steps out of the powder room, smoothing her sweater.

"Oh, sweetie. I didn't mean to frighten you." Diana pulls me into a perfumed hug, awkward since I'm holding the laundry. Her bony ribs press into my arms. "I said hello when I came in, but you must not have heard me over Paul's TV."

Paul's TV. Paul's house. She never passes up an opportunity to remind me.

I release from her grip, taking a step back. "If you're looking for your son, he's not here. He had a work thing."

"I'm not here to see him, dear. I'm here to see you. I heard what happened. That must have been some shock, finding that poor girl. Are you okay?"

Diana's voice is soft and soothing, every syllable rounded with a velvety mountain cadence. Not a coarse twang like mine and Chet's. She sounds like she comes from money, and she looks it, too, in styled hair and an oversized cream sweater that hangs artfully off one shoulder. Her boots are low and Western-inspired, chunky heels and pointy toes. She looks like a million bucks.

It helps that she's beautiful, all dark hair and ivory skin and a body she keeps lean with daily barre and Pilates. Even if she had Paul when she was a teenager, even if she slept hanging upside down by her ankles every night, there's no way someone her age—I've done the math, and the woman is well into her fifties—looks that good, not without a little help. But either her surgeon is really, really good, or somewhere along the line, Diana Keller made a deal with the devil.

"I'm fine, thank you. It was sweet of you to check on me."

This is how we always are with each other. Cautious. Polite. Full of bright smiles and friendly words we volley back and forth, more for Paul's benefit than for ours. Honestly, I'm surprised she wasn't here sooner.

"I'll make us some tea and you can tell me everything. Or would you rather have something stronger? I can pop open a bottle of wine if you prefer."

My stomach sends up a twinge of nausea. "Tea's perfect. Thanks."

"Sit, sit." She waves a manicured hand at the counter stools.

Invited to sit in my own home—scratch that, Paul's. I edge around the island and sink into a chair, watching her bang around his kitchen like she owns the place. I wonder what Micah would say if he were here. Micah sees Diana as a second mother, the kind he calls weekly and sends flowers to on birthdays and Mother's Day. Paul says Micah spent as much time in their house as he did his own. Is Diana one of the people I'm supposed to tell "no comment"?

"So how did you hear? About the woman in the lake, I mean." I don't mention her name. *Sienna*, assuming Jax was right. I gesture to the window I just spotted him through, a sheet of solid black glass. "Who told you?"

Her hands still, and her eyes cut to mine. "Everybody. Everybody told me. People in town are losing their minds, especially the tourists. The mayor's making the rounds, but I don't know how he'll be able to put out this fire. It's all anybody can talk about." She grabs two cups and saucers from the cabinet and a black tin from her handbag. "Peppermint okay? Miss Mary's is the best."

I smile, trying not to be offended she brought her own tea. "Peppermint's fine."

For the millionth time today, I wish Paul were here. Diana is a lot to handle on an ordinary day, and after the stress of this one, I'm not sure I can sit across from her and pretend my nerves aren't jangling. Too many lies to keep track of, too much bad blood boiling between us, and Paul not here to act as a buffer.

Diana chatters away, popping open the tin and rummaging through the drawer for the infuser, which it takes her three tries to pry open. The loose tea doesn't want to cooperate, either. It comes out in a surge, raining down over the infuser and onto the counter. She swipes it with a palm into the sink. Not for nothing, but Lipton is a whole lot simpler.

"Charlotte, did you hear a single word I just said?"

I snap back to the conversation, trying to inventory the words I missed, but it's like grabbing a handful of water. I come up empty.

"I'm sorry—what?"

"I said it's just so strange. I can't get over it. A body floating under the dock. I mean, what are the odds?"

If Paul were here, he could work the numbers. He'd know how many houses are lined up along the shore, and he'd use it to calculate the likelihood of the lake sending her to our yard instead of Micah's or grumpy old Mr. Guthrie's on the other side.

"I bet the odds are a lot higher than you'd think."

"It's a saying, dear." A quick pause, her nails, a light baby doll pink, tapping on the counter. "I heard she was staying at the Crosby Shores, which means she wasn't from around here."

"She was a tourist." Diana looks surprised, so I add, "Micah was here most of the day with the divers, and—"

"There were *divers*?" She presses a palm to her chest,

fingertips fluttering over a bony clavicle. "How many? What did they find? Where were they looking?"

"A whole bunch of them, and under the dock, mostly. But it didn't look like they had much luck. Micah said whatever evidence was on her probably washed off long before she ended up here."

"But people don't just fall into the lake in the middle of the night, not in this weather. Did somebody push her or, I don't know, whack her over the head? Do they think she was *murdered*?"

"I'm pretty sure that's exactly what they think."

Diana blanches. She reaches for the teapot, settling it under the hot water tap by the stove, twisting the valve to gushing.

"Doesn't it freak you out?" I ask. "Another woman under the dock, I mean. Because you know what people are going to say. You know who they'll suspect."

She scowls, her gaze whipping to mine.

"I didn't say they're right, just that everybody will think it. And now Micah's saying I should keep the doors locked and the alarm on all the time, which doesn't make me feel any better. He makes it sound like whoever did this might do it again. It could be a serial killer, for all we know."

My gaze wanders to the windows and beyond, to the shadows shifting in the darkness on the other side, and I wonder what's out there besides the trees. It makes me want to shut the lights off so I'm not so exposed. It makes me wish there were curtains.

Diana's voice pulls me back into the room. "Who are they talking to? Who are they questioning?"

Chief Hunt's words bark in my head: *no comment*. He and Diana are friendly—as friendly as someone can be

STRANGER IN THE LAKE

with that man. She puts up with him because of his son, even inviting the Hunt family over for Thanksgiving dinner. I'm still waiting for her permission to bring along Chet.

"You should probably ask Micah. I'm sure he knows more."

Diana glances over her shoulder, steam dancing around her head like smoke. "I'm talking to you, Charlotte. You just said they were here all day. I'm asking *you*."

I try not to be offended by her words, her snappish tone, the way she's looking at me like I'm a bug she'd like to squash. I lift my hands, let them fall to the marble with a slap.

"Diana, honestly. I've already told you everything I know."

"Well, it's not very much." She shuts the tap with a flick of her wrist, grabbing the pot and swinging it around onto the island. A steaming glug of water sloshes out the spout and onto the kitchen floor.

Why do conversations with Diana always make me feel so inadequate?

"I'm only repeating what I heard, and Micah was pretty specific. I'm not supposed to go spreading anything around. He said the police are holding back details on purpose."

"What kind of details?"

I open my mouth to respond, but a rattling starts up underneath us, a slow and subtle beat I feel in the soles of my feet. I turn to the stairs and scream, "Chet, turn it down!"

The noise builds steadily, a coal train rumbling through the hills, gaining speed and moving closer, swelling into a deafening roar.

"Chet's here?"

For sure I caught that bitter note that crept into her voice, the way the skin around her eyes went tight, but I don't have time to deal with it. The panel just inside the mudroom is beeping—the loud music tripping the glass break sensor on the alarm. I pop out of my chair.

I rush to the mudroom and tap in the code, then ping-pong from room to room, retracing my steps from earlier. I check under the magazines on the coffee table, the cushions of the chair across from the couch, the breakfast table and the kitchen charger. I look everywhere I can think of.

"What are you looking for?"

"My cell phone. The alarm company's about to call and ask me for the secret word, but of course Paul told me it forever ago and he just left me here to deal with everything all by myself. There was another dead woman in the lake and he *left*." It's the first time I've said the words out loud, and they come out angry and acidic, like the way I feel.

I cup my hands around my mouth and holler down the stairs. "Chet! Too loud!"

Right on cue, my phone rings, a shrill clanging coming from a pile of mail by the microwave.

Diana tips her head at the sound. "Dixie Cup." Her lips spread into a thin smile, a victorious one. "Paul's security password is Dixie Cup."

Of course she knows. Because if nothing else, these past four years have returned Diana to her post as the most important woman in Paul's life. Swooping in when he lost his beloved first wife, filling his freezer with individually portioned meals, patting his hand and promising him things would get better. That he would find another, that he would love again.

Except not me. She never meant he should fall in love with me.

And so that look on her face right now? That smug little grin? It's why instead of answering the phone, I hear myself say, "I'm pregnant."

15

I fall asleep, unexpectedly and deeply, my eyes popping open sometime around four. I roll over and catch a whiff of Paul, the smell of his skin and aftershave, and I reach for him before I remember. Paul's side of the bed is empty, his scent caught inside the fabric of the T-shirt I salvaged from the hamper. It was the only way I could get settled in this big bed all alone.

I stare at the ceiling and the worries return, nicking at my consciousness, shimmering in the dark air of the bedroom. I worry about Paul tumbling down some gorge or freezing in his hammock under the trees. About Diana a few miles down the road, screaming into her pillow at the news she's going to be a grandmother. About the lies that keep piling up like Jenga blocks, only a matter of time before a sloppily placed tile sends the whole mess toppling down.

Without warning, a wave of nausea pitches up my throat.

I lurch out of bed and sprint to the toilet, barely making it on time. My last meal was hours ago, pasta that comes up in a series of sour waves. I throw it all up, over and over, until all that's left is bile. I flush the sick down, but the dizziness, the shock of it, doesn't pass.

I brush my teeth and pull on some clean clothes, leggings and an oversized sweater because no way I'm going to work today. On the other side of the window, the ground is white with snow, a good coating this time, a couple of inches at least and more coming down. Even if I could get to the office, what would I tell Paul's staff? He never misses work, and everybody there has access to his calendar. I'd really like to not have to pile on yet another lie.

On the way out of the bedroom, I lift my cell phone from the charger and awaken the screen. No missed calls. No texts. No nothing.

Paul is an experienced hiker, and the area around Lake Crosby is remote enough that service, if there is any, would cut in and out. How long does an iPhone battery hold a charge in snow and sweat and freezing temperatures? If he's smart, and he is, he's powered it down and is saving the battery in case of emergency.

Emergency. My heart pinches, and I start catastrophizing. Broken bones, unconscious at the bottom of a cliff, frozen to death in that ridiculous hammock of his, ripped to shreds by a bear.

"Alexa, what's the weather?" I say on the way into the kitchen.

Her smooth voice cuts through the morning silence. "In Lake Crosby, it's currently twenty-seven degrees Fahrenheit with a windchill of thirteen. Today you can look for lots of snow."

I don't have to look very far. The windows are white

with it, swirling snowflakes pelting the glass like insects around a light. At the bottom of the hill, the crime tape is still strung in a wide arc around the dock like party streamers, a slick yellow ribbon dancing in the wind. I hope the police took whatever they needed from our backyard before it got buried.

At the view, my stomach growls, not from hunger but from habit. A lingering reflex from all those times the roads were too slick for the school buses to pass, and Chet and I would have no other choice but to stay home. Trailer-park kids don't wish for snow days like normal kids do, and we don't spend all spring counting down to the first day of summer. Not when the free school lunch is our biggest, most nutritious meal of the day.

Even now, even in a house full of food, the scars still sting—and I'm not the only one.

Krissy Hinkel from two trailers down is banned from the Piggly Wiggly for life, after the umpteenth time getting caught shoplifting candy bars. Johnny Winger from across the yard never goes anywhere without food, his pockets bulging like a squirrel's cheeks. I have secret piles of junk food, Doritos and Twinkies and industrial-sized boxes of Little Debbies, stashed under every bed and at the back of every closet in this house. Chet now wants to spend all day every day working with food. We all have our coping mechanisms from a constantly rumbling belly, some of them healthier than others.

In the pantry, I climb on the stepladder, remove the lid from the slow cooker on the top shelf and pull out a fistful of Slim Jims. I stare at the bouquet of gas station sausages, and I can already taste them on my tongue, the salt and meat and preservatives, can feel the smoke tickling my sinuses, that delicate tension before my teeth puncture the skin. *Empty calories*, Paul would call them, but he's wrong. When you grow up starving, there's no such thing.

The doorbell rings, and I toss them back in the slow cooker and scramble down.

The front yard is empty, all but a mishmash of fresh footprints that stomped down the snow by the front door, then moved in long strides around the left side of the house. I lean my head out the door and follow their path, my gaze landing on the word written across the snow in a series of angry red slashes.

KILLER.

I gasp and slam the front door.

A prank. A horrible, awful, vile prank. Who would do such a thing?

The answer slices through my mind: *plenty of people.* Half the town already thinks it. It's probably a miracle that this is the first time.

Except...

I race down the hall to the laundry room, launching myself onto the washing machine like a gymnast. I sit on my knees and press my face to the window, craning to get a better look. The red letters have bled into the snow, carving out miniature trenches like cherry-flavored syrup in a snow cone.

My gaze scans the footprints. Whoever did it came this way, around the side of the house in the direction of the stairs. Which means he was close—too close. He might still be outside.

I hop down and race back to the kitchen, sending up a silent thanks I'm not alone in the house. I lean over the railing to holler down the stairs. "Chet, get your butt up here. I need you."

The lower level stays dark and silent. No voices, no movement. If Chet's down there, he's still sound asleep.

I pull up Micah's number on my cell. His phone rings once before his voice pushes through a background of white noise, like he's got me on car speakerphone. "Hey, Charlotte. What's up?"

"There's somebody outside the house. One set of footprints, big ones."

I creep to the mudroom and press my face against the window, my gaze roaming the deck. There's snow, lots of it, a perfect fluffy carpet someone just walked through. I jiggle the knob, breathing a sigh of relief to find it locked up tight.

"Could be Sam or one of the cops, coming to finish up something he forgot yesterday. Weather's not ideal, but—"

"They're not from a cop." I glue my gaze to the back window, but all I see is a snowy haze. Either he's gone, or he's tucked just out of sight. "Whoever it was wrote something awful in the snow. He rang the bell, then took off before I could open the door. The footprints look fresh. I'm pretty sure he's still nearby."

"What'd he write?" Chet's voice comes from right behind me.

I shriek, whirling around to find him in nothing but cut-off sweatpants, washed a soft, grubby gray. His hair is a ball of frizz and tangles, licked up on one side like a lop-sided Mohawk.

I plant my palm in the middle of his chest and shove. "You asshole. You scared the *crap* out of me."

"I noticed." He scratches a hip and leans his face into the glass, looking out on the falling snow. "What's going on? Who're you talking to?"

But it's Micah's voice, all business coming through the

phone, that I concentrate on. "Stay inside. I'm turning around, but I'm halfway to town and the roads are bad. It's gonna take me a minute."

More like seven or eight. Maybe longer, depending on if he's made it across Knob Hill or not, and assuming his truck can make it back over. At the first spit of snow, even four-wheel drives like Micah's have trouble keeping their tires between the lines of Lake Crosby's winding roads, and not even a tank could make it down our driveway. He'll have to park at the top and walk down—another solid minute.

"Is the alarm on?"

"Yes. You told me yesterday to set it." I glance at the alarm pad to be sure. A red light tells me it's armed. "Alarm's on," I tell Micah, jiggling the mudroom door handle for a second time, "and the back door's locked."

"Check the other doors. Windows, too. I'll stay on the line. If you see anything, somebody in the yard or more footprints, I want to know about it."

The urgency in Micah's tone burns like ulcers in my belly. I order Chet to check the doors and windows downstairs, then race from doors to windows back to doors, rattling knobs and inspecting locks. By the time I return to the kitchen, Chet is coming up from the lower level. He gives me a sarcastic thumbs-up on his way to the espresso machine.

"Okay, we're locked up tight."

"Good. I'm on Pine Creek Road." On a normal day, in normal conditions, a two-minute drive. "Put Paul on."

"Paul's not here. It's just me and Chet."

A pause. "Can you get to Paul's gun?"

"His gun, seriously?"

Chet turns around, his brows disappearing into his shaggy hair, but I shake my head. Like every good country boy, Chet knows how to handle a gun, but only in theory. He's too clumsy, much too unpredictable. I can see him now, trudging through the snow in his cutoff sweatpants and a pair of Paul's snow boots. It would be like handing a butcher knife to a toddler.

I shake my head again. "No. No guns."

Chet rolls his eyes and turns back to his coffee.

"Put on some clothes," I whisper, frowning.

He ignores me, digging through the cabinet for a mug.

"You live in the middle of nowhere," Micah says. "You should know how to use a gun."

"I know how to use a gun, Micah. I just don't want to."

"Because she was at the receiving end of one once," Chet hollers toward the phone, not helpfully. He knows I don't like to talk about it, and it was twice, actually. The first by some scumbag who thought our father owed him money, and the second time at the gas station, a meth head who cleaned out the register.

"Stay in the house," Micah says. "I'm coming down."

The line goes dead, and I move to the front window just in time to see him coming down the hill, sliding from tree to tree, his coat flapping open behind him. He lands at the bottom with both feet, then takes off around the side of the house.

I hurry back to the mudroom and stare out the window, willing him to appear on the other side. I stare until my vision goes hazy from the swirling snow and the adrenaline, and maybe a little bit of panic—though I seem to be the only one. Chet is banging around in the kitchen behind me, pulling breakfast ingredients from the fridge and slapping them to the counter. I jump at the rattle of the coffee grinder, as loud and jarring as a chain saw.

I flinch when Micah appears in the window, covered in

snow, fat flakes lodged in his hair and clothes. He motions for me to meet him at the mudroom door.

"What's out there?" I say, once I've turned off the alarm.

Micah blocks the door with his body. "You don't want to know."

"The hell I don't." I stuff my feet in my boots and grab my coat from the hook, yanking it on as I push past him to outside.

"Okay, but don't say I didn't warn you."

He follows me around the corner, to the narrow passageway between the side of the house and the stairwell. Like the rest of the deck, it's covered in a thick blanket of snow, all but a bright red patch at the top of the stairs where something has bled out, staining the snow and melting most of it away. Whatever this messy heap used to be, it was warm when it died.

I take in the bloodstained fur, the lumps of waxy fat, innards the color of raw chicken, and a surge of nausea has me sucking in a breath. I pull my coat closed, wrap it taut around me. "Oh my God, I think I'm gonna puke. What the hell is that thing?"

"A pretty decent-sized opossum, or at least it was, before something mauled it."

"A bear?"

Wouldn't be the first time one has wandered into our yard, though they don't typically come this close to the house, not unless we've left out some food or garbage. And despite what people think, bears aren't violent, not unless they're provoked. No way an opossum, not even a rabid one, could have gotten a bear riled up enough to do this.

Micah bends at the waist, leaning over the carcass. "See here? See how this skin is cut away, these bones sliced clean in two? Hunting knife, I'm guessing. A fairly big one."

The nausea folds into a new spasm, reaching with claws into my chest. I take a step back, grounding myself with one hand on the siding.

A big knife. There was an unidentified person on my back deck with a big knife. I think of Jax out here just last night, the warning he flung as a parting shot. *Watch your back.* Jax has a big knife, and he's known for skinning bunnies on the benches in town, but he does that for food, not as threats or for his own sadistic pleasure.

Or so I've always thought.

The footprints have already grown faint, filling in with a fresh coating of flakes.

"I'll get Sam to send somebody out. Maybe they can lift a print, but I wouldn't hold your breath. By the time he gets here, everything'll be covered, including this carcass. He'll pick up what he can, but you'll probably have to wait until things thaw out to get the treads really clean."

Micah's right. Even with a shovel and an ice pick, that much blood means the stain isn't going away anytime soon. The deck will need a good hosing down, and with Paul's industrial-strength pressure washer. Yet another mess for Paul to deal with when he gets back.

"Did you see what he wrote?" I swallow, the image of that awful word slashed through the snow bumping around in my brain. I press a palm to my stomach, greasy and empty.

"I saw." Micah goes quiet, watching me. "It's just someone looking to get a rise. Don't let them."

"As much as I hate to admit it, it's kind of working. Is it…? What did they use to write it with?"

"Blood, and from the looks of things, from more than just one opossum. More like a cow, probably." Micah shakes his head, sighing. "Don't you pay it any mind, you hear me? Other than to make sure the doors are locked and the alarm is armed at all times."

"You don't think it was just a prank?"

No. Micah's carefully blank look tells me it's not a prank. "I think it's safe to assume that whoever comes that close to your door with a knife isn't going to hesitate to use it. Now's not the time to be taking any chances, especially when Paul's away. When's he back?"

"He said today or tomorrow, but now with this weather..." My stomach trips up with the lie, the knife, the blood. I wave a hand, scooping snowflakes out of the air. "There's no telling."

Micah takes this in with another grimace. "And Chet? How long will he be staying?"

One night, that's it, I'd hollered after him as he raced out to the car for his duffel bag, but we both knew I didn't mean it.

"I didn't exactly give him a deadline."

"Let him stay until Paul gets back at least. Where'd he go again?"

I shrug, holding my expression steady. "Work. That's all I know."

Another day, another lie, teetering at the top of the pile. If Micah notices, he doesn't let on. I see only worry stirring in the depths of his gaze, the way his mouth goes tight. He rubs a hand across his lower jaw, then tugs me toward the mudroom door.

"Come on. As long as I'm here, you might as well make me a cup of Paul's fancy-ass coffee."

We step inside, where Chet is still barefoot, but he's scrounged up some jeans, thank God, and a Falcons T-shirt that's seen better days. On the stovetop behind him, pans sizzle on all five burners—bacon and batter sprinkled with fresh blueberries.

"Hey, Sheriff. Want some pancakes?"

"Nah, just a double espresso, extra strong. Thanks."

Chet's not just making pancakes; he's working the opposite side of the island like a short-order cook, moving between the espresso machine and the stove, sliding there just in time to tease the batter loose from the pan or flip the bacon with lightning-quick twists of a hand. While the second side darkens to toasty brown, he slips a cup under the coffee nozzle and works the knobs. This chef thing might not be such a bad idea after all.

The doorbell rings as I'm digging a coffee cup from the cabinet, and I peek around the corner. Sam stands on the other side of the glass in his uniform parka over heavy snow boots, staring off to the left of the house. To that awful word, faded to pink in the fallen snow.

I open the door, and he looks at me with bloodshot eyes, dark circles against a bright white background. A shadow of stubble decorates his chin. He points a long finger at the snow graffiti. "It wasn't me. I just want to lay that out there first thing, that I had nothing to do with it."

I roll my eyes, lean a shoulder against the doorjamb. "Maybe not, but I bet you wanted to."

"Hell yeah, I wanted to. I'd take out an ad in the newspaper and write it with smoke in the sky if I thought it would do any good." He puffs a humorless laugh, unable to stop himself. "But you've made it pretty clear you're more interested in this big, fancy house filled with designer clothes and that diamond as big as your knuckle than you are in the truth."

His words land on me like a bucket of icy water, and I shove my left hand in my pocket. "Paul cries at sad movies, you asshole. He chops firewood for grumpy old Mr. Guthrie, and he gives bonuses to his staff every Christmas, even the ones who don't do much of anything, and he loved her. He *loved* Katherine."

"In the wrong hands, love can be just as deadly as a loaded gun, Charlie. All you gotta do is take off the blinders."

I gesture to the eastern side of the house, step back to close the door. "Opossum's around back, at the top of the stairs."

Sam stops the door with a toe. "Is Chet here? I need a word."

"What for?"

"For a word." His gaze flicks beyond me, to deeper into the house. "I also have a couple of follow-up questions for you and Mr. Keller."

I stand there for a long moment, trying to decide what to do. I could call Chet to the door, have Sam fire off whatever questions he has from right where he's standing, on my doorstep in the freezing cold. But I also heard the bit about the follow-up questions and it occurs to me that Chet banging around the kitchen might be a good kind of distraction, and same goes for Micah. With those two in the room, Sam will at least keep things civil.

"Take off your shoes." I turn away, leaving Sam to deal with his own coat. I don't want to see his face when he clocks the house's most impressive features—the steel-and-wood staircase that hangs like magic from the wall, the glass-front refrigerator and stainless-steel appliances, the twin couches on a massive wool rug thick as a cloud. Don't want to know if his expression looks anything like mine did when I first saw the place, an equal mix of envy and awe.

In the kitchen, I busy myself with the gathering of plates

and silverware, digging napkins out of the drawer while Sam doles out greetings to the other men. Chet points him to a counter stool with a greasy spatula. "Hungry man's breakfast, coming up."

"I just ate," Sam says, but everybody knows Sam has the kind of metabolism that gets him banned from the all-you-can-eat buffet. Doesn't matter how long ago he ate; he can always eat again. "I'd like to ask you a few questions, if you don't mind."

Chet's back is turned, flipping a row of bacon on the frying pan, and it takes him a couple of seconds before he realizes Sam's talking to him. "Who, me? Sure, man. Shoot."

Sam shifts his feet, stabbing a thumb over his shoulder. "We can do this in the other room if you prefer."

Chet points to the stove. "I've kind of got my hands full. Ask away."

I set everything on the counter with a hard clatter, glaring at Sam as he flips through a notepad to a page filled with his tiny scribbles. He sinks onto the counter stool next to Micah. "Want to tell me what you were doing at the Crosby Shores B and B Monday night?"

Chet shrugs, sliding a steaming pancake onto the pile on a platter. "Playing darts and drinking half-priced beer, like pretty much everybody else in town. The place was jammed."

"Did you talk to anybody?"

"Dude. I talked to *everybody*. They were short-staffed and folks were starting to get rowdy, so I gave Piper a hand behind the bar. She paid me in booze. Is that what this is about? Because I didn't drive home. Piper told me I could sleep on the cot in the back."

Sam digs his cell phone from his pocket, pulls up a picture. "According to multiple witnesses that night, you spent quite a bit of time talking to this woman." He slaps his phone to the marble, faceup. I take in the blond hair, the light blue eyes on a pretty face, and my heart clangs to a stop.

It's her. The woman in the lake. And Chet was talking to her.

"Do you recognize her?" Sam says.

I stare at Chet's back, willing him to not turn around, to shake his head, to say no, he's never seen her before.

He peers over his shoulder at the photo and his mouth curls in a sheepish grin. "Hell yeah, I talked to her. As you can see, she's smoking. What's her name? Savannah? Sierra?"

"Sienna," Sam says.

Chet points at Sam with the spatula. "Sienna, that's right. What happened? Did she rob a bank or something?" He laughs for a second or two until it dawns on him that no one else is joining in. He looks at me, and the smile drops off his face. "What? What'd I say?"

"Chet, that's her," I say, my cheeks stiff. "The woman Micah pulled from the lake."

Chet blinks. His mouth goes slack. He looks from Sam to Micah to me, then back to Sam. Behind him, the pans hiss and sizzle.

"No shit. Seriously?"

"Seriously." Sam watches him with an expression that's wiped clean, a blank slab—somehow scarier than his usual scowl. "And now I'd like to know the last time you spoke to her."

I scurry around the island, stepping in front of my brother like a shield. "Samuel Anthony Kincaid, now you're just *trying* to piss me off. You know Chet as well as I do.

You know full well he didn't have anything to do with how that woman ended up in the lake."

"Fine. Then let your brother answer."

I fold my arms across my chest, but I don't move out of the way. "Fine."

From behind me, Chet says, "What was the question again?"

"Oh my God." I whirl around, my hands flying up at my sides. "The last time you spoke. When did you last talk to her?"

"That night. She paid her tab and went upstairs, at well before last call. She didn't even drink that much. Said something about needing to be sharp the next day. She made it sound like she had a big meeting."

Sam squints. "Did she say with who?"

"No."

"Anything else?"

"No. She was alive and eating breakfast the next morning when I left, around eight or so. I haven't seen or spoken to her since. I swear."

Sam scribbles everything onto his notepad. My heart thuds as I stare across the island at the paper, trying to read the words upside down. Something about the security cameras—a reminder to check the feed? I look at Chet, who's turned back to the pans.

"She had a blow to her head," Sam says, "a good-sized lump and a fresh concussion. It wasn't what killed her, but it was hard enough to knock her out. Her lungs were full of lake."

"Which means?" I say.

Micah answers for him. "Means she was still breathing when she went under."

Sam confirms it with a nod. "The official cause of death was drowning."

Micah's gaze latches on to mine, and I must look as traumatized as I feel because he says, "She wouldn't have felt anything, if that makes you feel better. She would have been unconscious."

No, it doesn't make me feel any better. In fact, it's almost worse. That woman was alive when she slid into the lake. Somebody could have fished her out, given her mouth to mouth. She didn't have to die.

"Micah's looking for a murder weapon with a long, flat surface," Sam says. "Most likely an oar."

Micah makes a frustrated sound. "Good thing there aren't many of those around here."

Sam gives him a tight smile, but I can't find an ounce of humor in Micah's wisecrack. Whoever killed that poor woman did it twice—first with a whack to the head, and second by watching her sink. Whoever did it must have really wanted her dead.

My gaze creeps to Chet, but it's just not possible. Flirting, I can believe. Clobbering her upside the head and shoving her into a freezing cold lake? No way.

I look back and Sam's watching me. "What about Mr. Keller? Is he home?"

"No. He's out scouting properties." It's an excuse I come up with on the spot, mostly for lack of anything better. Vague enough it could mean anywhere, realistic enough to be believable.

"He's not answering our calls."

Welcome to the club. "He's probably out of range or something. If it makes you feel any better, he's ignoring me, too. But I'll make sure to tell him to give you a call the next time I talk to him."

Chet grabs a fistful of berries, drops a few in his mouth. "I don't get it. If she was staying in town, how'd she get all the way to Skeleton Cove?"

Sam shrugs. "Wind. Currents. Some combination of the two, maybe, but that's up to Micah to figure out. Probably too many factors for us to ever know for sure."

"By the time I'm done in the water, I'll know for sure," Micah says. "I need for this weather to clear. Then give me another day or two and I'll know."

Sam's gaze flits to mine. "Those security cameras on the back of the house. Are they working?"

"I think so. Paul said something about them being motion-sensitive, so they only record when they're activated. I don't know how to pull up the footage, though."

"I've already started the process for a warrant."

I bristle. "I said I don't know. Not that you couldn't see."

"The warrant is procedure," Micah says, "mostly to cover all the bases. Defense attorneys love to use any little missed step to eliminate evidence."

Sam confirms it with a nod. "And that's something I want to avoid. We'll be asking for anything the cameras picked up starting on Tuesday evening and up until the moment you spotted her. Time of death was somewhere between 4:00 and 6:00 a.m."

His words send a billow of heat to my skin, and the room hollows out, the smell of bacon and vanilla burning like acid in my lungs. That means she hadn't been in the water for all that long when I found her. The numbers on the nightstand clock flash across my brain, crimson as fresh blood. It was 6:04 when I woke up to an empty pillow next to me.

What time did Paul leave? When he reappeared, covered in sweat and mud and blood, was it really from a fall down Fontana Ridge? I sink onto a stool and remind myself to breathe.

"God, poor Sienna." Chet's voice is tinny, ringing in my ears. "Did you figure out where she's from? What she was doing in Lake Crosby?"

"We did, but we're not releasing any details, not until we get ahold of her next of kin. The folks down at the B and B are under a strict gag order, but you know Piper." Sam shrugs, more resigned than unconcerned. His tone is as serious as ever. "We threatened her with jail time. We'll see how much good it does."

None, probably. Nothing keeps in this town, not in the bed, not at the dinner table, not at the bar or B and B. And especially not with Piper.

Chet settles the platter on the island, bobbing his spatula between us. "Who wants the first?"

"Sam." I push the stack of plates his way, pass him the sugar and jam, which I know he'll choose over butter and syrup. I know where this conversation is going, and I can't even think about food.

He dumps on the jam, smearing it around as he asks the next question. "But since she was found on your property—"

I stop him right there: "It's Paul's property."

The irony is not lost on me. This past year, I've tried so hard to think of this place as home. To not cringe when I come up on a framed photo with another woman in it, to not fret that all my belongings, every stitch of what I own, could fit in the hallway linen closet. I tell myself I don't care that the pantry shelves are too high and the pillows too soft and I'm not supposed to eat on the white linen couches, or that I'd made myself small and unobtrusive so I'd fit in

Paul's preexisting life. Now, as soon as this place turns into a crime scene, it's not my home but his. I only live here.

Sam puts down his fork. "Since she was found on the property where you currently reside, I need to ask where you were the morning of November 20, say from 4:00 a.m. on."

My heart stops for a full second, like a slow-motion crash. "Okay."

Sam waits. Shakes his head. "Okay what?"

"Okay, ask away." I sit completely still, reminding myself to breathe. In my head I'm doing the math. Fontana Ridge is a little over three miles from the front door. The timing is doable but just barely, and only if Paul sprinted.

Sam rolls his eyes. "Where were you from 4:00 to 7:00 a.m. on the morning of November 20?"

"Upstairs asleep." I say it without blinking, with so much conviction that I almost believe it myself, but I can feel myself dipping into panic because I know the question that comes next.

"And Mr. Keller?"

And Mr. Keller. A liar and a secret-keeper, maybe, but not a killer. No way.

My heart gives three telltale thuds, *boom boom boom*, but I manage to keep my face calm. "In the bed next to me."

But Sam was here when Paul ran up yesterday morning, saw the blood and mud from his supposed tumble down Fontana Ridge. Good thing Paul's a fast runner.

"His alarm went off at six," I say before Sam can ask.

A lie and an alibi, wrapped into one.

16

Jax's car reeked of weed.

Correction: his dead mother's car reeked of weed, three puffs from the remnant of a crumpled joint Micah produced from his pocket, one toke apiece before it singed Jax's fingertips and he flicked it into the wind. He had to admit, it took some of the edge off his anger, but he didn't like the way it turned her car, a fully loaded Jeep Cherokee his dad gave her for her last birthday on this earth, into something out of *Wayne's World*. The 38 Special blasting from the speakers wasn't helping matters either.

But Paul drove a two-seater, so it was either this or Micah's Acura NSX, a gift from his mom the day he got his license. Micah's dad might be a cop, but the money came from his mom's side, thanks to her great-great-granddaddy's tobacco fields. But Micah's Acura had a back seat built for a duffel bag, and it was a stick, something only Micah knew how to operate. Jax's car was the obvious choice.

He hit the button for the windows to air the cab out and took a sharp right. Fast-food wrappers and empty bottles rattled around on the floorboard.

"Where are we going?" Paul said, pointing behind them. He was seated smack in the middle of the back seat, the seat belt straining as he leaned his upper body over the console. "Town's that way."

"I'm taking a detour."

Micah twisted on the passenger's seat. "This ain't a detour, man. This is the wrong way."

"Would you both just shut up and enjoy the ride? Listen to the music and just…chill. I know where I'm going."

His friends were just high enough to let it go, and chatter turned to the most likely place to score some booze. Jax sank into silence. US 64 was a sloppy two-laner lined with gorges and dented guardrails under a canopy of trees, obscuring everything in darkness. It was hypnotic, the way the road dipped and disappeared just beyond the headlights, how it was the yellow lines that seemed to be whipping by instead of the car shooting forward. Jax laid on the gas, leaning into the curves in a way that had even Micah grabbing for the ceiling handle.

Jax looked over with a laugh. "Stop being such a pussy."

"Stop driving like you have a death wish."

"Pull over," Paul said from the back seat. He was flush to the bench now, the seat belt tight across his chest, his hands gripping the seat on either side of his legs. "Let me drive for a while."

It wasn't the worst idea. Everything about Paul was neat

and precise, including the way he drove, like Jax's great-aunt Eleanor. Both stuck to the speed limits and kept their hands at ten and two. They liked order and craved control. He'd be a lot safer with Paul behind the wheel.

But Jax wasn't looking for safety. He was looking for something that made him feel alive. The road stretched on, rising and switching back, rising again. Paul and Micah fell still.

At the end of a straight stretch, Jax veered onto the shoulder and slammed the brakes, his tires fishtailing in the gravel.

"Holy shit," Paul muttered, slumping against the back seat. "You really could use some anger management. Has anybody ever told you that?"

Jax laughed despite himself.

Micah leaned into the windshield, frowning. "Rhodes Overlook, are you kidding me? It's summer, not to mention nighttime. There's no way we're seeing the bear."

It wasn't a bear but a bear shadow, one that only appeared in the fall. Months from now, people would flock to this spot from all over, leaf watchers waiting for the sun to dip behind Whiteside Mountain and cast a bear-shaped shadow on the treetops below, rippling branches of red and orange and russet. His mom used to bring him every October.

Jax killed the engine and marched across the road to the outlook.

A flashback, to those late afternoons with his mom. Eating sandwiches and chips out of a cooler in the trunk, standing shoulder to shoulder with strangers on the edge of a lichen-crusted ridge, cameras dangling from their necks. It was something they did every year, just the two of them, a mother-son tradition that lasted until long after he stopped giving a shit about the shadow. Good thing it was dark, because he never wanted to see that stupid bear again.

He stepped over the railing. Jax knew from all the times his mother would pull him back by his shirt that one more foot and the ground would drop out beneath him.

What would happen if he took that step? Just…walked out onto the air? He'd have to crash through the branches and needles first, but eventually he'd hit something solid. At the thought of what that would feel like, blood pulsed through his veins, infusing his organs and bones with life, which was really messed up since the only thing he could think about lately was death. His mother's. His own. One small step and it would all be over.

Behind him, a car door swung open to a rhythmic dinging.

"Jax, man, come on. Let's go." It was Micah's voice, but Jax knew without looking that those were Paul's shoes crunching in the gravel. He stopped right behind him, a silent, supportive presence.

What Jax needed was a sign. A butterfly landing on his arm, maybe, or a twinkling in the nighttime sky like his mom winking at him from that fluffy cloud. He looked up, and all he saw was blackness. No stars. No movement. Nothing but Jax, standing at the highest, loneliest point on earth.

"Don't even think about it," Paul said, his voice low and quiet enough that Micah across the street couldn't hear it. "I'm serious, Jax. Take one step and I swear to God I'll murder you myself."

Jax puffed a laugh. Leave it to Paul to both sense his gruesome thoughts and try to turn things around with humor. That was one of the things Jax loved best about his oldest friend, that he always knew what Jax was thinking without him having to say the first word. It was why they were such good friends, because neither of them ever felt like he had to explain.

But it was Micah, with his wild hairs and coal-dark streak, who surprised Jax the most. Micah stepped up beside him, toes flush to the edge, leaned his upper body over empty air and screamed. He just…opened his mouth and let loose. He screamed like Jax did when he reached the top of Balsam Bluff, long and loud and hard enough to make his ears ache and his eyes water. And then he filled his lungs and screamed some more.

Jax exchanged a look with Paul, who grinned.

The two of them joined in on the third go-round, Jax clenching his fists and giving it everything he had. He pictured his dad back at the house, his fingers stabbing the computer keys, and Pamela on her knees upstairs, clutching a Bible to her chest. To stand here, screaming with his friends into the vast, hostile wilderness, felt sad and pointless and stupid.

But for once, for however long the moment lasted, Jax didn't feel so alone.

17

Chet and I use the rest of our snow day wisely: stretched out on opposite ends of the buttery sectional in the basement, binge-watching an ancient season of *Naked and Afraid*. If Paul were here, he'd be catching up on emails or working on a sketch upstairs in his study, away from the noise. Paul likes schedules. He likes crossing off his to-do lists, the charting and mapping of his goals. He is physically incapable of doing nothing.

The McCreedys, however, are masters.

"Ten bucks says that dude is going to get eaten," Chet says, gesturing to the potbellied and bearded man on the screen. "And what kind of idiot chooses a fire starter in a jungle? You need a knife so you can hunt for food and fight off all the wild animals. Duh."

"What was she like?" Chet glances over with a frown,

and I add, "Sienna. Was she nice? Did you have a real conversation with her?"

"Sure, we talked. She was sweet. Funny." He doesn't take his eyes off the screen. "Good tipper."

"What'd the two of you talk about?"

"I don't know, all sorts of things. She asked me if I liked living here, what I did for a living, stuff like that. It wasn't anything serious. I got the feeling she just wanted to relax and have a good time."

I nudge him in the ribs with my toe. "You didn't give her one, did you? Because I heard you say she was hot. Please tell me the two of you didn't swap more than stories."

Chet snatches the remote from the table and hits Pause. "Seriously? You seriously want me to talk about my sex life with my sister?"

"Did you?"

It certainly wouldn't be the first time Chet has sweet-talked his way into some pretty girl's panties, a tourist looking for adventure with a handsome local. He's everything you'd look for in a town like this one—a little rugged, a little dirty, a lot charming. The female tourists love Chet, and Chet loves the female tourists.

"No. Now can we please just shut up and watch the show?"

He pushes Play and rolls onto his side. Conversation over.

We're deep into the fifth episode when my phone rings. Gwen, and I push her to voice mail. The second and third time, too, mostly because I have no idea what I would say to her. Gwen has access to Paul's calendar, which he updates with maniacal obsession. Whatever "work thing" I'm supposed to be using to excuse his disappearance won't be listed on there, and Gwen would call me out on it. And it doesn't make any sense for him to have gone anywhere with all this snow.

The phone screen lights up, and I tilt it toward my face. Gwen again, with a text this time.

SOS answer the goddamn phone!

It's followed by another call. With a sigh, I kick off the blanket and carry the phone to the hallway.

"Where the hell is Paul?"

No "hello." No "how are you?" Just this angry demand, one that I wish I knew the answer to.

"Scouting a property."

What worked just fine for Sam and Micah hasn't a chance in hell with Gwen. Gwen has worked for Paul since long before I came on the scene. She knows Paul scouts potential properties all the time, but she also knows he puts the trips on his calendar and makes sure he's reachable by cell. And he always checks the forecast before he goes so he won't get stuck in whatever weather is brewing between the mountaintops.

"What property? Where?"

"I don't know. He only said he might not have service. Did you try his cell?"

"Of *course* I tried his cell, all day yesterday and today. It doesn't even ring, just shoots me straight to voice mail. A scouting trip's not on his calendar."

"He said something about it being super top secret."

Another ridiculous lie. Gwen is Paul's longest employee, the closest thing to a partner he's got. He doesn't keep secrets from Gwen, not when it comes to Keller Architecture business. Anger wells in my chest, and I consider the words I'd really like to say. *I don't know where he is. He left me here holding a bag of lies. Go home and take a snow day. That's what I'm doing.*

But as angry as a part of me is at Paul, a bigger part knows he doesn't deserve all the blame. I lied, and then I lied again without him asking me to. So when the lies rolled off my tongue for the second and third time, I told myself I was looking out for Paul, but that's horseshit, isn't it? The truth is, by protecting Paul, I was also looking out for myself.

"You know what?" she says, sighing. "I don't have time for this. I need Paul's laptop, otherwise we're going to miss the Cedar Hill deadline."

Her words dull the sharpest edges of my thoughts. Cedar Hill is a development on the other side of Bald Rock, a potential build of up to thirty million-dollar homes situated along the Eastern Continental Divide. A big developer out of Atlanta invited only three firms to submit a bid, plans that showcase their vision for mountain luxury living. Paul has been working on the bid for months.

I frown, sinking on the steps. "The bid's not on the server?"

Another sigh, this time louder. No, the bid's not on the server.

"Hold on," I say, rising and heading up the stairs to the mudroom. I hang my head around the corner, and there it is, Paul's bag on the bench under the coat hooks, leaned up against the wall. I unclip the buckles and toss open the flap. His silver MacBook Pro is inside.

I pull it out, tuck it under an arm. "Got it. I'll email them over right now."

"You can't. The internet's down in town. TV and landlines, too. Some bad accident on 64 cut the cables or something. I need them on a stick. Either that, or I need the whole laptop."

My gaze goes to the window, a patch of swirling white blocking the view of the lake and trees. Gwen may have made it to the office, but for her it's only a three-block walk. For me, the only way there is by boat.

I drop the laptop back into Paul's bag and turn for the stairs. "I'm on my way."

By the time Chet and I get to town, my clothes are soaked and my nerves frayed. I was wrong before when I thought we got a couple of inches. More like six or seven, and it's nowhere near done. The snow is a swirling white curtain, turning the world opaque, and even slow going, moving through the snowstorm was like boating blindfolded. Three times I pointed the nose straight at the shore, pulling back on the gas just in time.

The dock appears in a wall of white, and Chet scrambles to throw out the fenders. We hit the wood with a jarring thud, knocking Chet clear off the bench. I clear the lines of water, cut the motor and clamber out on shaky legs.

Chet juts a thumb up the hill, the opposite direction of the office. "I'm going to see if anyone's out. Want something from the deli?"

"A sandwich would be great. Thanks. Bologna with extra mustard and pickles. Oh, and a strawberry milk over ice. Tell them to put it on the company's tab."

He cocks his head at my unusual order, then heads one way while I head the other, a sharp gust of wind chasing me up the hill to town. It whips my coat taut and clears the snow at the top, where I pause to catch my breath. The streets are deserted, an eerie winter wonderland lined with buildings and white lumps the size of parked cars. I spot tracks, both human and car, already filled with several inches of powdery snow.

At Paul's office, amber light trickles through the glass,

the promise of warmth in the subzero air. I push through the door, and Gwen pops off her chair.

"Oh, thank God." She rushes over, snatches the laptop from Paul's bag. "T minus forty-nine minutes and counting."

I sink onto the chair at my desk, watching her fire up the laptop and type in Paul's password. Laptops around here are communal property, and Paul requires everyone to use the same password, exactly for moments like this one. I see from her expression the moment she finds the files, and then she clicks in an external drive and waits for everything to copy.

"How are you going to submit without Wi-Fi?" The logistics are something I hadn't thought about earlier, in the stress of getting Paul's computer across the lake. If Gwen doesn't have internet to receive the files, she doesn't have internet to send them, either.

"I called Patrick at the Department of Transportation. He said their satellite can be sketchy in weather like this, but I'm welcome to come down and try. Cross everything, 'cause it's going to be a Hail Mary pass. Not even postal workers are out in this mess."

"Thank you for doing this. I know Paul will really appreciate it."

She puffs a sarcastic laugh, a phlegmy sound. "Yeah, well, he better, because when he gets back I'm going to kill him. This snowstorm has taken five years off my life. If I hadn't put about a billion hours into this project myself, I would've blown it off, kind of like Paul is doing now." The laptop beeps, and she yanks the external drive out and drops it in her bag. "Wish me luck."

"Luck."

She snatches her coat from the back of another chair

and leaves in a huff of swirling snow. A blast of icy wind slams the door behind her.

I shrug off my coat, drape it over the back of my chair to dry and step to Gwen's desk, where Paul's laptop sits open. I smile at the wallpaper, a selfie of us, a close-up from a trip to Charleston last summer, all big smiles and tanned cheeks. The Cedar Hill files are lined up neatly along the right side of Paul's head, and I skim them from top to bottom. His entire life resides on this hunk of plastic and metal. His correspondence, his finances, his calendar and to-do lists.

And the camera footage. The one Sam is sending a subpoena for.

The security website is bookmarked under House, the password the same one he uses for everything. It takes me a couple of minutes to figure out how to pull up the footage, then to limit the clips to the ones recorded after 5:00 p.m. on Tuesday. My heart gives a hard kick when it spits out dozens of clips. Why so many?

I click on the first one, at just past five, the one of Paul and me returning from town. I smile at the way he helps me out of the boat, with an easy tug into his arms. He swings me around and dips me over an arm right there on the dock. Something catches in my chest at the image of us, so happy and obviously in love. I think of Sam watching this same clip. Maybe then he'll finally believe my feelings are real.

I move on to the next clip, working through them one by one, my shoulders relaxing a notch with each one. A deer on the edge of the lake. A fox shooting down the hill. Dark smudges moving on a dark screen, too faint to make out. But what's clear is that in none of them is there a man, Paul or otherwise, tossing a body from the dock.

When I get to the footage of me heading to the dock in

my nightgown, I switch to Paul's email and send the log-in information to Sam. While I'm there, I scan the subject lines in his inbox. New product notices, sales pitches, de-tailed back-and-forths about current and future projects. Except for a couple of junk ads for penis enlargement sur-gery, nothing sticks out as unusual. The mailboxes are or-ganized just as meticulously as you'd expect from a guy like Paul, the projects listed by name and date, the contents separated into subfolders. I scroll through them, clicking on a folder marked Personal, but there's not much here I don't already know. His house, his health insurance and tax as-sessments. I back out and close the program.

The finder is more of the same. Work projects filed by address and dates, personal folders with copies of pass-ports and tax reports. I'm about to move on when I spot it, a folder marked Katherine.

Something tight and icy-hot spirals across my scalp at the sight of Paul's first wife's name, a yellow folder of mem-ories and who knows what else sitting on his hard drive. I hover the mouse over her name, wavering between dread and curiosity.

If I open this file, I can't unsee what's in it. I won't be able to pretend I don't know. There's no going back from this.

And yet I've already reached the point of no return, haven't I, simply by seeing her name on his hard drive. Even if I don't look inside this folder, for the rest of my life I will wonder what's in it, this digital mystery stashed on his laptop.

And that, somehow, feels even worse.

I click her name, and there are two subfolders, Legalities and Memories. I don't know which one is scarier.

The first file contains pdf documents, filed by name and

date. Her birth and death certificates, their marriage certificate, bank statements and tax returns. Her will is complicated, trusts and properties and a whole bunch of legalese I don't understand, no list of assets other than that they all went to Paul. I back out and click the most recent bank statement, a portfolio summary from J.P. Morgan, and my eyes bulge at the amount. Before Katherine died, her investments had a market value of almost six million dollars.

Maybe this is why we don't talk about money, because if we did, he'd have to tell me that the majority of his wealth came from a former swimmer who sank to the bottom of the lake she did laps in every summer morning. It's a hard pill for even the most trusting, most gullible wife to swallow. No wonder Sam thinks the worst. If I didn't know Paul so well, I might, too.

I back out and keep scrolling, and a file catches my eye: Fertility Eval. A chart, a long list of medical tests and terms. It doesn't take me long to get the gist. Katherine was infertile, something about ovulatory dysfunction and a diminished ovarian reserve, and I think back to Paul's reaction on the boat, his obvious joy when he found out he was going to be a father, and an invisible fist punches into my chest and squeezes my heart. Finally something I've beaten her at, but it doesn't feel like a victory. It feels like a tragedy, especially for Paul.

I shake it off and move on to the Memories folder, and it's pictures. Thousands and thousands of them. Smiling. Kissing. Gazing lovingly into the other's eyes. Capturing moments from the time they met, in grad school at Cornell, to the weekend before she died. Glamorous shots from their wedding, grainier shots at parties and on vacations, candid shots at home—Paul's home, the one I can't quite think of as mine because it's her hyacinth bulbs that push through the dirt each spring.

I zoom in on a shot of her sunning on my favorite chair on the dock, and she really is lovely. Long and lean, with high cheekbones and eyes so aqua it's hard to look away. I take her in, but it's Paul's face I concentrate on. He looks happy. Relaxed. I measure the edges of his smile, compare them to the one he aimed at me two days ago when I told him I was pregnant. Did he smile bigger with her? Was his face brighter?

And what was it Sam said? *All you have to do is take off the blinders.*

My eyes flutter shut, and I steel myself against something ugly and dark.

The door bangs open, and I jump so hard my body loses contact with the seat. Chet shakes off the snow and his coat, hanging it on the door handle.

"Deli was closed. Everything is, even the post office. It's like a ghost town out there. What? What'd I do now?"

I shake my head. "It's not you. It's just…" I gesture vaguely to the laptop screen. "I was going through Paul's computer. I don't like what I found."

Chet leaves a trail of snow and ice on his trek across the office, nodding knowingly. "Porn?"

"What? No, not porn." I frown. "Stuff about Katherine."

It takes him a second or two to place the name. "Wait—isn't Katherine his wife?"

"*First* wife. *Was.* The wife he refuses to talk to me about, ever. She was loaded, Chet."

"Well, of course she was. Her daddy was Pete-O-Pedic." He sings part of a jingle anyone in fifteen counties would recognize: "'Buy your mattress from a local dealer, get it for a little cheaper.' Remember those commercials?"

I remember. They only played them every five minutes on the radio. Those stores were everywhere until Mattress King swooped in and bought Pete out. He died of a heart attack less than a year later.

Chet leans over the desk, craning his neck to see the laptop screen. "Whoa. No wonder you're so bent out of shape. She's hot."

I snap the laptop closed. "Oh my God, you are literally the worst brother in the world."

"What? She was. And how'd you get on his computer, anyway?"

"I know his password. Everybody here does. We all have the same ones."

Chet points at me over the desk. "See? You're good, then. A husband with something to hide is going to lock down his technology. One hundred percent."

"Then why keep the pictures on his hard drive?"

"So what if he does? She's not here, and you are. From where I sit, that means you're winning."

It's such a maddeningly male thing to say and on so many levels. As if my love life is some kind of game, a competition to win Paul's heart. As if the first wife's death automatically guarantees the second wife's security, like love is a matter of proximity and wives are interchangeable. But mostly, that I should just suck it up and let it go.

Chet studies me from across the desk. "I scrounged up some intel for you, but now I don't know if I should tell you."

"What kind of intel?"

"I swung by the B and B." He leans in, lowers his voice to a shout-whisper. "I talked to Piper."

"I thought you said nobody was out."

"Not on the streets. They were all hunkered down in the

bar, pounding Jack Daniel's. Something like twenty people, all of 'em plastered. The place was a madhouse."

"And? What'd Piper say?"

"Nothing. Not one goddamn thing, but Wade was there, too, and he sure was talkative."

Wade. The guy leaning against the side of the B and B two days ago, when I came to town looking for Paul. The one who called me Charlie and Paul my old man.

Chet leans with both elbows on the desk. "Wade said he talked to Sienna the day before she died. She talked to a lot of people, apparently, and she was asking all of them about Jax. The cops are looking everywhere for him. They think Jax had something to do with Sienna ending up in the lake."

Jax, who was looking for Paul hours before a woman washed up dead. I see him stepping out of the shadows at the back of the terrace, the skittish way he looked everywhere but at me. *Tell Paul I need to talk to him.*

"But according to Wade, it wasn't just Jax she was asking about. She was also asking about Paul."

The room goes hot. "My Paul?"

Chet gives me a *who else?* look.

"What about Paul? What did she want from him?"

Chet shrugs. "Like I said, Wade was baked. I couldn't get much more out of him that made sense. You know how he tends to…"

Chet's voice bleeds away, and new worries snag in my brain. Why was Sienna looking for Paul? Did she know who he was when she approached him in town, or did I feed that info to her when I introduced myself as a Keller? And Wade isn't exactly known around these parts for his discretion. If he told Chet, he's told other people. People like Sam, who will automatically think the worst.

Chet pushes up from the chair. "Hey, you got something to drink? I'm parched."

"Check the fridge." I gesture behind me, in the general direction of the kitchen.

He wanders off, and I sit here for a moment, the breath turning sluggish in my lungs. If what Wade said is true, if this woman was here asking about Paul, if he *knew* her, then he looked me in the eyes and lied like it was nothing. What else has he lied about? What other secrets has he stuffed down, hidden in files on his hard drive or buried around the house like rotten Easter eggs? Happy couples don't keep secrets, and they don't lie. What does all this say about us? What does it mean for our future? For the future of the baby growing in my belly?

And then the darkest, ugliest question rises above the rest, sticking to my brain.

What time did Paul get out of bed, *really*?

18

The snowstorm blows off on a warmer wind, clearing the clouds into a bright blue sky. Late-afternoon sunshine heats the hill behind the house, a blinding white field of smooth crystals melting like ice cream in the summer, sliding into the lake in slushy chunks. According to the news, we got a full eight inches, a record for this time of year, all of which is supposed to be melted by this time tomorrow. Welcome to winter in the South.

Word of Sienna's murder has also made the news, though the details are scarce. They haven't mentioned her name or where she washed up, only that she was fished out yesterday morning. I keep Paul's laptop tuned to a local news station and roam from room to room, poking through closets and dressers, searching for anything that might explain why a dead woman under our dock might have been asking about my husband.

I save the study for last, settling in at Paul's desk and digging through the drawers. I rearrange the pens, sort the paper clips and rubber bands, flip through a stack of unopened bills, Post-it notes and papers. I spread a pile of business cards across the desk, examine the names, put them back in the drawer with neat, exacting edges. He's been gone too long. He could have made it around the lake three times by now.

Footsteps at the door snap me to attention. Chet wanders in, stirring in a mixing bowl with a wooden spoon. He's in jeans and a long-sleeved T-shirt, one sleeve dusted in a fine white powder. I mute the volume on the laptop.

"Hey, taste this, will you?" He scoops up a bite and holds the spoon across the desk, waving it in front of my nose. "Tell me if it needs anything."

I wrinkle my nose at the wet blob of orange and pink. "It's not pimento cheese, is it? I hate pimento cheese."

"Nope. Let's just say I took a few liberties." He wags his brows and the spoon in the air. "Stop being a baby. Taste it."

I sigh and take the spoon from his hand. Lick the blob with the very tip of my tongue. Frown, but only out of surprise. A pleasant surprise. I put the spoon in my mouth and it's an explosion on my tongue, salty and sweet and...

"Is that nuts?"

"Nuts and cheese and some strawberry preserves, a little bit of powdered sugar. I thought we'd have it on some French toast tomorrow." Chet grins, leaning back on his heels. "You really like it?"

"No—I love it." I give the spoon one last good lick and hand it back. "Seriously, Chet. This tastes like candy. Where'd you learn this stuff?"

He lifts a shoulder, suddenly bashful. "Annalee was always watching those cooking shows. You know, the ones where they give you half a coconut and some peanuts and you have to use it to make a gourmet meal. I guess some of it rubbed off."

"You're really talented. If I owned a restaurant, I'd hire you in a second, and I'm not just saying that because I'm your sister."

But because I'm his sister, I'm also counting the places in town that would be lucky to have him. The diner, Buck's Bistro, even the pub puts on a decent Sunday brunch. Paul knows all the owners. When he's back, I'll ask him to put in a good word.

And just like that, my cheerfulness bursts like a soap bubble.

Because what's going to happen when Paul walks through the door? After the relief at having him back in one piece, I mean. We can't just pick up from where we left off, those innocent moments before my early-morning trek down to the dock. I need answers, and to questions I'm terrified of asking. Especially now that there's a baby on the way. He can't keep me in the dark, can't keep holding me at an arm's distance. I need more from him.

Chet drops the bowl onto the desk and sinks onto the calf hide lounger by the window, swinging his feet up and crossing them at the ankle. "I know I'm supposed to be the ignorant one, but—"

"Don't do that, Chet." I shake my head, my shoulders slumping. "Don't make those kinds of jokes about yourself."

"Word on the street is it's no joke." One side of his mouth lifts into a half-cocked grin. "Anyway, you're supposed to be the smart one in the family. So how come you're acting so dumb?"

I frown. "What do you mean?"

"Well, your husband skips town two seconds after you

find a dead lady in the lake, and you're running around here trying to pretend that you're okay with it, even though anybody with a set of eyes can see that you're not. Let me see if I've got this straight." He pulls one hand from behind his head and ticks his points off on his fingers. "Lady asks about Paul. Lady turns up dead. Paul splits. You provide cover." His hand wriggles back underneath his head. "You gonna tell me what's going on here, or are you gonna lie to me like you did with Sam and Micah?"

I stare across the space at my brother, so much more observant than anybody ever gives him credit for. Chet didn't come in here for my opinion on his latest food creation or help in finding him a job. He's seen me poking around the house all afternoon, heard the silent debate raging in my head. He knows there's something bothering me I'm not telling him.

I realize with a pang that I want his opinion. I need another person's honest, no-holds-barred take, and I want that person to be Chet.

"You can't tell anyone. I mean it, Chet—not a soul. If Sam or Micah or anybody else asks, you have to play dumb."

"We've already established I can do that." Another slow grin, more deadpan tone.

I roll my eyes. "This is serious. I'm being serious. You have to promise and swear you won't say a thing."

He draws an X on his chest. "Not one word, swear to God."

I tell him everything. About finding Paul talking to Sienna the day she was murdered. About his lie to the police, and me following his lead. About him taking off with a backpack stuffed with food and a nylon hammock to find

Jax, all the ways I've covered for him since. About Jax pressing his face to the window just last night.

Chet swings his feet to the floor and sits up, frowning. "Jax was here? What for?"

"I'm not entirely sure. At first, I thought it was to tell me something happened to Paul, which is why I opened the door. He knew about the woman drowning—even knew her name—and then he told me to watch my back."

"Dude. That's…that's crazy. Weren't you scared?"

"The weird thing is, it didn't feel like a threat. He wasn't aggressive, like, at *all*. I think he was trying to warn me." I think back to his words about Paul and the body count, his expression when he looked through the woods to Micah's, the way he shifted from foot to foot. "He seemed more spooked by me than I was of him."

"He's at the receiving end of a manhunt. Of course he's spooked." Chet leans back into the recliner, watching me from across the room. Particles of dust dance in the air between us, glittering in a beam of sunlight. "But I guess the bigger question is, are you?"

"Am I what, spooked?"

Chet nods, and I don't have to think on my answer for long. Micah and Sam might say Jax is dangerous, but I'm less sure. If he'd wanted to hurt me last night, he could have, and in a thousand different ways. He didn't seem like a killer, just a lost and tortured soul.

"I'm not afraid of Jax."

Chet gives me a meaningful look. "I'm not talking about Jax."

My gaze falls on our wedding picture at the edge of Paul's desk, happy faces in a shiny silver frame. My head is tilted up to his, leaning in for the kiss that sealed the deal. "Hello, wifey," he whispered against my lips, and I thought my heart would burst with joy.

Unlike Sam and the rest of my friends, Chet never asked me if I was sure. He never tried to talk me out of it or told me I was insane for marrying a man who everybody says got away with murder. He never accused me of choosing money over sense.

But that doesn't mean he never thought it.

"I love Paul," I say, and my voice goes squeaky on his name. "I wouldn't have fallen in love with him if I thought he was capable of hurting me. Of hurting another person that way. And I know it makes me sound ignorant and gullible, but even after what Wade told you, I *still* don't think it. There are a lot of things I don't know about Paul, but he's not a killer. No way."

Chet picks at a thread on the hem of his shirt. "So I guess that means you're staying."

"Of course I'm staying. Leaving now would be doing the very thing I got so pissed at Sam for—making assumptions about a man's guilt instead of assuming his innocence. People drown all the time, even strong swimmers. Look it up. The only reason they suspected Paul at all is because of the money, which he doesn't need. He'd be doing just fine without it."

"What if he wanted it, though?"

"Is that what you think, that Paul killed her for the money?"

Chet shrugs, rolling his head on the lounger to face me. "I heard all those things people said about him after his first wife died, and maybe I believed some of it at first, but it doesn't match up with the Paul I know. He's a nice guy. It's complicated."

See? I'm not crazy.

But there's another reason I can't just up and leave, one I haven't told Chet yet. I hold his gaze, count to three. Three heartbeats, three breaths. I'm suddenly as nervous as when I peed on the stick.

"I'm pregnant."

"Shut up." He pops onto both elbows, a grin tugging on his lips. "Are you kidding me? You better not be kidding me. You're really pregnant?"

"I'm not kidding you. I really am."

I remember the thrill I felt on the boat, the way Paul picked me up and swung me around the tiny space between the seats, and I try to hold on to that flash of happiness. Without him here, it's fading fast.

"Aw, hell." Chet swings his feet to the floor. I'm two seconds away from waterworks, and Chet hates it when I cry. He says it makes him twitchy. His gaze stays steady on mine. "You're gonna be a great mom. Look at how you did with me. You took care of me, and I'm not even your kid. A baby is a good thing."

"How? How is this baby a good thing? It's going to live at the edge of a lake that's sucking down women left and right, raised by what everybody says are gold-digging and maybe murdering parents. This baby is not exactly coming in on a winning streak."

He shifts on the lounger. "That's not... You always say not to pay any mind to what people are saying, and they're not seeing what I see, that this baby will have two parents who actually like each other. Y'all eat meals together and hold hands on the couch and smile more when the other's around. I'm no expert, but it seems like the biggest battle is already won."

"You're just saying that to make me feel better."

"A little." He gives me a sheepish shrug. "But I kinda mean it, too. I don't know. I'm as confused as you are."

I laugh. If nothing else, Chet is honest.

The doorbell rings, and I'm out of the chair in an instant, breath tingling in my lungs. I'm praying it's Paul, who left in such a hurry he forgot his keys. First I'm going to hug him and then I'm going to strangle him, or maybe the other way around. Or maybe both at the same time.

I sprint into the foyer, and it's not Paul's face pressed to the window. It's Micah's.

Micah, who I've lied to now, what—three times? Four? I've lost count, and I know enough about lying to know that forgetting can't be a good thing. You have to keep track of all the lies you tell and to whom. You have to tie up all the threads and not let a single one dangle. One good tug on mine and the whole thing unravels.

He waves, then points to the wall. "Alarm," he mouths through the glass.

Chet steps up behind me, breathing hard. "Uh-oh," he mutters.

My joints feel locked up like superglue, but what other choice do I have?

"Just a sec," I shout through the glass. I smile brightly, hold up a finger and whirl around to face Chet. "Not a word," I whisper. "You promised."

Chet gives me a *who, me?* look.

I step to the panel, tick in the code and let Micah inside.

19

I gesture for Micah to follow me into the kitchen, where Chet is already popping open two Heinekens. On the island before him is what has kept him busy all afternoon—a thick wooden cutting board covered in onion peels and vegetable skins, surrounded by bottles and boxes and mixing bowls. Dinner, by the looks of things, a salad of broccoli and carrot and sliced almonds, thin strips of cucumber swimming in sour cream, two giant T-bones resting on a platter. Behind him, lined up like soldiers, two potatoes wrapped in silver foil sit on a rack in the upper oven.

"Wow, this is some spread," Micah says, taking in the food, doing the math. Two of each means none for Paul.

"Chet's practicing to be a chef. You should see what he does with pimento cheese. He makes it taste like dessert." My words are too fast and my voice too bright, like a spotlight on the melting snow outside.

"Here you go, Sheriff," Chet says, handing over the beer. "Got any news about Sienna?"

I widen my eyes at Chet—*real subtle*—but Micah doesn't seem to mind the question. "Yep, but not anything I can tell the two of you. Dad's holding a press conference tomorrow morning, though, so maybe give it a watch." He tips the bottle at Chet, then me. "Cheers."

I pour myself a glass of water, but I can't drink. My stomach is in knots, my hand shaking the glass. I set it on the marble with a hard smack.

"I hear you took the boat to town." Micah pauses to receive my nod. "Don't do it again, okay? This entire end of the lake is an active crime scene. I put up no-entry signs at either side of the bend by Piney Creek, and if you see anybody out on the water between now and tomorrow morning, I want to know about it."

"What happens tomorrow morning?"

"We'll be back in the lake as soon as it's light, looking at currents, trying to determine her trajectory from the moment she went in the water until we fished her out so we know where to point the sonar." His eyes flash with excitement. For Micah, there's no better day than one he gets to strap on his flippers and an oxygen tank and skim the lake bottom like a catfish, sifting through the silt for evidence. "We'll be starting in the cove, though, so if anyone tries to sneak past us, we'll see it."

I nod, the tightness I've been carrying around all day releasing just a tiny bit in my chest. Micah and his divers will be out on the cove tomorrow, which means no more surprise visits from Jax, no more vile words carved into the snow.

Micah swivels his head to Chet, watching from the other side of the counter. "In the meantime, Dad says for you to stop harassing Piper."

A red flush sprouts on Chet's cheeks, and his gaze darts between me and Micah. His expression says *fuuuuuuuuuck*.

"I wasn't harassing her," Chet says slowly, thinking about every word before it comes out of his mouth. "Piper and I were just...talking. About stuff."

Micah gives him a knowing nod. "What kind of stuff?"

Chet coughs into a fist. "Basically, she told me to leave her alone because she doesn't want to go to jail."

Micah laughs. "That's what she told him, too, though nice to have it confirmed by someone who's not Piper." He leans a hip against the counter, reaching down to scratch a knee. "I ran into Gwen on my way out of the B and B. She was spitting mad. She said Paul missed some big deadline?"

Chet's dip sours in my stomach, hardening into a painful lump. Micah talked to Gwen, who'd already told me she'd trudged all the way down to county GIS but couldn't get the email to send. The signal was too weak, the files too massive. After all that work, they weren't able to put the bid in. Gwen must have been livid, and I'm sure she gave him an earful.

I nod. "When Paul's back, he'll call them to explain, see if they'll accept his bid a day or two late. Surely they can't hold him responsible for the snow, or for a traffic accident that took down the internet. Isn't weather like an act of God or something?"

Micah is silent for a beat or two, and I know what he's thinking, that Paul didn't miss the deadline because of the snow or the accident. He missed it because he took off on an errand so important that he forgot all about the bid he'd been working on for months.

Micah takes a long, pensive pull from the bottle, then settles it onto the counter. "You know, back in high school, everybody made fun of Paul for turning in his term papers a whole week early. Professor Paul, we used to call him, including the teachers. He never waited until the last second to turn in anything."

There's a question in there somewhere, but I'm not about to touch it. Micah is right. It's not like Paul at all to miss a deadline. If I keep my mouth shut, I won't have to tell another lie.

"Here's another thing Gwen and I can't seem to understand. How's Paul scouting anything in this weather?"

I swallow, trying to keep my breath steady. I want Paul to be here. I want him to swing his arm around my shoulders and explain it his damn self. "He left before the snow hit."

"How come he's not answering his phone?"

"No reception, I guess. Either that, or he forgot his charger."

Or both. Or he's too busy lying in a broken heap at the bottom of some bluff.

The kitchen is a pressure cooker. Micah is playing us. He talked to Gwen, and he knows Paul's history. He knows the way Paul thinks, what makes him tick, what would make him run off in such a hurry. The walls shrink in, the ceiling moves lower, and the hot air blowing through the vents hurts my ears.

Micah sets the beer on the counter with a sigh. "Charlotte, what do you say we cut the crap? Because I think you know exactly where that crazy-ass husband of yours went, and if it's the place I think he's gone, then you'd best be telling me so I can do something about it. You won't hear it on the press conference tomorrow, but all signs point to Jax for Sienna's murder."

My body is tight with unreleased fear. Micah knows where Paul went, and he's worried about him, which means I should be, too.

"Look, I don't want this getting all over town, but the cops have been to Balsam Bluff."

I frown. "What's in Balsam Bluff?"

"Jax has a cabin on the western side."

This is news to me. Jax has a cabin, and in Balsam Bluff no less. A popular hiking area crisscrossed with trails and picnic spots deep in the Nantahala National Forest, a good thirty minutes by car from here.

But the western side is undisturbed wilderness, an untamed, undeveloped forest where the few humans wandering the hills are either lost or up to no good. How Jax got away with erecting a cabin on government land is anybody's guess. You can't stake anything there without an act of Congress.

Chet doesn't buy it, either. "Dude, that makes zero sense. For one thing, nobody has a cabin in Balsam Bluff. And even if Jax did live there, which he doesn't, he's not going to be anywhere near there by the time the cops arrive. You don't find Jax. Jax finds you."

"That may be so," Micah says, "but they found Sienna's coat in Jax's cabin. Her scarf is MIA."

I think of Jax, standing in the glow of the porch lights on the back deck, and something sparks in my chest. "What does the scarf look like?"

"Cashmere. Cream and knitted. With dangly things on the ends."

"Fringe." I close my eyes, and I see his neck, wrapped in the creamy material. I remember thinking the scarf was too pretty for his big frame, the pattern too complicated and girlie. I think back to when I saw Sienna in town, the scarf she had double-wrapped around her neck and stuffed into her black wool coat.

But the parts of it I could see were cream.

Jax knew her name. He was wearing her scarf.

I open my eyes, and Micah is watching me. "Jax is dangerous, Charlotte. Volatile and violent and completely unpredictable, and he has been for a while. The cops have evidence he murdered that woman, something I'm guessing Paul at least figured when he took off after him. That's where Paul is, isn't it? He went to warn Jax the cops were coming for him."

I look at Chet, standing stiff like a soldier on the other side of the island.

You can't tell Micah, Paul said on his way out the door. *Promise me you won't say a word until I get back.*

In the end, though, I didn't make that promise, did I? I was angry about him leaving, angry he might not make it back in time for my doctor's appointment tomorrow, moved to next week because of the snow. He said he had to go, that we'd talk about everything when he got back.

But when will that be? Paul has been gone for far too long already. What if he's hurt? What if Jax hurt him?

"There are cops from five counties crawling all over Balsam Bluff, looking for a man who's considered armed and dangerous."

There's so much to latch on to here, but one word is ringing in my ears: *armed*. Jax owns a gun, which shouldn't surprise me. This is North Carolina. Everybody owns a gun. But Paul is unarmed and Batty Jax has a gun.

Micah turns the bottle in a hand, scratching absently at the lettering with a thumbnail. "If Paul is there, if the cops see him and think he's Jax, there's no telling what will happen."

Paul's words echo through my head, just as surprising as when I heard them the first time.

Promise me you won't tell Micah.

I grab on to Micah's sleeve, the words tumbling out of me. "You have to find him, Micah. He left with his backpack and three days' worth of supplies, but he should have been back by now. He—"

"I knew it." Micah slams the beer bottle to the marble so hard foam shoots out the top. "I *knew* that idiot would be halfway to Balsam Bluff by the time I came up the hill. You'd think he'd learn, after looking down the end of Jax's barrel as many times as he has, but Paul has always been such a goddamn martyr. One of these days this bleeding heart of his is going to get him killed."

Just then, from the depths of the house, a door bangs open. Chet tilts his head, listening for the source of the noise, but I already know. I race to the railing and lean over the stairs to the lower level, right as the alarm pad chimes. A computerized voice fills the air: *basement door open*. It's the only way in without a key, but only if you know the code.

There's movement just out of sight in the downstairs hallway, the thump of something hitting the ground. And then, finally, a familiar slope of shoulder, a patch of filthy brown hair.

"Paul!"

20

They decided pretty quickly that Micah, with his eighteen years and stuntman swagger, would be the best bet to win over any liquor store cashier, especially if they could manage to find one who was female. The first three, flashy package stores that catered to the tourists on the outskirts of town, were staffed by men who knew too damn well who Micah was, and what his dad would do to their permits if he found out they'd sold his underage son alcohol. At each one, he came out empty-handed.

In a fit of frustration, they drove all the way to Sylva, to a seedy shack run by locals who knocked back as much as they sold. They watched through the window as Micah flirted with the cashier, a permed blonde in jeans too tight, her smile too big, too desperate. But Micah leaned on her counter and turned up the charm, reemerging moments later with two bottles wrapped in brown paper bags, one clutched in each fist. He held them high above his head, like trophies.

"Way to be cool about it, asshole," Jax muttered, but he was only half-serious, the other half-impressed Micah actually pulled it off.

He strutted with the bottles across the gravel lot, dodging cars and tromping on trash, and Jax smiled despite himself. A lot of the time Micah was insufferable, but all that screaming earlier had loosened up something in Jax's chest, made the night a little more bearable. Micah was a blowhard, but only a real friend would know what Jax needed at the exact moment he needed it. Jax couldn't help but love the guy a little for it.

He reached across the passenger's seat and popped open the door. "What'd you get?"

Micah grinned, wagging the bottles. "Do you prefer your tequila with a worm or without?"

Paul grimaced. "I prefer beer."

"Quit your bitching, man. Beggars can't be choosers and all that. Besides, liquor's quicker."

Jax wasn't going to argue with that. He started the car and Micah dropped in, passing a bottle to the back seat, tugging off the bag on the second, holding it up so Jax could see. Tequila. Fast and cheap and dirty.

Micah twisted off the cap with a click. "Happy Saturday, gentlemen. Let's get plastered."

21

"Are you okay?" I push past the others lined up next to me along the railing and step to the mouth of the stairs. Paul is hunched at the bottom, loosening the laces on his boots. "Do you need help?"

"I'm fine. Just beat." He kicks off his shoes and glances up.

I gasp. Paul's face is a horror show. The cut on his brow is angry and infected, a purple scab pushing up from skin that's swollen and rash-red. Dark stubble has sprouted on his chin and cheeks, and it's clumped with dirt and grime. One of his eyes is sunken into skin bruised a dark purple; the other is swollen shut.

I rush down the stairs. "Oh my God, what happened to you?"

"You're lucky he didn't do worse," Micah says from above our heads. "He could've put a bullet in your head and buried you somewhere we'd never find you, you stubborn moron."

Paul ignores him, shedding clothes as he comes up the stairs. His coat, two thermal shirts stiff with dirt and sweat, his woolen cap and fleece neck warmer. He drops the filthy pieces to the ground as he heaves his body up, pulling himself up by the handrail. He reeks of blood and sweat.

I give him an arm, and he looks over with a tired smile. "I missed you. Everything okay?"

I'm not entirely sure how to answer this. Everything's pretty much the opposite of okay, but this also isn't the best time to sift through all the things that are wrong. Not with an audience. I nod, wrapping my arm around his waist and nudging him up the stairs. "Everything's fine."

Of all my lies, this one's the most absurd.

Paul moves in slow motion, each step an effort when on a normal day he bounds up them by twos and threes. I scan his body for more injuries—wounds pushing through the fabric of his clothes, spots soaked with blood—but there's nothing but hard muscle and sharp bone, more angular than usual. He's lost weight, a good five pounds at least.

Micah shakes his head, staring down the staircase in sturdy silence.

"Did you sleep at all?" I say, counting new lines around his eyes and mouth, everything deeper than it was a couple of days ago. Or maybe that's just the dirt smeared across every inch of him, shoved into every wrinkle. He's like a charcoal drawing of an old man, black and white and defined.

He tries for a smile, but it comes up a wince. "For about five minutes. I'll be fine. I just need some food and a bed."

"On it," Chet says, pushing away from the banister.

"You better hope you didn't muck up this investigation,"

Micah says. "If you stepped even one foot in that cabin, if you polluted the space with your DNA, then you'll not just be an idiot but a suspect."

Paul pauses halfway up the stairs. "He didn't do it, asshole. Jax wasn't anywhere near the lake when that woman went in, but I sure do appreciate your sympathy."

We reach the top, and Paul is panting like he just sprinted up Clingman's Dome. He elbows past Micah and collapses onto a counter stool with a groan.

"And you know this, how? Because Jax looked you in the eyes and pinkie-promised?" Micah laughs, a harsh sound. "Why are you always such a sucker where that man is concerned? Hasn't anybody ever told you not to believe the madman in the woods?"

"You know," Chet says, clutching a loaf of white bread and a peanut butter jar he fetched from the pantry, "Jax and I once had a twenty-minute conversation about the traffic light they put in at Fringe Tree Street. He said roundabouts were a lot safer, and then he spewed off all sorts of statistics to back him up. That dude's smarter than he likes people to believe, and a lot less crazy."

Paul shoots Micah a *told you so* gesture, but he's too busy glaring at Chet to notice.

"Does Jax have an alibi?" Micah asks, turning back to Paul. "Of course he doesn't, because he *was* there. Multiple sightings in town the afternoon before that woman fell into the lake. Multiple witnesses saying she was asking about him, and then her things were found in his cabin. He lied to you again, Paul. You fell for his bullshit, again."

Paul frowns, but only one eyebrow dips. The other is too swollen to budge. His hands are filthy, the dark lines of dirt under his nails like black half-moons against the white marble.

"What bullshit?" I say, but no one answers.

Micah's body is restless. Impatient. He takes three steps closer to Paul, moving into his line of sight. "Dad's made it his personal mission to find Jax, and you and I both know that man always gets what he wants. If you want to help Jax, and I know you do, then tell me where he's hiding."

"Right." Paul coughs up a laugh with zero humor. "Because we all know what'll happen then, don't we? Jax'll be dead before sunrise."

"So you *do* know where he's hiding."

Paul shakes his head, looking away.

Micah leans in, planting both elbows on the cold marble. His voice rises, a brewing storm rattling the windows and walls. "Paul. Where is Jax?"

"I don't know." Paul shouts it, his cheeks going pink with rage. He takes three puffed breaths, three painful seconds to wrangle his anger back under control. "I don't fucking know, okay? He knocked me out. He punched me in the face and left me there. By the time I came to, he was long gone."

That explains the black eye, at least, but it's four or five miles to Balsam Bluff. If Paul didn't sleep, what has he been doing all this time?

Micah shoves off the island, straightening to full height. "What is it people say? That the definition of insanity is doing the same thing over and over and expecting things to change. So maybe I was wrong. Maybe you're the crazy one here, not Jax. Maybe you're the one who needs psychiatric help."

Paul grunts. "Are we almost done with this lecture? Because I really just want a shower and my bed."

Chet wags the knife in the air. "Sandwiches incoming, extra heavy on the PB and J." They're more gooey filling than bread, stacked in a messy pile. He slices them down the middle and passes Paul the plate.

He wolfs the sandwiches down like he hasn't eaten in days, only occasionally pausing to chug a glass of milk, greedy tugs that spill down the sides of his mouth. He wipes it away with a sleeve, but it doesn't slow him down. He shoves the next sandwich half in his mouth and keeps going until there's nothing on his plate but crumbs and a cranberry-colored smear. If Diana were here, she'd scold him for his lack of table manners.

"Feel better?" Micah says.

Paul nods, and he does look better. The sugar and the full stomach have brought some color to his cheeks, softened the beard and the bruises.

But that cut he got sliding down Fontana Ridge looks worse. A hardened scab on skin that's shiny and inflamed. Deep enough that it's going to leave a scar.

Micah slaps the counter. He reaches in his pocket, fingers jingling his keys. "Then maybe you'll hear me this time when I say that you can't save Jax this time. Nobody can."

Five minutes later, Paul is in the shower, his clothes in a crusty pile on the bright white bath mat. He hasn't said the first word since Micah stormed out. At first, I attributed Paul's silence to exhaustion, the thirty-six hours of searching the woods finally catching up with him.

But then I noticed his shaking hands, the muscle jumping in his jawline. I've only ever seen him that way once, when a contractor tried to swindle him out of $100,000. Paul is furious, literally quaking with outrage, and I wonder who it's aimed at—Micah or Jax or himself, for getting in between the two. From the ruckus in the kitchen, it's clear that whatever's going on with those three runs deeper than whatever I witnessed here tonight.

"You missed the Cedar Hill deadline."

The least unpleasant of all the things I have to say to him, a warm-up question disguised as a statement. I watch the smoky shadow of Paul's body through the steamed-up glass, the soapy outline of his hair, but I can't quite make out his expression.

"Yeah, Gwen left me about a thousand messages. I didn't listen to all of them, but after about three or four I got the gist." He leans his head into the spray, scrubbing with both hands. Suds scatter against the wall, fat white bubbles trickling down the foggy glass. "I'll see what I can figure out tomorrow, but…" He sighs, flips off the water. "Right now I'm too tired to care."

And clearly, too tired to shave, as well, but at least he's clean.

I pull a towel from the rack and hand it over. "Are you going to tell me what happened, or are you going to make me guess?"

"Honestly, there's not much *to* tell. Jax wasn't at his cabin—and before you ask, yes, I knew he had one, and, yes, I went inside. From what I could tell, the cops hadn't been there yet, but if they dust for prints, they'll find a million of mine. I drank some water and ate some of his food, and I rifled through his things. If anything of hers was there like Micah said, I didn't see it, but I wasn't looking for it. The only thing I cared about was refueling and finding Jax."

"It was her coat and scarf, apparently."

"Oh, then maybe? I might have seen something hanging over a chair, but I don't remember. I was only inside for long enough to catch my breath, and like I said, I was distracted." Paul drags the towel across his back, swipes it over his hair, the necklace glinting gold against his wet skin. "After that, I tracked him around Balsam Bluff for hours, until I figured out he was messing with me. Snapping branches, putting down footprints where I'd find them, then doubling back and pointing me the other way, getting me all turned around. He used to do that when we were kids, too. I can't believe I fell for it."

"He was here, Paul. Jax, I mean. He was on the back deck."

Paul's fingers pause on the terry cloth, and his gaze whips to mine. "He was? What for?"

"I don't really know. He said he'd seen you—he knew about the cut on your forehead—and he wanted me to know he didn't put it there. He told me to watch my back." Paul's face pales around the bruises and cuts. "Paul, why are you protecting him?"

"Because he didn't do it. He's not the reason Sienna ended up in the lake."

He says it without hesitation, without pausing first to think, which is how I know he's telling me the truth—or at least his version of it.

But he also said it too quickly to notice the slipup until it was already out there, slithering in the space between us. Or maybe he saw it on my face, in the way I flinched at her name. Because how would he know? The police still haven't released her name and I haven't told him.

"That's what Jax called her," Paul says. "He told me her name was Sienna, right before he punched me in the face."

It's possible he's telling the truth. But still. The words you don't say are sometimes just as meaningful, just as deafening, as the ones you do.

"Why do you think Jax will end up dead if you share his whereabouts with Micah?"

"Because Micah will tell Chief Hunt and Chief Hunt will…" Paul shakes his head, and that muscle ticks in his jaw again. "Jax just wants to be left alone, and he doesn't like feeling caged. If the cops find him, if they point their guns at his head and shout for him to hit the ground, he's going to get himself killed."

"That seems a little extreme."

"There are all sorts of extenuating circumstances here. Things you don't understand."

Another flicker sparks in my chest, more at his tone than his actual words, and I push off the wall, moving to the center of the room. Yes, I knew there were circumstances. No, I don't understand them. But only because Paul likes to shove things into a box and bury them at the back of his brain, never to be thought or spoken of again. And he doesn't have to say it like *that*, like my lack of knowledge is because I'm stupid.

"I don't understand, Paul, because you never talk about it. You've told me nothing about your friendship with Jax, about how it ended, about whatever awful thing happened to turn him into Batty Jax. And don't tell me the awful thing didn't concern you, because I can see by the look on your face whenever his name comes up that it did."

"How do I look?"

"Sad. Guilty."

He doesn't say a word, but he doesn't have to. His silence tells me I'm right. He wraps the towel around his waist, tucking in the corner so it hangs low on his hips, and leans into the mirror. "Jesus, I look like Frankenstein's monster."

I roll my eyes at the obvious attempt to change the subject. "Chet talked to Wade, and Wade said Sienna was asking about you. Not Jax. *You*."

Paul frowns at me in the glass. "Wait—who's Wade?"

"He works at the B and B."

"Sienna asked this Wade person about me? What about me?"

"I don't know. Where to find you, I guess. He didn't give many details."

Paul shakes his head. "That…that doesn't make any sense. She stopped me because of my coffee, and she didn't ask me anything that was even remotely personal. We certainly didn't introduce ourselves, not until you came along. You're the one who said the name Keller, remember."

"Okay, but that's not how Wade's telling it. If he told Chet, he's told everybody else, too, including the police. Sam was already asking where we were yesterday morning from 4:00 a.m. on."

Paul pulls his toothbrush from a drawer, squirts it with toothpaste. "What did you tell him?"

"That your alarm went off at six."

His gaze finds mine in the mirror. "You lied for me?"

His words set off an electrical storm in my chest, and the big ball of emotion I've been carrying around for two days bursts into flame. "What was I supposed to say, Paul? You left me here to deal with everything, and I didn't know where you were. I didn't know if you were alive or dead or what the hell was happening. And then somebody skinned that animal on the back deck and—"

"Wait. What?"

I nod. "An opossum on the back deck. It was disgusting. And when the snow melts tomorrow it's going to really smell. They also wrote something awful in the snow."

Paul dumps his toothbrush in the sink and turns to face me. "What did they write?"

"KILLER, in blood. Enough to have come from a cow, according to Micah. I've been living in lockdown, terrified

whoever killed that poor woman is coming back for me."
I study Paul's face, the tight skin around his mouth, the
way the color has drained from his cheeks again. "What?"

"I'm just… Jesus, Charlotte, I'm so goddamn sorry. I
didn't want any of this to touch you." He says it quietly,
purposefully, like he's been practicing the words in his
head for days.

"Any of what, Paul? That woman was asking about you.
You go on an early-morning run around the same time she
slides into the lake, and you come back covered in mud and
cuts. They pull her out from under our dock, you lie about
knowing her, and then you disappear."

"Hang on, hang on." He steps closer, his bare feet swishing against the tile. "Do you think I had something to do
with that woman's death? Do you really think I would kill
some stranger, then dump her under my own dock? Is that
what's going on here?"

I lift both hands from my sides. "You have to admit it
looks bad."

"That's not an answer."

I bite my lip and look at him, and I can see him go still. I
see him thinking. The skinned opossum rattled him, got his
bones humming before he pushed the subject away into…
what? How did this conversation get so turned around?
And why does having him home make me feel even more
alone, this terrible slippery fear rising all over again? That
Sienna washing up under the dock was only the start of
this nightmare?

He shakes his head, hurt and disappointed. "I thought
you were… I don't know. Not immune to what people were
saying, but I thought you were *different*. I thought you knew
me."

The skin of my face tightens, and the fire in my chest

moves higher, scorching the back of my throat. My body is gearing up for a good cry. Tears hang in my eyes, but I will not let them fall.

"I *do* know you," I say, my voice high and tight. "That's why I lied about what time you got up. To give you an alibi."

"You didn't have to do that."

"Yes, I did, Paul. Because think about it. If I'd said anything else, you'd be in handcuffs right now. Especially after Katherine and the evidence you left all over Jax's cabin. Micah knew where you were the whole time."

He watches me for the span of a few deep breaths, and I try to read his expression, but I can't. Not with the room going foggy with my tears, not with Paul's bruises and cuts and that one eye bulging like a rotten apple. It's like looking at Paul in a fun-house mirror, ugly and unfamiliar. I have no idea what he's thinking.

He moves to the end of the counter, picks up his cell from the charger and punches at the screen. In the bathroom's silence, I hear Micah's voice answer.

"Charlotte was mistaken about the time I got up yesterday morning. It was more like five fifteen, and I was out the door fifteen minutes later. I passed Billy Barnes's place as he was coming out his front door, probably around six or so. Tell Sam if he wants a revised statement, he can drop by tomorrow sometime."

He presses End, and the phone clatters to the counter. "I'm going to fix this."

"I know," I say, even though what I really want to say is *how?* How are you going to bring back that woman? How are you going to bring back *us*?

These past two days have tipped the emotional scales in our relationship, pitched some of the weight from him to me, and I'm not sure I like where we've landed. It feels unbalanced, precarious, wobbly. Like one of us could topple over the edge any minute, and it's not just the way Paul is swaying on his feet.

"Can we finish this tomorrow? I'm beat." He turns for the bedroom without waiting for my answer, then stops halfway there. "What time do we need to leave?" I frown, and his gaze flicks down to my belly. "Don't we have a doctor's appointment tomorrow?"

And suddenly, I realize why he hasn't slept, why he busted his ass to make it back tonight instead of stringing his hammock between two trees. So he could be here for my doctor's appointment. The one that, thanks to the eight inches of snow, has been rescheduled. The office left a message on my cell this morning.

"It's moved to next week."

He nods and turns for the bedroom, dropping the towel on the rack on his way out of the room, leaving me alone— yet again—with more questions than answers.

The first thing I think when I open my eyes is *Paul*. He's tangled in the covers beside me, his breathing deep and even. He didn't stir when I crawled in beside him, at some time just past one, which could have been thirty minutes or three hours ago. I feel around on the nightstand for my phone, check the time. 3:34 a.m. A sliver of a milky moon lights up the glass of the window.

I push back the covers and slide out of bed.

It's not the thought of Paul that woke me, actually, but two little words that pressed up from somewhere deep, creeping through my subconscious to poke me awake. *Extenuating circumstances.* Paul used those words to explain away the things I don't understand, secrets from his past he tends to keep locked up tight. In his head, on his laptop, behind the three hundred pounds of solid steel bolted to the wall in his study.

The safe was the one place that I didn't look, a place I didn't even *think* about looking. Paul's mention of it was too hasty when he left, and so insulting I'd shoved it to the back of my mind. If it weren't for his emergency chase after Jax, I'd never know the code. Whatever secrets Paul might be harboring, he'd stash them there, the only private place in this palatial home, stowed away behind a five-digit combination lock.

I slink down the stairs in my nightgown, not bothering to remember the code Paul rattled off on his way out the door. Not since he followed it up by telling me where he wrote the combination, on the inside flap of the Le Corbusier. The book Paul once told me he comes to regularly for inspiration.

"'Mass. Surface. Plan,'" Paul had quoted, flipping proudly through the pages, and I nodded like it made any sort of sense. "'The house is a machine for living in.'"

The Le Corbusier is what I look for first, running a finger down the spines on the bottom shelf until I find the right one, bloodred with golden lettering. I pull it out and flip it open on the floor.

Paul's neat handwriting is on the inside flap. "AIA Design & Honor Awards, Atlanta, GA 30319."

I leave it on the carpet and step to the far shelf, to the row of hardback novels at eye level, moving them into neat piles on the floor. Not the most clever place for a safe, maybe, but Paul always jokes that thieves would be sorely disappointed in the contents anyway—a couple thousand bucks if they're lucky, but no real valuables.

He told me in case I needed money, but I happen to know

that cash is not the only item in here. Important papers and documents—that's what I'm here for.

I tap in the zip code on the digital pad, tug on the handle, and the lock slides open with a metallic thunk.

In the dim study light, I survey the contents: a gun, a box of bullets, a neat pile of papers and files a few inches thick, stacks of crisp bills held together with green rubber bands, and a small red box, the kind that contains jewelry. I peek inside and find two matching gold bands—one hers and the other his—then shove it to the back of the safe with the cash. I pull out the paper files and carry everything over to the desk.

I flip on the desk light and start at the top, moving through the files one by one. The first is marked Personal, and its contents are exactly what you'd expect: Paul's birth certificate, Katherine's death certificate, a copy of our pre-nup and Paul's last will and testament, updated to list me as sole beneficiary this past March. I close the file and move on.

The rest of the files are filled with property deeds, grouped together according to their location. For years now, Paul has been buying up lots under PJK Real Estate Investments, LLC, clusters of individual properties that, grouped together, make up a subdivision. It's a brilliant strategy, one that with minimal investment—a paved road, a fancy sign and a big iron gate at the entrance—more than doubles the value of a lakeside lot. If you're the investor, all you need is patience and a butt-ton of money. Apparently, Paul has both.

My fingers pause on a file labeled Pitts Cove.

I flip it open and it's more of the same, property deeds for the land lining the northernmost finger of Lake Crosby. Uninhabitable land, as the cove's waters are bordered by cliffs, muddy swampland and a curvy state road. There's no flat spot for Paul to put a subdivision on, and even if there was, nobody would ever plunk down money for a house there. Pitts Cove is rumored to be haunted, thanks to the Camaro filled with human bones those recreational divers accidentally swam up on earlier this year, buried for two decades under a hundred feet of water. Skeleton Bob, the ghost shows dubbed him, and the nickname stuck. There's not a soul in a hundred miles who would ever want to live there.

And Paul owns it all, every square foot.

22

The rest of the night is filled with dark, sticky dreams. Of Skeleton Bob, doing doughnuts across the silty bottom of Pitts Cove, one bony arm dangling out the window of a rusted-out Camaro. Of Jax, flitting in and out of the waves above his head while Micah circles him like a shark. Of Paul at the water's edge, hollering for them both to quit goofing around and come on shore.

A buzzing on the nightstand pops my eyes open on a gasp, and I snatch my phone up and silence the ringer, even though I needn't have bothered. Paul's already gone. His side of the bed is cool, the goose down comforter flattened like a rumpled snowdrift. I roll onto my back, my hair fanning prettily on the pillow—silk, a gift from Diana. *For your hair, dear. So the blowouts will last longer.* The time on the screen says 8:47. The text was from Paul, an FYI he's on the way to the doctor for the cut on his brow.

I lie in the flickering morning light, processing that Paul left without waking me for part two of our conversation. I picture him slipping out of the bed silently, carefully, so as not to wake me. I see him dragging clothes up his battered body in the closet, cringing at the noise of the zippers and snaps, tiptoeing across the carpet, and I'm caught between anger and amazement.

My stomach lurches, its daily morning protest propelling me to my feet. I make it to the toilet just in time, dropping to my knees on the cold tile as the bile surges up my throat.

It's not like I haven't dragged the internet enough to know that I'm one of the lucky ones. My morning sickness is mostly confined to the morning, and once I choke down a cracker or slice of dry toast, my stomach typically settles. Mama used to brag about how she puked for nine months straight when she was pregnant with me, so sick she begged the doctors to induce her at six months—though that was also around the time people started giving her dirty looks in the bar, so her motivation wasn't entirely pure. Still, as much as she hated being pregnant, I'm pretty sure she hated being a mother even more.

I sit on my heels and flush with a shaky hand, my throat burning. If only I could flush my thoughts of my mother, too, watch them swirl like last night's steak dinner down the drain. I hate the way this pregnancy has cleared new space for her in my brain, allowed thoughts of her to bubble up more and more often.

Sunning in a banged-up folding chair in the yard, her skin slick with baby oil. Smoking cigarette after cigarette while Chet and I run wild, pelting us with the butts she'd fling into the yard. Every time I spot a cigarette stub smeared with lipstick on the ground, I think of her.

But also, memories of her French-braiding my hair,

her fingernails tickling my scalp. Of clomping around the trailer in her favorite boots, the hot thrill when she'd gloss my lips or spritz me with her perfume. *There*, she'd say when she was done. *Now you're prettier than me.* In the space between her words, I understood: pretty can get you a man. Pretty can snag you a better provider than your father.

Stop.

Maybe it's the hormones, but the memories suddenly sting more than they used to, a hot poker pang that throbs for hours. I banish the woman from my thoughts and step into the shower.

Paul's return last night conjured up more questions, especially after my middle-of-the-night peek into the safe. More than once, I considered marching into the bedroom, shaking him awake and demanding some answers. Why Pitts Cove? What happened with Jax, *really*? I try to think about it logically, to shove aside my feelings for Paul and examine everything with clinical detachment, but I can't. I'm too emotionally entangled.

In the kitchen, I stand for a moment at the window, looking out at the lake. In the few months I've lived here, it's become a morning ritual, watching the sun climb up the trees, golden flashes that light up like a sea of stars. Most of the snow is gone now, only an occasional white patch in the shaded spots—down by the dock, under the trees, a big smudge on the opposite shore.

No, not snow. A boat.

Micah and his crew, I think, except…

I lean into the glass and squint. Pointy bow, beefy hull, deadrise sharper than usual—a boat made for water sports. Even from here, even in the dim morning light, I can see there's no one at the helm or hanging over the sides.

It's Paul's boat. Unmanned and adrift—or at least it was,

until its draft got caught in the rocky shore. It's sitting all wrong in the water, pitched at a sharp angle.

"Shit."

I think back to yesterday, when I slid the boat up to Micah's dock. By the time I climbed out, Chet had already tied two lines, but since I didn't know how long the boat would be there, I made him tie up two more. The spring lines were good and tight, the slipknots solid. I checked. There's no way that boat could have gotten loose, not without someone helping it.

Shit shit shit.

I grab the keys from the mudroom hook and run down the stairs, flipping on lights as I go. "Chet? Chet, wake up." I rap a knuckle on the guest room door, open it a crack. "Somebody untied the boat and set it adrift."

His groan comes from the larger room behind me, from a lump on the far end of the couch. "Go away. It's *not* morning."

"Did you hear me? I said the boat's loose. It's caught in the rocks on the other side of the lake."

The lump moves, and he lifts his head. "For real?"

"For real. Get dressed. I need you to hike around the lake and bring it back."

"What, *now*?"

"Yes, now." I toss him a sweatshirt hanging inside out over the back of the couch. "And hurry, before it gets *really* stuck."

His grumbling is muffled as he pulls the hoodie over his face. "You do know it's not actually my boat, right? If anything, you're the one who should be traipsing through a freezing lake to bring it back, not me. I'm just the houseguest." He shoves his feet in his jeans and hauls himself off the couch. He steps into his boots with a sigh. "You owe me for this."

I hand him the keys, disarm the system and shove him out the door. "I love you. I'll make it up to you. Now go."

I head up the stairs, ticking off the incidents in my mind. The opossum. The boat. The snapped branches and planted footprints Paul told me about last night. None are exactly life-threatening, unless you happen to be an opossum. Still, it was a targeted threat, and Micah agreed. If he peeks out his back window and sees the boat, I already know what he'll say: Batty Jax, at it again.

In the kitchen, I tune the television to a local channel, dropping the last bagel in the toaster on my way to the fridge. Not much there other than yesterday's leftovers stacked in clear Tupperware containers. I'm working on a grocery list on the back of an envelope I dig from the drawer when the chief's mountain twang, thick as paste, fills the air. My fingers freeze on the pen.

"...update on the investigation up to this point. Early Wednesday morning, November 20, at sometime before 7:00 a.m., a Lake Crosby citizen discovered the body of an adult female, floating in the waters of Lake Crosby. The police were called to the scene, as was a unit of underwater crime investigators from Asheville, divers trained in both body and evidence recovery. The body was removed, then transferred to the medical examiner at Harris Regional for autopsy and processing."

Oof. No mention of Micah and the Lake Hunters by name, an intentional slight. I think about Micah watching on the big TV in his kitchen, and I can just about hear his fist punching through the wall.

"The ME has determined the official cause of death to be drowning, but also informed us that the victim had a contusion to the head that preceded her death. This contusion would have rendered her unconscious, and we're working under the assumption that it was not an accident. To be clear, folks, this is a murder investigation."

He pauses as a murmur works its way through the crowd.

"Though I appreciate the public's need for information, I am not prepared to discuss the details of this investigation at this time. The only thing I can tell you is that we've identified the victim as Sienna Anne Sterling, age twenty-nine, from Westerville, Ohio. Her family has been notified, and they ask you to please give them space and privacy during this difficult time. Thank you."

The chief gathers up his papers to a barrage of shouted questions from somewhere off camera. He tosses an annoyed look past the cameras, but he doesn't lumber off the dais. One of the voices, high and female, rises to the top like cream.

"Chief Hunt, do you have any suspects?"

The chief rolls his eyes. "Yes."

"Can you give us their names?"

"Nope. Next question." He points at the bottom left-hand corner of the screen.

"Do you have any indication as to the murder weapon, and has any other evidence been recovered?"

"Yes and yes, but that's all you're getting out of me on that subject. Anybody else?"

A jumble of voices, then another feminine tone pushing through: "Sir, it's been reported that the Lake Crosby home where Ms. Sterling's body was found is the same home where, four years ago, another woman, the homeowner at the time, drowned under mysterious circumstances. Any chance the two deaths are connected?"

The pen falls from my hand and onto the floor, rolling

under the refrigerator. Katherine's name was on the deed? I'm living in *her* home, not Paul's?

I stare at the screen, and I recognize the emotion that flashes across Chief Hunt's expression, the way it crumples his forehead and drags the corners of his mouth toward the floor. I saw it just last night after Paul returned, on the face of the chief's son.

He leans onto the podium with both forearms, the papers clutched in a fist. "Young lady, who do you work for?"

"WXPT, Channel 19, from Kingsport, Tennessee."

"Did y'all hear that? This lady here from WXPT in Kingsport is going about, making reckless suggestions on live television, planting rumors that are guaranteed to take on a life of their own. Everybody listen up, because I'm about to nip this one in the bud. We are investigating the murder of Sienna Sterling and only Sienna Sterling. The Katherine Keller case is closed. Anyone who implies anything otherwise is guilty of spreading fake news."

And with that he stalks off screen. Press conference over.

The cameraman scrambles, and the shot shimmies into a pretty blonde behind a news desk. She rattles off a quick recap of everything we've just heard, then follows it up with a longer list of all the things we don't know, things like suspect and motive and evidence. She doesn't mention Katherine's death again, but it's there, throbbing between the lines, filling up the empty pauses.

Chief Hunt was wrong about nipping things in the bud; that seed has been planted and watered now. It's already sprouting roots that are twisting around the truth, strangling it like kudzu. I peek around the wall to the front of the house, where people are milling around up at the mailbox. Reporters, staked out at the top of the drive.

I return to the kitchen, fishing the pen from under the

fridge and adding to the list. *Katherine. Sienna. Pitts Cove. Micah and Jax and Paul. Lies.* So many lies. I look at the words, and my whole body tingles with the feeling the universe is laying something out for me. Giving me important pieces to the puzzle, spreading them out on a table for me to see, but there are too many to sort through. The more pieces I get, the more I can't tell the edges from the middle. Nothing fits together, nothing makes sense.

My phone buzzes with an incoming text—Paul, telling me he's picked up his car and will be spending the day visiting build sites. I toss it onto the counter, breathing through a wave of anger. An early doctor's appointment is one thing. Following it up with more appointments means he's avoiding me.

The tightness in my chest doesn't loosen as I stare out over the lake. The sun is good and high now, the sky a cloudless dusty blue, bright against the still-shaded water. Lake to the back, wall of reporters to the front, trapping me in this place. I spot movement down the shoreline, a flash at the far end of the cove. I recognize the lazy gait, those long legs and broad shoulders. Chet, right before he disappears into the pines.

My baby brother was so easy to fall in love with, velvety pink and squirming in that grubby blanket, blinking up at me with those pretty eyes. The first time my mother shoved him in my arms, my heart squeezed and soared at the same time. I remember thinking it strange that love could come in such a tiny bundle.

When it happened again with Paul, falling in love felt as easy as slipping into a warm bath. I gave him my heart, and I saw it as a sign. *See?* I remember thinking. *You are not your mama. Your heart has room for more.* I thought loving him made me a decent person. I thought it made me better than her.

I never stopped to think about what turned her love ugly. I never wondered about all the things that could make love flip over to show its underbelly, cold and dark and dangerous. I never considered how easy it might be, or how once love slips away, if it's possible to ever get it back.

But as I stare out the window at the glittering lake, these are the things I'm thinking about now.

"Helloooo." Diana's voice echoes off the foyer walls, slicing through the weatherman's chatter on the TV. I hit Mute as the front door closes with a thud. "Anybody home?" Her heels click on the hardwoods.

I've lived here long enough to know that she does this, lets herself into her son's home, treats it like it's her own. Who knew a big house surrounded by woods could come with zero privacy because Diana could walk in any minute? I shove a smile up my cheeks as she comes around the corner, her arms holding a giant white basket wrapped in cellophane.

She sets it on the counter and moves closer, peeling off her sunglasses and inspecting my face. "You've got your color back, I see. Feeling better, are you?" She smells like gardenia and vanilla.

"Much better, thank you. Paul's not here."

I didn't mean for it to come across like that, like I know she's only here for him, but there it is.

I needn't have worried. Diana doesn't seem the least bit offended. "I know. I just got off the phone with him. Dr. Harrison says it's too late for stitches, but he cleaned up Paul's brow and gave him a shot in the butt. I told him on a handsome face like his, scars add character. Just look at

Harrison Ford, for example, or that guy who played Wa-
terman."

"Aquaman."

"Whatever." She reaches for the basket, drags it across
the island by the cellophane. "I picked you up a little something."

Whatever it is, it's not little. I take in the size of the
basket, the thick layer of tissue paper bouquets conceal-
ing whatever's underneath. A normal person shells out a
couple of extra bucks for a gift bag from Walmart, but not
Diana. Diana shops at the kind of stores where the wrapping is as extravagant as the gift.

"I… You didn't have to do that." An unpleasant tightness gathers in my chest at her thoughtfulness.

"I know, but I couldn't resist." She grins, claps her hands
three rapid-fire times, and her enthusiasm is like a saw
against my skin. "Go ahead. Open it."

I tug on the canary yellow ribbon wound around the top
of the cellophane, and the plastic opens up like a flower, the
filmy petals floating to the countertop with a soft crinkle.
I remove the tissue paper, pretty pastel bouquets arranged
in a tight layer to conceal what's underneath. A rubber gi-
raffe smothered in polka dots. A chenille bath towel with
floppy elephant ears hanging from the hood. Pacifiers and
rattles and blankets and clothes, a mountain of miniature
sweaters and footed pants and onesies as soft as butter. I
pull out a knitted hood shaped like a miniature strawberry,
tiny enough to fit on my fist, and set it on the marble with
the others.

"I know it's early still," Diana says, admiring a sweater
with a teddy bear embroidered across the front, "but I went
in that baby store just to take a little peek, and before I
knew it, I'm standing at the cash register with a mountain

of stuff. We didn't have all this when Paul was born. The cribs and the rugs and the changing tables and— Oh my God, the mobiles! So precious. I would have bought you one of those, too, but I couldn't decide. Have you thought about colors yet? Do you have a theme for the nursery?"

When Chet was born, our mother wrapped him in an old T-shirt and put him in a box on the floor. If he cried in the middle of the night, she'd shove him, box and all, into my room. Of course I don't have a theme for the nursery. I didn't know I was supposed to.

"Diana, this is all…"

"Too much?" I look up in surprise, and she laughs. "Go ahead—you can say it. It won't be the first time I've been accused of being too much. I know I have the tendency to go overboard, especially when it comes to my family."

I smile. "I guess I can't fault you for that. But it is a lot. Does a baby really need all this stuff?"

"Well, no. Of course not. A baby doesn't *need* any of this, but that's the whole point." She picks up a stuffed lamb, holding it by its fuzzy neck. One eye is shut in a saucy wink, its lashes stitched to the fabric with shiny black thread. "Grandmothers are supposed to spoil their grandchildren, especially the first one. I'm supposed to spend a ridiculous amount of money on stuff they'll grow out of within a year. That's part of the bargain."

She says it without an ounce of malice, and I tell myself it's not a dig of some kind, not a subtle swipe at my penniless, motherless existence. My mother will not be dropping by with expensive gifts. I will not have to tell her to back off. She can't be bothered to love her own children, much less a grandchild.

Diana shakes her head. "You know, I had actually given

up on the idea that Paul would ever have kids. I'd resigned myself to the fact I'd have to live the rest of my life without knowing what it was like to be a grandmother. If he'd married someone his own age, that window would be closing up about now." She pauses, looks at me. "I guess I have you to thank, don't I?"

It's the closest she's come to saying she approves of Paul's choice of wife, and it's like all those times when my mother told me I was pretty. I find myself liking Diana a little more for the compliment.

"You should know that Paul and I didn't plan this. We weren't looking to get pregnant this early on in our relationship, but I guess sometimes life has other ideas."

"You *do* want this baby, though, don't you?"

I pick up a silver teething ring tied with a tulle bow, and it really is beautiful, so beautiful I'd never even consider buying it myself. A blast of longing hits me hard, a physical tug in my chest—for this baby, for things with Paul to go back to the way they were before yet another dead woman's body washed up in the lake. For Diana to like me, even if only because of my ability to give her a baby Keller.

"Yeah. I do. I want this baby with everything inside of me, and so does Paul."

"Good, because now that I've gotten over the surprise of it all, I can't tell you how excited I am." Her gaze wanders to the items spread across the island, and she laughs. "Clearly I'm excited. Though I hope all these gifts didn't scare you off, because when all of this—" she sweeps a hand in the general direction of the lake "—dies down, I'd really love to throw you a shower. At the club, maybe, or a restaurant in town. Up to you."

I bristle a little at the *this*—murder is so darn inconvenient—but I'm not about to slap the hand extending an olive branch. I give her my brightest, happiest smile. "I'd love that, Diana. Thank you."

23

23

On the day Katherine Marie Keller drowned, the woman who four years later still haunts this town and my marriage, I had just clocked in at The Daily Bread diner in town. It was an hour before opening time, and we were gathered around a table by the window for our morning meeting, a run-through of specials and instructions that our manager Leonard always started with prayer. He'd just flipped to the appropriate page in his Bible when sirens sounded on the other side of the glass—too many of them whizzing by. Police. Ambulance. Rescue squad. Leonard made us hold hands and pray, loud and long, for whatever God's creature they were dashing off to save.

The lunch shift was in full swing when the news reached the diner. People shaking their heads and whispering, holding hands and saying prayers for the poor, lost soul. Katherine was dead before they pulled her out of the water.

I wasn't the only person in Lake Crosby who found it suspicious an experienced swimmer would drown in a lake she swam in every day. Those treks to Waterfall Cove and back were how Katherine stayed fit, her workouts so regular that the boaters knew to watch out for her. One of them, a fisherman, spotted her on her way back, a brunette in a crimson bathing suit executing the perfect butterfly. Strong. Powerful. Two hundred yards from home.

The mountain came alive with questions. How does a perfectly healthy woman drown in water she swims in every day? Did she run out of breath? Get a cramp? And why did she have fresh bruises on her right ankle?

That last one is what keeps Sam awake at night still. Four small round bruises just above her foot, plus one larger one by her heel. Fingerprints, Sam claims, though the medical examiner never went that far. The ME documented the bruises, but she didn't find much else. No alcohol or drugs in her blood, no other injuries. Nothing to give anyone reason to think Katherine's death was anything other than a tragic accident. The case was closed before it was even opened.

And Paul? Paul was on a run when she went under. I know this from the photographs in the paper, his beet-red cheeks shiny with sweat, his look of terror to come home to a driveway filled with police cars. Some reporter pointed a camera at his face at the exact moment Chief Hunt delivered the bad news. Talk about a money shot. There's no way he could have faked that kind of grief.

And yet that reporter's question won't stop playing on repeat in my head. *Any chance the two deaths are connected?* Jax's words thump bass lines in my ears: *That's two. Watch your back.*

Diana is long gone by the time the back door bangs open,

and I jump clear off my chair. My heart settles when I see Chet, drenched from the waist down, his boots dangling from two fingers. He drops them, and they land on the tile with a splat.

"Did you get the boat?"

"I got the boat. Froze my ass off in the process, but I got it. I hope you got insurance, though. The seats were slashed to shreds, and so were the ties. Sliced clean through."

I think of the opossum, rotting in the early-morning sun on the back deck, blood and guts and white bone. That awful word that's bled—literally—into the grass. That's twice now someone has crept up dangerously close to do damage with a knife, both times when Paul wasn't here.

Just like he wasn't here when Katherine drowned. Or when Sienna slid into the lake. A fluke? That explanation feels too convenient, much too easy. So what, then?

I consider calling Paul, telling him to get his ass home or else, forcing him to finish the conversation we started last night, the one he ran away from this morning. I feel like all I've done is ask, and I've gotten very little in return. Paul clammed up. He sneaked out for a reason.

When you're ready to hear the truth, you call me. Not Paul, but Sam's voice, an echo cutting through my mind, the last words he said to me before he stormed out of the wedding. Maybe I'm ready to hear what he has to say about Paul. Maybe it's time to judge for myself.

The muddy puddle under Chet's feet is spreading fast. It seeps over the tiles and over the grout lines, creeping closer and closer to the hardwoods.

I grab some kitchen towels and toss them on the puddles. "Go get dressed. We're going to town."

Thirty minutes later, Chet and I pull in to the gravel lot of Dominion Marine Salvage, otherwise known in these parts as the boat junkyard. Where boats go to get chopped into pieces and sold in repair shops and on eBay. Mostly legit, though Lake Crosby boats do tend to disappear and Donny Dominion spends his winters lounging on a beach in the Panhandle, so your guess is as good as mine. Either way, the place is dead this time of year, not to mention on a stretch of deserted road on the outskirts of town.

In other words, perfect.

"Up there," Chet says, pointing to the far end of the lot, where I spot Sam leaning on the hood of his car, scrolling through something on his phone. The day has warmed up to somewhere in the low fifties, but Sam has always run hot. He's soaking up the early-afternoon sunshine in short sleeves and no jacket, immune to the frigid breeze rustling in the trees. He hears the gravel crunching under my tires and pushes off the car.

"You're late," he says as we're climbing out. His phone rings, but he silences it and slips it in his pocket. Chet's the only one of us who gets a smile, and even then, it's half-assed. Sam's anger runs deep, and it spills over to all the McCreedys.

"Hello to you, too. You look like hell, by the way." Even from here, parked a good fifteen feet away, I can see he looks exhausted, the lines around his eyes and mouth deeper than just yesterday. His scruff is two days old, maybe three. I close my door, and the clap echoes across the water. "Have you been getting any sleep?"

"Do catnaps at my desk count?"

So no, then. Not sleeping.

I slide my hands into my back pockets, stepping right up to Sam, staring up at him. It feels strange to be standing near enough to see the amber flecks in his eyes, the scar from a long-ago biking accident that slices his brow. The last time I was this close, I planted two hands on his chest and shoved, hard enough he fell backward over a chair. He looks skinnier, too.

"What about food? And before you crack some joke, I don't mean coffee and sugar doughnuts. I'm talking about real food. Something with vitamins and protein."

I used to fuss at him like this all the time, egging him on to eat better, to dress nicer and study harder, and he used to roll his eyes and tell me he already had a mom and didn't need another. Subconsciously, at least, there must be a reason I'm doing it now, trying to shoot us back to that place when we were on better terms. A kind of apology, maybe, or because I miss his friendship. All I know is that it feels good to be doing it again.

He checks his watch. "Do you mind if we hurry this along? It's pretty much all hands on deck down at the station, and I need to be getting back. Why did you want to meet?"

"I saw Jax."

And just like that, his impatience drops to the gravel beneath us, replaced with something sharp and intense. "When? Where?"

"On my back deck." A tiny stab of guilt spears me between the ribs, but I manage to hold Sam's gaze. "And two nights ago."

"You're freaking kidding me, right?" He shakes his head, looks away in disgust. "I was at your house just yesterday. You looked into my face and you didn't say a goddamn word." He flicks his gaze to Chet. "Did you know about this?"

Chet stuffs his hands in his coat pockets, turning his back to the wind. "Dude. You know as well as I do there ain't nobody on this planet can tell Charlie what to do. Least of all me."

Sam reaches for his phone, sliding it out of his pocket. "You know that cops in five counties are looking for him, right? You know he's wanted on suspicion of murder."

"I do now."

"Jesus, Charlie. When a suspect is seen on your back deck, you tell the cops. I shouldn't have to tell you this. Did you talk to him?"

Unlike Sam, I remain calm. I recount my conversation with Jax, word for word. His not-so-subtle implication linking two bodies to Paul. The weird way he peered through the trees to Micah's. And just like Jax did, I save the best part for last.

"Watch your back? He said for you to watch your back? And you *still* didn't tell me?"

"Jax shouts poetry at the tourists and presses his face to the shop windows, puffing up his cheeks like a blowfish. I thought he was an innocent kook. I thought it was a warning, not a threat. So, you can quit with the reprimands or we're leaving." I pause, just long enough to let him suck back down whatever he was about to say. "Though while I'm here, I might as well tell you the boat got loose this morning. Chet says the seats were slashed and the ropes sliced clean through. You can't help but wonder."

I leave it at that, with *wonder*. It's as much as he's getting from me. We both know what I meant by it.

Sam shakes his head, incredulous. "You really do have a death wish, don't you?"

"Oh, stop. I'm telling you now, aren't I?" I pause, chewing on a lip. "This also seems like as good a time as any to tell you I'm pregnant."

"Congratulations." He says it with so much disgust, I

actually flinch. "You don't need that man to help you raise a baby, you know. The Charlie I used to know didn't need anybody. She could do pretty much anything on her own."

"Everything but get herself pregnant." My wisecrack lands like a belly flop, and Sam looks away. "Come on, Sam. You know this baby was made out of love."

"That may be so, but Paul is still a murder suspect. Billy Barnes didn't see him on Wednesday morning."

Billy Barnes. The man Paul claimed to have passed on his early-morning run. The alibi isn't holding up. The revelation is like getting punched; I'm breathless from the shock. My gaze pulls to Sam, his face set in hard lines as he watches it all sink in.

"Did you plant that Kingsport reporter?" I say, suddenly livid. "Did you get her to start that rumor?"

Sam doesn't seem the least bit offended at the accusation. "Here's what you don't get, what you've never gotten—that I'm not the only one with suspicions. In fact, I'd be willing to wager that most people with a functioning brain are seeing the same thing I'm seeing—a man who stood to gain more money than he could ever make in one lifetime with his rich wife gone. Sure, okay, I'll admit he got away with it the first time, but two female bodies under the same dock? That's too much of a coincidence to be a coincidence."

"You just told me you were looking at Jax for Sienna's murder."

"Okay, but ask yourself this—why is your husband running all over creation avoiding questioning? What has he got to hide?"

I look out over the lake, refusing to give Sam a reaction, even though his words strike a gong in my chest. All morning I've been thinking something similar.

"Did he tell you about the police report Katherine filed two weeks before she drowned?" My gaze whips to Sam, and he pauses, taking in my expression, which I couldn't clamp down on fast enough. "He didn't, did he? Somebody'd skinned a skunk and smeared it all over the leather interior of her car. She didn't think much of it, either, at the time. Just needed a police report to make a claim on the insurance. The stank pretty much totaled it."

That explains Paul's face when I told him about the opossum, at least. What it doesn't explain is why he failed to tell me about it. Because I saw his expression in the mirror. I know he made the connection.

Chet shuffles his feet, gravel crunching underneath the soles. "Sam's right, Charlie. Things are lining up too tight. Maybe you should... I don't know...put some space between you and Paul. Just until the dust settles."

I shake my head—not because I don't agree, but because I don't want to. These are some of the same things Sam told me a year ago, and I hadn't listened then, either—and not just because of his crappy timing. It was because of the words he used when he dragged me into that corner of the country-club kitchen, the way he'd said them with his lips curled in disgust. That Paul was a monster and a murderer. That I was an idiot and a fool. There's not a bride on the planet who would have listened to all that ugliness.

For me, it was as easy as breathing. I chose Paul that day, and Sam here still hasn't forgiven me.

He leans a hip against the freezing metal of his car. "If you're not going to listen to Chet or me, at least talk to Micah. Ask him why he told me Paul and Katherine's marriage had hit some rocks, that their relationship wasn't as smooth as Paul would like everybody to think. That toward the end there, there was a lot of fighting."

This time, I can't hold back on my frown. Micah tattled on Paul to an officer of the law. He told a cop that Paul and Katherine were fighting in the months before her death. And not just a cop—Sam, who from the very start suspected Paul. Who would like nothing more than to slap on some cuffs and cart him down to the station. Micah had to know what he'd be implying with such a statement. Why would he say such a thing?

Unless it was true. The thought whispers through my mind before I can stop it, but I can't go there. If that's the case, if Paul and Katherine's marriage was falling apart when she drowned, then how could I ever believe another word he says?

I feel myself losing it, that grip on everything I've been fighting so hard to hold together—my belief in my husband, my marriage—and so I do the only thing I can think of. I say what I brought Sam here for and, in doing so, take the heat off Paul and swivel the spotlight onto someone else.

"I hear you found Sienna's coat in Jax's cabin but that her scarf was missing."

"From Micah, I presume." When I don't deny it, Sam scowls. "He shouldn't be running around town talking up this case. He knows better. Next time you see him, tell him I said to keep his mouth shut."

I roll my eyes and describe the scarf for Sam, every detail I can remember about the color and the fringe and the fussy pattern, the way it was long enough to be looped around a neck multiple times. I can tell by the way his eyes turn to slits that it's hers. That scarf belonged to Sienna.

"How do you know all that?"

And there it is, my ideal opening. The perfect place to admit I saw it hanging from Sienna's neck that first day. To step off this hamster wheel of lies and half-truths and come clean. Let the chips fall and trust they will fall the right way.

But that's not how things work in a town like Lake Crosby, not with Sam steering suspicions. The story he would weave together from very few facts, the fabrication he so desperately wants me to believe. I refuse to give him the ammunition.

Because Sam is right about one thing. I *am* stubborn. Sometimes it takes me a long time to learn my lessons, but I always learn them.

I turn for the car, revealing the only part of the answer he needs to know. "Because when Jax showed up at my back door, her scarf was wrapped around his neck."

24

June 12, 1999
10:36 p.m.

Somehow, they ended up in a tobacco field. Jax wasn't sure how it happened, didn't really remember much other than the music blaring and Paul shouting to slow down and suddenly they were airborne, flying over the field like the Dukes of fucking Hazzard. Jax hung his head out of the window and yee-hawed, or maybe it was Micah. They landed with a thud in the dirt and plants, teeth rattling in their heads, everybody laughing but Paul.

"Are you *insane*?" Paul unhooked his belt and flung himself between the seats. "I know you have a death wish, but Micah and I don't. We'd really like to live, and we sure as hell don't want to do that in a jail cell or worse, because if we get arrested Micah's dad will kill us."

Jax looked at Micah, and the two collapsed into giggles. They were way past buzzed now, wasted on too much tequila and thin mountain air. In the back of his head, Jax knew he shouldn't be driving.

But he was also too drunk to care.

"He's right," Micah said, clutching his stomach. "My dad will murder us, and then he'll bury our bodies somewhere nobody will ever find."

They were right. Jax didn't doubt Officer Hunt's anger could boil over into revenge, or that he was capable of covering up a triple murder. Micah's dad was scary as hell.

Suddenly, Jax's door lurched open. He blinked, and there were two of Paul.

"Get out of the car."

"It's my car."

"Stop messing around and get out. You're done driving."

Jax opened his mouth to say he was nowhere near done, but somehow, Paul had already unhooked Jax's seat belt. He grabbed a fistful of Jax's T-shirt and hauled him out of the car, then shoved him through the open back door. Jax landed facedown in the leather.

Micah clutched his stomach, laughing like a hyena.

Paul dropped into the driver's seat and stabbed a finger across the console. "You shut up. I mean it, Micah. Not one word. I need to concentrate."

Jax closed his eyes and they were moving again, bouncing across the dusty field, mauling some poor farmer's tobacco crop.

25

"Here she is. I found her." Chet twists in the passenger's seat of my Honda and wags his cell phone in the air. "Sienna Anne Sterling."

For the past twenty minutes, we've been sitting here in the deserted Dominion lot, vents spewing hot air at our heads. Sam is long gone, but Chet and I haven't moved other than to scroll through our phones because I'm desperate for more information. I need to know what Sienna was doing here, why she was going around town, asking about Jax and Paul. I need a sign if I can trust my husband or not.

Chet passes me his cell phone, and there she is, the stranger I found in the lake. Those light blue eyes. That light blond hair. I'm staring at her Twitter profile.

I expand the screen and read from her bio. "'Yogi. Vegan. True crime slut. Aspiring podcaster blowing shit out of the water in Lake Crosby, NC.'" I look at Chet. "That's her. What shit?"

"I don't think she means it literally."

"Well, I know that. But she was in town to look into some old crime, and this bio makes it sound like she'd found something." I say the words and realization creeps up my body, paralyzing me to the seat. Sienna came here to ask about a past crime. I found her talking to Paul. She was asking Wade about him. And now she's dead.

The phone slips from my fingers and onto my lap. "Oh my God. Oh my God. I think I'm going to throw up."

"Then give me back my phone before you yak all over it."

He snatches it from my thigh, and I lean my forehead against the steering wheel and try to breathe around the panic. What if Sienna came here looking into Katherine's death? What if when I found them, she was asking Paul about his swimmer wife who slipped under the waves and drowned? The doubts rise, pouring up and out of me, filling the air in the car with a sweet, sickly dread.

Chet yammers away, oblivious to my distress. He scrolls through her Tweets, reading them aloud with a running commentary. An expensive yoga retreat in Florida. Restaurants she's tried. Books she's read. Nonsense about the Kardashians. I hear him, but he's miles away. Right now, it's just me and Paul in this car, a man with six million dollars' worth of motive and no real alibi.

"Hey, listen to this one," Chet says, twisting in his seat. "'Why were Lake Crosby police so quick to write #SkeletonBob off as a runaway?'"

I lift my head from the steering wheel. Blink. "What did you just say?"

"I said she wonders why the cops were telling people

that Skeleton Bob was a runaway. I don't remember anything about him running away from home."

I snatch the phone from his fingers, and there it is, her Tweet from October 28. A little over three weeks ago. Relief slackens my bones, and I think I might cry. I think my body might melt into the grubby upholstery because she didn't come here for Paul.

"She was here because of Skeleton Bob." He was the unsolved crime she came here to solve. Skeleton Bob, not Paul, not his late wife.

"Well, duh. What did you think, that she came here for Katherine?" Chet's eyes go wide with realization. "Oh. You did, didn't you?" He laughs, a breathy sound. "That would have been awkward."

"Not funny, Chet. This is serious. We need to tell Sam."

Chet shrugs. "I'm sure he already knows. Once we plugged in her last name, she wasn't all that hard to track down. A couple of clicks and he'll end up like we did, right here on her Twitter profile. As a matter of fact, he's probably already been and gone."

I click on the hashtag, #deathinthedeep, and the Tweets fall into a neat column. Dozens and dozens of them from @SiennaAnne.

June 13, 1999: drug dealer and all-around bad guy Bobby Holmes disappears without a trace. When the cops closed the case without a body, the general consensus was good riddance. Nobody cared, for twenty years. #SkeletonBob #deathinthedeep

Bobby Holmes deserves more than fifteen minutes of fame. He deserves justice. Was his death an accident or a crime? The truth depends on who you choose to believe. #SkeletonBob #deathinthedeep

New details in the Bobby Holmes case, coming soon to a podcast near you. Not as open and shut as the police would like us to believe. #SkeletonBob #deathinthedeep #thetruthiscoming

I keep scrolling, but it's more of the same. Tweets as advertising, meant to drum up interest for a podcast that didn't yet exist. Unless there are recordings somewhere—her cell phone or laptop, maybe. At the very least, there would be notes, interviews, an electronic trail.

I frown, my gaze skimming the Tweets. "But Bobby Holmes wasn't killed. He crashed his car into the water and drowned."

"Mama was convinced he was in witness protection, remember? She was like, 'Wherever that boy is, it ain't some shithole town in Montana. Bobby's smart, and he knows how to negotiate. He's probably living large on the beaches of Mexico by now.'"

Chet grins at the memory, but I don't want to go there. Our mother was always spouting off some stupid conspiracy theory, the more ridiculous, the better. For her, Bobby Holmes was a hero, a street-smart whiz kid who knew how to work the system. It didn't matter a lick that he was a criminal, as long as he never got caught—unlike her husband, whose own incarceration was such a disappointment.

"My point is, nobody's calling his death a crime, not even the police. Bobby landed in the lake by accident."

Chet tilts his head, frowning. "Still. Now that we know he was at the bottom of Pitts Cove all this time, it doesn't feel like the cops looked very hard. Wouldn't he have busted through a guardrail or left skid marks or something?"

"There are always skid marks on that curve."

"True. But when they happen at the same time that a person goes missing, seems like you'd have to try real hard not to put two and two together."

Chet's right, and he and Sienna have landed on a point all those ghost hunter shows missed: that nobody tried very hard to find Bobby Holmes. Without him blaring heavy metal music out the windows of his Camaro or squealing his tires in the church parking lots, the town settled back into its slower, quieter ways. For everybody but his sister Jamie, Bobby's disappearance wasn't so much a mystery as it was a relief. They were perfectly fine with forgetting he ever existed.

And then up came that rusted-out Camaro, dredging up another fifteen minutes of fame—this time for his bones. The assumptions people made were not kind. Bobby was wasted when he skidded out of that curve. High and drunk and too far gone to swim his way out. A victim of his own bad karma. That's the thing about people like Bobby—it's easier to write them off when you already thought of them as disposable.

Only, Sienna didn't write him off. While Bobby's death had faded to a memory for everyone else, she was digging up new details.

I point to the column of Tweets. "New details, plural. What do you think she means?"

"Let me see that thing." Chet grabs the phone from my hands and clicks to another column, scrolling through a long line of Tweets and replies. "See all the checkmarks on these profiles? That means these guys are legit. Big-time podcasters with thousands and thousands of followers, and she was in full-on Twitter conversations with them. Talking shop, picking their brains, asking for advice, stuff like that. Especially this guy Grant. They seem like good Twitter buddies."

He pulls up a thread, a lively back-and-forth that at times is downright flirty. She asks what he's working on, questions him on his equipment and how he handles hostile witnesses, about a conference coming up in the spring. She offers to buy him a drink. He suggests dinner instead. Her answer is a kissy-face emoji and two clinking glasses of champagne.

"Message him," I say. "Ask him what he knows. Maybe she told him something."

Chet scrunches his nose. "Worth a try, I guess." He opens a private message window. "What should I say?"

I reach for the phone and start typing.

Hi Grant, you don't know me, but I noticed your conversation with Sienna Sterling and thought you should know she died this past week. Murdered and found in the same lake as the Skeleton Bob she came here to research. My sister was the one who found her.

Chet reads it, then shrugs. "He might not have any clue what I'm talking about."

I hit Send, and the message reappears a split second later in a bright blue bubble. "Or he might know exactly what you're talking about."

26

On the way home, Chet takes a detour on 64, rolling to a stop at a 1970s ranch of dark brown brick.

"Are you sure this is the place?" I take it in through the windshield. Landscaped yard, a fresh coat of paint on the door, lacy curtains hanging in the windows, everything neat and tidy. Either Jamie Holmes won the lottery, or her brother, Bobby, was selling a lot more than drugs.

"This is it," Chet says with a nod. "I brought her groceries just last week."

I look over, surprised. "I didn't know you still visited Miss Jamie."

He shrugs. Like me, Chet is no stranger to soup kitchens and donation boxes, so he knows what it's like to be on the receiving end. The shame, the hopelessness, the constant butting up against stereotypes of stupidity and laziness. He may have clawed his way to the other side, but so far, he hasn't been able to make it stick. He doesn't have the money to be buying groceries for himself half the time, let alone another person—and yet he did, he *does*, for Jamie Holmes.

"You little bleeding heart, you."

He rolls his eyes, shoving open the door to a blast of cold. "Just don't go blabbing it all over town, will you? I have a reputation to protect."

The two of us pick our way across the grass to the front door, where Chet knocks hard enough to crack the wood. Jamie Holmes is a little deaf.

A little lame, too. I can hear her limping on the other side of the wood, the *whomp swish, whomp swish* as she makes her way across the room. I hike my bag higher on my shoulder and give her all the time she needs.

"Well, well, well," she says, and loud enough they can hear her in town. "If it ain't Miss High and Mighty and her baby brother, Chet. How y'all doin'?"

She softens her words with a grin, and there's a hole where a tooth used to be—the third that I can spot. I take in her rumpled clothes, her gray skin and uncombed hair, the clear tube hanging from her nose like a skinny mustache. It trails down her chin and snakes around her left side, disappearing into the oxygen tank she drags with her everywhere. Jamie is only fifty, but thanks to the bum knee and faulty heart valve, she looks twice her age.

"Hi, Miss Jamie," I say. "You're looking good."

She laughs, a painful hacking sound. "Liar. Now get your skinny tails in here before you let in all the cold."

I wait for her to step back, which takes a minute. Jamie's tank is in the way, the wheels snagged in the shaggy carpet. Chet leans around her to turn the thing around, a sleek piece of metal and plastic on caster wheels. Once she and her tank are pointed in the right direction, I follow her in and shut the door.

Jamie limps into her living room, a cramped space on the front side of the house crammed full of durable, mismatched furniture. A gilded coffee table next to a modern wing chair, an LED floor lamp, a leather couch buried under discarded clothes and junk, newspapers and food cartons and crumpled lottery scratch-offs. I shove everything aside and sink onto a corner. Chet perches on the armrest.

"Can I get y'all some tea or lemonade or something?" She parks her tank next to a plaid La-Z-Boy.

"We're fine, thanks. How are you feeling?"

"Oh, like crap." She collapses into the chair and gives a hard yank on the handle. The footrest pops up like magic, revealing ankles swollen to twice their normal size, meaty white skin cinched by the elastic of her sweats. "I'm panting like a dog in heat, and I haven't felt my toes in a decade. How do you think I feel?"

I'd ask what the doctors say, but Jamie doesn't see a doctor. She doesn't take medication, either, at least not regularly. Whatever money she has is not spent on medical care, and she probably shouldn't be driving. If she can't feel her toes, she sure as hell can't feel the brake pedal.

And yet...my gaze lands on her oxygen tank, the latest, lightest model. Maybe Medicaid, but what about the yard and paint job outside? What about all this furniture? I glance around the room, taking it in, clocking the electronics—an iPad, a laptop, a sixty-inch flat screen on the wall, and that's only the pieces I can see. Miss Jamie hasn't worked in years. There's no way she can afford all this.

Miss Jamie waves a hand through the air. "Are y'all gonna tell me what brought the two of you all the way over here, or are you gonna make me guess? Though I've been watching the news. I know it was you who fished that poor lady from under the dock, wasn't it?"

"It was. And we're here because there's a rumor going around Lake Crosby that she was here because of Bobby."

I say it slowly, gently, because I was standing on the shore the day they dredged Bobby from the depths of Pitts Cove. I saw the way she dropped to the dirt and worked herself into a coughing fit so violent that even the paramedics looked spooked. My gaze lands on an old picture of him, hanging from a nail rammed into the wall. The crooked teeth, close-set eyes, greasy dirt-blond hair I remember hanging out the window of a bright yellow Camaro. As tragic as his death was, his sister was the first thing I thought of when I saw his name on Sienna's Twitter feed, what dredging him up all over again is going to do to Miss Jamie.

She shifts in her recliner, agitated. "God, the people in this town. You'd think gossip was an Olympic sport. Twenty years and they're still making up tales about poor Bobby."

"Actually, the rumors are coming from her," Chet says. "The lady Charlie found under the dock. Sienna Sterling was her name."

I lean forward on the couch. "She didn't happen to stop by here, did she?"

Miss Jamie shakes her head, her gaze bouncing between us. "I don't get many visitors these days, no. What would she want to talk to me for?"

"On Twitter, she was calling Bobby's death a crime."

"Well, of course it was a crime. It was a crime the cops took five whole days to file a missing persons report, and even then they didn't spend more than ten minutes looking for him. They came back two days later with the nonsense that he ran off. Case closed. But I know my Bobby.

He wouldn't have just up and left. Not without telling me. Not without something real scary chasing him out of town." She reaches down and twists a knob at the top of the tank, and air hisses through the tubes. "Or somebody."

"Why do you think they waited so long?"

Jamie is quiet for a minute, all but a high-pitched wheezing coming from her lungs. "I know you know Bobby's business."

I nod. That's one part all the gossips got right. Drugs. Bobby dealt all kinds of drugs.

"And I know you know where we lived at the time."

Another nod. In a pimped-out trailer on the ugly side of the lake, smack in the middle of what's now the parking lot for a frozen yogurt shop. That's how I know Miss Jamie, because she moved into Bobby's trailer shortly after he disappeared. Chet and I lived four doors down.

"Then you know why the cops didn't much care when he disappeared. What's one less piece of trailer-park trash to them? Especially one who wasn't exactly operating on the right side of the law. Those ghost shows always make him out to be an idiot, but that ain't right. My Bobby had brains. He had street smarts." She taps a finger to her temple. "A genius IQ. Whatever charges the cops flung at him never stuck."

"What about the rumor Bobby was chased out of town by another drug dealer? That had to have come from somewhere."

"Yeah, from mean ole Chief Hunt, though he was Officer Hunt at the time. That man always had it out for Bobby. Whooping his siren at him in town. Doing drive-bys during peak business hours. Showing up here, hauling him out of bed just to rattle his cage. Chief's the one who planted that story in people's ears, you know, so he didn't have to explain why he wasn't actually doing anything to find Bobby.

For a while there, I suspected Chief of doing it himself. I thought he was the one who made Bobby disappear."

I can see why. Chief Hunt climbed the law enforcement ladder because of two things: the status that came with his wife's wealth, and the strong-armed way he went about cleaning up Lake Crosby's streets. He closed up all the meth labs, tossed the drug lords in jail. He patrolled the streets, pulled over anybody who even looked like they were thinking about a drink. People joke about having to drive all the way to Sapphire for some decent weed, but it's the truth— and all thanks to Chief Hunt's iron fist.

"Sienna suggested there were some new details in the case," I say.

Jamie frowns. "What kind of new details?"

"That she didn't say. But apparently she was planning to reveal them in a podcast. Have you heard anything about it from the police?"

"What, you think Chief Hunt's coming over here to fill me in? That jackass don't tell me jack. When those divers found Bobby, I learned it from the news. The *news*, Charlie. Chief didn't even have the decency to come over here and tell me himself. It's like he's forgotten I even exist."

Talk of Bobby has worked her up something good, turned her wheezing into something that pulses worry in my chest. I look around for a landline in case we need to call for an ambulance, wondering if the cell tucked in the pocket of my bag will do me any good on this side of the mountain, where service is spotty at best. I glance at Chet, and he looks worried, too.

I scoot to the edge of the couch. "Things are about to get ugly, Miss Jamie. I don't know how much of it will be true and how much of it is gossip, but I remember what it did to you last time around. You stay strong, and call me anytime you need to talk, or if somebody shows up here looking to take advantage. I'll send Chet here over to chase 'em off."

He nods. "Gladly. And I'll bring you some of that seven-layer dip you like so much, too."

She pitches back in her recliner, tilting herself almost horizontal, looking up at us over her heaving belly. "You two turned out a whole lot nicer than your mama did. Anybody ever tell y'all that?"

"Only once or twice." Chet grins, pausing to pat her ankle. "You take care of yourself, Miss Jamie. I'll see you next week."

I'm at the door when my curiosity gets the better of me. "Miss Jamie, who does your landscaping?"

"Huh?" Her head lolls my way, her eyes at half-mast. She waves a hand through the air, but it's sloppy. She's losing steam fast. "Oh, hell if I know. They come through here with their blowers and their weed whackers, and then they're gone. Never ask me for a penny."

I smile. "Do you have a sugar daddy on the sly?"

Another phlegmy laugh. "Not hardly." She pats the tank next to her like a favorite pet, her fingers resting on the knob. "I keep waiting for Amazon to figure out they've got the wrong address and take everything back, but they never do."

"Sounds like you found yourself a guardian angel."

She closes her eyes and sighs. "If you see him, tell him what I could really use is a new heart."

As we file out the door, my hand goes instinctively to my stomach, and I'm struck with the thought of how fragile we all are, how vulnerable and temporary. How one moment we can think we have it all, a home and a family and good health, and the next—*poof*—it's all gone.

27

Chet and I return home to a kitchen full of people—Paul and Diana and Micah and Chief Hunt, standing in a cluster by the island—and an air thick with sudden silence. The kind that comes after wrangling words and heated voices. The kind they stopped hurling around the second we walked through the door.

Paul turns, watching me with that beat-up brow and blackened eye, an angry kaleidoscope of black and purple and red. His expression sucks up all the air in the kitchen.

"What is it? What's going on?"

I dump my bag and keys onto the counter and look around for clues, but there's nothing but marble on the countertop between us, and in a house where visits revolve around topped-up glasses and trays overflowing with finger foods. But whatever this occasion is, Diana is dressed for it. Full makeup, silky top, leather motorcycle jacket over dark jeans, her hair slicked back into a high ponytail. She looks like a Charlie's Angel, cougar edition.

"I'm here to talk to Chet," Chief Hunt says, and a memory flickers. Of a younger version of him busting in our door, tackling my father to the ground, hog-tying his hands and feet. I was only six at the time—too young to remember the details, but that doesn't mean my bones don't still shake at the image of their bodies hitting the floor, that I don't hear my father's grunts or taste the fear and shame climbing up my throat. Memories are strange that way. They don't have to be real to feel visceral.

But my fear of Chief Hunt, the way the sight of him sends my heart flapping around like a caged bird against my ribs—that is 100 percent real.

Chet parks his boots at the edge of the room. "Did Annalee send you? Because I told her I'd pay her back."

"This isn't about Annalee, Chet. This is about Sienna Sterling."

"Okaaaay." His gaze flicks around the room. When it lands on mine, I recognize alarm and something else that makes my skin prickle. I recognize fear, the same kind I'm feeling. "What about her?"

"A witness is on record saying she saw you coming out of Ms. Sterling's room in the B and B at some time just before eight on Tuesday morning. One day before Ms. Sterling was killed."

Chet doesn't move. He just stands there, stock-still and wide-eyed, for a good five seconds. My breath turns solid and I stare at him—*say no say no say no*. Chet doesn't shake his head, but he doesn't nod, either.

"Maybe."

"Maybe, what?" Chief Hunt scowls, stepping closer,

looming in the kitchen. "Was that you coming out of her room Tuesday morning or not?"

"It was more like seven thirty, but yeah. It was me."

"Chet!" I say, too loud and far too flustered because I want to strangle him. I think of the conversation we had downstairs on the couch, the way he swore they didn't sleep together. Hiding his shenanigans from me is one thing; hiding them from the police is another thing entirely. He *had* to know this would come out at some point.

"Interesting. Especially since you told one of my deputies the last time you talked to Ms. Sterling was at the bar the night before. Monday night."

Chet winces. "That's 'cause once we got upstairs, we didn't do much talking."

"So you lied."

"I didn't lie. Not technically." Chet looks at me for backup, giving his head a nervous shake. "I told Sam we didn't talk, and we didn't. We did…other stuff. But after I left her room, I didn't see or speak to her, like, at *all* that day. I didn't even know she was the one y'all fished out of the lake until Sam showed me her picture."

"Did you have any contact by phone or text? And I'd suggest thinking real hard before you answer because we already have her phone records."

Chet's shoulders slump, and he sighs. "She gave me her number at the bar that night. That's how I knew to come up. She texted me her room number. There's not a single guy on the planet who would've said no."

Chief Hunt sticks out a meaty hand. "Show me the string."

"That's private."

Chief Hunt rolls his eyes. "There are a million ways I can go about getting those texts, son, and every single one of them only makes you look more guilty, not less. You might as well just show me. Unless you have something to hide."

After a second or two, Chet digs around in his pocket for his phone. "Fine, but I just wanna state for the record that I didn't show anybody these pictures she sent, and the plans we made to meet up on Tuesday night never happened. She went silent, and I ended up crashing on Jed Allen's couch. Annalee had kicked me out." Chet unlocks his cell and pulls up the string.

I watch Chief Hunt's expression as he scrolls through the texts, the way his lips purse and one brow crawls up his forehead at photos with what looks like a hell of a lot more than a simple flash of skin. My mind is racing, but I can't think straight, can't think of any way to stop this runaway train. All I know is that I need the questioning to end and everybody to leave. Chet slept with Sienna Sterling the day before she died. Jesus Christ.

Chief looks up from the phone. "Where were you on Wednesday morning from, say, 2:00 a.m. on?"

"Like I said, asleep on Jed Allen's couch."

"Was Mr. Allen there at the time?"

"Yeah. And so was his girlfriend."

"Can either of them confirm it?"

"I mean…everybody was asleep, but I guess."

"I'm going to need a list of your whereabouts from the time you left the B and B until noon on Wednesday, along with a list of names and numbers of people who can back you up on it. Bring it by the station by closing time today. Oh, and if you delete this string from your phone, I'll throw your ass in jail for evidence tampering."

He doesn't wait for Chet to respond, or for Micah or anyone else to say goodbye. The chief hands the phone back to Chet and stomps out the door, leaving behind him a silence so complete I hear the engine crank on the front driveway. I stare at Chet. Chet stares at the floor. Diana stares at us from across the island, that stupid perfect corkscrew ponytail draped down one shoulder, and I hate that she's here. I hate that she's a witness to all this.

I smack Chet with both hands on the chest. "Chet, what the hell? You said you didn't sleep with her."

"That's because you're my sister. I'm not telling you that kind of stuff. Gross."

"This is serious!"

"You think I don't know that?" He groans, scrubbing his face with both hands. "I messed up, okay? When Sam showed me her picture on his phone, I completely freaked. I swear I didn't know she was dead, and I'd never hurt her. You know me. I wouldn't."

I fold my arms over my chest. "What else? Because I can't fix it unless you tell me now. What else are you not saying?"

"Nothing, I swear. We were gonna meet up but she got busy. The last time we texted was Tuesday afternoon. She said she had something to do that night but would text me when she was done. She never did. Here." He shoves his phone at my chest. "Take a look if you don't believe me."

I clutch his phone in my hand but I don't look at the thing. I'm too busy breathing through the fury, the panic.

Paul steps up next to me, a supportive presence, but his words are aimed at Micah. "Can you talk to your dad? We need to know what we're dealing with here, what, if anything, the police are holding back. She told Chet she had plans on Tuesday night. Can you find out if the police know what they were?"

Micah laughs, a harsh sound without humor. "You know as well as I do that man tells me nothing. I have zero control over what happens next. He's just following leads, is all, and Chet did sleep with her."

I wince.

Paul turns to Chet. "I take it you can make that list?"

Chet gives him a shaky nod. "Yeah, but seriously, man. We were all asleep. Is sleeping even an alibi?"

"Yes," Micah says. "Especially if there was some kind of security system holding you inside, or if you can find a neighbor to confirm your car was there all night. Your phone's another piece of the puzzle, assuming it was on you that whole time. They'll use it to verify if you were where you say you were, so be as specific as possible. Retrace your steps, and make sure to write down everybody you saw or spoke to that day. Every name you can think of, even if you didn't have an actual conversation with them. The more people saw you around town, the better."

Chet thanks him, then scurries off to Paul's study. Suddenly, I'm thinking about the Hostess cupcakes stashed in a shoebox at the back of my closet upstairs. Chocolate and sugar and preservatives. I want them so bad I contemplate marching up there. I want them so bad my teeth ache.

I whirl to face Micah, then Paul. "Chet didn't do this. You know he didn't."

Diana sinks onto a counter stool. "Well, then he shouldn't have lied. It doesn't look good, you know. No wonder Chief Hunt is so angry."

"That's very helpful, Diana." I stuff as much condescension as I can in my tone—a page from her playbook. Paul's palm presses onto my back, but I shake him off. "Thank you for pointing it out."

"Let's all just calm down for a second," Micah says. "Let's think this through. As far as I know, the manhunt for Jax is still full steam ahead. There's an APB out in three states and volunteer agents from Macon, Haywood, Transylvania and Swain counties beefing up the search. Even if Chet's DNA was found inside Sienna, and I'm not saying that it was, consensual sex is not a crime. And if he's telling the truth about seeing her last on Tuesday morning, that means he wasn't the last person to see her alive. There were multiple sightings of both her and Jax in town all that day and into the evening."

Micah's words do the trick. I blow out a sigh, and my shoulders relax a good inch.

And then I think of something else. I saw Jax in town on Tuesday, too, when he stepped out of the shadows of the terrace. I am a witness.

Tell Paul I need to talk to him.

I whirl around to Paul. "Jax was looking for you. He wanted to talk to you. Why?"

Paul frowns. "I don't… What are you talking about? When was he looking for me?"

"On Tuesday when I came to pick you up, Jax was waiting outside your office. He said, 'Tell Paul I need to talk to him.' The next thing I know, Sienna turns up dead and you run off to find him, and he shows up here wearing her scarf. Now it's looking like all those things are somehow connected, and I want to know how."

The blood drains from Paul's face. "What exactly are you asking me?"

"I just want to understand, Paul. What is happening?"

Micah pushes to a stand, moving around the island, coming closer. "Back up a second. Jax was here?"

I nod. "Wednesday night. In Sienna's scarf and Paul's boots."

Micah cuts his gaze to Paul, shaking his head in disgust. "Why am I not surprised? What other handouts have you been sliding his way? Wait, wait—let me guess. Food, for sure. Money, too, probably."

Paul doesn't deny either. He casts a pointed look at Diana, a silent communication like the ones we sometimes share, our married couple's telepathy. Only this is a message I can't quite read. I study her expression, trying to identify the emotion smothering her face. Worry looks like fear looks like disapproval. Or maybe all three.

But of course Paul has been taking care of Jax all this time. Why else would Jax be waiting for Paul on that terrace? Why else would Jax show up here?

The answer churns in my stomach, sending up a wave of nausea that makes my mouth water. I stare out the window and try not to throw up while the conversation moves on to the progress Micah and his team have been making—very little. Not a stitch of evidence, no sign of anything that would have been on her when she slid into the water. Her cell phone, maybe, or her jewelry.

"A pair of gold hoops, a pearl bracelet, a watch and her grandma's diamond-and-ruby ring," Micah says, "all of which are pretty much impossible to find in a lake the size of Lake Crosby. Don't go spreading that around town, by the way. Dad's trying to keep the list of jewelry quiet."

"You can't honestly think you're going to find her jewelry in the lake," Diana says, filling a glass at the sink. "The killer would have to be a real idiot to put it in the same place he dumped her body."

Micah's phone beeps, a muffled sound from deep inside a denim pocket. He fishes it out and checks the screen. "Looks like the guys have picked up something. Keep the doors locked and the alarm on, and don't even think of stepping outside without backup. If Jax is desperate enough, we all know where he'll end up."

Micah disappears out the back door, and a tingling starts on the top of my head. It spreads down my scalp, ringing in my ears with the one word he didn't say.

Here. Jax will end up here.

28

Buddy's BBQ is little more than an ancient, rusted-out trailer shoved to the back of a clearing, but like most every night, the place is hopping. Packed with throngs of diners standing in clumps around the counter, spilling down its rickety deck. Cars are parked every which way on a stretch of trampled-down dirt, a field that's more weeds than grass and scattered with picnic tables. On the opposite end, a giant smoker burps smoke into the nighttime sky.

Paul leans into the windshield. "Are you sure about this place? It looks kind of...unhygienic."

They're the first words he's said since leaving the house, not that I've said much, either. I'm still worried about Chet, still pissed at Paul for sneaking out this morning and staying away all day, still confused about whatever had Jax and Paul looking for each other around the time a woman was murdered.

STRANGER IN THE LAKE 239

And I can't shake that feeling, that cold and oily wave that went through me when I thought Sienna was here because of Katherine, because of Paul. I can't just scrub those suspicions away. They hold power now, simply by the act of thinking them. Even if I don't believe them anymore, what does it say about me that I did? What does it say about my marriage?

I kill the engine, drop the keys in my bag. "Don't worry about the germs. By the time the food makes it to your plate, they've all been fried or smoked off."

"Somehow that doesn't make me feel better."

We step onto the deck, and the gazes sweep over me and Paul with a disapproving thud. This is a Wrangler jeans and baseball-cap kind of crowd, and Paul's brand of designer casual might as well be a three-piece suit. I scan the row of faces pointed our way, and I recognize every single one. Nobody smiles. Nobody says hi.

"Tough crowd," Paul mutters.

I point to an empty picnic table under a pine tree. "Go save that spot. I'll get the food."

I step to the window and Buddy doesn't smile, but then again, Buddy never smiles. He lifts a chin in greeting, wiping a hand down his grubby apron. "What do you want?"

"Two heavyweights all the way with strings. Two Cokes."

Buddy huffs an approving grunt. He doesn't have a menu, and only a regular customer would know the lingo for their most popular sandwich, chopped brisket topped with everything but the kitchen sink. The strings are code for french fries. He turns and hollers the order into the trailer, then leans his head out of the window far enough to see Paul, sitting woodenly on the hard bench. He waves when he sees us looking.

Buddy ducks back inside. "Who's that?"

"That's Paul. My husband."

"What happened to his face?"

"Jax happened. Paul went searching for him in Balsam Bluff, and Jax didn't want to be found."

Buddy grunts, I think in approval. "Balsam Bluff is the last place Jax'll be. He's too wily for that."

And thus the reason for me bringing Paul here. Buddy hears everything. He knows things, and assuming you're the right person and you don't ask for his BBQ recipe, he's typically generous with his information.

"What's the word on the street? About the tourist, I mean."

Buddy's eyes go squinty, and he stares me down. He knows I haven't been around much since marrying Paul, and he knows this reception I'm getting from his regulars is why. I feel their gazes on me now, hear their murmurs and whispers behind my back, even though none of them will look me in the eye. It's a proper mountain snub; I'll give them that. But I'm hoping Buddy here is a different story.

He looks past me, shakes his head. "That Chet thing. That's just a distraction."

Something loosens in my chest, and I blow out a sigh. "A distraction from what?"

"Unclear. But I don't trust that Chief Hunt. Too many tales of him planting evidence, strong-arming false confessions. That's why this thing with Jax, it just feels too convenient."

"You think Chief Hunt is dirty?"

Buddy frowns. "I didn't say that. But ask anybody here. They'll tell you that man don't play fair." He slaps a palm to the countertop. "Food'll be up shortly."

He ducks back inside and that's it. Conversation over.

I wait for the food, contemplating Buddy's words. I knew Chief Hunt was mean and power-hungry, that his policies were biased against the working class, that the sight of him kicked my heart into gear.

But dirty?

Buddy reappears, shoving two cans and the baskets of food at my chest, and I suddenly can't think of anything other than how starving I am, the smell of smoked meat and fried potatoes waking up a new, animalistic hunger. I haven't eaten much since finding out I was pregnant, and then Sienna washed up and killed whatever was left of my appetite. Now my stomach is so empty it's howling.

Paul and I inhale our food, washing everything down with icy soda that chills me to the bone. The sun dipped behind the trees hours ago, and the temperature soon followed, nose-diving to somewhere in the midforties. One last weekend of sunshine before the rain moves in. I pull my coat tight around my body and shiver.

"I need to ask you something, and I need for you to tell me the truth." Paul glances around, but our picnic table might as well be an island. Nobody wants to sit close enough to us to overhear. Still, he leans in, lowering his voice. "Are you afraid of me?"

No. The answer sounds in my mind, immediate and clear, but the word sticks to my tongue because I'm not entirely sure it's the truth. When Paul lied, when he left on this crazy errand to Balsam Bluff, I wanted so desperately to believe in him that I made excuses for his behavior. But now, with the information I have today, I see the flaws in my thinking. This is a man who looked into a police officer's eyes and lied, and convincingly. Who's to say he isn't doing the same with me?

So am I afraid of him? Maybe.

Paul nods. Looks away. "That's fair. If I were sitting where you're sitting, I'd be scared of me, too." His gaze wanders back to mine. "But I swear to you, Charlotte, on my life and the life of our unborn child, I didn't touch Sienna."

"Why did Jax want to talk to you?"

"He needed some cash, a few supplies. I swear to you, it wasn't anything more than that." I roll my eyes, and he reaches across the empty baskets and wrappers for my hand. "You have no reason to believe me. I get that. But it's the honest to God truth."

I stare at him, and he stares back, his gaze strong and steady. Is he lying? Telling the truth? I don't know what to believe.

"Listen, first thing tomorrow I want you to go to Sam. I want you to tell him you saw me talking to Sienna. Say you didn't make the connection until tonight, when I told you it was the same woman."

"You want me to turn you in?"

He nods.

"Why the sudden change?"

"Because I've been thinking about it, and this was my blunder. I won't have you paying for following my lead, for saying something you knew was untrue in an attempt to protect me. You said it yourself. All it would take is one person who happened to be rolling by in their car, or some nosy neighbor who spotted us through an upstairs window, and we're caught—both of us. This way, you beat them to the punch."

"What about you? Sam will arrest you on the spot. I don't know what the punishment is for lying to a cop, but—"

"Five years." Paul's shrug is going for nonchalant, but it doesn't quite get there. "I probably wouldn't get that long, but this is a capital felony case, so they'd have to give me some jail time."

My stomach churns, and the back of my neck goes cold. Five years. That feels like an awful long time. "How do you know?"

"I talked to an attorney."

This surprises me, though I suppose it shouldn't. Paul, with his methodical thinking and color-coded to-do lists. Of course he's talked to an attorney.

He squeezes my hand. "At least think about it."

"I am thinking about it, and I don't like it one little bit." I snatch back my hand, drop it onto my lap. "Five years. Why did we lie?"

"I already told you. I panicked."

"Yes, but why? Why are you running around like it's your job to save Jax? What am I missing here?"

He clicks the top of a ketchup bottle up and down a few times, then scrubs his face with both hands. "Jesus, this is all such a clusterfuck."

"I'm not an idiot, Paul. I know there's more you're not telling me, a lot more. You promised me answers."

"I never said you were an idiot."

"No, but you're doing a damn good job of making me feel like one. Every time I turn around, I'm learning some big new secret."

"I don't keep secrets from you. It's just…stuff I haven't gotten around to telling you yet. Like the fact I love green asparagus but can't stand the white kind, or that when I was nine, I fell out of a tree and got fifteen stitches in the back of my head. It doesn't mean I'm keeping it from you."

"What about the skunk somebody smeared all over Katherine's car?"

He picks up an empty can, shakes it, then drops it back to the table. "What about it?"

"Oh my God. Really? I saw your face when I told you about the opossum. You didn't say a word. I had to hear about the skunk from Sam."

Paul frowns. "Okay, but did he also tell you they caught the guy? Some asshole who confused Katherine's car for his cheating wife's. The opossum was meant to scare you, yeah, but the message was intended for me. Micah told me what they wrote in the snow."

A headache starts up at the base of my brain, a low-slung throbbing of confusion. Paul always has an answer for everything, which means he's either telling the truth or is exceptionally good at lying. I study his face, the light illuminating him in shadowy patches. The spiderweb of fine lines around his eyes, the deeper ones on either side of his mouth, the way the thinning scab is pulling on his brow. He looks at me, his eyes flecked with gold, and God help me, I want so desperately to believe him.

But I don't.

"What about Jax? Why have you been helping him all this time?"

"I already told you. I owe him my life. I owe him everything."

I've heard the story multiple times. Jax dragged Paul out of the lake by his ankles when they were kids. It's why Paul won't stick a toe in the lake, because he almost drowned, and Jax saved him. "Because he pulled you out of the lake? I know it scared the crap out of you, but—"

"That's not the time I'm referring to. I'm talking about another time. After Katherine."

He pauses, and I brace for whatever new bombshell he's going to drop on me now. All this time I've been waiting for him to bring her up, and now here we are, and I'm not sure I want to hear it. This is the scary part.

"Jax was there for me in a way no one else was. Not even Micah. You know how people were looking at me back then. God, like they're looking at me now, at this dump of a restaurant. Like I'm pretty sure you're looking at me, too."

I shake my head, hard, then stop myself. The denial happened automatically, like an old instinct, that instant before I realized that he was right. I have been looking at him like that. "I know you loved Katherine. I know that. But you never talk about her, and then I saw the files on your laptop. The pictures and the other stuff. The finances. Her infertility. And then I hear that all this time, I've been living in her house—"

"The ownership was just a technicality. Our accountant suggested we put the house in her name, but I designed it. I laid the first brick. It's just as much mine as it was hers."

"And yet I'm just hearing about this now."

"What do you want me to say, that I loved her? I did. I loved her. I've loved her since we were juniors in college. That's why it is so infuriating that people would think I had something to do with what happened. Yes, I got a lot of money after she was gone, but I'd pay ten times that to have her back."

Even Paul looks shocked at the words that just tumbled out of his mouth. His back slumps and his face goes apologetic. He smothers my hand in his. "I didn't mean it like that. I just meant I didn't want her to die. I certainly didn't cause it."

It's true I don't know everything about this man, but I know when he feels something deeply. Paul loved Katherine. If she were still here, I wouldn't be. It's as simple as that. And honestly, haven't I known this all along?

The food turns solid in my stomach. "Micah said you were fighting before she died."

Paul jerks in surprise. "He told you that?"

"No, he told Sam." I don't have to add that's even worse.

Paul goes still, hurt and anger coloring his cheeks along with something else—confusion? He shakes his head, but he won't quite look me in the eyes. "I mean, sure, we argued now and then, but nothing… Why would Micah say that, and to Sam, of all people? Micah had to have known what he would think."

"And Pitts Cove?"

"You mean the deeds?" Paul pauses to receive my nod. "I own dozens of lots on multiple coves. It's no secret that Pitts is one of them. Gwen knows it. The people down at the Register of Deeds know it. Those are public transactions subject to public knowledge, available for anyone who asks. It's an investment, not some nefarious scheme to… I don't know…bury some old bones."

"State Road 32 is the one Bobby Holmes used to drive into the cove."

"I know that. But Walsh Capital was petitioning the county to reroute 32 away from the lake. Walsh is basically the Walmart of developers. Fast. Flashy. Cheap. In and out like a plague of locusts. They wanted to scoot the road back and plop down a time-share. The kind with prefab condo buildings and a miniature golf course. Paddle boats shaped like swans and sunset lake cruises. Do you know what that would do to a place like Lake Crosby?"

It would turn this town into a tacky resort destination and attract the wrong kind of tourists—the kind looking for cheap lodgings and fast food. The shops in town wouldn't have customers plunking down hundreds of dollars for Chanel sunglasses, and the restaurants and country clubs and golf courses would sit empty. Everyone, from the business owners to the people scrubbing their floors and toilets, would suffer.

"Seems the town council wouldn't allow such a thing. You didn't have to buy up all the land."

"I didn't say rerouting 32 was a bad idea. Done right, it would create a big, flat, lakefront parcel accessible by a brand-new four-lane road. In someone else's hands, someone committed to maintaining the look and feel of Lake Crosby and its surroundings, it could be a gold mine."

"In other words, you."

He lifts both hands from the table. Paul has always been a shrewd businessman.

"But how come this is the first I've heard about it? If I hadn't looked in the safe, I wouldn't know about Pitts Cove or any of the other properties."

"None of this is a secret. There are copies of the deeds all over the office, in the file cabinets and on the server. I just don't talk about them much because they're long-term investments. I can't do anything until I own all the land, and that takes time."

He looks me in the eye as he says it, and his words come without the slightest hesitation, not even the tiniest pause to think. So far, all his answers have come this way, and they all make a weird sort of sense. I want to believe it, but I can taste the lie buried underneath his words, the way this explanation is meant to deceive.

"You own all the land on Pitts Cove," I remind him. "Every single inch."

He nods. "True, but I can't really do much with it just yet. The timing's not exactly ideal."

"Because Pitts Cove is haunted?"

He laughs, the first genuine one I've heard from him in days. "Come on. You don't really believe that, do you?"

"No, but plenty of other people do. There's not a soul around who doesn't know what happened there, who's been sitting on the lake bottom for the past twenty years. Nobody wants to live there."

He shrugs. "So I'll sit on the deeds a little longer."

Before Paul, I thought being rich meant a full refrigerator. I thought it meant an insulated roof over my head and the ATM spitting out cash every time I tapped in my pin code. I never dreamed it meant sitting on a million-dollar investment until a collective memory fades. Who knows how long that will take? Maybe decades, maybe never. But Paul doesn't seem the least bit worried.

And he's so good at this, at explaining away all this baggage he's kept locked away for years. It's part of what attracted me to him—not the baggage, but his battle scars. The way we'd both emerged from our respective tragedies, damaged but still breathing.

Now, though, the answers seem too easy. The deeds, Katherine's finances, his complicated history with Jax. I'm still missing an essential piece of the puzzle, and he's still intentionally leaving it out. If Sam were here, he'd say it's because my husband is a killer.

I think back to our roadside chat earlier today, those ugly words he said about the man I married. That Paul doesn't have an alibi for Wednesday morning. That he and Katherine had been fighting before she died. That last one he'd heard from Micah—Paul's lifelong best friend, the best man at our wedding—and he wasn't the only one of Paul's friends issuing a warning. *Watch your back*, Jax said to me, and I didn't want to listen to him, either.

I look at Paul—the man I love, the father of my unborn

child, the man I stood before in a church and made such beautiful promises—and I can't separate the truth from the fiction. What is real? I have no idea.

"Are you cold?"

I shake my head. "No."

"But you're shivering."

I sit on my hands, but it doesn't stop them from shaking.

"Come on. Let's get you home before you freeze."

Paul gathers up the trash, stacking everything in a neat pile, tossing it into the barrel a few feet away. When he returns, he reaches out a hand, and I let him pull me off the bench. Tessie Williams, a former friend who filled her belly with shrimp cocktail and champagne at our wedding, snickers with her boyfriend as we pass.

We stop at the car, and I'm digging out my keys when he wraps a hand around my wrist. "Are we good?" No smile this time, but the message is clear. *Do you believe me? Do you still love me like you used to?*

Before this week, I wouldn't have had to think about my answer, not even for a second. From the first time Paul and I met at my gas station counter, my feelings for him haven't wavered. Not when my friends stopped waving when I walked down the streets of town. Not when every restaurant like this one fell silent, even though it's filled with folks who talk plenty behind my back. Not once have I ever doubted my love for Paul, or that marrying him was the right thing.

But now… He steps up to me, so close I can feel his breath on my skin, his warm body pumping blood next to mine, my own cells responding. He looks like the man I've loved for fourteen months now, the one I fell for the instant he smiled across the counter, the one who can make me shiver just by touching me, but tonight the shiver is from fear. Fear I've made the wrong choice. Fear that by ignoring the rumors and pushing away all my doubts, I'm just as self-serving as my mother.

Fear of Paul, of what he's done.

I look at him, and my heart revs with a heavy, cloying dread. "Yes, Paul. Everything's perfectly fine."

I've gotten so goddamn good at lying.

29

June 13, 1999
1:27 a.m.

Jax opened his eyes, and the first thing he noticed was the quiet. No blaring music, no engine vibrating under his seat, no Paul and Micah arguing up in the front. Just crickets and the cool mountain air, blowing through the open windows. He shivered and sat up.

"Hey, Paul," he shouted. "Micah."

No answer. His friends were gone. Jax was alone.

The door handle was like water in his fingers. He couldn't get a solid grip. After three tries he somehow managed, shoving open the door and sliding out onto the dirt. He caught his balance, then turned in a slow circle, trying to get his bearings—hard to do when the world was spinning.

He rubbed his eyes, searched for movement in the dark shadows. It was like looking through a dark, wispy fog.

A trailer park. He was standing in the middle of a dark and grubby trailer park, one he didn't recognize. Then again, why would he? He wasn't friends with anyone who lived in one, didn't run with that kind of crowd. The trailer-park kids weren't exactly college-bound.

He took in the square and stubby shapes, dozens and dozens of them lined up like boxy shadows, all dark but one, pushed up against the woods at the far end. That one was lit up like a fairground ride. Colorful Christmas lights, strung across the roof and around every window. A lava-red glow coming from underneath the cinder-block risers. Jax leaned forward on his toes and squinted. Was that a hot tub?

"Hey, Paul. Micah." He slurred their names into the nighttime sky, his voice bouncing around the hills. "Get your sorry asses out here!"

A sleepy voice shouted from the darkness behind him. "Shut the hell up!"

What time was it?

He stuck his head through the driver's window, but the car was dark. The engine was off, the dash black. He reached for the keys and swiped air. Excellent. Now what? He couldn't walk home. He had no idea which way to go or how far. And it wasn't like he could call a taxi in this sorry mountain town.

So Jax did the only thing his tequila-saturated brain could think of. He laid on the horn. One by one, lights popped on all around him, the dark shapes coming to life. Somewhere to his right, a baby started crying. He leaned on the horn again, a long series of beeps that echoed through the hills.

Somewhere around the fifth or sixth time, a door swung open and a woman tumbled out, shooting across the dirt in a tank top and red bikini underwear. Her bare legs were scary skinny and her hair wild, like she'd been sleeping in a wind tunnel. She marched right up to him and smacked him on the chest.

"Goddamn it all to hell, you woke up the baby. Do you know how hard that kid is to get to sleep, and now your caterwaulin' woke him up. Are you going to come in there and put him back down? Because I sure as hell ain't. What the hell is wrong with you?"

Where to start? With his dead mom? With his missing friends? With this woman's shouting that was only making her kid cry harder?

"I'm so wasted." He meant it as something like an apology, but this woman just rolled her eyes.

"I got a nose. I could smell you from ten miles away."

Behind her, a girl appeared in the doorway. She was six, maybe seven, and cradling the wailing baby to her chest. She had that same crazy hair as the lady in front of him, those same skinny legs sticking out from a tattered nightgown. "Mama, I think he's hungry."

The woman ignored her daughter, sizing him up instead. "Tequila?"

"Jose Cuervo." His tongue stumbled around the words, mushing them up and sticking the syllables together: "Hosaycuervo."

"Where?"

"Where what?"

"Where's the tequila? It's the least you can do for waking the baby."

It was then Jax felt a pang. Something wasn't right with

this woman. Her pupils were the size of dimes, the skin on her arms all scabbed up. Track marks or scratches or both. He looked beyond her to the girl, standing on the pile of cinder blocks that served as steps. The baby cried and cried.

"Mama, he needs a bottle but there ain't one."

"Shut up, Charlie. Get your butt back inside."

What killed Jax the most was that the little girl didn't look surprised. She didn't look sad or disappointed. She just looked…accustomed. This jittery-ass woman angling for Jax's booze was her mother. This was their life. The girl just stood there, clutching her wailing baby brother against her chest, blinking at him with those Bambi eyes, willing her crack-whore mother to come inside and feed her baby brother. Jesus, somebody call child services or something.

By now the woman was digging through his car, throwing doors open and rooting around on the floorboards, her skinny ass in the air while her baby howled. She emerged with the bottle of tequila—now empty. She grimaced and flung it to the dirt.

"You got more, right?"

Was this a dream? Was this woman really begging him for booze while her kids went hungry?

He stared at the lady and her kids on the cinder-block steps, and he wondered which was worse: losing the mother who glued your family together or growing up with a mother like this one. The answer came to him instantly, along with a sour wave of tequila that landed on the dirt by his feet.

These kids. These poor, miserable kids had it so much worse than Jax ever could.

And this was how Jax knew he couldn't be saved, why a hundred baptisms by Pamela's crazy pastor into the waters of Lake Crosby couldn't save his black and evil soul—

because looking at that scraggly girl and her wailing baby brother made him want nothing more than that second bottle of tequila.

30

The good thing about living in a house of glass in the woods is that you know when someone's coming. You hear the whir of a motor as they steer around a curve in the drive, murmured voices carried on the wind, the way the birds and chipmunks go still and quiet. It gives you just enough time to pat down your hair and slap on a smile before they step up to a door or a window.

The bad thing is there's no hiding from the two strangers, peering through the glass.

A man and woman, both in their late fifties or early sixties, their faces far too grim and somber for a sunny Saturday afternoon. They could be anyone, and yet my gut knows exactly who they are.

I freeze at the edge of the foyer, taking in the woman's white-blond hair, her birdlike build, her full lips and pale skin behind dark sunglasses. She clutches flowers to her chest, a spray of big white buds that falls over an arm.

Funeral flowers.

I open the door, and she nudges her husband with an elbow.

"My name is John Sterling, and this is my wife, Sharon. We're looking for the owner of this house. I understand his name is Mr. Keller?"

He has an accomplished air about him—a doctor, an accountant, the owner of a chain of shoe stores—but with clenched fists and a sharp, angry edge. Grief in the form of fury, and I don't blame him. If I were in his shoes, standing on the doorstep where my daughter washed up dead, I'd be pissed off, too.

"His name is Paul. He's my husband. I'm sorry but he's not here." Neither is Chet, and I wish he was because I am not emotionally prepared for this. I'm not sure I'm equipped to comfort grieving parents on my own. "I am so sorry for your loss."

The last sentence is the one I should have led with, I realize too late.

"Thank you," Mr. Sterling manages with a jerky nod. His face is grim and rock hard. "Were you...were you here when it happened?"

I nod, trying not to wince at the memory of her pale skin, that one glass-blue eye staring into the sky. "I'm the one who found her. I called the police."

Mrs. Sterling gasps, whipping off her glasses and staring across the pavement like I'm her daughter's savior. Like I am the one who rescued her from the lake, except that I didn't. By the time I got to her, she was already dead.

I stare into eyes the color of a weak sky, just like her daughter's.

It's to her that I make the offer. "Would you like to come inside?"

* * *

The Sterlings step across the threshold and pull up short, planting their shoes at the edge of the foyer rug and staring with obvious shock. Not at the house, at the size of the place or the way it looks ripped from a design magazine, but at the lake, glittering on the other side of the plate glass.

Mrs. Sterling sees it and bursts out crying. She clutches the flowers to her chest and just lets loose, a continuous sobbing that racks her body so hard I worry she might pass out. Her husband stands next to her, both hands shoved in his pants pockets, glaring out the window in grim silence.

I give them space, shimmying my cell from my back pocket, and text Chet.

OMG the Sterlings are here. Where are you?

Three little dots dance around at the bottom of my screen, and then:

Still in town. Want me to come home?

My gaze creeps to the Sterlings, lit up golden by the setting sun, and I wonder what Chief Hunt has told them. I wonder if they've already been to the B and B, if they've talked to Piper. If they've heard what their daughter was doing on her last days in Lake Crosby...or more specifically, who. My thumbs fly over the keyboard.

Actually, prob better if you stay away. Wait there until I give the all clear.

"Chief Hunt said she was under the dock." Mr. Sterling turns away from the glass, and for a split second, his expression matches his tone, glittering with accusation. As if I was the one to drag his daughter up from her watery grave like some kind of lake monster. He squints, watching me from across the room. "Is that true?"

His wife gives him a pleading glance over her shoulder. "Hush, John. I can't do this right now."

I slip the phone in my pocket and reach for the teapot, settling it on a tray with some cups and saucers.

"When, then? When would you like to do it? That lake out there was our daughter's final resting place. It's the reason we're here." His face is purple and his voice a cold, hard slap. I don't blame him for being furious, but his anger seems more than a little misplaced. His wife didn't do anything. She's suffering, too. And clearly, she's in need of some comforting.

He aims his animosity at me. "I need to know where she was *exactly*."

Mrs. Sterling shakes her head, clapping her free hand over her ear. "I don't... I can't hear this right now."

"I need to know, Sharon."

"John, *please*."

Chet and I are used to heated arguments. We're used to slamming doors and loud voices and cuss words shouted over our heads. We've learned the best way to not get beaned with a plate is to stand still and keep quiet, and fade into the background.

But there's no background here. Not in a house that's basically one giant room, not with two grieving parents looking to me for answers.

"You should know that they handled your daughter with the utmost care. Especially the lead diver, Micah. He's our neighbor, and a dear friend." I don't mention he's Chief Hunt's son, as that would only muddle things that have no business being muddled. I think of how he refused to bring her to shore any other way than by doing it himself, by plowing through the ice-cold water, even though he knew his father would refuse to give him any credit. "He could not have been more gentle."

Mrs. Sterling is crying again, dabbing at her eyes with a sleeve. I eye the drooping roses in her other hand, the buds fainting over the crook of her arm. "Here. Let me put those in water." I gather up the flowers, and she doesn't protest.

"Does this Micah person know how Sienna got in there?" Mr. Sterling says, following me into the kitchen. "Do the police have a suspect?"

I lean the flowers in a pitcher I pull from the shelf and settle in the sink, then fill it with a couple of inches of water. "That's a question for Chief Hunt, I'm afraid. I'm not up on the latest with the investigation. I only know what I saw on TV."

Another lie, of course—the latest in a long string of them. But it doesn't seem like a good idea to be spouting off his questioning of Chet or any of what Micah told me about Sienna's jewelry, or that I saw her scarf hanging from Jax's neck. Better to let the police decide which information they want to share.

"They won't tell us anything," Mr. Sterling fumes. "What kind of operation doesn't tell the parents what they're doing to find their daughter's killer? This is ridiculous. It's *bullshit*."

It *is* bullshit, and I'm pretty sure his question was rhetorical.

I fill the teapot with hot water, drop in a bag of Lipton and carry everything over to the couches. "Please, let's sit down."

I point Mrs. Sterling to a couch, but the problem with

a house that's built around lake views is that there's not a seat in the house without one. She sinks onto the cushion facing the kitchen, giving her a clear shot of Micah's dock farther up the cove, but at least from where she's sitting, she can't see ours.

I sit at the opposite end, busy myself with the arranging of cups on the coffee table.

Mr. Sterling has too much nervous energy to sit. He paces along the edge of the carpet. "I *told* her to let it go. I told her this podcasting business was dangerous. If somebody got away with murder all those years ago, you better believe they'll murder again."

"I saw her Twitter feed, all the stuff about Bobby—Skeleton Bob. Why did she think he was murdered?"

"Because of the necklace."

"John." Mrs. Sterling flashes a glance in my direction. "We're not supposed to talk about the necklace."

I sink onto a chair and shuffle through my memories of the weeks after Bobby and his Camaro emerged from the depths, dripping in mud and gunk. After two recreational divers swam up on Bobby's car, Micah and his boys brought it to the surface and turned the accidental discovery into a walking advertisement for his company. It was on every front page and television screen in the Southeast, and made Lake Hunters into a household name. Thanks to Bobby Holmes, Micah became a local celebrity.

But I've heard all the stories. I've read all the articles. None of them mentioned a necklace, and Sienna wasn't wearing one. I tick off the jewelry Micah told us he's combing the bottom of the lake for—hoop earrings, a pearl bracelet and watch, a ring. He didn't mention a necklace. I'm certain of it.

"That necklace got our daughter killed. It's the reason

Sienna is dead." He is pacing now, in long strides perpendicular to the couches, back and forth across the carpet. "I will shout about that thing in the town square if I have to. I won't shut up until they find who did this to our daughter."

His wife frowns. "We don't know she's dead because of the necklace."

He stops abruptly. "Don't be ridiculous. That necklace is a clue. Sienna always said that necklace was going to make her famous, and it did, didn't it? Our daughter is famous, but it's because she's dead. Because she was *murdered*."

"I don't understand," I say. "What necklace, and how did she connect it to Skeleton Bob? Because there are thousands of people on the lake every summer. It could have come off a skier's neck last decade, or somebody could have flung it out of a car ten minutes ago."

"Because of Jeremy—he's the diver who found the car. He took the necklace from the car and hung it around his neck. He wore it like some kind of trophy. But Sienna saw the engraving on the back, and she traced it to here, to the lake. That's when he told her what really happened."

I sit very still, a freezing cold finger climbing my spine. How many necklaces are there in the world? Billions, probably. But a necklace she could trace to Lake Crosby? What are the odds?

"What did the necklace look like?"

My voice sounds all wrong. Too high, quivering in my skull like an airplane going down because surely, surely they're not talking about the same necklace.

"A dog tag with the town's coordinates," Mrs. Sterling says, and her words leach to the lining of my stomach. "You know. The intersection of longitude and latitude smack in the center of the lake. It was gold."

Not just gold. Solid, weighty twenty-four-karat gold. Only the best for Diana's boys.

Fresh tears are brimming in Mrs. Sterling's eyes, and she buries her face in her hands. "I just can't believe this is happening. We made it through childhood without her choking on a marble. She didn't get shot up at school or die in some fiery crash when she got her license. Every time we reached this big milestone in her life, I thought, whew, we made it through another phase alive." She looks up, her cheeks slick with tears. "And now *this*. How did this happen? Mrs. Keller, do you have children?"

I shake my head, try not to throw up. "No."

"Well, be glad. Being a parent is a constant worry. It never goes away, *ever*. Not even when they're grown and gone. It's the burden of being a mother."

I don't even know what to say to that. My mother didn't worry, not even a little bit, but I have bigger problems. *Tell Paul I need to talk to him*, Jax said, right before a girl with his necklace turned up dead, and Paul took off into the woods. Only a guilty man would do that. A man with something to hide.

"Where's this necklace now?"

"That's the problem," Mr. Sterling says. "Nobody can tell us. Not the police. Not the people in the B and B."

Mrs. Sterling nods, her summer-blue eyes boring into mine. "It's gone. The necklace has vanished."

31

I don't wait until the Sterlings are done with their impromptu memorial. As soon as they've carted the flowers out the back door, the second they've rounded the corner for the stairs that will lead them down to the dock, I'm reaching for my cell. Chet's number rings and rings, then pushes me to voice mail.

"Chet, call me. Sienna came to town with a necklace that connects Bobby to Jax. Did she say anything to you about it, or was she maybe wearing one? Either way, it's MIA. Call me the second you hear this."

I hang up and stare out the window, at the lake and hills and light that's fading fast.

Being responsible for a man's death would drive a person batty. It would drive me batty. Chet, too, probably. Maybe Jax ran Bobby off the road. Maybe Jax saw it happen and jumped in to save him, losing his necklace in the process.

Or maybe it was worse than that—maybe he was sitting next to Bobby in the Camaro when they crashed. Maybe he was driving.

The thought wipes me clear inside, a bright white light that's blank and blinding. For a second or two, I think I might pass out from the enormity of it. It would explain so much. Why Jax kept quiet about it for all these years. Why he traded his golden-boy status for a reputation as the town loon. Why he crumbled under the weight of all that guilt.

And now the necklace links Jax to Bobby Holmes to Sienna, a shiny, definitive token someone was willing to kill to make disappear.

And what about Paul? How much did he know? I stare out the window and will my mind to come up with a safe explanation, with an answer that makes some sort of sense. My brain bubbles with half-formed thoughts, but the same one keeps rising to the surface: Paul doesn't have an alibi for the morning Sienna went into the lake.

Would he do that? Silence an innocent stranger in order to keep Jax's secret safe? Would he weigh loyalty to an old friend over another life? I think these things until my bones are ready to jump out of my skin. The Paul I know would never do any of these things, but if the past few days have proved nothing else, it's that I only know the Paul he's wanted me to see.

The Sterlings are down by the shoreline now, standing at the far edge of the dock. Mrs. Sterling tosses the roses in one by one, while her husband watches from three feet away. The wind picks up her hair, whirls the petals from the flowers. There's a storm brewing, the clouds low and heavy over the mountain and in my heart, and I don't know what to believe.

My phone beeps with a text from Paul.

Home in 15, see you soon <3

I grab my keys and race to the car.

The rain starts as I'm rounding the bend to Knob Hill, fat splatters on the windshield, knocking against the roof, sliding in rivulets down the glass. I flip the handle for the wipers and they squeak and whine, leaving greasy streaks on the windshield. It makes it hard to see past the next curve, to judge if the car coming at me is Paul's or another SUV. If he was where he said he went, to the Curtis Cottage on the southern end of the lake, he'll be taking a whole different road home than the one I'm on now.

A silver Toyota whizzes past, and I blow out a sigh of relief. The road before me is empty, and it feels darker than before. I reach down and flip on my headlights.

I dig my phone from the cup holder and call Sam on his cell.

"Kincaid." It comes out gruff, the word hurried, and for an irrational second I wonder if he knew it was me when he picked up, if he still has my name in his phone.

"Sam, it's me. Charlie. Is it true Sienna had Jax's necklace?"

A pause. "I take it you've talked to the Sterlings."

"Is it?"

Sam sighs. "That's the rumor going around, but I'm still working to confirm. Nobody's laid eyes on the necklace but the Sterlings and presumably the killer, and until we locate Jax, we can't prove he no longer has his. I've got a call out to a detective in Ohio. They've gone to question the diver."

"Paul owns all of Pitts Cove, Sam. He has for years."

"I know."

"Do you think he knew about Jax's necklace in Bobby's

car? And not just because you hate the guy. I'm talking about real, concrete evidence."

"Why, because trying to conceal what was at the bottom of Pitts Cove isn't evidence enough?" A string of thunderous claps shakes the Civic down to the tires, and Sam pauses long enough to let it pass. "But okay, here's what I know. I know Jax showing up on your back deck is a regular occurrence, once about every six or seven days. I know that his visits usually last somewhere between twenty to thirty minutes, and that by the time Jax leaves he's showered and fed and wearing clean clothes. I know Paul never lets Jax leave without giving him a prepay card, which he pays for on the company AmEx. I know these visits are friendly and usually end in a hug."

I stare out the slice of road lit up by my headlights, the way it goes blurry between swipes of the windshield wipers. "How do you know all that?"

"The cameras on the back of the house. You mailed me the log-ins, remember? They only go back sixty days, but there were enough of them for me to see all that. The prepay cards I heard about from a couple of cashiers in town. Apparently, Paul buys 'em in bulk."

Sam gives me a moment for the message to sink in. Paul has been in touch with Jax all these years. He's brought him food and clothes and a cell phone. He's looked after him. I think of Jax stepping onto the back deck in Paul's boots, the acres and acres of land he bought up around Pitts Cove, that time he made me ring him up for an expensive prepay card I assumed he wouldn't use—and he didn't. He tucked it in a pair of his old boots and gave them both to Jax.

It's not some nefarious scheme to bury old bones, Paul said when I asked him about Pitts Cove, and I wasn't sure I believed him.

Staying silent about a crime is a crime. If Paul knew Jax was somehow responsible for Bobby's death, then he's spent the past twenty years helping a man stay quiet about another man's death, which in my book can't be explained away. Jax should have reported it the second he popped to the surface, and Paul should have the second Jax ran blubbering to him.

"Where are you?" Sam says into my ear, and I almost drop the phone. I'd forgotten he was there, waiting on the other end of the line.

"Heading to town to find Chet."

"Okay, well, be careful, and maybe lie low for a day or two, will you? Something's not right here, and I'm still puzzling out what it is. My gut tells me everything's connected, and that includes Katherine's death. I'll call you as soon as I've got a handle on the situation."

We hang up, and I'm dropping the phone into the cup holder when something darts into the road. A brown blur, flying across the windshield. I stomp the brakes and give a jerk to the wheel, and the tires Chet's been hollering at me to replace for months now lose traction on the wet asphalt. The car slides sideways, hurtling me toward an incline that will drop me ten feet, maybe more, into a creek. I overcorrect, hands slapping at the wheel, then overcorrect the other way, but it's too much for the old Civic. The car lurches into a spin, flinging me around like a fairground ride. After five or six turns, my back fender connects with something solid, and a loud, metallic *chunk* slams me back into my seat, snapping my head sideways. My skull slams into tempered glass, and everything goes deathly silent.

No, not silent. There's the steady patter of rain, the wind in the tops of the trees, another rumble of thunder. And heavy breathing—mine.

I sit very still for a moment, taking stock. My head hurts, and my chest where the seat belt tried to cut me in half. I press a hand to my lower belly, but there's nothing. No pain, no cramping. Other than the whack to the head, I think I'm fine.

My car, however, not so much. I twist around, looking out the smashed back window on the passenger's side. I've landed flush against a tree, a pine at the edge of the road. The impact folded a deep dent in the Civic and stuck a branch through the glass, letting in the sharp tang of sap and green wood and rain. I twist the keys, but nothing happens. The engine's dead.

I look around for my phone, which in the second or third spin flew from the cup holder. I search the passenger's seat and console, stick my hand between the seats. I'm feeling around by my feet when, suddenly, the windshield lights up. Headlights gleaming in the gushing water.

Not Paul. Please don't let it be Paul.

I freeze, peeking over the dash.

A flash of relief at the sight of Micah's truck, followed by trepidation. Micah is one of Paul's best friends. How much does he know? He rolls to a stop by my front fender, throws open the door and slides out, hitting the dirt at a jog. I eye him through the cracked windshield with suspicion.

He yanks open my door. "Are you okay? Jesus. Can you move?" Already the rain has soaked his hair, his clothes, splashing from him onto me.

"I'm fine, but I can't find my phone." Even I hear how ridiculous it sounds, to be whining about my phone when my car is crumpled against a tree, but it's not the phone I'm worried about. It's Chet. I need to talk to Chet. I need him to be a sounding board, to help me sort everything out. He's the only one I can trust.

"Come on. You need to go to the hospital. I'll take you." Micah wraps a hand around my bicep to help me out, but I shake him off, a violent, physical no.

"I need my phone." I unhook my seat belt and hurl myself over the console, reaching with both hands onto the floorboards. "I need to call Chet. He's waiting for me in town."

He slides his cell from a pocket, flips on the flashlight. "Here. Get out. I'll find it for you."

I stand in the pouring rain while Micah fishes around under the seats, finally locating the thing wedged between the back door and a box of tile samples I was supposed to return days ago. He hands it to me, and I check the screen. Other than a text from Paul—Home. Where are you?— there are no messages. No missed calls.

I dial Chet again, get his voice mail, *again.* I hang up and look around, eyes drilling into the rain and dark woods, trying to decide what to do. I could get Micah to take me to town, but there are a million places Chet could be by the time I get there, including back at the house. What if he's there already, his phone charging on his nightstand downstairs while he's busy in the kitchen? How do I call the house without talking to Paul?

And then something else occurs to me. "Did Paul send you to find me?"

"No. I was coming from town, headed home when I spotted you." Water drips down his glasses, soaks his collar, splashes off his sleeve when he hitches a thumb over his shoulder. "Can we talk about this in the car?"

"What's going on here, Micah? And tell me the truth, because I'll know if you're lying. I'm starting to piece things together."

He squints at me behind his glasses. "What kind of things?"

"Nope, it doesn't work that way. You tell me and I'll know if I can trust you."

"I understand that, but we're in the middle of a police investigation. What I can tell you is that Jax has been a source of contention between me and Paul since the second he walked into the woods. Longer than that, actually. Paul was the reason Jax and I were friends. He was the glue."

"Is Jax the reason Bobby was at the bottom of Pitts Cove?"

Micah nods. "There's a piece of evidence putting him in the car, yeah. They're still sorting out the rest."

"That's why Paul never talks about Jax, isn't it? Why he bought up all of Pitts Cove. Paul knew what was down there, didn't he?"

Micah watches me for a long time, the water dripping in streams off his chin. He sighs, his breath cutting a shaft in the foggy rain. "It sure as hell looks that way."

His answer hits me square in the stomach because it makes a sick sort of sense. Paul knew. He knew, and then he *left* Bobby down there. For twenty years.

I look to the shoulder, a thin line of mud and puddles that ends in scraggly brush, searching for a good place to vomit. "I can't go home, Micah. The Sterlings were just there. They told me about the necklace, which I'm guessing you've been looking for, haven't you?"

He nods. "I couldn't mention it. You understand that, right?"

"But...didn't Bobby Holmes go missing around the same time Jax wandered into the woods? How is it possible nobody made the connection?"

"You didn't."

"I was a kid." Six going on sixteen, thanks to my jailbird father and a mother who left me alone with a newborn baby for long stretches of time. Too busy caring for Chet to care why the trailer at the end of the park suddenly went dark and quiet. Of course I didn't make the connection. But the police should have.

Micah lifts his hands, lets them fall back to his sides with a splat. "Selling drugs is a dangerous business. When Bobby disappeared, people assumed he skipped town or ended up at the wrong end of a drug deal gone bad. I heard a million scenarios, and not one of them involved Jax or the bottom of Pitts Cove. It wasn't something people assumed because there was no reason to assume it."

"And Katherine?" I say her name, and my voice wavers. "Is it true she and Paul were fighting before her death?"

Micah winces. "Everybody argues, even the perfect couple. And for what it's worth, I regretted saying those words the second they came out of my mouth. Sam latched on to it like a bulldog, but he couldn't prove anything. That's got to count for something, right? Now can we please get out of the rain?"

I nod, and he grabs my arm and leads me to his truck. I'm numb, shaking from the cold and wet and shock. I let him pack me into the passenger's seat of his truck, then sit there in the stuffy air while he jogs around the front to his side, his big body lighting up in the headlights like a firefly. The cab is thick with the smell of roasted chicken coming from the grocery bags by my feet, heavy brown paper with the gourmet market's logo. It clings to my lungs and coats the windows in a milky fog, turning the woods and road hazy.

Or maybe that's just my tears.

The cell phone buzzes in my hand. Paul, probably wondering where I am. I hit Ignore, and my cell goes dim, then black.

Micah climbs in, cleaning his glasses with a bandanna he pulls from the seat pocket. "Look, maybe you should… I don't know…call him back and talk this out."

"What's there to talk about? Paul lied to me about Pitts Cove. He fed me some bullshit story about Walsh Capital and a plan he hatched with the mayor, but I'm no idiot. Swampland is not an investment."

"No," Micah murmurs. "It's not." He slides his glasses up his nose and cranks the engine. The radio kicks on, a country music station, as does the heat. He fiddles with the controls, flips on the defogger.

"And why is Paul always out for a run when women get sucked into the lake? What is up with that? It's so awfully damn convenient, don't you think? Especially since Billy Barnes doesn't remember seeing him on Wednesday morning. Paul doesn't have an alibi for the morning yet another woman washes up under his dock. Even Jax said as much. He said, 'That's two.' He told me to watch my back, and I thought it was just Jax being batty."

"Look, it might be nothing."

"If you believed that, you would have just said it was nothing."

Micah doesn't respond, and his silence is answer enough. I turn to the window, feeling sick.

"What am I going to do? I don't have anywhere to go. I don't have a job. Knocked up with a baby I didn't plan and don't have the money to care for, not on my own." I rake my fingers into the soaked hair at my temples, squeezing with the heels of my hands. "I am married to a criminal. I am having a criminal's baby. Oh, God, I really *am* my mother."

My cell lights up on my lap with another call from Paul.

I hit Ignore, then pull up his contact card and tap Block. I don't ever want to talk to him again.

Except I have to, don't I, because of our baby. A baby attaches me to Paul until the end of time. It tangles us up in a bond so much more complicated than marriage. My throat goes thick, burning with coming tears.

Micah sits silent, watching me across the dim space, and his expression makes my stomach hurt. He doesn't think the baby is good news, either.

"Maybe I should take you to Dr. Harrison, let him check you out just in case."

"No, I'm fine. Really. I just need Chet."

Micah's phone buzzes in the cup holder. I know who it is long before he shows me the screen. Paul's face jiggles in the air between us. "What do you want me to tell him?"

"Nothing. You haven't seen me."

"At least let me tell him you're okay. If he gets wind of your car wrapped around that tree, he's going to have a fit."

"Not a word, Micah. I'm serious."

Micah stares at me, and the phone rings and rings. He swipes to pick up right before it flips to voice mail. "Hey, Paul. What's up?"

My husband's voice comes through the phone in fits and starts, too faint to pick out anything other than speed. Paul is in a hurry, the words rushing out of him.

"No, sorry. I haven't talked to her all day. Is her car there?"

A long pause. Micah gives me a reassuring smile.

"Well, I wouldn't worry too much. She probably just ran into town or something. I'm sure she'll show up soon. Hey, listen, I'm kinda in the middle of something here. Can I call you back in a little bit?" Another pause. "I know, but try to chill out, will you? I'm sure everything's fine. I'll call you back as soon as I can."

He hangs up, tosses his cell on the console. "So what now?"

"I don't know. Take me to town, I guess? That's where Chet went earlier."

"Let's stop at my place first." With a quick glance over his shoulder, Micah puts the truck in gear, pulls onto the road and points the nose toward home. "You need to get out of those wet clothes, and so do I. After that, we'll figure out a game plan."

32

Of all of Paul's projects, Micah's house has always been my favorite. Some old great-aunt's dusty log cabin, transformed into a sleek, modern masterpiece, all wood and glass and steel. Paul scaled the place for Micah's six-foot-two frame, the rooms and the fittings and the furniture all oversized, gargantuan tables and deep-seated couches made for large bodies and long limbs. I want to climb onto that big couch of his and sleep for a week.

He parks in the garage, then flips on the lights as we come into the kitchen, dumping his keys and bags onto the counter. He tosses me a couple of towels from a top drawer. "I'd offer you some whiskey to warm you up, but after what you just told me in the car, you're going to have to settle for hot tea."

I drop one under my feet and use the other to sop up the worst of the rain from my hair, biting down on my molars to stop my teeth from chattering. "Tea would be perfect. Thanks."

He fills an electric kettle at the sink, flips on the switch. "Bags are in the cabinet above the microwave. Make yourself at home. I'll go see what clothes I can scrounge up."

He disappears upstairs, and I select a box of green tea, then wander into the living room with the dish towel, bypassing the matching leather couches for a spot at the back window. Like Paul's, Micah's house is perched high on a hill, flush with the treetops for spectacular views of the water. Tonight there's nothing but blackness where the lake should be, but that's not the direction I'm looking. I'm looking through the trees, staring at the house I've called home for the past year.

It's lit up like a bonfire, golden light pouring from every downstairs window, the kitchen and the living area and Paul's study. Paul must be home, looking for me. Even the sides of the house I can't see are glowing, the wet trees and grass glittering with reflected light. I stare through the branches, trying to pick up movement behind the glass, but I can't tell if the motion is coming from inside the house or from the wind shaking the trees.

The ceiling squeaks above my head, bare feet moving across an uncarpeted portion of the floor. The low hum of his voice, worming its way through the wooden planks. It probably wasn't fair to Micah, asking him to lie to a friend, but I didn't know what else to do. I just pray he's not up there talking to Paul.

I slide my phone from my pocket and text Chet. I'm at Micah's. If you talk to Paul, do NOT tell him where I am. And freaking call me asap. I need you.

I turn at Micah's footsteps on the stairs, a thick stack of clothing balanced on an arm. He's changed into fresh jeans and a hooded sweatshirt, but his hair is still damp. "Here," he says, handing me the pile. "Something in here should fit."

"Thanks."

I carry the clothes into the bathroom and select the least gigantic pieces from the pile. A shrunken pair of sweats I roll up at the ankles, a light blue sweater that once belonged to a female. I fold my things and leave them on the sink to dry.

"Whose sweater is this?" I say, coming back into the kitchen.

"Yours now." Micah is at the counter, filling two mugs with boiling water, dropping in bags of tea. He glances over his shoulder with a sheepish smile. "But if some angry woman comes up to you in town, demanding to know where you got it, maybe don't mention my name. As I recall, things didn't end well."

They never do. Micah Hunt should come with a warning sticker: *not husband material*. His relationships rarely make it past more than a few months, which is why I don't bother remembering their names until I've seen them more than three times by his side—and even then I sometimes confuse their faces. Micah has a type: young, blonde, pretty. His girlfriends all look the same.

He picks up the mugs, points me to one of the couches. "I probably shouldn't be telling you this, but the diver confessed to swiping the necklace. He says it was resting on the rear dash under the shattered back window, which had collapsed under the weight of all that water. The local cops have tossed him in jail. Tampering with evidence is a crime." He settles my mug onto the coffee table and plops with his onto the opposite couch.

"So that puts Jax in the car."

"That puts Jax in the car." Micah grimaces, shifting on

the couch. "You know, I have to think that whatever happened that night would have been an accident. Jax was a mess, but he was always a good guy. Reckless and careless, maybe, but not malicious."

"No, what was malicious was leaving Bobby down there all these years and not telling a soul. For pretending he had no idea what happened. For lying about it for twenty years." I'm talking about Jax, but the same would apply to Paul, too. How could I ever be with Paul after this? How can I share a house, a bed, a life with a man who lied about something so monumental? "So what do you think happened? Was Jax… I don't know…hitchhiking and Bobby picked him up? Were they taking a joyride when the car slipped out of the curve?"

Micah swings a big arm over the back of the sofa and watches me across the coffee table. "Probably too many possibilities to think about."

"Maybe, but you said it yourself. Jax and Bobby didn't exactly run in the same circles. Most likely they wouldn't have been palling around."

I pause a moment to think, mulling around the possibilities in my mind when I hear my mother's voice, so clear it could be coming from the next room.

Come on, Bobby. Just one little hit.

"What about drugs? Jax could have gone to Bobby for drugs."

It's not all that far-fetched. People always think it's the trailer-park kids who are looking to numb their woes in narcotics, but the kids I grew up with couldn't afford pills—not until they were old enough to get a job, and even then, it wasn't pills but heroin, strong and cheap. The rich kids, though, the ones with big allowances and parents too distracted with their sixty-hour workweeks… Those kids lived in a world where anything was possible. Coke. Oxy. Adderall. They were always making a pit stop at Bobby's trailer. My mother always said they were some of Bobby's best clients.

I think these things, and at the same time, a memory. A fleeting image of her falling naked in the dirt. Of a pretty man—no, a *boy*, puking. It flits away before I can grab hold.

"What are you thinking?" Micah says, watching me from the opposite couch.

"I'm just thinking about how we lived down the street from him. From Bobby, I mean. My father was already... well, you know. But Chet and I lived four trailers down."

Micah's face flashes genuine surprise. "That's...that's quite a coincidence."

"Is it?" I shrug, reaching for my steaming mug. "The shacks down by the river, that row of apartments off 64, the trailer parks. There are only so many places for people like us to live."

He tilts his head at the *people like us* comment, but he doesn't dismiss it. "Why haven't you mentioned this before? And you must have been, what—two? Three?"

"Six." I did the math this past spring, when they pulled Bobby's skeleton from the cove. I was six that summer he disappeared. Not old enough for any real memories, only a bunch of blurry images that connect into the same, sad story. Chet crying. People raising hell out in the yard. Our mother passed out on the couch. "Enough people talk about my trailer-park past. I'm not going to go around reminding the rest."

"I don't talk about it."

"I wasn't referring to you." I smile and sip my tea.

"But six. That's old enough to notice when a boy from your neighborhood goes missing."

"Honestly, the only thing I remember about Bobby was the noise." I thread my fingers through the handle of the mug, soaking in the heat. "His car, his music, his clients coming by at all hours of the day and night. When Bobby disappeared, I wasn't the only one who was relieved. Bobby stopped raising hell, and Chet started sleeping through the night."

My phone springs to life on my lap, a flurry of texts from Chet. I scroll through the messages.

Sorry I disappeared on you, but you won't flipping believe who I ran into.

Grant! Sienna's Twitter friend. And he had a LOT to say. He's working on a podcast.

Actually maybe I should tell you in person. It's kinda bad.

Leaving now, call you from the car.

Paul's been blowing up my phone FYI.

That last one he follows up with an emoji with its mouth zipped shut, and I relax a little against the cushion. Chet is on the way, and Paul still has no idea where I am.

"What about the investigation?" Micah says, dragging my attention away from my phone. "You must have seen the cops coming around. They didn't question you?"

I give him a rueful smile. "You think the cops came around? How cute." I wrinkle my nose at his expression, bury it in my tea. "Sorry. I know he's your dad and all, but that investigation was a joke. Nobody looked very hard for Bobby. They closed the case after only a couple of days. He wasn't even officially declared dead until they found his skeleton in his car. Ask Jamie. She's still salty about it."

"Who's Jamie?"

"Bobby's sister. She lived in his trailer for a while, and she was always looking out for me and Chet, feeding us, letting us hang out at her place when our mother would go missing, which was all the time. I just saw her, actually. Somebody's been buying her stuff, paying for her medical supplies, taking care of her yard service. My first thought was Jax, but where would he get the money?"

"From the bank. He has stacks of it from the trust fund his mother left him."

"But then why would Paul give Jax all that cash and hand-me-downs? That doesn't make any sense."

"You don't remember anything else?"

"Not really." But even as I say it, I get a flash.

Shut up, Charlie. Get your butt back inside.

I close my eyes, trying to put myself back there, in that grubby trailer park on the ugly side of the lake, in the dirt yard littered with trash and cigarette butts and somebody's smelly old sofa. I hear my own cries and Chet's wails, get a whiff of pine tree and dirty diaper. I feel Chet squirming against my chest and the sharp pang of hunger tearing at my belly. The burn of shame, of disgust and self-pity when our mother was wasted again.

Bobby laughed at her. I hear his mean chuckle, those ugly words he used to mock her. He called her a crazy bitch. I hear the words clear as day, and other voices, laughing. There were others, too, and they were laughing.

I open my eyes, and two pictures swim in and out of focus, pulling apart then shimmering into one.

Micah, seated on the couch across from me.

Micah, doubled over in laughter at the trailer park. A younger version of him, but still.

"Oh my God," I say. "You were there, too."

33

June 13, 1999
1:42 a.m.

The light is what Jax noticed first, bright and blinding and sudden, so sudden it made his eyeballs ache. A blazing light that turned night into day, like someone flicked a switch in the yard and inside that meth-head mother, turning her shirt and her skin see-through. Next, he noticed her face, the way her mouth went round and her eyes wide with fear. Then finally, he heard country music and the roar of a souped-up engine, a sound that had been there all along now that he thought about it, but that was the whole damn purpose, wasn't it? The tequila was so that he wouldn't *have* to think.

Jax swung around, shading his eyes with an arm.

"Mama, look out!" the girl screamed.

The woman dived for the dirt, but Jax didn't move. He

just stood there, squinting into the headlights, thirty feet away and closing fast. He spread his arm wide, welcoming it.

At the very last second, the tires cut right, sending a blur of shiny yellow carving a fat arc around him, kicking up dirt that rained on a trailer's metal siding like pellets from a BB gun. He watched the car fly past, clocked it skidding across the yard until it came to a messy stop at the far end, parallel to the lit-up trailer. It was shockingly loud, a noise that bounced off the trees and ricocheted through the trailer park, shrill in Jax's ears.

Through the open windows he spotted Micah, laughing it up with the driver.

Bobby, that was his name. The loser who flunked out in tenth grade. The freak who sold drugs under the bleachers. This was his car, his crazy Christmas trailer. He killed the engine and lit what Jax thought was a cigarette, until Jax noticed the way Bobby held in his breath. The pothead sampling his own wares.

Micah unfolded himself from the passenger's seat in a cloud of smoke, his movements slow and syrupy.

"Where's Paul?"

Micah tapped a finger to the Camaro rooftop. "Passed out cold. Dude can't handle his liquor."

That was because Paul drank like the teenager he was. Jax, too. But Micah... When it came to booze, he was light-years ahead. Drunk and high on who knew what and still relatively steady on his feet. Not like Jax, who couldn't seem to stop swaying.

The woman pushed past him, bare feet churning up the dirt. "Hey, Bobby. Gimme some of that. Just one little hit. That's all I need. Just something to tide me over."

Bobby looked through the window with obvious disgust.

"Put some clothes on, Francine. You do know you're out here in your underwear, right?" He swung the door open and stepped out in redneck gear—boots and Levi's and a leather jacket that hung from scrawny shoulders. His hair was greasy and so was his face, his forehead gleaming in the darkness.

"Come on." The woman lunged for the joint dangling from the corner of Bobby's mouth. "I'm good for it. You know I am."

Bobby held her back with an arm, craning his upper body out of reach. "Back off, you crazy bitch. You still owe me for last time."

"I'll pay you tomorrow, I swear."

"With what? We both know you ain't got no money."

Jax looked over at the little girl, who'd sunk to the stoop, her face screwed up with tears. Jesus Christ. He hoped like hell he wouldn't remember any of this tomorrow.

A familiar fire sparked in his chest. "What is *wrong* with you people? Stop laughing. Nothing about this is funny."

Micah either didn't hear or he didn't care. The woman was still swiping at the air. Bobby was still twisting away, holding the joint high above his head. Micah clutched his stomach and laughed and laughed, hooting like they were some kind of street performers.

"Micah, shut up." Jax banged on the hood of his Jeep with a fist. Micah was doubled over by now, wiping at his eyes, slapping his leg with hilarity. "Oh my God, you are *such* an asshole. How is this even remotely funny? This is *tragic*."

Jax's voice broke on the last word, and here came the tears, damn it. More than three months after his mother's death, in the middle of the night in the middle of nowhere, surrounded by a bunch of people he didn't want to see. Fucking figured.

Jax turned away in anger, in shame. He'd walk home. He'd sleep in the woods. He couldn't stay here another miserable second.

"It's okay," the little girl said, and for a split second, Jax thought she was talking to him, until she ducked her head and pressed her cheek to the baby's forehead. "Everything's gonna be okay. I'm gonna take care of you and we're gonna be just fine, I promise."

That was it. Party over. Bobby's shiny yellow Camaro was just sitting there, with the door open and the keys hanging from the ignition. A getaway car if he'd ever seen one. He leaned his upper body inside, spotted the keys and Paul, crashed on the back seat. His head was slung back, his mouth hanging open. And bingo—he was clutching that second bottle of tequila.

Jax grabbed it and chugged. He chugged until his eyes watered and his brain cleared and his belly lit up with liquid fire, and then he dropped behind the wheel and reached for the keys.

34

Micah stares at me from the opposite couch. "I thought you said you didn't remember anything."

"I didn't. I don't. It's just snippets, really, but…"

But now I can't tell what's real and what's my mind twisting up on itself. The image of Micah is so vivid it feels almost tangible, but dreams are like that too sometimes, those blurry moments right before you're good and awake. Our mother scrounging around for liquor and drugs, that was a constant, and there were always people hanging around the trailer park, there to do business with Bobby. Maybe I'm seeing something that wasn't there, putting Micah's face on another person's body. I was only six. How real can it be?

Come on, Bobby. Just one little hit.

Mama said it, I'm positive. I squeeze my eyes shut and new pictures flash behind my eyes, turning from black and white to technicolor. Mama's red underwear. A grubby yellow blanket. Expensive blue jeans.

My phone lights up on my lap, Chet calling from the car, but I let him go to voice mail. Those first blurry memories have broken through the darkness, knocked something loose in my brain, and I don't want to let go of the images.

"My mom wanted some of Bobby's cigarette. No, not a cigarette. A joint. She was begging him for a hit, and he laughed at her. He pushed her down in the dirt."

"Jesus, that scrawny lady... That was your *mother*?"

"And the baby in my arms was Chet. He was a really light sleeper. The noise from Bobby's place was constantly waking him up."

Micah laughs, a strangled sound. "Damn. I thought maybe I'd seen you working the register at the gas station, or busing tables in town or something." He shakes his head slowly, not bothering to wipe away his surprise. "But I should have known because you look just like her—minus the bad skin and tweaker teeth. Oh my God, your mom was a tweaker. Too strung out to notice she was outside in her underwear while her babies were bawling on the stoop."

Micah's tone hits me wrong—too high and mighty, and I shift on my chair.

"Bobby laughed at her, and so did you."

There's a voice in my head screaming at me to just let it lie. To shut up and pick up my phone, silent and dark on the cushion next to me, to tell Chet to hurry. But the memories have edges now, and this one's too big, too consequential to keep inside.

"What can I say? We were real shits back then."

"Not Jax," I say, and suddenly I understand. This is why I've never been afraid of him, why when he showed up—a raggedy fugitive on my back deck—I opened the door without hesitation. "Jax got mad. He felt bad for me."

"No, he felt *sorry* for you. There's a big difference."

Micah's words knock me like a slap, even though it's true. Jax did feel sorry for me that night. I get a lightning-quick glimpse of the look he gave me from behind the wheel of Bobby's car, the sudden lurch of the car shooting forward only to go nowhere. I hear the laughter, the shouting. I shake my head, trying to string the images together in a way that makes sense, but I can't. None of it makes any sense.

But still.

If I hadn't said anything just now, Micah wouldn't have, either. He would have gone right on acting like he'd never met poor, sad Bobby. He would have gone right on blaming Paul and Jax. The mood changes in an instant, the seriousness of where this discussion is headed settling like a rash on my skin.

"And Paul? Was he there, too?"

Micah nods. "Passed out on the back seat of Bobby's car."

And that's when all the pieces fall into a place, a combination of memory and conjecture.

A secret under water for twenty years.

Paul, almost drowned.

Jax, saving his life.

"Micah, what did you do?"

There's a breath where I think he's going to deny it, a pause that hangs heavy in the air. I hear the percussive tick of a clock somewhere off in the kitchen, the smooth hiss of my own breath.

"I got in the car with a drunken idiot who crashed us into the cove. That's what I did. And you can stop looking at me like that. None of this would've happened if Jax hadn't been such an asshole. Leaning over cliffs, chugging tequila, driving like a maniac. This is his fault. Not mine."

I imagine it then, the squeal of the Camaro's tires, smell the rubber burning against asphalt, feel the weightlessness as the car takes flight. A car as solid as Bobby's would have hit the water and sunk fast. If Jax had just enough time to drag up one person, if he could only choose one, which would it be—the trailer-park drug dealer, or his lifelong best friend?

If this is true, if I'm right, then so was Paul. Pitts Cove *was* a long-term investment, just not in the way he wanted me to believe. It had nothing to do with rerouting State Road 32 or turning swampland into an exclusive lakeside community. For Paul, buying up Pitts Cove was about keeping old bones buried not just for Jax but for himself as well.

And those bones would *still* be down there if that recreational diver hadn't swum up on his car and swiped that gold necklace as a trophy. No wonder Paul reacted like he did when I found him talking to Sienna, or the next day, when she washed up dead under the dock. Even if he wasn't the one who put her there, even if all he was trying to conceal was his hand in Bobby's death, Paul would have known what identifying her could lead to.

And Micah. Micah is a Lake Hunter, for crap's sake. What, did he strap on his tank and flippers and sink to the bottom of Pitts Cove every couple of months just to check in on Bobby? To report back to Paul and Jax that he was still down there, untouched and undiscovered?

"This is going to come out, Micah. Y'all had to have known that the second Sienna showed up here, the truth about Bobby would come out."

"Not if we'd kept our mouths shut, like we planned. We made a pact that night. We swore we'd never tell a soul."

"I'm pretty sure that ship has sailed."

"Why? Because of some girl with a necklace?"

"Because of a dead girl with a necklace. And I'm guessing you've seen her Twitter feed, so you already know about the podcast. There's got to be notes or recordings or something on her phone or laptop or uploaded to some website. Probably all of the above."

Micah watches me with those same eyes, that same serious stillness. His voice is eerily low. "Maybe. But they'll have to find it first."

The air in the room turns heavy and solid, like the barometric pressure outside. Micah knows every crack and crevice at the bottom of the lake. If he's done what he's implying, then he stashed her things somewhere deep and dark, somewhere no one will ever find them.

"And besides. I was at home the night Bobby disappeared. There's pictures of me at the dinner table, Dad and Mom and me. Dad's always been real good about documenting family moments. He writes the place and date on the back of every photo."

I don't believe him, not for a second. No way in hell Chief Hunt is that sentimental. If those pictures exist, which I'm sure they do, the dates were fudged exactly for this purpose—to serve as an alibi. Micah's been planning to let Paul and Jax take the fall alone, and his father is helping him.

Which means Chief Hunt is in on this, too.

Micah leans to his left, sliding his still-full mug onto a side table. "You know, when Paul came home that first day, telling me about this woman he met while getting gas, I was thrilled for him." He says it like a compliment, his voice warm and affectionate, but I'm not fooled. I see the way his shoulders have gone stiff, that muscle ticking in his jaw. "You didn't see him that first year after Katherine died, how those rumors tore him apart. Diana was ready to put him on suicide watch. It was that bad. But then you came along, and he started smiling again."

"Twenty years. You sat on this secret for twenty years. You and Paul literally stood by and watched a man go batty from the guilt. And for what? To save your own skin?"

"Oh, come on. Jax was never a friend. He was someone I tolerated because Paul liked him. And it's not like we planned it or anything. This wasn't premeditated. We were young and we were stupid, and may I remind you once again this was Jax's fault. Jax was behind the wheel. He was driving."

That feels right, Jax behind the wheel. Only…my head explodes with images, with sounds. An argument threaded through with blaring music and laughter. Fists flying.

Thunder booms overhead at the same time a bolt of lightning splits the night, turning darkness into day like God flicked on a flashlight, there and gone in an instant. Barely long enough for me to pick out a cluster of trees, a pile of slick firewood on the back deck, a drenched Jax—right before everything goes black.

Jax.

Something prickles up the back of my neck—shock, disbelief, a disturbing kind of unease. What is Jax doing here? How long has he been watching? I stare at the glass, searching for his shape in the shadows, but all I see is the reflection of the room, Micah twisting around on the couch.

"What?" he says, turning back, studying my face. "What did you see?"

"Nothing. The storm's close, that's all. That lightning hit right outside."

The room goes deathly quiet, an empty, heavy sound

that expands and fills me with dread. I think about what I should do now that I know the truth. I could run. I could leap over the couch and arm myself with a kitchen knife. But I can't make my body move because it's Micah. Paul's friend and mine. The one person who never made me feel unwelcome on this side of the hill. When he smiles at me, I smile back, half wondering if this is a dream.

"I thought you were different than her," he says, and I'm guessing we're back to Katherine. "The way you look. Where you come from, your white-trash upbringing. But the more I got to know you, the more it made sense. You and Katherine are a lot alike, you know. You're both smart. Relentless. So goddamn righteous. You won't be able to sit on this secret, will you?"

"Katherine knew?"

"Paul told her. That asshole broke the pact we made that night, that we'd take this secret to our graves. But Paul blabbed it to Katherine. She was trying to talk us into turning ourselves in. She gave us a motherfucking deadline. That's what they were fighting about. What we all were fighting about."

On the other side of the glass, the woods light up with a streak of lightning, followed by a boom that shakes my bones with meaning.

Fury flashes across Micah's face, flaring his nostrils, pressing his mouth into a thin line. "I don't take kindly to ultimatums. Ask any of my ex-girlfriends."

It's not an admission but his words still wash over me like a wave. Could Sam have been right? Were those marks on Katherine's ankle really fingerprints?

I picture Micah swimming up underneath her with his flippers and a tank strapped to his back. Nobody would have looked twice when he walked into the water in his dive gear. He would have been invisible to everyone but Katherine. My cheeks tingle with shock, burning like they've been slapped, leaving me gasping.

"You didn't. You *wouldn't*."

He pushes to a stand, and I think about Chet in his car, somewhere between here and town. How long ago did he leave? How long before he gets here? Micah is so big, so strong. Fast, too. There's no way I could outrun him. My fingers creep across the cushion, but Micah gets there first. He grabs my phone and tosses it onto the opposite couch.

When he turns back, everything about him is hard. His face. The set of his shoulders, the tilt of his head. His voice when he glares down at me.

"She didn't give me a choice."

"Oh my God. Micah! Katherine was your friend. Your best friend's wife. And you *killed* her for what—to save your own skin?"

"Well…yeah. That's exactly why I did it—that and because of her ultimatum. It was either that or go to jail, and I am not going to jail. Do you know what they'd do to the son of a police officer in there?" He shakes his head, a slow side to side. "No way. I am not going to jail for Jax's mistake. Not happening."

How did Micah do it? How did he drink our beer and do flips off our dock and pose for pictures with his arm around Paul's shoulders and a smile that said everything was just fine?

"What kind of monster are you?"

It's probably stupid to say it out loud, but I've already tipped irreversibly off course here, soared well past the point of no return. If Micah has gone to all this trouble to conceal being in the car with Bobby, he's not going to let me go. These truths, the worst ones, die here with me tonight.

There's only one way for this to end.

I blink, and he's yanking me up off the couch by my bicep, sloshing tea all over his designer mohair couch. I struggle to break free, but he's like a brick wall, his grip hard and unyielding.

"Charlotte, stop. I'm not going to hurt you."

But I already know Micah Hunt is a liar.

One chance, that's all I get.

I use the only weapon I have. I swing back an arm, send the mug thunking hard against his temple. The impact vibrates up my arm, douses us both in hot tea, but it was a direct hit. Micah growls in pain, in anger.

The backhand to my jaw is both shocking and disorienting. The world goes upside down and I go flying. My foot catches on a leg of Micah's coffee table, and I hurtle over it and crash to the floor, rolling across the carpet in a messy heap. My mouth fills with a warm gush of blood, and some of it trickles out of me and onto the carpet, bright red liquid soaking into his custom Berber carpet. *Evidence*, I think, right before my head connects with a wall. If nothing else, they'll get him for me.

And then...

Nothing.

35

I come to on the floor, and for a moment I do nothing. I just lie there, trying to get my bearings, waiting until my head stops throbbing. The air is cool, and so is the ground under me, a smooth, hard concrete. I fill my lungs, catch a whiff of rain and petroleum.

A garage. I'm in Micah's garage.

I crack an eye and there he is, gathering up equipment at a far wall of the garage. A mask, his flippers, a tank.

I lurch to a sit, scooting backward on my ass across the concrete. I'm not fast. I'm nightmarishly slow, but there's nowhere for me to go anyway, not in a room with four solid walls and Micah standing between me and the button to lift the garage door. My back hits a cold wall and that's it, that's as much air as I can put between us.

"Ah, you're awake. Sorry about the force of my backhand in there. I guess I don't know my own strength."

I press a cheek to my jaw, still on fire where he hit me, the skin by my right ear tight and tingly like a sunburn. I scan the walls for an exit, but they're solid sheets of drywall without a single window. There are only two doors—the double garage door to my left, and the door leading into the kitchen. The button that lifts and lowers the garage door is just inside.

I'm trapped. There's no other way out.

He leans over and checks the gauge on the tank, and my pulse ignites. He's going to drown me like he did Katherine.

Full-beam headlights flash on the windows, a series of rectangular sheets of glass high across the top of the garage door. Micah scowls over his shoulder, taking in the car coming down the driveway and me, watching from the floor.

"That's Chet." Micah stalks across the garage, stepping over the puddle his truck has dripped onto the ground. He reaches into his waistband, pulls out a gun and leans down, both hands propped on his knees. "Okay, so here's the deal. You make any noise, I shoot your brother. You open that garage door or break out a window, I shoot your brother. You do anything that makes him even look at me funny, and I shoot your brother. Are we clear?"

A car door slams, and footsteps sound on the concrete right outside. A swishing noise as my brother jogs up the steps.

"I said, are we clear?"

My gaze lands on the gun and I nod, my heart knocking against my ribs. Clear as crystal.

The doorbell rings, and Micah presses a finger to his lips, then disappears inside the house. I hear the *thwunk* of the dead bolt sliding into place, then a big stretch of silence before his voice worms its way through the wall.

No, not the wall, the pressed wood of the garage door.

The voices are coming from right outside. I picture Micah's front porch, the steps leading down the side to the patch of concrete. Fifteen feet at most, separated by a thin sheet of wood shavings and glass.

"Hey, Chet, what can I do for you?"

"I'm here for Charlie. I've been trying to call her, but she's not picking up."

Too late I realize my mistake. I missed my chance to have said something, called for help and told Chet to play it cool in those precious seconds of dead air when Micah was in the house, but I wasn't thinking. I run to the truck, clearing the wet glass with a hand. No key, of course there's not. Micah took it with him when he went inside.

Think, Charlie, think.

"I took her home a half hour ago at least," Micah is saying, and he's good; I'll give him that. His voice is relaxed and casual with only the slightest smidge of worry. And Chet's always been too trusting. He'll never know Micah's playing him. "Did you try there?"

I whirl around, spotting a toolbox on a bottom shelf, and I race over and root through it for the sharpest, most dangerous tool—a box cutter. One of the cheap, snap-off models, but there's a few good inches of blade left. I slide it into my waistband and listen.

A pause. "I thought she was avoiding Paul."

I look at the glass panels across the top of the garage doors. Too high for me to look out, but if I jump up I can reach the bottom. Maybe I could wave my hands around, hope that Chet sees them when he's driving away. Or no—maybe I can hang something in them, a sign. I look around for paper, for anything to write on.

"I talked some sense into her," Micah says. "Told her the only way to work things out is to communicate. She went home so they could talk through whatever it was they were fighting about."

"But my phone says she's here. I just checked the app, and she's here."

I freeze, my heart kicking against my ribs, and I don't know whether to cheer or cry; I'm so scared he'll hurt Chet. I hold my breath and listen for what comes next.

"She must have forgotten her cell phone. Stay here, and I'll run and grab it for you."

Micah's footsteps fade into the house, and I know I don't have much time. I run to the far end of the garage, press my mouth to the crack and shout-whisper as loud as I dare.

"Chet, listen to me. I need you to leave right now. Call Sam, tell him to get over here and to hurry. But play it cool. Act normal, and don't say anything that'll tip Micah off." I pause, waiting for a response or maybe the sound of his footsteps racing to the car, but all I hear is rain and a sudden gust of wind that shakes the trees. "Chet, did you hear me? *Leave.*"

I leap backward at the sound of the door opening.

"Here you go," Micah says. "Tell those crazy lovebirds I said to kiss and make up, will you?"

"Thanks, man. I sure will. See ya."

The front door closes with a thud, and I know I don't have much time. I race to the window at the far right end, by the patch of empty driveway where guests are meant to park. I spit on my finger, blood and slobber and slime, and then I jump, tracing the letter *H* in the glass with my spit. It's faint and it's a Hail Mary pass, but if Chet hits it with his headlights, he might actually spot it. I lick my finger again and keep going.

My writing is sloppy and my lungs and legs burning with effort, and I'm nowhere near finished by the time a car door slams. An *H* and *E* but only part of an *L*, a slimy but partial mirror image of my call for help. I press my palms to the door and pray Chet sees. *Look up look up look up.*

Chet's motor revs as he swings the car around, a four-point turn that flashes his headlights on the windows, shafts of light glowing against the glass. One window lights up, then the other, the letters pink and slimy and plain as day. I hold my breath. *Come on, Chet. All you have to do is see.*

Chet guns the gas, and the headlights flit away. The garage goes dark. Chet winds the Jeep back down the drive. I collapse to the floor, the tears coming hot and heavy. Chet's gone. He didn't see.

The door opens, silhouetting Micah in white light from the kitchen. He gathers his equipment from the floor and motions for me to follow. "Come on. Let's go."

"Where are we going?"

He looks down at the tank in his hand, the mask dangling from a finger. "Please don't make this any harder than it needs to be."

My wits and adrenaline, that's all I've got left—that and a box cutter. I feel its sharp edges pressing into my waistline as I haul myself off the floor.

I drag my feet as much as I can on the hill, buying myself some time until we make it to the dock, though I can't imagine what for. Micah is only a pace or two behind, too close to make a run for it, and I'd never make it very far, not with a gun pointed at my shoulder blades. The rain has mostly stopped, an intermittent patter interspersed with thunder rumbling in the distance, but the lawn is slippery and I'm still barefoot. I move in slow motion, feeling the outline of the box cutter against my skin. Sometime between moving from the garage and the back door, I've managed to slide it into my sleeve, but I'll be dead before I can whip it out. I brought a knife to a gunfight, and a cheap-ass one at that. My only hope here is a miracle.

Or Jax.

I scan the hill for him, but if he's here, he's well hidden—and honestly, I'm not 100 percent sure it was really him I saw, standing on Micah's back deck. The flash of lightning was so unexpected, so bright and sudden, my mind could have been playing tricks on me. Jax at the trailer park. Jax on the other side of the glass. It's possible he was just part of the memories I was trying to conjure up at the time.

"So how does this work?" I gesture to Micah's dock, a light brown U floating on the glittering black lake. Thirty yards, maybe, but not more. "Do I jump? Do you push me in? And how are you going to explain me wearing your sweats and some random woman's sweater?"

"It's Katherine's." I glance over my shoulder, and he laughs at the expression on my face. "She was always slinging her stuff around, leaving it everywhere. But to answer your question, they'll probably assume you got it from Paul."

"But…won't people be suspicious? When I wash up under Paul's dock, I mean." We both know that's where I'll end up.

"Yeah, of Paul. Drowning women is his tactic. Not mine."

"Only it *is* yours. Because you pretty much admitted to killing Katherine that way, and I'm guessing Sienna, too, probably. It makes sense, especially now that I know you hid her stuff."

Silence Sienna, bury her electronics and jewelry somewhere it will never be found, let the currents sweep her to Paul's dock. Like Jax said, *that's two.* Problem solved.

"No, Jax killed Sienna. And before you ask, I know it was him because Paul wouldn't have had the stomach for it. I love the guy, but he's always been kind of a pussy."

At the sound of his name, the reality that I'll never see him again rises hot and urgent in my chest, but I swallow it down and keep moving. The low-hanging clouds above my head. The hill drenched in shadows and a sweet, drifting perfume. It feels like a dream. A nightmare. I focus on the light trickling from Paul's house farther up the cove. On the piece of plastic and steel against my skin. I straighten my arm, and the box cutter slides out of my sleeve and into my hand.

I whirl around, terror bubbling in my throat. "Micah, please. Please don't do this. We can figure something out."

"I like you, Charlotte. You're a lot of fun, and I meant it when I said Paul's been his old self since he met you. I hate what this is going to do to him."

"Then don't do it! I'll go find Chet and we'll leave town. I swear! I'll never speak about this again."

I'm lying, of course—to him, to myself. There's no way I could leave this place, no way if I did that I could ever live with that lie. It would be doing exactly what I'm accusing Paul of, sitting on an awful, unforgivable secret. If Micah knows me at all, he will see right through this lie. He's already told me too much. He can't afford to let me go.

"I really wish you hadn't remembered that night," he says, reading my thoughts, and *this is it*, I tell myself. *This is where you die.*

He's urging me forward when I slide the box cutter into his side. It cuts through his skin like butter, just slips right in. He jerks in surprise, and the thin metal snaps in my hand. Three, maybe four sections of blade, stuck in his stomach—not deep enough to hit an important organ. Barely far enough to draw blood.

"You stabbed me." His voice is incredulous. His gaze falls to the bright orange handle in my hand, my thumb rolling out the last segment of blade. "With a Stanley knife."

"It's a box cutter. And I wish I'd aimed for your neck."

Micah laughs. "You're insane. You know that? I'm really going to miss hanging out with you." He snatches the box cutter from my fingers and gestures to the dock with his gun. "Now go."

This is happening. This is really fucking happening. I think of the baby I will never see and the life she or he will never lead, and the hillside blurs with my tears.

He nudges me forward, and slowly, I turn for the dock. "When you flipped Sienna over, Paul knew who she was, and he lied about it to Sam. I saw him talking to her the day before." Keep him talking. Drag this out and pray. It's the only strategy I've got left.

"I know. Paul told me. He was pretty torn up about it, too."

"But why would he lie about knowing her if he was innocent? He doesn't have an alibi for the time she was killed. Maybe it *was* him."

The lawn dumps us onto a patch of gravel and dirt, and wet mud squishes between my toes. By now my bare feet are so cold they're going numb, a sharp mess of pins and needles that's making it hard to walk.

"Because by the time I fished her out, all three of us knew what she was doing in town. She'd been talking it up in all the restaurants and bars, getting folks riled up about some big new development around Skeleton Bob. When I pulled her out of the lake, Paul and I both knew who put her there."

"You."

Micah sighs, long and loud. "You're starting to wear on my nerves, Charlotte. It was Jax. Why else would Paul run off to Balsam Bluff if not to protect him?"

An excellent question. One I haven't figured out the answer to yet.

"It wasn't me." Jax's voice carries over the water from our left, and I almost collapse in relief. I whip around and so does Micah, aiming his gun into the darkness. He swivels from bush to tree to rocky patch, finally settling on a dark smudge behind a tuft of tall grass.

Batty Jax, and he's holding a rifle.

"But I gotta say, man, bravo. Killing that girl, setting things up to make it look like me or Paul. Didn't matter to you which one of us took the fall. So long as you and your dad could pretend you had nothing to do with any of it."

Micah rolls his eyes, but he doesn't lower his gun. "Oh, Jesus, not you, too. Why does everybody think that I killed her?"

"Process of elimination. If it wasn't Paul or me, it had to have been you. You're the only one left."

In between the words, a distant and ghostly wail carries across the wind and water.

Sirens.

If Micah notices, he doesn't let on. "Her coat was in your cabin, dumbass. Charlotte saw you wearing her scarf."

"Yeah, because Sienna gave them to me. She didn't want me to be cold."

Micah laughs, a sharp, angry sound. "Right. Next you're going to say that wasn't your necklace she was waving around town. That she—"

"I told her the truth!" Jax stabs the rifle in Micah's direction, his shout echoing over the water. "When she showed me that necklace, I confessed. I told her we were wasted. That for some reason I will never understand, we piled into Bobby's car. That I was the idiot who drove us into the cove. She recorded the whole thing. I talked to her for hours and you know what? It was a goddamn relief to finally tell somebody."

There's a long, stunned silence. Jax's face is a shadow, just two white eyes glaring down the barrel of his gun.

Micah sputters. "You stupid, demented, pathetic asshole. What the hell were you thinking? Do you know what the penalty is for manslaughter? There's no statute of limitations on that shit."

Jax spreads his free arm wide. "Look at me, man. I've already lost everything I ever cared about. I'm already living in hell. I'm pretty sure jail can't be worse than this." He drops his arm, his tone flat and final. "It's over, Micah. I'm done."

"No." Micah's voice rises in anger, in panic. "You idiots might be done but it is not over. We'll say you traded your necklace for a joint. We'll say Bobby stole it."

In Micah's desperation, he's not thinking clearly. By now too many people know—Chet and me and Sienna's friend Grant. Micah looks across the cove, to the swirling blue and red lights painting colors on the trees and lake surface. Two, maybe three minutes, tops.

Another voice floats down from the opposite side of the hill. "Micah. Put down the gun."

Paul.

My heart alights, and I search the hill for his familiar form, finding it half-hidden behind a mountain laurel the size of a tree. I take in his stance, the glint of metal in his hand—his gun from the safe. Chet stands a pace or two behind, a ragged shadow in the darkness. There's the flash of white teeth as he gives me a grin, and I can't help it—I laugh with relief.

Micah's gun is steady on Jax, but his gaze swivels back and forth between the two, from Paul to Jax and back again, at the two guns pointed at his head. "Gentlemen, I believe this is what's called a Mexican standoff. You know the first one to pull the trigger wins, right? Who's it gonna be?"

Silence. I hold my breath and wait for a shot.

Micah lowers his arm, the gun dangling from a fist. "Fine. *Fine.* But I would just like to reiterate for the record that we wouldn't be standing here right now if you bastards had just followed the plan. Sit tight, act normal, say nothing. Isn't that what we agreed to do? But Paul here couldn't keep his stupid mouth shut and Jax… Jax had to go and lose his marbles. Batty Jax. You can't make this shit up."

"I can't live this way anymore." Jax's voice cracks, weary with emotion, with what sounds like tears. When he steps out from behind the clump of grass, his rifle is pointed at the ground. "This guilt…it's too big for me to keep carrying around. It's too heavy. Every time I close my eyes, Bobby is right there. That…that look in his eyes when he couldn't break free of the seat belt, the sound of his underwater scream when I went for Paul and not him. He grabbed my ankle, and you know what I did? I kicked him in the goddamn face and then I dragged Paul to shore."

I can see it. I can see what a burden it's been for him. We all knew Jax was suffering; we just didn't know from what.

Micah laughs, a bitter snarl of a sound. "You stupid motherfucker. Even now, even all these years later, you still think this is all about you. *My mom died. My father doesn't love me enough. Paul's my best friend, not yours.*" Micah's face goes ugly and mean, contorting with his awful words.

"That's always been your problem, but I'm here to tell you this time it's not. This thing with Bobby, it's not about you."

"What are you talking about? Of course it's about me. I was the reckless one, the idiot who insisted on driving even though I couldn't see straight. I was the one who leaned into that curve, took it way too fast."

Micah fills up his lungs and roars, *"It wasn't you, ass-hole."* Three quick puffs of air, sharp in the dark quiet, and I struggle to focus on his words, slipping through the hills like smoke. It wasn't him, what? "Bobby's car was a stick."

For the longest time, no one speaks. There's just sirens and black night and Jax, breathing hard.

He shakes his head. "No, it was—"

"You wanted to drive," Micah says. "Hell, you tried to, but you couldn't. You killed the engine, about launched us all through the windshield. I wouldn't stop laughing, so you dragged me out of the car and tried to fight me, but your punches never landed because you were too plastered."

The memories flicker, spinning and blurring before they fall into place. How Jax dropped behind the wheel. How the car lurched forward only to stop. The laughter, the fight-ing. I didn't understand it at the time, but I understand it now. Jax didn't push down on the clutch when he started the engine. I know, because the same thing happened to me once in Chet's Jeep, right before he taught me how to operate a stick.

Jax grunts. "No. That's not right. I remember getting into the driver's seat. I remember holding the wheel. It wasn't a stick."

"Yes, it was," Chet says, and all heads swing in his di-rection. The sirens are deafening now, screeching around the curves at the top of the hill, and he shouts to be heard above them. "Bobby's car was a Camaro Z28 1LE. Chevy's lightweight race car package. Built for the track, but most people buy 'em to drive on the roads. Especially roads like the ones around here."

Chet again, with his car facts, stuff nobody else knows or cares to retain.

"So?" Jax's voice is impatient.

"So all LEs are manual transmissions. Chevy doesn't make them any other way."

I stare at Micah, and oh my God. For twenty years, he's kept this sickening secret that he's responsible for the crash.

No, it's more than that.

For twenty years, Micah has fed them this lie like a bowl of ice cream, scooping it up and shoving it down their throats often enough, and with enough passion that they believed it. He fooled his so-called best friends with this stitched-together story and held Jax's sanity hostage. He let Jax believe that it was his fault, his crime, when all this time, it was Micah's.

My gaze flits to Jax—to poor, batty Jax, and it's hard to see his face in the dark, but I see his stance. The way his arms swing up once again, the way he aims the rifle at Micah's chest. I don't need to see his expression to know what happens next.

"Charlie, *move*," Chet hollers, but he doesn't have to tell me. I'm already scuttling farther up the dock, putting some space between Jax and his target, moving all the way to the edge. I don't know how accurate a shot Jax is. Don't want to be in range when he pulls that trigger.

Micah puffs up his chest, spreading his arms wide. "Do it. Go on—shoot me."

Cars screech around a curve in Micah's driveway, and I shudder at what Sam will think when he comes around the side of the house. Jax will look like the aggressor. Paul must be thinking the same thing, because he yells at Jax to put down the gun.

Micah sputters, pounding a fist on his chest. "Right here. Somebody shoot me, damn it. *Do it.*"

There's commotion high on the hill, bodies spilling down it like an army of ants, voices shouting to get down, to put the guns down. Jax freezes, everything but his expression. He's close enough I see it now. Not the anger I expected to see but a smile—a real, actual smile. Slowly, smoothly, he lays the rifle on the grass.

Revenge comes in all shapes and sizes. Sometimes the best revenge, the worst kind, is to do nothing at all.

I see it too late, the way it creeps over Micah's features—the hardness, that look of determined exhilaration. Daring death. Doing something crazy.

His body shifts, and three things happen all at once.

Jax lunges.

I scream.

Micah pulls the trigger.

36

A gunshot on the lake sounds like the sky is cracking open, shattering your eardrums and swallowing up every other sound, ripping through your bones like a bullet.

Only it wasn't my bone the bullet ripped through. It was Micah's, and by his own hand.

Paul was on me in a millisecond. "Don't look," he shouted, covering my eyes, but he was too late. I already saw the way Micah's limbs were splayed every which direction on the dock, how his eyes were open but the top of his head was a mush of hair and meat and white bone. I saw how Paul sank to his knees and vomited onto the lawn, how Jax's body seemed to sway with the patch of grass he stood before. I saw it all.

And then the hill came alive with light and sound, with men shouting and waving guns and handcuffs, and I saw the look on Paul's face when Sam read him his rights. It was like the clouds cleared and God shone a spotlight on all those things I'd missed before. That my husband was old. That he was full of secrets. That I was better off before he stepped up to my counter at the gas station, when I was so eager to claw myself out of that muddy trailer park, I didn't realize I was trading one set of problems for another. Pretty things for a man still in love with his first wife. No, Paul didn't kill Katherine, but his secrets are the reason she's dead, and in my heart that feels unforgivable. There was a hint of truth to all those whispers in town. I should have listened.

"Paul told me he met Sienna the day before she died," Sam says, watching me from the other side of the kitchen counter. Behind him, on the other side of the glass, the lake is high wattage in the early-morning sunshine. A glorious morning, one that makes me long for sunglasses.

Chet steps up beside me, but neither of us say a word.

Sam's gaze sits steady on mine. "I just think it's weird, don't you? That Paul forgot to mention it the first time I asked him, I mean. He claims you found him talking to her in town, but that there's no way you would have recognized her. Something about the distance or the angle, I don't know which, and before you say anything, don't. This is where you're supposed to nod your head and agree."

I don't disagree, but I don't nod, either.

Sam sighs, pushing at his eyes with a thumb and forefinger. He's still in the same clothes he was in last night, a flannel shirt and faded jeans as if he got the call as he was settling down to dinner. I'd say he slept in them, but the hollowed-out shadows under his eyes tell me he got about as much sleep as I did, which was none. Every time I closed my eyes, I saw the dark stain on Micah's dock. I smelled the blood and gunpowder and fear, the way bone and brain drizzled down like rain. It was so much easier to stay awake.

"Charlie, what do you say we cut the crap? I've got confessions on record from both Jax and Paul that make them accessories to manslaughter on top of a heaping pile of other charges. They're going to prison, probably not as long as I'd like them to, but they're going."

"Is this the part where you say *I told you so*?"

"No. This is the part where I say if there's anything you're holding back on, then you should tell it to an attorney. As soon as we're done searching Micah's house, we're coming here next."

For some reason, his words rile me up, and my shoulders hike to my ears. "Why would I need an attorney when all of this is news to me? I don't have anything to hide. I didn't know about Bobby, about Katherine, about any of it. I learned all these things last night, like everybody else in this room. But if you're looking for someone to blame, you may want to check with Chief Hunt and Diana, because from everything I heard, I'm guessing they knew all along."

Sam runs it down for us, how Paul's and Jax's statements have opened the floodgates. How our old friends and neighbors from the trailer park are stepping forward one by one, claiming their eyewitness accounts were ignored or buried. How a power-hungry Chief Hunt actively participated in the cover-up, then twenty years later did it again, when Sienna's investigation connected his son to Bobby's death.

"We're searching Chief's house. Micah's, too. If something's there, we'll find it."

"No, you won't. Micah told me Sienna's things were somewhere no one will ever know to look. The bottom of the lake, probably."

"Micah wasn't the only one with motive and opportunity. So far, we haven't found one person who can verify your husband's alibi."

Chet leans onto the countertop with both elbows. "Dude, you can't be serious. Jax was wearing her scarf."

Sam swipes a hand down his face, his fingers digging into his temples. "Jax was at his sister Pamela's house the night Sienna was murdered. He tends to do that when the weather turns nasty, crashes at her place, then takes off as soon as the sun's up. She's already given a statement, and I believe her. The Pentecostals are pretty solid in their belief that lying is a sin."

And Pamela lives all the way on the other side of the lake. A good twelve miles from the marina, maybe more. Too far for Jax to hike back and forth in one night.

Which brings us back to where we began: Micah or Paul. Both have motive. Both insist they didn't touch Sienna, but an innocent man denying his guilt would use the same words as a guilty man. Their arguments would sound the same.

Exhaustion washes over me, dragging down on my skin and bones, turning my thoughts sluggish. How did they do it? How did they keep a secret that monumental for twenty long years, feeling it heavy over your head all day every single day? Knowing that all it would take was one tiny nudge for the whole thing to come tumbling down, cracking open for all to see.

"And Diana?" I say. "How much did she know?"

"Paul and Jax are pretty tight-lipped whenever her name comes up. They're very protective of her."

Chet and I share a look. Of course they are. She's been guarding their secret like a pit bull all these years. I'm sure as far as they're concerned, silence is her reward.

Sam gathers up his things, his keys and notebook and cell, and Chet walks him out.

I sink onto a stool and think about what I'm going to do, now that the bottom is blown out of this marriage, now that I don't have a job, a place to live, a bank account overflowing with cash. Maybe Paul didn't kill a person. He didn't shoot a bullet through another man's heart or hold a woman under water until her breath ran out, but he still kept quiet about something so important, so momentous that for me there's no way back. There's no reset button on this thing.

"So, I talked to Tim McAllister earlier," Chet says, stepping back into the kitchen. "His grandma's place at Shady Grove is up for rent now that she's moved down to Florida, and he's giving us the first look. Fully furnished, and the price is right."

"That's because it's in Shady Grove."

A pretty name for a hideous trailer park off Highway 73. Not so much a grove as it is a muddy clearing lined with a few dozen trailers, all of them run-down and propped up on grubby cinder blocks. They surround a cluster of cracked picnic tables and a rusty swing set, the seats and metal chains long gone. Any rental contract should come with a free tetanus shot.

"I'll take the couch, and I promise not to hog the bathroom or leave my crap all over the place."

Call me thickheaded, but that's when the realization hits. This move is for me, too. I'm moving from this place to a trailer. I'm ending up right where I began with a baby in tow.

Chet reads the look on my face, and his voice softens. "It's only for a little while. We'll be out of there by the time the baby comes. I swear."

"How?"

He shrugs. "We'll figure out a way. We always do."

He's right, even though a real McCreedy would be packing up all the valuables right now. She'd swipe the silver, stuff the cash from the safe in a bag and take off into the wind. She'd put this ridiculous sham of a marriage in her past, bail on this accidental pregnancy. If I were anything like my mother, I'd be long gone by now.

But I'm not like her, which is why I'm leaving here with what I walked in with all those months ago. Two pairs of threadbare Levi's, five polyester sweaters, some underwear and T-shirts and my most comfortable pajamas, stuffed into a Hefty bag by the front door. As far as I'm concerned, this part of my life is like Vegas: what happened here stays here, hanging from velvet hangers upstairs in the closet.

All but one tiny memento, a little seed sprouting in my belly.

I shimmy the diamond off my finger, place it on the counter next to the sink and turn to Chet. "Okay. I'm ready."

37

The average person can hold their breath for somewhere around a minute. That's sixty seconds for the clock to tick down and the scales to tip in your body. Oxygen levels plummet while carbon dioxide builds in your bloodstream, blazing like fire in your lungs until instinct kicks in, and you suck an involuntary breath. Air. Water. Either one will put out the flame.

Paul or Bobby. That was the choice presented to Jax that night. His best friend or a drug dealer he barely knew. It wasn't fair, and his decision wasn't difficult. Jax chose his best friend, and if he had to do it all over, he'd choose Paul again in a heartbeat.

What Jax wouldn't repeat are all the things that came next, after he'd dragged Paul to shore and blown air into his lungs. After Micah had quit puking his guts into the bushes. After everybody had stopped flailing around and bawling. After all that, when the reality of what just happened set in and Micah said they didn't have to go to jail. Sit tight. Act normal. Say nothing. For the rest of his miserable life, Jax would regret making that stupid pact.

Micah made them seal it with blood like they were twelve or something, slicing a gash into their palms with the sharpest rock he could find. He made them swear on the lives of everyone they ever loved and ever *would* love. And they were just drunk and desperate enough to agree.

Especially Jax. The driver who wasn't.

Even after all of Micah's revelations out there on the hill, Jax can still only call up fleeting snippets of that night with Bobby. The earthy scent of tobacco leaves. Empty bottles rolling around the floorboards. Vomit surging up his throat and nose. A baby's cries piercing the nighttime quiet. The rest is just a big black hole in Jax's head, an empty void of nothingness until then suddenly, everybody was screaming and there were only a few inches of air left in the car as it sank in the lake.

Micah's dad, when they showed up dripping on his doorstep, threw one hell of a tantrum. Jax still shudders when he thinks about it, the way Chief's cheeks turned purple as he screamed and cussed and kicked a hole in the foyer wall. The words he said, the awful names he called his own son. Worthless. Pathetic. A retard. Micah just stood there, shaking from anger or embarrassment, maybe both. But he knew better than to say the first word.

It was Chief who fetched Jax's car from the trailer park and covered up the tire tracks leading into Pitts Cove. Who made arrangements, quick and dirty, so the case was closed before any witnesses could step forward to say the man who was about to become police chief had a murderer for a son. For twenty years Chief Hunt sat on the truth, not to protect his son but to cover his own ass.

Jax meant what he said. It was a relief to finally tell, to clear Bobby's black stain from his conscience. Only his confession got a woman killed. Not by Jax's hands, just like Jax isn't technically the reason Bobby ended up at the bottom of Pitts Cove.

Jax came so close to shooting Micah out there on that hill. His finger was taut on the trigger when it occurred to him that blowing a hole through Micah's chest would be a gift, that it would serve him in the same way the woods had been a relief for Jax. Alone and unseen. Ignored. Jax fooled himself into thinking it was some kind of penance, when really it was an escape. When people stop looking at you, do you really exist? Fading away was the only way he knew to survive.

Stupid fucking Micah. Jax will never forgive him for what he did. To Bobby, to Jax and Paul. He can hear Paul crying in the next cell for his beloved Katherine. For Charlotte and their unborn child. The cruelest punishments don't always come behind bars.

But Jax is still guilty. He still has to pay.

Maybe that's what his sister, Pammy, means when she says everybody has their own cross to bear, a heavy burden that burns like a thorn in their flesh. Pammy's thorn chased her to the church, Jax's into the woods, his solitude a salvation and a damnation at the same time. In the quiet of the forest, Bobby only grew larger, louder in his mind. His laughter echoing in the trees, his shadow lurking behind every log. Every time Jax closes his eyes, it's Bobby's face he sees, floating behind the bubbles of his final scream. The desperation, the pleading, the terror when Jax went for Paul instead. The images will stay with Jax for the rest of his miserable life.

There's a rattling at the door, a chinking of keys against the metal bars. Sam, coming for a statement.

Sacrifice.

Penance.

Atonement.

Justice.

In the end, we all reap what we sow.

38

Two days later, on a crisp Monday afternoon, Diana summons me to her house, a sprawling cottage of stone and shingle on the outskirts of town. She doesn't tell me what for, or ask if I've been to see her son, languishing in the jail cell next to Jax's. "I'll explain once you get here" was all she would say, so here I am—too curious for my own good.

The door pops open, and I look back at Chet, watching with one hand draped over the steering wheel of the still-running Jeep, his fingers tapping against the dash. Chet thinks I should wash my hands of the Kellers, let them sort out their own drama.

But like I told him before he dropped me off, I'm not here for Diana or for Paul. I'm not even here for myself.

I'm here for another Keller, the one it is my duty to protect.

"Charlotte, thanks for coming." The caramel-colored Pomeranian on her arm barks like we've never met before, and she gives him a little jiggle. "Dolly, hush. She'll settle down once you're inside. Can I get you something to drink?"

I give her the best smile I can muster. "I go by Charlie now."

Diana seats me on an overstuffed chair in the sun porch, a glass-walled, terra-cotta-tiled room at the back of the house. Paul once told me this is why he became an architect, because of these cramped, low-ceilinged spaces connected by narrow hallways, every inch of it crammed with fussy antiques and complicated decor. It made him yearn for open spaces and clean lines, and I can see why. Even without the sun beating through the windows and Diana a few feet away in the kitchen, gathering refreshments, the room feels stuffy and oppressive.

"I just want to start by saying I'm sorry." She settles a tray onto the table between us. Peppermint tea and raw honey and a porcelain plate piled with cookies she'll never touch. "About Micah, I mean. What he did to you and Katherine. I had no idea he was that evil."

She passes me a steaming cup, but I leave it on the table. "Like father, like son, I guess."

"I suppose." She sinks into her chair, scooping up the dog at her feet and settling it on her lap like a fuzzy pillow. "Still. I always thought those crazy stunts of Micah's were some kind of… I don't know…misguided attempt to prove his worth to his father—that man has *never* been nice, and you can quote me on that." She strokes her dog with a hand, raking the fur with her fingernails. "It's funny when you think about it. Micah spent his whole life trying to act so brave, when really he was a big ole scaredy-cat. Scared his daddy wouldn't love him, scared of what people would think if they knew what he did. And in the end, scared to face up to his own sins. He took the coward's way out. Of all the awful things he did, that one's the worst."

I don't really know what to say to that, so I say nothing at all. I could point out her son lied, too, that he sat on secrets so monumental it cost him two wives, but Diana already knows these things. I press my lips together and wait for whatever it is she brought me here to say.

"Paul says you haven't been to see him yet."

"I'm not ready to talk to him." I lift one shoulder. "Honestly, I don't know if I'll ever be ready."

"I see." She pauses to twist some honey around a polished silver spoon, then drops it into her tea. "You should know that these past twenty years have been torture for Paul. I know my son. I saw how he suffered after Katherine. He was convinced her death was the universe's way of punishing him for what happened to Bobby. Paul didn't want to lie to you, but he'd already lost one wife because he told her the truth. He couldn't go through that again."

Resentment swells, both at her words and her puffed-up tone. Something didn't just *happen* to Bobby. Three drunken idiots drove him into a lake and left him for dead, and Paul's suffering can't wipe away his guilt. But Diana has always been her son's greatest defender. She's always had blinders on where he and Jax are concerned.

My eyes, however, are wide open.

"But Paul *did* lie. He swore he wasn't keeping any secrets from me, when really he was sitting on a big one. And now four people are dead. And okay, so maybe Paul didn't technically kill them, but he had a hand in their deaths. He should have come clean after Bobby, but instead he doubled down. He should have confessed that very night."

I believe this with everything I am. Murder and you are

a murderer. Lie and you are a liar. This is how the world works. Loyalty to an old friend, even one you love like a brother, can't wipe away the fact you were accessory to a crime.

Diana shakes her head. "But it wasn't just anyone he was keeping quiet for, dear. It was Jax. The boy who risked his life to pull Paul from a sinking car. With the facts he was working with at the time, it felt like a fair trade. Paul's life for his silence."

"What about loyalty to me? I mean, granted, I didn't think to include the word in our wedding vows, but I kind of thought *love* and *honor* and *cherish* covered all the bases. Isn't loyalty implied?"

"Yes, Charlotte, but—"

"I already told you. It's Charlie."

Diana sighs, a quick burst of impatient air. "Charlie. But please try to think about it from Paul's point of view. Jax chose Paul. He let another man die so Paul could live. There is nothing Paul wouldn't do for Jax. Nothing I wouldn't do for him. Jax is family."

Emphasis on the family, as if that explains everything. And for Diana, I suppose it does. All that time I spent feeling like an outsider proves that I need more than a marriage certificate to crack that Keller nut. I need something I don't have, something I'll never have, especially since I am no longer willing to try. This person I tried so hard to become, this dream I worked so hard to attain, it doesn't fit me anymore.

She looks out the window, to the trees and the lake and the rolling hills on the other side, and her forehead crumples with new lines. "I mean, honestly. The second I heard that woman's jewelry went missing, I knew that it couldn't have been Jax. What would he want with some cheap costume pieces, anyway? He has no need for money, and he's not that conniving. Jax is a good man."

"He managed to keep a skeleton buried for twenty years. Clearly, he's no saint."

Her gaze, still defensive and hard, whips to mine. "Yes, and you can see what that did to him. Jax has paid deeply for his hand in Bobby's death, and so has Paul. Both of them have lost so much."

The image of Paul's face flashes, fierce and proud and happy as he watched me make my way down the aisle, and my heart pinches with the memory. My whole life stretched out before me that day. The life I wanted. The life I thought I deserved with a handsome husband, a pretty home, a bank account overflowing with cash. If only I had looked more closely at the man behind the offer.

"Yes, and now Paul has lost me. Because I can't be with him after this, Diana. I just can't. If that makes me uncompromising, then so be it. This baby deserves better. I deserve better."

Her shoulders slump with disappointment. "That's too bad. Because I hate thinking of that baby growing up without a father."

"A divorce won't change the fact that this baby is Paul's. And I'm not saying I'm cutting him out of our lives completely, just that I can't be married to him anymore."

She gives a swirl to her tea, watching the way the liquid spins around her cup. "What I meant is, it's hard enough to raise a child, but doing so on your own is a special brand of difficult. The midnight feedings, the constant worry. The money." She sips, watching me over the lip of her teacup. "Babies are so very expensive."

Her tone is parked in Neutral, but her words still hit me wrong, like jumping into the lake before the sun has had a chance to warm up the water. "I don't plan on asking Paul for anything more than what I'm entitled to according to the prenup, if that's what you're fishing for. Child support and health care, at least until the baby is born. That's all I want."

"Of course you are entitled to those things. I wasn't implying anything otherwise. But you should know that this case is going to trial, and people will be watching. In fact, they're already watching, and they've seen how you've moved out of Paul's house and into some rickety trailer. You can't raise this baby in a trailer."

A hot flash of indignation, but I manage to keep it out of my tone. "Plenty of people raise babies in trailers. My mother did. Not very well, but that had nothing to do with the trailer. The point is, a baby doesn't care where it lives as long as it's loved and cared for."

Diana tries very hard not to roll her eyes. "What I'm saying is, it doesn't have to be that way. You don't have to struggle."

It takes a few seconds for her meaning to sink in, and then I laugh out loud at the irony. After all these months trying to chase me away, after all the ways she's cut and stabbed and poked at my feelings, now she wants me to stay.

"Let me get this straight. You want me to stand by my man. No, no, wait. It's more than that. You want me to waddle around town with my big belly on display so people will look at me and feel sorry for Paul. You want us to sit behind him at the trial so the jurors will think we're a united front." I place both hands on the table and lean in. "You want to pay me to stay."

"Not you, dear. The baby. A trust fund in his or her name, with you as the administrator. Enough so that you can buy a house of your own, take care of your child and never have to work again." She settles her cup back onto the saucer and sinks back in her chair. "Think of it as a sort of insurance. You do this one little thing for me, and I'll make sure you're set up for life."

I blink at her in disbelief, in horror. "That's not insurance. It's a bribe."

"Be smart, Charlie. I'm offering you security, a future without money worries."

"Seriously, lady. You have lost your ever lovin' mind. I don't want your money. I don't want Paul's. All I want is to get off this crazy train and go back to my side of the hill, where people might not have as much but at least they're not killers—"

The words die in my throat because it hits me then. The thing Diana said before, about Jax and the costume jewelry. I close my eyes and struggle to recall the missing pieces Micah rattled off in the kitchen that morning with Chet and Paul and Chief Hunt and Diana. She was there. She heard it, too.

"What is it? What's wrong?" Diana says, but I ignore her.

A pair of golden hoops. A pearl bracelet and a watch. A ruby-and-diamond ring that once belonged to Sienna's grandmother. That's what Micah said. He told us to keep it quiet, too, that the police weren't releasing the list of jewelry to the media.

I open my eyes, and she's watching me. "How did you know about Sienna's jewelry being costume?"

Diana frowns. "What are you talking about? Micah said—"

"Micah told us what pieces he was looking for, but he never said the jewelry was fake. And even if it was, he's not the kind of guy who would have known the difference. Even if he held the pieces in his hand, he wouldn't have recognized gold from gold plate, or that those stones in her grandmother's ring were colored chips of glass."

There's a voice in my head telling me to leave it, to leave this house and never look back. But my heart is pounding, my skin tingling with realization, and I never could let things lie.

I lean forward in my chair. "But *you* would."

Diana, who insists on only the best. Who once paid a jewelry designer to pour pure twenty-four-karat gold into three identical wax molds and engrave the town's coordinates on the back. Who had not one man she loved to protect from the truth coming out, but two. Jax is family, she just told me. There's nothing she wouldn't do for him.

Her whole body changes in that instant of understanding. Everything about her hardens—her eyes, her mouth, her expression. I sit there for a moment, watching her scramble for her game face, but she doesn't quite get there. And it's too late. I've already seen it. I already heard.

She tucks a hank of hair behind an ear, fidgets. "I don't like what you're insinuating."

"You do know what this means, right? Jax has an alibi. He was twelve miles away at the time of Sienna's death, and three people heard Micah deny killing her, right before he admitted to killing Bobby. Why would he admit to one and not the other?"

Diana doesn't answer. The only sound is a clock ticking in another room and a light snore coming from the fur ball on her lap. She stares at me and I stare at her, but she doesn't say a word.

"This means all signs point to Paul. Your beloved son, the last of the three with both motive and opportunity. You're really going to let him go to prison for something he didn't do?"

She waves off my words with a hand. "It'll never come to that. I've already retained the best defense attorney in the South, who assures me Paul won't get much jail time, if any. And they can't prove something that never happened. Whatever evidence the police have on him for Sienna's death is purely circumstantial." But she doesn't sound very certain.

"You people are bonkers. Do you know that?" My rising tone wakes the dog, who jumps to its feet on Diana's lap, yipping. She slides a hand around its snout like a muzzle. I was crazy to think this woman would ever accept me into her family, just like I'd be crazy to let a murderer anywhere near my child. "There's not enough money in the world to make me want to stay in this family. You're unhinged."

"I'm just a mother protecting her son." Her gaze dips to my belly. "You'll understand soon enough."

"That's where you're wrong. I'll never understand. You killed a woman to protect your son's secret and in the process blew his life to smithereens. You deserve everything you have coming to you."

Her eyes narrow into slits. "Is that a threat?"

I stare at her across the teacups and that ridiculous dog, and my heart gives a warning thud. It wasn't a threat, not an intentional one at least, but she's already killed one woman to keep her son's secret. Maybe it was a crime of passion—an impulse, a threat that threw her into a sudden rage—or maybe it's something more sinister. Maybe she lured Sienna to the lake, to a place where the murder weapon was within reach. Either way, who's to say Diana wouldn't do it again?

Leave.

Suddenly, it's the only thing I can think about, getting out of this house, this family. I glance around the room, taking inventory. The cut crystal figurine, the base of the candlestick, the pokers by the fireplace. For the first time,

I am afraid of the woman before me. I have no doubt she saw silencing Sienna as a necessary sacrifice to protect Paul, but Diana's reasoning is just as faulty as her son's. Loyalty can't cancel out a wrong. Love, no matter how big and broad, can't balance these scales.

Only justice can.

"Congratulations," I say, standing. "You finally achieved what you've been trying for all this time, because I'm done. I'm walking out this door and out of this family, and there's not enough money in the world to stop me."

I'm out the door seconds later, jogging down the steps to Chet's Jeep, motioning for him to hurry up and start the car.

Every person has a single defining moment. A moment that veers their life in a new direction, that changes them at a cellular level and makes them question everything they thought they knew, that colors every thought and decision afterward. For Paul and Micah and Jax, it was that moment they landed in the lake. It turned Micah into a killer, drove Jax into the woods, made Paul secretive, turned him inward.

But this moment, this one right here, this is mine.

39

It's only six blocks from Diana's house to the police station, but Chet takes the long way, weaving up and down side streets so I can give him the highlights of my visit with Diana. The bribe. The jewelry. What I plan to do now that I know.

Because my goal hasn't changed. I went there to protect the littlest Keller, and that's still my plan, in the best way I know how.

"You'll be here when I come out?" I say as he pulls to a stop in front of the door.

Chet's eyes go wide, and he gives me an enthusiastic nod. "Dude, I am going nowhere. Now get in there and give 'em hell."

By now it's late afternoon, and the station is mostly empty, all but Doris, who runs the reception desk, and Sam, riffling through a file cabinet behind a waist-high wooden partition. He pulls out a well-thumbed file and points it at a sign on the wall to my left. I missed visiting hours by a whole twenty minutes.

"You can't be serious."

He gives me an apologetic shrug, though he doesn't look the least bit sorry. "Rules are rules." He sinks into a swivel chair at his desk and pretends to ignore me.

Frustration rises, bubbling in my chest and up my throat. "Sam, please. If you and I were ever friends, you'll give me this. Ten minutes, that's all I need."

He looks up, his head tilted to the side. "Were we ever friends? Because, honestly, I can't remember."

"You know we were." I think back to his face when he stormed out of the church, the way he shoved the door open with a sharp bang, and I actually flinch. "To tell you the truth, you kinda broke my heart."

"Yeah, well, you broke mine first. So I guess that makes us even, doesn't it?"

At that, Doris gives up all pretense and her head snaps up, her gaze flicking between us. By bedtime, everybody on both sides of the mountain will know what happened here, how after all this time, Sam and I finally had it out. He waits, watching me from the other side of the partition.

"You were right. Is that what you wanted to hear? I married a guy you warned me about, and now it's blown up in my face, just like you said it would. Does that make you happy?"

"No, Charlie. None of this makes me happy." He still looks pissed, but the sharpest edge is gone from his tone. "And for what it's worth, I remember us being friends. That's what makes this so damn hard. Because for a while there, I honestly and truly thought we were on the road to being more than friends. I thought that's where this thing between us was headed."

I nod because I know. If I'm being completely honest, I've always known. All those times Sam went quiet, watching me with a blend of frustration and longing. All the times he stood too close or stayed too long, like he was waiting for something to happen. He wanted me, and I wanted Paul. No wonder he spent this past year angry.

"I should have been more sensitive to that, and I'm sorry. If I could go back and do it all over again, there are a lot of things I'd do differently. Like tell you how much I loved you, just not in that way. But that was the whole problem. I loved our friendship too much to risk it."

"So you sabotaged it instead."

"You can't help who you fall in love with, Sam. If you've learned anything from this shitshow, surely you know that."

He puffs a pained laugh, and when I smile at him, he smiles back. It's not a big smile. It's not an easy one. But it's a crack in that big, angry wall he's put up between us, and I'm just stubborn enough to keep hacking.

With a sigh, he slaps the file to his desk. "Ten minutes, starting now."

He leads me down a hallway and parks me at a table in a windowless room that does double duty as a kitchen. A counter is shoved against a far wall, battered and basic: a fridge, a double sink, an industrial-sized coffeepot lined with dark sludge. A vent above my head pumps in stale air, drying my throat into brittle paper.

Two seconds later the door opens, and in steps Paul, his jaw thick with two days' worth of stubble. He's wearing clothes that aren't his—a grubby thermal and beige pants two sizes too big. They're rolled at the ankle, a messy furl of wrinkled fabric that drags on the ground. He looks at me with eyes that are red and swollen, and the emotions cycle through me, love and regret and sorrow and fury.

Behind him, the lock slides into the slot with a metallic thunk.

"You must really hate me."

I hate him and I love him and I hate him and I love him. But the man I fell in love with—the one whose first wife's death left him with broken and ragged edges that matched up against mine, the one who promised to care for me in ways my own parents didn't—that man exists mostly in my head. Paul showed me only the sides of him he wanted me to see and the rest he shoved somewhere deep inside, and I traded whatever doubts I had for security. I lived in his house and I ate his food and I never demanded to know the real Paul. How can you love a man who's only a shadow? How can you hate him?

He gives me a resigned nod, reading the answer in my silence. He moves closer, pulls out the chair across from me. "I wanted to tell. For twenty years, I wanted to, but I owe Jax my life. I—"

"Stop." I slap the air between us with my palms, and Paul freezes, his hand still on the chair. "Seriously, just shut up. I didn't come here for an apology, and I'm not looking for an explanation. I already heard both from your mother."

Paul frowns. "Okay."

I gesture for him to sit, and he sinks into the chair. He folds his hands and sits up straight, waiting, and I notice the two pale strips of skin where his Rolex and wedding band used to be. Confiscated when they tossed him in jail.

"What did Sienna's jewelry look like?"

He startles at my sudden change of topic, and I can't really blame him. This is a question that's either coming out of nowhere, or it's not. He either has an answer ready, or he doesn't. I intend to find out which.

He shakes his head. "I'm sorry. What?"

"Sienna's jewelry. Micah described it for us last week in the kitchen. Chief Hunt and your mother were there, too. We talked about how the killer would have been stupid to dump it in the lake. Remember?"

"No. I don't know."

"Think about it."

Paul humors me, and for the span of ten breaths. I watch his frown of concentration, those spider-fine lines fanning out from his eyes that mean he's thinking really hard. I give him all the time he needs.

Finally, he lifts his hands from the table. "A watch. A piece from her grandma with some kind of stone. Some earrings, maybe? That's all I remember."

"It was a pair of gold hoops, a pearl bracelet, a watch, a ruby-and-diamond ring that once belonged to her grandmother. That's what Micah told us. He also told us the police weren't releasing the list of jewelry to the media. I checked, Paul, and it's nowhere. No one has mentioned those pieces specifically."

"Okay." Paul drags out the word, still sounding for all the world like he still doesn't know where this conversation is going. I stare across the table, taking in his furrowed brow, his measured breaths, the way his gaze stays strong and steady on mine, and I can't decide if he's playing me or not. His mother knows everything about him, but does he know what she's capable of?

"The thing is, there's no way your mother could have known unless she saw the jewelry for herself."

"Could have known what?"

"Diana told me they were costume. She called them

cheap." I watch a shadow flit across his face, but he remains silent. He doesn't move, either, other than to clasp his hands a little tighter, his knuckles going sharp and white. "Except how could she know that unless she saw it herself? Unless she held them in her own hands?"

"What exactly are you accusing her of?"

"Exactly what you think I am, and for the record, she didn't deny it. Not even when I said they'd be looking to you for Sienna's murder. Jax has an alibi, and Micah told all of us he didn't kill Sienna. By then he'd already admitted to killing Katherine and driving the car that killed Bobby. Why not just come out and say he killed Sienna, too? At that point, he had no reason not to."

"I don't know. Because Micah was a monster. Because he wasn't the person I thought he was."

"And your mother? Is she the person you think she is?"

There's a long stretch of silence, and I let him sit with things for a minute, giving him time for the full weight of his realization to sink in. Diana, who loves her son so fiercely, she'd silence anyone who got in his way. He winces, closing his eyes.

"When I heard there was a woman waving Jax's necklace around town, I figured that was it. Finally this long, hellish nightmare would be over. For twenty years I've been waiting for someone to arrest me, but Mom kept telling me to sit tight. She told me to trust her, that she'd take care of it." His eyes snap open, his gaze sticking to mine. "I thought she meant she'd talk to Chief Hunt or something. I never thought... Jesus."

I puff out a breath, not a laugh exactly, but close. If Paul's words are true—and I'm not saying they are—then I'm not the only one guilty of having blinders on. We see what we want to see, and we disregard the rest. I know this better than anyone.

"So when Sienna washed up under the dock, who did you think killed her?"

"Micah." Paul stabs a finger into the table and leans forward. "That's why I went to find Jax, because Chief Hunt was never going to let his own son go down for murder. I knew they were going to try to pin it on Jax. Blame the crazy person. Plant some evidence or, hell, I don't know, drum up a witness or two. But never, not once, did I think it was Mom. You have to believe me. It didn't even cross my mind."

I don't respond, because the truth is, I don't believe him. I don't know if what he's saying is real or yet another falsehood from his bag of lies. A woman who was only asking about coffee, a deal to build million-dollar homes on swampland. So many stories, and I am done taking this man at his word.

"Your mother offered me money to stay through the trial, maybe longer. She said she'd set up a trust fund under the baby's name but give me control of how to spend it." I pause, shifting in my chair. "I don't know how much, but I'm guessing a lot. I didn't exactly give her time to finish."

"You don't need her money. You can have half of mine. Screw the prenup—I'll split everything straight down the middle. My attorney will draw up the papers first thing tomorrow."

"I don't want Katherine's money."

"Okay, mine, then. All of it. Every cent. It's not as much as hers, but it's more than enough to care for you and the baby."

"Guilt gifts, like the ones you've been buying Jamie Holmes."

"This isn't about guilt, Charlotte. This about paying my debts. Taking care of people caught in the crosshairs through no fault of their own. I know money doesn't fix things, but I figured if I could just...take some of the pressure off, maybe it would make things easier."

I can't deny money makes things easier, just like Paul doesn't deny he's been paying for the upkeep on Jamie's home. I should have known it was him and not Jax. Paul's love language is money. What's some electronics and a monthly landscaping bill to a man with so many millions? He has more than enough to spare.

"I want to take care of you, Charlotte. And our child. Please let me."

"That's not why I came."

He shakes his head. Frowns.

There are footsteps outside in the hallway, moving closer. Sam coming to get me.

"I came because I need you to understand what it feels like to grow up like I did, under the shadow of parents who've done awful things. That shit leaves scars, and I wouldn't wish that pain on anyone, least of all an innocent child."

My words hit him like a punch, and his eyes shimmer with regret, with pain. "I get it. Of course I do. And for the rest of my life, I will hate myself for what I've done. To you, to our baby. Our child will suffer because of me, because of the mistakes I've made, the wrongs I've done. I know I don't deserve anyone's forgiveness, least of all yours, but I need you to know that I'm sorry. I am so goddamn sorry."

He breaks down then, sobbing into his hands, and I know what he wants to hear—that I accept his apology, that I understand and forgive him. That our baby will be okay, that together we will see to it.

But I can't say any of those things. Maybe one day I'll be able to, but not today. Not yet.

The lock chinks in the door, and I know I don't have much time.

"Paul. *Paul*." I slap a hand to the table to get his attention, waiting until he looks up from his fingers. "Years from now, when our baby is old enough to understand, I am going to tell him or her what you did, and I will use it as a lesson. To teach right from wrong, how to pick the good from the bad. And when I do, I sure would like to be able to say that, in the end, when push came to shove, your father did the right thing."

The handle twists, the door creaking open, and I plant both hands on the table and lean in close to make sure my next words land, that he hears them and understands.

"Do the right thing here, Paul. Or I will."

40

I steer Chet's Jeep around the last hairpin turn on the driveway, and there it is, the sleek box of steel and glass hanging from rocks high above the glittering lake. I remember the first time I saw it, from the passenger seat of Paul's fancy SUV, the excitement I felt when I counted all the windows and doors. Twelve, and that was only across the front side.

By now it's winter, and the wind is achingly cold as I make my way to the front door, icing over my skin and rustling the plants in the pots on either side of the stoop. Hellebores, Katherine's favorite. I know, because I heard it on "Gone Swimming," episode 5 of Grant's podcast, along with the fact that she was a master gardener, ate cold pizza for breakfast and detested country music. Silly, trifling details I'd been longing to hear for so long, and I heard them from a stranger.

But thanks to the podcast, media attention has been brutal. Reporters chasing me through town, ambushing me at the coffee shop and in the grocery store, shoving microphones like furry ice cream cones under my nose. My answer to them is the same every time—"no comment"—but like Micah once said, they're a persistent bunch.

The people in town have been kinder, rallying around me when things get too crazy, herding me into one of the shops and letting me escape through the back door. Oh, sure, they still whisper about me behind my back, still give me sideways glances, but Chet says they're coming around, and so is Sam. Especially now that I've moved back to his—no, *my* side of the hill, his icy demeanor is starting to thaw. We're not back to being friends yet, but we'll get there.

He hasn't said as much, but I can tell Sam respects me for refusing to take part in Grant's podcast, even though he offered me a number that made my eyes bulge. Chet called me crazy when he heard, but I don't expect him or anybody else to understand. I'm done profiting from Paul Keller.

Paul opens the door and I take him in, his familiar face with a few more wrinkles, the thread of gray at his temple, and I brace for the pang—sadness combined with lingering bitterness for the lies and betrayals he brought into our marriage. But Paul did the right thing that day I went to see him at the police station, and I owe it to our daughter to do the same.

"How are you? You look good." His gaze dips to our daughter in my belly, a little small for her five months, but otherwise perfect.

"I feel good. The doctor says everything's right on schedule." I pull a slip of paper from my bag, small and gray and grainy. "Here, I brought you a picture."

Episode 12 was the ugliest of all: "A Mother's Love." Diana's genteel Southern cadence, her pretty voice saying all those horrible, awful words after Paul coaxed out a confession. His forgiveness, the promise of his forever devotion and love, but only if she turned herself in. She plunked herself down at Sam's desk and told him how she'd lured Sienna to the edge of town then bashed in her skull with a garden shovel, which she ditched along with Jax's necklace and the costume jewelry in a firepit at the Singing Waters campground. By the time Sam got to it, there was nothing but melted plastic and charred metal, licked clean of her fingerprints by weather and flames. But there wasn't a lawyer on the planet who could keep Diana out of jail after that confession.

As ugly as Diana's episode was, I could relate to a lot of what she said. That her entire world revolves around this beautiful being, a tiny piece of herself she was designed to love and protect. That motherhood changes you, that it leaves behind a ghostly afterbirth you can never quite scrub off. It didn't happen to my mother, but I can feel it happening to me, this growing fire to give our daughter everything I never had. Security. Three meals eaten together at a table. Love. The things I was so desperate for when I met Paul, before I got blinded by all the glittery stuff.

I look around now, at the thick rugs, the expensive furniture, the sad man standing before me, and I feel nothing but pity.

He wipes his eyes with a sleeve, steps back to let me in. "Make yourself at home. I just have to run upstairs and grab the papers."

The papers I'm to deliver to his attorney because he can't, the ones granting me a divorce. Paul signed them without protest.

He takes the steps by twos and threes, his legs still strong thanks to the treadmill shoved against the window where the dining table once stood. Best view in the house, Paul always said, and now all he can do is look.

House arrest. People went nuts when they heard, but somehow that fancy lawyer of his managed to finagle a plea that included twenty-eight months in this glass palace plus a hefty fine to offset the costs of the monitor strapped to his ankle. Agreeing to testify against his mother helped some, but still. Money can't buy happiness or bravery. It can't save a marriage or bring a drug dealer back from the dead. But in these United States of America, especially here in the South, it can keep a white man out of prison.

It would have kept Jax out, too, but he pleaded guilty. The judge gave him sixty-four months, but Sam says he'll be out a lot sooner. Especially now that he's found religion, though he doesn't call it that and he never mentions the word *God*. Jax preaches in his podcasts, *The Path from Prison*, that every being is divine and that nature is our church. He talks about other things, too, stuff like astral projection and moral diversity. I have no idea what half of it means, but I listen to him anyway. I like the idea he's pushing, of people being basically good, that we make mistakes, but ultimately, everybody's in charge of their own destinies.

Just like I am with mine. Twenty-six and pregnant, on the verge of divorce but still standing. Studying for my GED and then, hopefully, college. It won't be easy with a baby, but Chet will help, and so will Paul. Between the three of us, we'll figure out a way.

"Can I get you something to drink?" he says, returning with the papers.

"No, I can't stay. I promised Chet I'd help him out at the food truck."

Lake Crosby's first of its kind. We park it every day at the edge of town, where Chet cooks and I serve until we sell out, usually by three o'clock every afternoon. Oh, the irony of us being back where we began—in a tiny metal trailer—but now we own it and it's chock-full of food.

Paul holds out the papers, but when I try to take them, he doesn't let go. "I really loved you, you know. Not the way I should have. Not the way you deserved. And I'm sorry for that. I'm sorry for not letting you in the way you deserved to be. I'm sorry for hurting you."

He pauses, and I believe him this time. I'm certain this apology is sincere.

"But I am not sorry for falling in love with you. I'm not sorry for our time together, because those months were the happiest I've been in a very long time." He smiles, and it's the saddest thing I've ever seen.

"They were happy for me, too."

It's funny when you think about it, and I've thought about it a lot, but I fell in love with Paul not despite his flaws, but because of them. The way they made me feel less alone, the way they fit up snug against mine.

But now that I've put a little space between us, I can see his scars weren't so much a complement but a camouflage. I'd found someone whose wounds overshadowed mine, and he came with a pretty house and a pile full of money. Of course I fell in love with him.

But I'm done being ashamed of our marriage. I'm not to blame for his lies.

Like Jax says, I am in charge of my own destiny.

And so what will I tell our daughter, when she's old enough to understand? I'll tell her the truth of what happened here, certainly, because there have been more than enough lies. I'll tell her the sins of her father are not her burden, and neither are they mine. I'll tell her that of all my many mistakes, she wasn't one of them. That I didn't choose her but she chose me, and for that I'll always be grateful.

Then I will say, listen: no one ever taught my mother to love her babies, but somehow you taught me. You are the reason I am not like her, just like you will never be me. Every generation is a new life. A new chance to get things right.

Now it's your turn. Your story begins and ends with you.

* * * * *

ACKNOWLEDGMENTS

Writing is solitary work, but bringing a book into the world is a team effort. Deepest thanks and undying gratitude to everyone who helped guide this book from story spark to finished novel, especially:

My agent, Nikki Terpilowski, who read so many drafts of this book that I've lost count. Thank you for being my toughest critic and fiercest advocate. We make an awesome team.

My editor, Laura Brown, for embracing this idea and helping me give Charlotte the story she deserved. My stellar team at Park Row Books, publicist Emer Flounders and all the talented and dedicated folks working behind the scenes in the art, marketing and sales departments. I'm so thankful to be part of the Park Row family.

My early readers and cheerleaders: Kristy Barrett, Tonni Callan, Laura Drake, Andrea Peskind Katz and Annie Mc-

Dowell. Thank you for your enthusiasm and guidance and friendship.

Authors are some of the kindest, funniest, smartest, craziest, most creative people I know, and I am honored to call many of them friends. A.F. Brady, Emily Carpenter, J.T. Ellison, Rea Frey, Wendy Heard, Amy Impellizzeri, Hannah Mary McKinnon, Mindy Mejia, Kate Moretti, Abbie Roads, Kaira Rouda, Joan Swan, Wendy Walker and so many others, thanks for the cocktails and laughs and brainstorm sessions, for being such amazing and brilliant partners in crime. Y'all make this bonkers business so much more fun.

I am blessed with a network of family, friends and loved ones by my side: my husband, Ewoud, who lets me talk about murder over dinner and still wants to sleep next to me at night; my kids, Evan and Isabella, who talk me up to their friends and face my books out at bookstores around the world; my parents, Diane and Bob Maleski, and brother Mark Maleski, who schlep hundreds of miles to come to my events and buy books I would have given them anyway; my girl gang Elizabeth Baxendale, Christy Brown, Lisa Camp, Nancy Davis, Scarlet Grootens, Angelique Kilkelly, Jen Robinson, Amanda Sapra and Raquel Souza. Your love and support means the world.

And most of all, thanks to you, the person holding this book. Thank you for reading my words and talking about them with your friends, for taking lovely pictures of my covers and posting them to the internet, for writing reviews and Tweets and blog posts. Because of you, I have the best job in the world.

*Read On for a Sneak Peek at
Kimberly Belle's exciting new domestic thriller,*
My Darling Husband

THE INTERVIEW

Juanita Moore: Mr. Lasky, thank you for speaking with me today, and sharing your story with *Channel 7 Action News*. I know rehashing what happened to your family can't be easy for you to talk about.

Cam Lasky: [squinting] Do you mind turning those lights down?

Juanita: Those lights are necessary for our viewers to see your face, and people are clamoring to see you. You haven't spoken to the media for months now, and for those of us who have been following your story, we are eager to hear it from your own lips, a firsthand account of what happened and how you've survived the months since. You've become quite the celebrity, though—

Cam: I believe the proper term going around socials these days is *celebrity asshole*. Can I say that on TV—asshole? We're not live, are we?

Juanita: No, we're not live. My editors will cut that one out, but if you wouldn't mind keeping your answers PG, it will save them a lot of work later.

Cam: [doesn't respond]

Juanita: As I was saying, the narratives that have come out since the home invasion haven't exactly painted you as a hero of this story. You are the aggressor, the fraudster, the money-hungry villain.

Cam: Too bad I don't have a mustache or I'd twirl it.

Juanita: Here are just a few of the stories circulating about you: that you're involved in the mob, the head of a satanic cult, that your kitchens served as clandestine meeting spots for a ring of international child traffickers—

Cam: Now, that last one's just ridiculous. And absolutely untrue. They all are.

Juanita: But still. Having all these unfavorable stories written about you must feel…

Cam: Invasive. Intrusive. Annoying. People love to make stuff up, don't they?

Juanita: I meant the criticism.

Cam: [shrugging] I'm used to it by now.

Juanita: The BBC did a series on America's biggest grifters and cited you as a classic example of an American business-man who will stop at nothing to succeed. Netflix is currently in talks to resurrect the show *American Greed*, with your story dominating their first three episodes. And a poll floating around Facebook last month declared you the most hated man in America behind Pharma Bro, Martin Shkreli.

Cam: Well, since Facebook says it, it must be true.

Juanita: And yet for months now, you have refused to talk to the media. Our many phone calls and emails and texts were left unanswered. You threatened legal action if my producer or I didn't leave you alone.

Cam: All true.

Juanita: Until yesterday, when out of the blue you contacted me to request an interview. You were quite insistent, in fact. Why is that?

Cam: Well, I guess I figured it was time to set the record straight.

JADE

2:51 p.m.

I'm pulling into the Westmore Music Academy lot when I spot him, the man leaning against the building's brick and carved concrete sign. Pocked skin. Black-rimmed glasses. Skinny shoulders hunched against the rain. Atlanta is getting plowed with the tail of a tropical storm stalled over the gulf, blasting soupy heat all the way up to Tennessee, and he's wearing that same cracked leather coat like it's January and not early August, his hands shoved deep in the pockets as if for warmth.

I gun it up the hill hard enough to make my tires squeal, tapping a button on the steering wheel. "Call Cam."

While the call connects, I glance in my side mirror, trying to pick him out of the trees and shrubs.

The grocery store. The nail salon and yoga studio. Yesterday at Starbucks, he passed me a stevia packet before I could ask for one, which makes me wonder how many times he's seen me there, stirring sweetener into my coconut latte.

Cam's deep voice booms through the car speakers. "I'm in the middle of something. Can I call you in thirty?"

My husband always answers, even when he's busy. *Especially* then. This is our steadfast rule ever since our oldest, Beatrix, took a spill on the playground when she was four, knocking herself out and breaking her arm in three places. Cam was in the middle of a renovation at the Inman Park restaurant at the time, covered in construction dust and arguing with contractors whose every other word was *over*. Overdue, overworked, over budget. Thirty times I called him that day, frantic and bouncing in the back of an ambulance while comforting a scared child and trying to keep a fussy toddler on my lap. Cam didn't feel his phone buzzing in his back pocket, didn't notice the screen lighting up with a long line of increasingly desperate messages from me.

The last one I left as they were wheeling Beatrix into Children's Healthcare.

"Your daughter is in the hospital, Cam. Maybe pick up your phone and call us sometime."

Mean and petty, I know, but I've never been so furious. Or so stressed. Or so downright petrified.

Beatrix was fine. Cam and I, however, lost five years of our lives that day.

Now I say to Cam, "He's here."

"Who's where?"

"That guy. The skeevy one I told you about, with the glasses and the comb-over man bun. He's here at Westmore."

"Well, maybe he has a musically gifted kid."

I roll my eyes, lift my hands from the steering wheel.

"Right. And he just happens to go to the same gym as me and shops in the canned goods aisle at Whole Foods whenever I walk through their door."

In the back seat, Baxter leans as far forward as his booster seat will allow. "Hi, Daddy!"

"Hey, buddy. You keeping your mom company?"

Except for his fine mousy waves, our son is a spitting image of Cam. Baxter gives an enthusiastic nod. "She took me to Bruster's, and then she made me get the frozen banana."

And he's still salty about it, too, no matter how many times I explain that food coloring is bad for his six-year-old body, and the scoop of Purple Dinosaur he's constantly begging for is more dye than ice cream. The banana dipped in dark chocolate is our hard-won compromise.

I twist around on my seat and hold a finger to my lips, my next words for Cam: "Of course he doesn't have a musically gifted kid. I'm telling you, Cam. This guy is following me. He *is*."

"Who is?" Baxter says, looking out the back window. "Who, Mommy?"

I ignore him and check my mirrors, all of them, but the man is gone. The line of parked cars, the hill between here and the busy road, he's nowhere. Even if I could see the sign from where I'm sitting, there are dozens of people on this stretch of street, pedestrians and runners, employees popping out for fresh air or to the nearby sandwich shops, people socializing on the covered benches. If he's still down there, it would be easy to conceal himself in the crowd.

And yet he made sure I saw him when I was turning into the lot, didn't he? The way he was dressed in all black like some kind of daytime cat burglar, how his shoulders straightened and his head popped up when he spotted my car, how he stared at me through the windshield like he was daring me to see him. Like he *wanted* me to see him and be scared. Maybe *that's* why he's been following me for days.

I gasp as something occurs to me. "Omigod, Cam. What if it's not me he's after, but the K-I-D-S? What if that's why he's been following me all over creation, because he's trying to get to them?"

"Why would he be after the kids?"

I cringe at the way he said the word, already dreading the conversation I'm going to have to have with Baxter later. "I don't know. For ransom. For creepy shadiness I don't want to say out loud because you're on speaker phone. Plus, I don't want to give it energy."

"Saying the words…" Something clangs in the background, metal on heavy metal. Cam waits until the noise dies down. "Saying them out loud doesn't bring something into existence, you know that as well as I do. And why would he be after the kids when there are a thousand other families in this city with fancier cars and bigger houses than ours? I mean, one look at our street and it's clear there are plenty of bigger fish."

"Yeah, but it's your face on the cover of *Atlanta Magazine*." When Cam walks into a place, everything tilts. Heads turn, bodies shift, gazes stick. Going to a restaurant with Atlanta's Steak King is like dining out with a rock star. The waitstaff, the chef, the other patrons in the restaurant—they all come over to bask in Cam's glow.

And Cam knows he's visible, even without his chef's gear. Thick black hair, a square jaw, straight white teeth he flashes often. My husband is handsome, but it's the combination with his height that gets him noticed. Six and a half feet of big, Mediterranean man.

"Go talk to the building's security guard. That's what he's there for."

"And say what? That there was a strange man standing on the sidewalk? The road is public property."

"True, but I'm sure the guard would want to know if one of their clients is being stalked. At least give him a description of the creep."

I shiver, the reality of this conversation inching up the back of my neck. Maybe I'm wrong. Atlanta is a big city that can feel like a really small town. I run into people I know everywhere. Maybe this is all some strange coincidence.

I rewind back to the first time I noticed him, a few days ago through the plate-glass window at Kale Me Crazy. There I was, seated alone at the bar with my phone and a smoothie I didn't want, killing an empty hour between playdates and pickup times by scrolling through Pinterest. I was feeling sad and nostalgic for the offices and boutiques I used to design, back before I met Cam. This was before his name became eponymous with Atlanta's high-end dining, before I came up with the sleek stone and metal look that would become a recognizable part of his brand, before I pushed out two babies in three years and closed up shop. But that day, I looked up and he was there, squinting into the sunshine and watching me.

A weirdo, but a random one, I assumed—until I spotted him later at the dry cleaner, at the deli across from my yoga studio, at the Starbucks and the canned goods aisle of the grocery store.

And now here he is again, today.

At my child's music school.

My skin prickles with alarm.

"I'm sure it's nothing, but next time you see this guy, point your phone at his face and tell him you're streaming live to Twitter. If it doesn't scare him off, you'll at least have a visual to show the guard."

His voice gets sucked up into more clanging, followed

by a heavy crash and multiple voices, all of them shouting. I realize it's been like this since the start, his voice pushing through loud and chaotic background noise.

"Babe, why does it sound like you're at fight club?"

"I'm at the shop on Bolling Way. There was a fire."

My stomach drops at his words. Bolling Way is Cam's signature restaurant, a booming scene surrounded by Buckhead's finest stores, a place that's packed from noon until midnight.

"How bad was it?"

"On a scale of one to ten? Four hundred and fifty-seven." He sighs, and it occurs to me that the concern I thought I heard in his voice wasn't for me and the kids, but disaster at his most profitable restaurant. A torched Buckhead kitchen means a big, giant hole in our income. "I'm here with Flavio. We're talking through our options."

Flavio is the location's general manager, and Cam's highest paid employee.

I'm opening my mouth to respond when I spot the clock on the dash: 3:01. A whole minute late, and to pick up a child who loses her shit at the tiniest adjustment to her daily schedule. "Oh crap, gotta go. Call me later."

I hang up, swipe my bag from the floor and Bax from the back seat, and race to the double glass doors of the building, looking over my shoulder the entire way.

I look for him after. Instead of turning left for home, I point my car right, steering past the spot where I saw him last, leaning against the sign. Four times I hold up traffic to search him out of the crowd, twice headed in the wrong direction, then two more times on the drive back past the building. I press my iPhone to the window and ride the brake the entire time, creeping by the entrance to the lot so slowly that more than one impatient driver honks.

But he's not there. The patch of trampled grass by the sign is empty. The man-bunned man is gone.

Baxter pushes up in his booster seat, straining to see out the window. "Mommy, where are we going?"

"We're going home." I'm headed in the right direction, but my hunt took too long. Now we're stuck in traffic.

"Then why do you keep turning around?"

"And why are you going so slow?" Beatrix adds before I can explain. She swipes a wet finger down the back window, pointing at two women speed walking past us. "Are you sure we're not going backward?"

Beatrix knows we're not going backward, but she enjoys being a smart-ass. Too clever for her nine years. Too sassy and energetic, too, and as tightly wound as the composite core strings on her DZ Strad violin—at least that's according to her teachers.

And as much as I love my daughter, they're not wrong. Beatrix has been a handful since the second she came into this world, bloodred and hopping mad. Colic. Sleeping issues. Sinewy muscles that hated to be swaddled. My pediatrician called her a high-needs baby, patted me on the shoulder and promised me most grow into normal, well-adjusted kids.

Something that for Beatrix will never happen.

My daughter is a musical genius, something I accidentally discovered when she was four, when after a quick dash through Fresh Market she hummed a perfectly pitched concerto all the way home. A few weeks later at Target, she picked out the melody with two chubby fingers on a keyboard, but it was the pink toy violin she begged to take home. Within a few months, I managed to find a teacher willing to give formal lessons to such a young student. The woman, a stern grandmotherly type, emerged from their first session pink-cheeked and throwing around the word, *prodigy*.

My Beatrix is special. Thanks to an accident of fate and chance and random genes, she will never grow into that normal child the pediatrician promised. She has this astonishing, one-in-a-million gift, but one that comes with an ear that hears her every mistake. A perfectionist with mile-high standards for herself, quick to become frustrated and anxious when her fingers don't cooperate.

But when they do, it is magical.

I grab two packets of Goldfish from the glove compartment, then pass them to the back seat. We're only a few miles from home, but I have learned to always come prepared. Juice boxes, snacks, iPads with every movie known to man. I'm not above parenting by distraction.

"Help Bax open his, will you?" I say to Beatrix, but I'm too late. They're already playing tug-of-war with the bag.

"Give it to me. I can open it on my own." Baxter kicks the back of my seat in protest.

"You can't do it by yourself," Beatrix says, her voice matter-of-fact. "You're too little."

"I'm not little! Give it here." Baxter swipes at the bag, but his big sister is too strong. He can't pry the packet from Beatrix's fingers. "Mommy, Beatrix won't give me my Goldfish. Make her give me my Goldfish!"

This happens hundreds of times a day, relentless bickering over anything, everything, nothing.

I take a deep, deep breath and try not to death-grip the steering wheel. How does this happen? How can it be that I spend every second my kids are out of sight missing them terribly, picturing their adorable little faces all day long, seeing their sweet smiles, imagining the feel of their bony arms around me, then I have them for ten minutes in the car and I'm counting the seconds until bedtime.

"Miss Juliet says you worked on a new piece." I stuff my words with enthusiasm and smile into the rearview mirror, trying to catch Beatrix's eye under those crazy white-blond curls, a cloud of a million tiny ringlets she wishes would lay flat like her brother's.

The distraction works. Beatrix sighs and lets go of the crackers. "Yeah."

"That's great. Which one?"

"*Fantaisie Impromptu*. But I think I want to play the piano."

I can't help myself; I laugh. School starts in two weeks, and thanks to Miss Juliet's nonnegotiable requirement for a minimum of three hours of daily practice, our schedules are already packed. With Beatrix's ear, she could probably pick up a new instrument quickly, but still. "When on earth would you find time to practice the piano, too?"

"Not 'too.' I want to play the piano *instead* of the violin."

I roll to a stop at the intersection, and my foot punches the brake a little too hard. I lurch against the seat belt and twist around on my seat. "Don't be ridiculous. You can't quit the violin."

Beatrix hears the horror in my voice. We all do. Even Baxter stops tugging on his Goldfish wrapper and waits for his sister's answer.

"Why not?"

"You know why." It's something we talk about often, how this spectacular gift comes hand in hand with a spectacular responsibility. "You can't throw away all the work you've done. You just can't."

"Says who?"

"Says me. Says your father and Miss Juliet. You're a violin prodigy."

She frowns and drags her gaze to the window. "I hate that word. I wish people would stop saying it."

I stare at my daughter's profile, trying to puzzle out if there's anything fueling this sudden change of heart, or if her announcement is for shock value only. Ever since that day in the toy aisle at Target, Beatrix's musicality has felt equal parts exhilarating and consequential, an all-encompassing talent that means my daughter's most important relationship is with an inanimate object. I've tried very hard to make sure she doesn't miss out on friends and school and normal, nine-year-old life, fighting traffic to squeeze in playdates and birthday parties when really she should be practicing, but quit? Put down the violin and let all that talent and hard work go to waste?

Like hell. Not going to happen.

The car behind me honks, and I turn back to the road.

"Mommy, what happens when a kangaroo jumps on a trampoline?" Baxter says apropos of nothing, his voice light and carefree. The pureness of him melts my heart.

"I don't know, baby. He jumps even higher, I guess."

But Beatrix is still feeling combative. "No, he doesn't."

"Yes, he does."

"No, he *doesn't*. Mo-om."

I'm still debating how to handle Beatrix's little bombshell when I slow to a stop in front of the house, an ivy-covered brick-and-stone high atop a hill, to grab the mail. I keep pestering Cam to put a lock on the mailbox, something to stop strangers from digging through our post, but he hasn't made the time.

Why bother? he said last I mentioned it. *All the important things are digital these days.*

I flip through the stack, junk mail and flyers folded around a lone bank statement. Not that there's much in this one; it's for the debit account which we run down every month. But the point is, not everything is digital. If anyone wanted to know how much money we have in any of our accounts, all they'd have to do is rifle through our mail.

I drop the papers in my bag, steer the car up the driveway and press the button for the gate while behind me on the back seat, things are escalating. Baxter punches Beatrix. Beatrix pulls Baxter's hair in retaliation. Both kids scream and cry.

I pull into the detached garage on the back side of the house, slam the car into Park, and hit the remote for the garage door.

Later, this is the moment I will keep coming back to, in our windowless garage with only one flickering lightbulb on the mechanical box above my car, the darkness descending as the big door rumbled to a close. To the smell of dirt and oil and something foreign, something that didn't quite belong but that I dismissed as carried in on the wind. To the chaos of holding my shit together while dragging two squirming children out of the car, of gathering up juice boxes and crackers and empty wrappers, of strapping backpacks and instrument cases to little shoulders because they're big kids now and Mommy shouldn't have to carry everything herself.

To how I was too busy, and far too distracted to see the body in the far corner.

How I didn't hear his rubber soles hitting the concrete floor, or notice the dark smudge of the man stepping out of the shadows.

How I didn't register any of it, not until it was too late.